The Ivory Tower

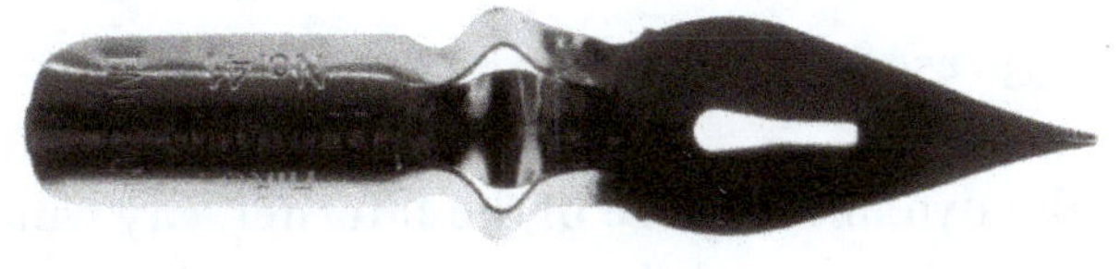

Fiona Price

Serenity Press books may be ordered through booksellers or by contacting:
Serenity Press
www.serenitypress.org

ISBN: 978-0-6486948-8-5 (sc)
ISBN: 978-0-6486948-9-2 (eB)
Printed in Australia

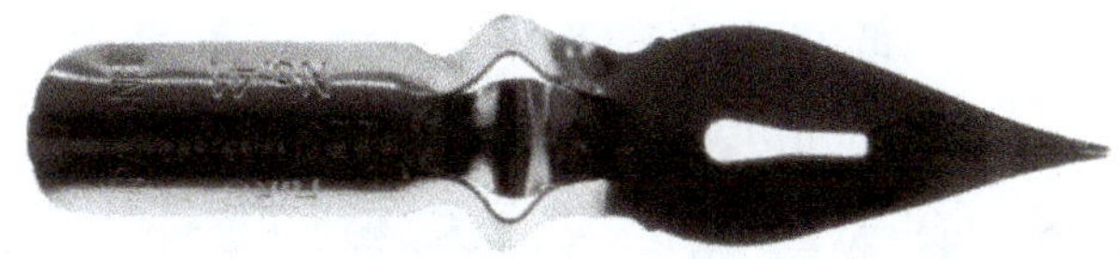

Contents

Part 1 – The Ivory Tower 7

Chapter One - Underbelly 8

Chapter 2 - Window to the Soul 16

Chapter Three - Getting Trashed 25

Chapter Four - Back to the Drawing Board 37

Chapter Five - Dated 46

Chapter Six - Principality 52

Chapter Seven - Motherlode 58

Chapter Eight - Brought to Book 66

Chapter Nine - Meeting Mrs Jones 71

Chapter Ten - Turning the Tables 79

Chapter Eleven - Indecent Proposal 86

Chapter Twelve - Going Postal 93

Chapter Thirteen - To the Letter 99

Chapter Fourteen - Bombshell 103

Chapter Fifteen - Eye for an Eye 108

Chapter Sixteen - Frames 115

Chapter Seventeen - Desktop 121

Chapter Eighteen - Washout 128

Chapter Nineteen - Making a Statement 136

Part Two – The Golden Tower 142

Chapter Twenty - Cutting Edge 143

Chapter Twenty-One - Winging it 150

Chapter Twenty-Two - Mother of Pearl 158

Chapter Twenty-Three - Missionary Position 164

Chapter Twenty-Four - The Road to Brazil 173

Chapter Twenty-Five - An Object Lesson 182

Chapter Twenty-Six - Homecoming King 190

Chapter Twenty-Seven - Crying Jag 197

Chapter Twenty-Eight - Picture Perfect 203

Chapter Twenty-Nine - Fatherland 214

Chapter Thirty - In Camera 220

Chapter Thirty-One - Suspended Animation 224

Chapter Thirty-Two - The Thin Pink Line 228

Chapter Thirty-Three - By Extension 236

Chapter Thirty-Four - Just Shoot Me 248

Chapter Thirty-Five - House Cooling 257

Chapter Thirty-Six - Retractions 263

Part Three – The Wilderness 270

Chapter Thirty-Seven - Bag Lady 271

Chapter Thirty-Eight - Finger Food 280

Chapter Thirty-Nine - Frequent Flyer 288

Chapter Forty - Oyster 293

Chapter Forty-One - Thin Air 301

Chapter Forty-Two - Watershed 308

Chapter Forty-Three - Second Sight 315

Part Four – The Castle 325

Chapter Forty-Four - Body of Work 326

Chapter Forty-Five - A Man's Home 333

Chapter Forty-Six - Box Office 338

About the Author 345

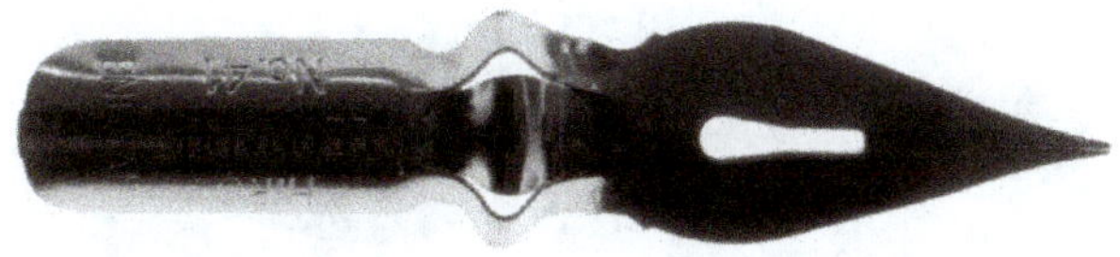

Part 1 – The Ivory Tower

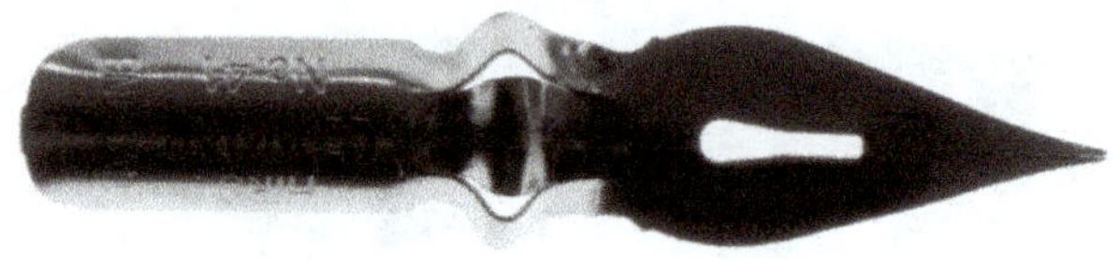

Chapter One

Underbelly

On the day I turned twelve, my grandmother Andrea took me to the red light district. We set out in a Honda she'd borrowed from work, white and glossy as a wedding dress with the university crest on the side. I wound down the window to let out the new car smell, hugging the notebook that came in a pack titled *Homeschooling Children: A Guide*.

When we reached the bad end of town, Andrea slowed to a crawl and told me to wind up the window. A blare of angry honking erupted behind us, and I shrank as if from gunfire, but Andrea was unruffled as a bullet-proof vest. She slowed further and three cars screeched round us, hurling curses and a couple of beer cans.

A parking spot opened and she pulled over, squinting at the throbbing neon signs. A raucous group of men prowled past like a six-headed monster. Their alien voices and big, bristly faces filled my stomach with spiders.

'Look at the woman on that billboard,' said Andrea.

I looked up. The woman's eyes were scrunched shut, and her wet mouth was open, as if crying out in pain. She was blonde, with a heart-shaped face, like the girl in the picture I kept in a drawer by my bed. My mother, aged seventeen, six months after having me and two weeks before she walked out.

Everything went still, as if the billboard had stopped the world spinning. Was that *her?* Could this be why Andrea had brought me here?

'What do you see?' she prompted.

Andrea's voice sounded blurred and far away. I couldn't answer. All I could find were questions for the mother who'd left me. *Is that you? Are you here? Why don't you come to see me? When are you going to come home?*

'Come on, Sage, we haven't got all night.'

Andrea's impatience brought the world back in focus. I bowed my head and mumbled an apology. When I looked up again, the woman on the billboard was a stranger once more, too busty and far too young to be my mother. 'She looks uncomfortable. Like someone's hurting her.'

'What about her body? Tell me what you see.'

What did she want me to say? The woman lay on her stomach with her head arched back. Her buttocks had eaten most of her shiny black G-string, and above it she wore nothing but a mane of brassy hair.

'Her skin's sort of … orange, and she's wearing practically no clothes. That's to look sexy for The Male Gaze, isn't it?' Andrea often talked about The Male Gaze. I felt proud of having used the phrase in a sentence.

'That scrap of lycra isn't *clothing*,' said Andrea with heavy sarcasm, 'it's garnish. Garnish for a dish of human meat. What else?'

'Her breasts are too big for her body, like the ones on a Barbie doll, and she's squeezing them together, like she's milking herself.'

Andrea made a cynical sound between a snort and a laugh. 'Yes,' she said, sounding pleased. 'And that, Sage, is exactly what she's doing. She's *milking herself*.'

I nodded as if I understood what this meant, making notes in careful black biro. *Woman on billboard, dressed for The Male Gaze. Barbie doll shape. Milking herself.* Underneath my words, the page flashed peach and pink.

As I wrote, I sensed someone watching the car. A woman, garnished in scraps of black leather that glistened in the street lights. She strode towards us and rapped a blood- coloured fingernail on the windscreen.

Close up, she looked older than the women on the billboards. There were creases between her eyebrows, and her mouth was ringed with lines that looked like tiny matches tipped with leaked red lipstick. My skin prickled as her weary, painted eyes scanned my short blonde hair, and paused on my half-grown breasts. I snatched up my notebook and flattened them from sight.

When Andrea had taught me about sex workers at home, I'd agreed that they deserved our respect. Yet now one was peering through the window of our car, I wanted to dive under the dashboard and beg my grandmother to drive me away.

Andrea threw me a disapproving scowl and wound her window down.

'You guys looking for company?' The sex worker's breath smelled of cigarette smoke. 'Or something else? Contacts? Tips?' Andrea shook her head and pulled out one of the green-and-purple flyers I'd seen in her study. 'Here,' she said, tucking a hundred-dollar bill inside and holding it out the window. 'If you need help, don't be afraid to call someone.'

The woman slipped the money into her boot and held the flyer up to the light. It was printed with the numbers and addresses of every women's refuge, drug clinic and rape crisis centre in the city. 'Uh, thanks.' She teetered back to her corner.

With clammy fingers I opened my notebook, and wrote *sex worker* in a wavering hand. I waited for Andrea to comment, but she just sat, her eyes faraway and sad. I closed the notebook and put down my pen, sensing my lesson was over.

Some minutes later, Andrea started the car and pulled away from the curb. As we drove off, I glanced back and saw the sex worker toss the flyer into the gutter.

The Humanities building where Andrea worked was the tallest on campus. By day, it cast a shadow that crept across the university, as if the grounds were the face of a sundial. I followed the shadow to the foyer and stepped into the lift.

Office doors on the top floor wore engraved brass nameplates. I made my way to the one that read *Professor Andrea Rampion, Head of Womyn's Studies*. Elsewhere, her department was spelled Women's Studies, but on her own door she insisted on a Y. Her office was her sanctum, where she crouched like a grey-crested eagle, scouring the campus for signs of sexism. Going in without her felt blasphemous somehow, even with my newly minted key.

Inside, the room was furnished in the velvet and carved oak that came with top-floor offices. Through the windows, the ivied walls and arches of the old end of campus spread out beneath an overcast sky. From here, students on the tree-lined paths looked like floating confetti on rivers whose banks changed through the seasons from pink to green to gold.

As I lowered my backpack to the floor, something scarlet caught my eye. Something closer and brighter than the students far below. I went to the window and the sun came out, shining through a skylight in the roof of the building opposite. Under the skylight was a dark-haired young man, lying naked on a bright red rug.

A flush spread over my face and neck, as if someone had doused me in hot water. I wasn't sure whether to bolt for the door or stand at the window and stare. The only naked men I'd seen were textbook illustrations when Andrea taught me biology. Seeing a live one from her office was like biting into an apple and finding a snake. Yet there he was, head propped on one elbow, alien genitals at rest on a nest of curly hair.

What was he doing there? Did he know people could see him through the skylight? Maybe he had no idea. Or maybe he did, and he was getting his kicks by flaunting his body at the Head of Women's Studies.

The thought of Andrea steadied me. Andrea always knew what to do about men. But she wasn't here and I couldn't call her—she hated mobile phones, and kept hers switched off except to check her voicemail once a day. Until she returned I'd have to face the window alone.

I backed into my chair and switched on my computer, clutching the mouse like a talisman to protect me against male nudity. How would Andrea react? I'd dreaded her lessons on sex education. With numbers and letters, she was matter-of-fact; with bodies, she was forced and self-conscious. *Sex is a natural part of life*, she'd say, looking unnatural as she said it. *To be enjoyed when you feel ready, alone or with someone you trust.* She reinforced this sex-positive message by giving me a vibrator when I hit puberty. The one time I'd turned it on, its dentist-drill buzz disturbed me so much that I hid it in my wardrobe and never touched it again.

Keys jangled outside the door, and I jumped, as if caught doing something forbidden. I grabbed the Staff Handbook and opened it at random as Andrea strode in.

My grandmother was a head shorter than me, but seemed taller. When she entered a room, a nervous hush fell, as though she headed an invisible army. Her jaw was square, and her hair was thick and iron-grey, not only on her head, but on the inches of ankle emerging from her pants.

'Hi, hon.' She dumped a folder labelled *Equity and Discrimination* on her desk.

I eyed her irritated face. 'Is something wrong?'

'University politics.' Her voice was disgusted and cynical. 'Even more wrong than global politics.' She glanced over my shoulder. 'Not considering *Fran* as a PhD supervisor, are you?'

I looked down and embarrassment flared. The random page I'd opened was a profile of Fran Mackenzie, Andrea's arch-enemy. 'Hardly,' I said in my most sarcastic voice, hastily turning the page.

Andrea sniffed. 'Can you make it home by six tonight? I've got a community meeting at seven thirty, and I need a haircut.'

'Sure.'

Andrea refused to support the beauty industry. We wore recycled clothing, used homemade soap, and cut each other's hair. Until I was eighteen, we had identical short hairstyles with a part on the side. Then, after my first semester at university, I'd stopped having it cut altogether.

Andrea hadn't been pleased. Long hair was an unnecessary vanity, a waste of resources, an inconvenience adopted for the enjoyment of men. I'd nodded repentantly, and agreed this was so, but kept on dodging the scissors. She wanted to know why, but I dodged that too, not daring to confess how I'd been shamed into growing my hair. Now that it reached almost to my waist, I kept it coiled and covered with a crocheted brown hairnet, conscious of her disapproval.

'Actually, Andrea,' I added in a shamefaced rush, 'there was something I wanted to tell you.'

She checked her watch. 'Well, make it quick. I have a meeting.'

'It's just that … there's a naked man down there. Through the skylight.'

'A *naked man?*'

Andrea marched over to the window and exhaled like a dragon breathing fire. Without breaking stride, she stomped back to her desk and stabbed a number into the phone. It rang and rang, muffled against her ear.

'For fuck's *sake.*' She hung up with a crash that made me jerk.

I huddled in my desk chair. 'Who were you trying to ring?'

'The buildings manager. Whose boss I'll have words with at this meeting.' She bent to give me an unexpected hug. 'I'm so sorry you had to see that, hon. Especially on your first day. It's despicable. Will you be OK?'

I nodded, more intimidated than soothed by her fierce, steely arms.

'Don't worry,' she added with a reassuring pat, 'you'll never see that naked man again.'

The door banged behind her as she left the office, and I slumped at my desk like a sandcastle hit by a wave. When her footsteps faded I picked up the handbook again, biting my lip.

PhD in Women's Studies. How could I be starting one of those? I didn't feel qualified, despite the enrolment forms on my desk, and marks high enough to win a doctoral scholarship. PhDs were for serious, clever people who knew what they were doing. Not pretenders who hadn't decided what they wanted to research, let alone found a professor to supervise their project.

I made myself open the handbook again and skimmed the staff profiles. When I reached Hilda Ziehler, specialist in feminist art, something occurred to me. There were art studios along the top floor of the building below the window. The man I'd seen through the skylight wasn't flaunting himself, he was probably posing for a life drawing class. And now I'd set Andrea on him.

I rushed back to the window. Through the skylight, the man was no longer naked. He was wearing a navy blue robe, talking to someone I couldn't see. Was he in a studio?

On the top floors, stoppers prevented the windows from opening too wide. I slid my head carefully through the gap and the catch on the frame lodged in my hair. Trapped between frame and sill, I struggled to free myself, and the movement caught the man's attention. He looked up through the skylight and our eyes met. The hairnet holding my bun together came free, and my hair spilled out the window, rippling in the wind like a long, pale scarf made of silk.

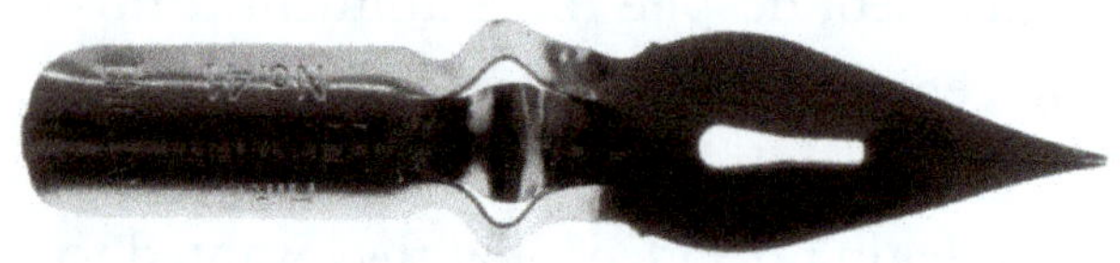

Chapter 2

Window to the Soul

I wrenched my head in, grazing one ear against the window frame. Strands of my hair were still hanging over the sill, and my fingers felt like noodles as I struggled to gather them. It took four attempts to rebuild my bun and secure it.

When I looked out again, the man grinned and waved, as if we were sharing a joke. A bubble of warmth welled inside me, and I gave a tiny wave in return. A cloud cast a shadow over the skylight for a moment, and when the sun reappeared he was gone.

For five minutes or so, I stood at the window, looking through the skylight at the bare, polished boards. He didn't come back, but his smile was still there, the way an image lingers after looking at a light. What was Andrea planning to do to him? She was famed for being ruthless with men in power. But he wasn't a man in power. He was probably a student, modelling for art classes to pay his way through university. The afterimage throbbed with a terrible guilt, as if I'd set a pit bull on a puppy.

Maybe Andrea hadn't got to him yet. I rang the building supervisor's number. When no one answered, I typed 'art class' into the university search engine and found *Life drawing, Mondays 3-5pm. Studio 3, Fine Arts building. Six week short course. Tutor: Sally Old.* I grabbed my keys and headed out the door.

The ground floor foyer of the Fine Arts building had the high-ceilinged cool of a cathedral. The painted eyes of long-dead professors watched from the walls as I hurried through the foyer to the lift. I'd left a note for Andrea saying I'd gone to the library, and the lie rattled inside me like dice in a cup.

The top floor corridor smelled of turpentine and clay. I walked past pinboards flapping with flyers and timetables, to an open door labelled with a '3'. Inside, a ring of artists stood at their easels; in the centre was a woman in a purple dress with a name tag that read 'Sally Old'. She looked quite young, maybe thirty. The man from the window was nowhere to be seen, but his red rug was laid out on the floor beside her. No longer under the skylight, but a few feet to its right.

'Here for the class?' said Sally, with a smile that made the stud in her left nostril wink. 'Thought we started at half past, did you?'

I gaped like a goldfish. 'I … yes. No. I mean … I thought I should tell you that … that I saw your model.'

'Ryan, you mean?' said Sally. 'Great, isn't he? Where'd you see him, Carol's class?'

Before I could clarify, a curtain in the corner of the room drew back and the man from the skylight stepped out in his robe. A ripple swelled my veins. His gaze fell on me and a curious frown formed on his face.

'Anyway, sorry to interrupt ...' I tried to sidle out with my back to the model, but Sally pressed a new box of charcoal in my hand.

'Don't sweat it,' she said. 'We all get lost. Get started and I'll fill you in later.'

Cornered by her kindness, I gave her my name and she added it to her class list. I retreated behind an easel and tried to breathe normally as the model ambled back to his rug. Close up, his hair was a dark, springy brown that bounced as he walked.

Had he recognised me? Surely not from a couple of stories away, through two layers of glass?

'Can we have Ryan back under natural light?' said the woman at the easel next to mine.

Sally shook her head. 'Afraid not.' Her mouth twisted wryly. 'That man who came up before was from Buildings. Someone in Humanities saw Ryan through the skylight and made a complaint.'

Goosebumps of horror sprouted all over me.

The model gasped, clutching his hair in theatrical anguish. 'A *complaint?* About seeing me in the buff? I'm crushed! *Crushed,* I tell you!' His voice was sunny and animated, like a character in a children's cartoon.

Sally grinned. 'Don't worry, Ryan. We still love you.'

He released his hair, looking mischievous. 'Maybe,' he mused, 'the person who saw me just didn't want to share the view with anyone else.' His gaze slid onto me, and this time I was sure he knew who I was.

My cheeks burned. I rummaged in my backpack to hide my face, wishing I could crawl all the way inside it and die. Why hadn't I just let it go? All Andrea had achieved was to make him move from the skylight. Now this man thought it was *me* who'd reported him, and then hurried to the class to *see him naked!*

'You wish, Ryan,' said Sally, taking out a small electric timer.

'A man can dream, can't he?'

'He can.' The timer emitted a series of tinny beeps under her thumb. 'But not when he's giving us five two-minute poses and two fives. Now,' said Sally, addressing the whole class, 'I'd like you all to start off with charcoal today. Later on, when the poses get longer, you can draw with whatever you like.'

The clink and rustle of other students preparing to draw filtered through my backpack. I peeked out. Ryan was standing by the rug in his robe, rummaging in his own bag. He pulled out a wooden sword and shrugged his robe to the floor. Beneath it, he was naked.

My hand whipped up to shield my eyes, as if I'd walked in by mistake when he was changing. In my peripheral vision I saw the other students looking him up and down. Not lustfully, but analytically. Holding pencils up to measure his proportions, pacing back and forth to assess him from different angles.

I lowered my hand. Sally was talking to a student about shading and Ryan was standing on the podium, sword in hand, as if public nudity was as natural as breathing. The only person in the studio feeling embarrassed and exposed was me.

Ryan brandished the sword as if fighting a duel, and Sally pressed her timer to start the session. The whisper of charcoal on paper filled the room. Willing the blood to recede from my cheeks, I selected a long piece of charcoal.

From this distance, Ryan's nakedness was less shocking. Less shocking and more ordinary, somehow. More human. Online and in magazines, bodies looked like mannequins, featureless and

Photoshop smooth. Here in the studio, Ryan looked unnervingly *alive*.

He was still, but his body was stirring with life. His eyelids fell and lifted, and his ribcage swelled and contracted under his skin. The side of his left knee had a crescent-shaped scar, and his limbs and chest were sprinkled with dark curls of hair. My eyes skirted around his genitals, but I sensed them there, dangling between his legs like a sinister fruit.

Sally called 'Change!' and Ryan turned side-on, placing the point of his sword on a stool as if claiming it for his empire. I sketched his profile but had only reached his nose when Sally called 'Change!' once again.

She came over as the third pose began. 'Big, loose sweeps of charcoal, Sage. Fill the page! We're here to draw, not save paper.'

Ryan donned a fedora for the first five-minute pose, and I found my hand had relaxed into the new, sweeping movements. I captured not only his outline, but his hands and the details of his hat in the available time.

Sally called 'Change!' again.

This time he went down on one knee, swept off his fedora and held it out, his eyes directly on mine. The charcoal I was holding snapped in my hand. I dropped my gaze to his fedora, readjusting the stub of charcoal with clumsy fingers. Blood flooded my cheeks once more, accompanied this time by resentment. Why had Ryan set up a pose where he was looking right into my face? Was he was mocking me, or trying to unnerve me?

Andrea would have felled him with a brutal remark; I went on strike instead. Knowing he could see me, I folded my arms and stood listening to the rasp of fifteen-minus-one pieces of charcoal. When Sally announced the break, I strode over to make a complaint.

'Hi Sage,' she said, setting the timer for ten minutes. 'Keeping up all right?'

'I … yes. Thanks.'

'Help yourself to tea or coffee. You were doing great once you loosened up. There were some really expressive lines in that last drawing.'

I struggled to refocus. 'Thanks. Um, about the model—'

'Good, isn't he? Always dynamic, aren't you, Ryan?'

'A dynamo in human form,' said Ryan, strolling toward us in his robe.

I scuttled over to the urn and stared at a plate of biscuits, trying to gather my thoughts.

'Hey, Sage.' It was Ryan's voice, so close behind I jumped.

Muscles puckered in my back. Staring me down hadn't been enough. Now he was *following* me. Andrea's lectures on sexual harassment and stalking pounded in my head. *Sometimes a harasser who's ignored will give up. Sometimes, he'll go on until he gets a reaction. The best thing to do is look him in the eye and confront him about his behaviour.*

'Your name's Sage, right?'

Beads of sweat formed on my skin. He was even closer now, so close I could feel the faint warmth of his body. I'd never been this close to a man before. Summoning my most assertive tone, I snatched up a biscuit and turned to face him. 'Yes. It is.'

He smiled, as if I'd cracked a mild joke. 'You've come down in the world since I saw you last.'

It occurred to me that confirming my name was a mistake. He knew where my office was. My name was unusual. What if he searched the university directory and tracked me down?

I gripped my biscuit and looked him in the eyes. They were the colour of dark chocolate, like his hair. Embarrassment overwhelmed me again and the biscuit disintegrated in my clenched hand. 'I don't know what you're talking about,' I said in a huff, as I swept the crumbs into the bin and hurried back to my easel.

'Relax!' said Ryan, keeping pace with me. 'Don't be embarrassed. I'm flattered!'

Four or five curious artists had turned to listen in. I dropped my voice to a hiss. 'I'm not here to flatter you.'

He pressed the back of his hand to his brow. 'Crushed again! So why did you come, then?'

'OK, everyone,' announced Sally, 'time to get started. Two ten-minute poses. Do you want a stool, Ryan?'

'Stool, schmool,' said Ryan, returning to the rug with a swirl of his robe. 'Seated ten-minute poses are for wimps.'

He took a plastic replica of the Statue of Liberty from his bag and thrust it in the air like a torch. This time I was facing his back. He had a light tan that extended up to the middle of his biceps and down to a curved line at the bottom of his neck, as if his T-shirt had left an echo on his skin.

When Sally next said 'Change!' I tensed, but he didn't face my way again. Neither did he speak to me in the next two breaks, leaving me to ponder his question: *Why did you come?*

On the surface, the answer was easy. Because I'd wanted to warn them that Andrea was on the warpath. Yet this wasn't quite enough to explain why I'd stayed, or the surge in my veins when I saw him again.

'All right, folks,' said Sally as the timer went off, 'that's it for today. Stack your easels in the corner, and go outside if you want to spray fixative on your drawings. See you next week!'

I unclipped my sheaf of drawings as a chorus of scraping chairs and easels filled the studio.

'Good work, Sage,' said Sally, collecting my box of charcoal. 'Coming back next week?'

The events of the day pressed in like a hostile crowd. 'Can I think about it? I've just started a PhD, and I don't know how much time I'll have for drawing.'

Sally nodded, not bothered. 'Sure, that's fine. Hope to see you again.'

She headed off to collect more charcoal, and I rolled my drawings into a cylinder.

'Need a rubber band?'

Ryan's voice. He looked thinner dressed, as if his clothes had taken bulk away from his body instead of adding it.

My cheeks stayed cool, and only the faintest wary eddy went through me. 'Actually, yes, thanks.'

He flicked a rubber band into the air, and it landed in my palm like a raindrop. 'Sorry if I embarrassed you before. I can be an embarrassment, sometimes.'

As I stretched the rubber band around my drawings, the print on his T-shirt caught my eye: a small boy standing on a giant lemon, holding a flock of bluebirds tied to strings.

'By the way,' he added, 'did you come up with an answer to my question?'

I hastily looked back at Ryan's face. 'Your question?'

'Why did you come to this class? Just … wanted to learn drawing suddenly?'

Self-consciousness returned, and I looked away. 'Um, yes. I suppose so.'

'Well, I'm glad you did. Nice to meet you, Sage. Catch you next week.'

He flourished a hand at me, slung his bag over his shoulder, and loped out the door, chocolate fountain of hair dancing above him.

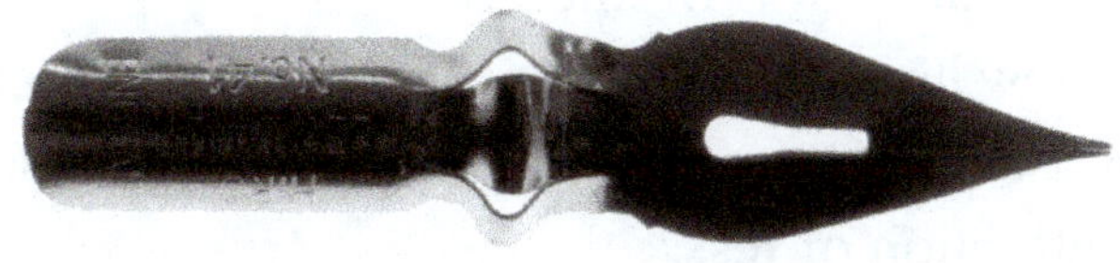

Chapter Three

Getting Trashed

I walked slowly home, the conversation with Ryan turning over and over in my head. It was three-and-a-half years since I'd spoken to someone my age who hadn't been introduced to me by Andrea. Three-and-a-half years since I fled university to finish my degree online from home.

When I started my degree in Women's Studies at eighteen, I'd been full of hope and excitement. In my imagination, university was a wonderful place, where I'd find myself a circle of brilliant young friends who shared my passions and ideas.

My collision with reality was shattering. I couldn't connect with other undergraduates at all. They spent their lives either staring at their phones or locked into pre-existing circles of friends I could never hope to enter. They used slang I didn't understand, talked about things I didn't know, and seemed more interested in drinking and celebrities than anything they heard in their lectures. The few that enjoyed discussing ideas were scary and aggressive, or so full of drawling sophistication I felt intimidated. My clumsy attempts to talk to them were met with rebuffs and incomprehension. Sometimes polite incomprehension, sometimes condescending, as if I should know better than to think I was of interest.

After a few humiliating weeks, I retreated and spent my time studying and debating feminist theory with staff. This was what caught the attention of Jess.

Jess was a student in my Gender Politics class. I lingered after class to talk to our tutor one day and saw Jess still at her desk, contemplating a list of essay topics as if afraid it might bite her. She looked about eighteen, like me, with a face made up of circles: curly hair, round rosy cheeks and wide, despairing blue eyes.

'You get this stuff, don't you?' she'd said, her lips tremulous.

I nodded. Andrea had taught me everything we'd covered so far when I was fourteen or fifteen. 'Do you?' I asked.

Jess shook her head. 'It's like a whole different *language*. I mean, like, what's *this* supposed to mean?' She pointed at the first essay topic. 'Para … diggum,' she read gingerly.

'Paradigm shift,' I corrected. 'It means a change in the way people think about things. Like when people stopped believing the sun went around the world and started believing the world went around the sun instead.'

Jess's wide eyes widened still further. 'My God,' she said, sounding awestruck, 'you are so totally going to own this subject. Half the time I don't even understand what you're saying.'

I gave an offhand shrug, but her innocent admiration touched me. 'Would you like me to help you?'

She nodded, as if I'd thrown her a lifeline. I spent half an hour taking her through the essay topics, and her earnest gratitude warmed me to the core.

At the next tutorial she sat beside me, and the following week she invited me to lunch after class. After a month of walking among aliens, one had finally rolled out the welcome mat.

Jess had just graduated from high school, where she had more young people in her circle of friends than I'd met in my entire life. As her new Gender Politics friend, my job was to listen to the tales of these friends and give a feminist analysis of their behaviour. Jess seldom asked me about myself, but I didn't mind. I had no tales of my own, and I enjoyed being entrusted with hers.

Near the end of first semester, Jess invited me to her nineteenth birthday party. She'd booked a private room for twenty in a karaoke bar to 'get trashed and sing trashy songs'.

At half past eight, Andrea dropped me off in Chinatown, where I steered through the crowds to a flight of granite steps. At the top was a bar, behind which lounged a bored Chinese youth, his eyes fixed on his phone. I gave him Jess's name and he pointed me down a corridor with a muddle of discordant voices leaking through the doors.

I opened the door labelled '4' and a wall of noise smacked me in the face. The room was windowless and dotted with orange vinyl couches. The only light came from a television screening what looked like a Korean rom-com and the phones glowing in everyone's hands. In front of the television stood three off-key young women holding microphones. One was fondling her body as she sang, one was taking a selfie of herself giving the microphone oral sex, and the third finished every line with an inaccurate swig from a bottle. Of the people nursing drinks and phones on the couches, the only one who gave me more than a cursory glance was a stocky young man with a humorous mouth and skin the colour of sarsaparilla.

He held out an oddly formal hand. 'Hi, I'm Sumeet.' His palm was cool and dry, and his voice was deep and lilting, with an Indian accent.

Sumeet had featured in several of Jess's tales. He'd arrived at her school from India when he was fourteen, and was one of the few guys who could see through Bitchy Caitlin, a redhead who thought herself the 'hottest thing ever'.

'Hi, I'm Sage.' I attempted a smile in return. 'Is this Jess's party?'

Sumeet nodded. 'Take a seat.'

I slid onto his couch a careful arm's length away. The song ended and the three women rambled over, looking me up and down as if they couldn't quite believe what they saw. For the first time in my life, I sensed there was something terribly wrong with me.

'You're Sage, the feminist, aren't you?' said the tallest of the women, with the smile of a circling shark. She wore a skin-tight black dress that bared most of her thighs, and her long, wavy red hair identified her as Bitchy Caitlin.

'How did you know?' I asked, trying to be friendly.

She darted a sidelong look at her friends. 'Call it a hunch.'

Her two friends giggled, still looking me up and down. Both wore low-cut tops that exposed half their breasts, one with a mini-skirt and one with black pants. Like Caitlin, they had long glossy hair, lashings of glittery makeup, and heels so high they walked with a strange, stilted strut.

I could have been of a different species from these women. Everything I was wearing had been bought by Andrea: my loose hemp shirt and pants, my Fairtrade canvas shoes and the green men's jacket she found at a charity shop. Andrea often bought second-hand men's clothes. *They're better quality than women's clothes,* she told me, with an eye roll to say this was only to be expected. My hair was very short, and the only thing on my face was a pair of Andrea's glasses, recycled and fitted with my lenses.

The thought of Andrea bolstered me against their stares. *Don't be cowed, be compassionate*, she would say. *They were raised in a world where a woman's worth is measured by her sex appeal. Where they're fooled into obsessing over diets and shoes to stop them from challenging male power.* I lifted my chin and told myself their sneers were an opportunity. Maybe I could help these women escape The Male Gaze and embrace real power through feminism.

'*Loving* the look, by the way,' added Caitlin, closing in for the kill. Her friends giggled so hard that they almost toppled off their stilettos.

My stomach caved in with shame. These women would die of laughter at the thought of learning anything from me. They were at the peak of their sexual power, and to them I was a loser and a joke.

'Are you girls being bitchy?' asked Sumeet.

I felt unsettled. On one hand, I didn't want a man to protect me; on the other I was desperately glad he'd stepped in.

'Us, Sumeet?' said Caitlin, in mock-wounded tones. 'We're *never* bitchy, are we, Kayla?'

'*Never!*' said the woman in black pants.

'Anyway,' said Caitlin, her perfect teeth glistening, 'nice to meet you, Sage. Come sing with us later.' She sashayed away to a couch with a wave, and the other two followed behind.

'Don't listen to those girls,' said Sumeet. My hand dodged his reassuring pat. 'They think looking pretty means they can act ugly.' He sounded kind, but his gaze scanned the legs of the three departing women in a way no man had ever looked at me.

The last of my pride crumbled. 'Is Jess here?' I asked, craving the reassurance of her admiring, dimpled face.

'Oh yes. Here in body, but not in spirit, you might say. Or maybe in too many spirits. Let me show you.'

He led me to a couch. Jess lay face down in a short red dress, her curly head joined at the lips to the man underneath her. All I could see of him was two denim-clad legs and a forehead edged with spiky blond hair.

'Jess,' called Sumeet, 'your friend Sage is here to see you.'

Jess detached herself from the man and looked up. Her left cheek was smudged with mascara. 'Sage!' She extracted the man's hand from her top and clambered off him, engulfing me in a hug that smelled of hairspray and cocktails. 'Thanks *so* much for coming!' Her voice was bright but unsteady.

'Happy birthday!' I said to her right ear, with as much enthusiasm as I could muster.

'My *God*, we need to sing something together! Shove over, Kurt.'

I balanced myself on the very edge of the couch. Kurt got up with a grunt, yanked his shirt over the lump in his jeans and slouched off in the direction of the bar.

Jess draped one arm around my shoulder and picked up a plastic folder with the other. 'What should we sing? How about "Toxic"?' she said, with a bright-eyed conviction that *everyone* would know "Toxic".

My spirits, which had begun to lift, stalled somewhere between my shoulder blades. 'Um … sorry, I … I don't really know the latest … bands. And things.'

Jess and Sumeet stared as if I'd come from another planet.

'Toxic isn't a band, Sage,' said Jess, in careful, almost pitying tones. 'It's a Britney song. From, like, the early 2000s. You *do* know Britney Spears, right?'

'Kind of.' The name Britney Spears did ring a bell. Not because I'd heard her music, but because she'd featured in an article I'd read on the commodification of women.

Jess and Sumeet exchanged a glance so incredulous I felt my face begin to prickle with shame.

'So,' said Sumeet, 'who *do* you know? How about … Adele? You know, "Someone Like You?"'

Withering under their saucer-eyed disbelief, I dropped my gaze to my hands. 'Not really.' I'd never listened to commercial music. Bubblegum, Andrea called it. Disposable music for the masses to chew and spit out.

They listed song after one, and artist after artist, and every time I shook my head my spirits sank a little further. I reminded myself that I knew plenty about important things, like politics and history and world poverty, and that pop music didn't actually matter. But there on the orange couch, behind a giant folder of songs, it felt like the most important thing in the world.

Ten crushing minutes later, Jess thrust the folder into my lap, told me to keep looking, and took Sumeet off to get drinks. Alone on the couch, I leafed through the greasy plastic pages. I found a handful of tracks I knew, but they were songs from Andrea's time, generations removed from the fluffy pop blaring from the speakers.

I shoved the folder aside and slunk to the toilets to pull myself together. Shortly after I'd locked myself into a cubicle, two sets of stilettos clattered in, and I recognised the voices of Caitlin and Kayla.

'Did you see Sumeet? He was almost *flirting* with her!'

'Yeah, but guys love that dyke stuff,' said Caitlin. 'She probably reminds him of lesbian porn.'

The stilettos positioned themselves in front of the mirror, to the sound of zips and tiny plastic clicks.

'So is she a dyke, or just a femmo?' said Kayla.

'God, she *must* be a dyke. I mean, seriously, check out the ugly glasses and the butchmeister haircut. Is she in the army, or what?'

It was at this point that I realised they were talking about me. I sank fully clothed onto the lid of the toilet, their words hitting my stomach like fists.

'And the *clothes!* My God, where do you even *find* clothes like that?'

'Some dyke shop. Made extra baggy for feral pubes and leg hair.'

Andrea would have marched out and mowed them down, but I curled into a ball, not wanting to listen, but unable to stop. Jess talked to me constantly about the people at this party: what had she said to them about me? Was I a circus freak she'd plucked from her 'femmo' class for her normal friends to laugh at? Was everyone who looked at me sniggering at the hairy dyke loser in bad clothes who didn't know a single pop song?

By the time Caitlin and Kayla left the bathroom, tears were streaming down my face. I smeared them on my sleeve and crept out to the mirror. Was I ugly? Did I look like a lesbian? What was so bad about my clothes? I stared into the glass for a good five minutes, and realised I had utterly no idea.

The loud, discordant karaoke bar was suddenly too much to bear. Head down and shoulders hunched, I ducked into Room 4 to thank Jess and say goodbye. She was back on the couch with Kurt.

I cowered in the shadows, waiting for her to disengage, but the kissing and groping went on and on and on. Sensing eyes on me, I looked up and realised two of Jess's guests—a man and a woman—were watching me watch Jess and Kurt.

The man gave me a sly, knowing grin. 'Yeah that's right, have a good look. You're really getting off on it, aren't you?'

He stuck out his tongue and waggled it from side to side. The woman laughed, and a burning wave of humiliation broke over me. I wanted to escape, but my body wouldn't move.

'Ask if you can join in,' added the woman. 'Or do you want Jess all to yourself?'

The spell broke, and I bolted from the room, crashing into chairs and half-falling down the steps in my desperation to get out, get away, get to somewhere safe from the laughter and contempt of these people I'd hoped might be my friends.

The streets outside were full of faces. Staring, judging, finding things wrong with me. I fixed my gaze on the pavement and walked and walked until the boiling shame eased to a simmer. By now the crowds of Chinatown had ebbed to a trickle of passers-by.

Spying a convenience store, I decided to go in and ask for directions to my bus stop. As I walked to the counter, a magazine caught my eye. One of the pop stars Sumeet and Jess had mentioned was featured on the cover. I picked it up, dropped it in a fit of self-consciousness and bought a broadsheet newspaper instead. Later, I took that paper to the back seat and read the Entertainment and Fashion sections that Andrea always threw out. I threw them out myself when I got off the bus, but only when I'd read them cover to cover.

Four days later, I saved Jess a seat in Gender Politics, but she didn't turn up. I rang her when I got home, and she told me she'd withdrawn from the subject.

'It just wasn't what I thought it was going to be,' she said, her voice stiff and cool.

A shadow of foreboding crept over me. 'What did you think it was going to be?'

'I thought it would be about women being strong and doing what they want, but it wasn't that at all. Mostly it was just preaching.'

'Preaching?'

'You know, about how there aren't enough women in politics, and whatever. I mean, maybe women don't *want* to be in politics.'

Part of me wanted to make her see why politics mattered, and how much she owed feminism, but another, deeper part sensed it was too late. The note of admiration had vanished from her voice; the welcome mat had been snatched from the doorstep.

'I'm sorry I left your birthday party without saying goodbye,' I said. 'I was feeling sick, and you were busy with Kurt, so I—'

'You really don't know how to have fun, do you?' snapped Jess.

I froze, shocked and stung.

'I mean, OK, so you're a *feminist*,' she went on, with a sneer in her voice, 'but that doesn't mean you're better than everyone else.'

My face went numb. 'I never said I was better than everyone else.'

'You don't say it, but you *think* it, don't you? You're always judging people. Well, sorry, but I like pop music, even if it is commercial and sexist. And I like guys, and wearing nice clothes. And if that makes me oppressed and stupid, well, at least I know how to have fun.'

She hung up. I pressed my fingers into my welling eyes and fumed. At Caitlin for ridiculing me, at Jess for siding with her friends, and at myself, for seeing how much truth there was in what Jess had said.

The front door opened, and I remembered it was haircut night. Andrea spread newspapers on the kitchen floor and I went to fetch the scissors. I closed the blades on tuft after tuft of grey hair, as if trying to chop Jess from my memory. Overnight, the world had become a sea of sneering faces, laughing at how I dressed and how very, very little I knew.

The last wiry tuft hit the paper. 'Can students do Women's Studies subjects online?' I asked.

'Our students are almost all women, Sage, and lots of them are caregivers.' Andrea's voice was impatient, implying that I should have known this without being told. 'We offer everything online. It's an equity issue.' She peered at me suspiciously. 'Why?'

I grabbed a cloth and bent to clean the scissors and hide my expression. 'I was thinking I might finish my degree from home, instead of attending classes.'

She shrugged. 'Suit yourself.' She didn't ask me why, and her offhand tone sounded almost like relief. 'I'll let Student Admin know.'

She took the scissors and waited for me to sit down. I looked at the chair, Caitlin's words burning in my guts. *She must be a dyke. Check out the butchmeister haircut.* 'I might skip the haircut tonight.'

Andrea's face darkened. 'Why's that? Too much time on your hands? Growing yourself a lure to attract *men*?'

I shrank from her words, but my feet wouldn't budge. 'No special reason,' I said to the scissors. 'I just thought I might let it grow.'

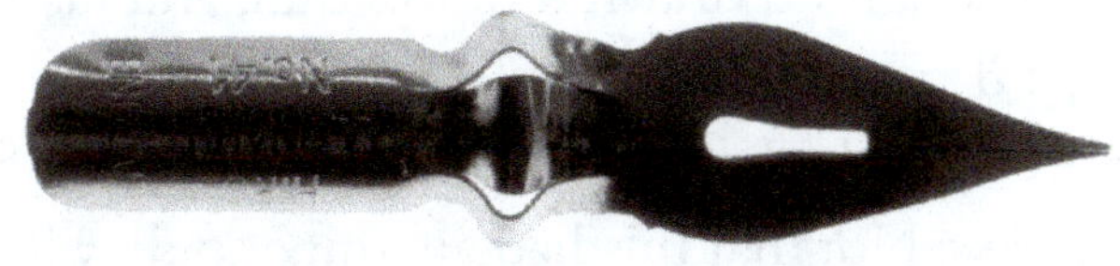

Chapter Four

Back to the Drawing Board

Something was beeping. The sound was coming from my head, as if an electric mosquito had sneaked inside my skull. I groped around blearily and the computer mouse fell in my lap. Startled into consciousness, I realised I'd fallen asleep on the space bar. The reason for this gleamed above me on the screen: Jacqueline Fisher's PhD thesis.

This thesis, wrote Jacqueline, *endeavours to interrogate the unidimensionality of the socially embedded and heteronormative paradigms of corporeal femininity, with post-structural reference to historically contingent constructions of pedagogical discourse.*

Four pages in, I felt new respect for Jacqueline's PhD examiners, who'd managed to read the whole thing. I tried to add to my notes on her work, but it was like giving birth to a building. With a resentful burst of energy, I pressed Print and reached behind the bookcase for the rolled-up drawings from last week's class. I had to go downstairs to the staffroom for the printouts, so I could toss these drawings in the recycling bin at the same time, and come back to Jacqueline refreshed.

I unfurled the roll of paper for one last look and found my five-minute sketch of Ryan in a fedora. A strange fizz went through me. Though I'd drawn him too thin, and his feet looked like turnips, I'd captured some of his bright, jaunty energy. In fifteen minutes he'd be back in the studio, posing for Sally's next life drawing class. Not that this had anything to do with me. I had an acclaimed PhD thesis to read.

The sign on the door said 'Staff and Graduate Students Only', which as of last week included me. With a twinge of excitement, I opened the door. A printer in the corner was churning out paper, and beside it stood Fran Mackenzie, small and neat with smooth red hair. I was suddenly hyper-aware that I was carrying several large pictures of a naked man.

'Sage,' she said, smiling as if I were a long-lost friend, instead of the granddaughter of her boss and arch-enemy. 'Taking drawing classes?'

I clutched the drawings to my chest, trying to screen them with my arms. 'No, no,' I said, my voice unnaturally high. 'I was just … looking at how women are portrayed in different media.' I glanced down. In between my wrists was my squeamish attempt at drawing Ryan's penis. I hastily swivelled the roll to hide it.

'Well, if you decide to look at popular media, let me know.' Fran turned back to the printer.

Heat rising in my cheeks, I located my freshly labelled pigeonhole, grabbed a sheet of paper and wrapped it strategically around the drawings. Had Fran seen the penis? What if she told people? *What if it got back to Andrea?* I peeled back the paper, peeked at the offending organ, and breathed a quiet thanks for my lack of drawing skills. Hopefully she'd thought it was an oven glove.

Fran approached, holding out my summary of Jacqueline's first chapter. 'Is this yours?'

'Um, yes. Thanks.'

I willed Fran to leave so I could throw out the drawings, but she paused, leafing through her printouts. Close up, I could see she was wearing makeup. My tongue made a silent click of disapproval. *Queen of the lipstick feminists*, Andrea called her. Fran attracted third-wave feminist graduates who posted outfit photos on Instagram and called our field 'Gender Studies'.

'I hear you're starting a PhD with us,' she said. 'Well done. Have you been assigned an office?'

I wrapped an extra layer of paper around the drawings. 'Andrea invited me to share hers.'

Fran's brows hit her hairline. 'Is that what *you* wanted?'

My hackles rose. 'Of course. Anyway, if you'll excuse me, I have to go.'

Still bristling, I stalked out to the lift and pressed the button for the ground floor, where there was a larger and more public recycling bin.

Like all the best arch-enemies, Fran had started out as Andrea's friend. Her daughter Freya was two years older than me, and Andrea used to invite them around to give me contact with other children. We saw them every couple of weeks for some years until Freya, then fifteen, arrived on our doorstep wearing makeup and heels. Andrea declared Freya a negative role model, and refused to let her in. The heated argument that followed ended in the Mackenzies being banned from our house, and began a long and bitter feud between Andrea and Fran.

The lift doors opened. I marched straight to the recycling bin and threw in the drawings. They unrolled and there was Ryan looking up from his blanket, just as I'd seen him through the skylight. I told myself to go back to the office, but my body refused to obey. My hands snatched up the drawings again, and my legs led me out the door and pelted across the grounds towards the studio.

'Today,' Sally Old's voice drifted down the corridor, 'we're going to try drawing with our non-dominant hand.'

I skidded to a gasping halt in the doorway of Studio 3. Sally was back inside the ring of easels, but the rug behind her was bare. Last week's drawings sagged in my grip.

'Hi, Sage,' said Sally. 'Catch your breath and grab an easel.'

I was levering an easel from the pile in the corner when the curtain across the room opened and Ryan stepped out. The room brightened, as if lit by his zest. Hair springing cheerily, he strode to the rug, clothes and bag of props on one shoulder.

His gaze fell on me and a flicker went down my spine. 'Hey!' he said with a grin. Not sheepish, like last week's, but bright-eyed and broad. 'Who invited *you* back here?'

A smile broke out before I could stop it. 'No one,' I said. 'I just thought I'd come back.' I dropped my head to hide my blush, and realised two things that embarrassed me further. One was that I'd been watching him ever since he appeared. The other was that the unsaid rest of my answer was *because I wanted to see you.*

The phrase roared in my ears. I scuttled away, hiding my face with my easel and trying to shut down those unthinkable words. Unthinkable because I wasn't the sort of woman who took drawing classes to court a man's attention. Absolutely not. I chose to take the class because drawing was a refreshing break from Women's Studies. Something I'd enjoyed. Something that hadn't been chosen for me by Andrea.

This unexpected thought distracted me until the drawing exercise began. Ryan assumed a comical muscle-man pose, with chin lifted and one bicep flexed. From where I stood I could see the tension in his arm, and the gleam of his eye. His lashes were as thick and dark as his hair, and his limbs were slightly browner against the ghost of his T-shirt.

'You OK there, Sage?' called Sally.

Everyone else had started drawing several minutes ago. I snatched up my charcoal. 'Um, yes, I was just … I was … I'm fine.'

'You're left-handed, then?'

Left-handed? What … oh. Drawing exercise. Non-dominant hand. I switched the charcoal to my left hand. After a few flustered minutes, my mind changed gear, and the man on the podium changed from Ryan to a shape marked with contours and shadows. Capturing these with my left hand instead of my right felt awkward but strangely freeing, like a window had been opened in a long-shuttered part of my brain.

Twenty minutes later, when the timer went off, the shape on the podium turned back into Ryan. He pulled on his robe and wandered around the circle of easels, looking at the drawings. I covered my clumsy left-handed sketches as he approached, but he didn't even glance at them.

'*So*, Sage,' he said in a portentous tone, 'have you figured out why you're here yet?'

Because I wanted to see you. 'Actually,' I said. 'I have. I think I need to do something that's not academic sometimes. To reconnect with mainstream society.'

My smile evaporated as the sentence left my mouth. What was I, a yoga teacher? No one at Jess's party would have spoken like that. I was about to blunder in to amend what I'd said when I saw his face fall.

'*Mainstream?*' His horror was only half-comical. 'I'm not *mainstream*. I'm offbeat! Cutting edge!' He seized the charcoal T-shirt he'd hung on a chair. 'Check out my T-shirt. I ask you, is this the T-shirt of a mainstream man?'

The front was printed with a drawing of four dancing figures framed by grape vines. The sinking feeling from the karaoke bar returned. This picture must be like a Madonna song, one of those things normal people just knew.

'It's from *Prince Caspian*,' said Ryan. 'The cover of the first edition.'

'Oh,' I said, trying to sound enlightened.

Ryan looked at me, a suspicious frown creasing his brow. 'You've read *The Chronicles of Narnia* by C.S. Lewis, haven't you?'

'Not really.' I contemplated my pencils, scared I was about to see that saucer-eyed look on his face. 'I was home-schooled.'

'And your parents didn't read books to you?'

'I wasn't raised by my parents,' I said, head still bowed. 'I was raised by my grandmother.'

Before Ryan could respond, the timer went off, and he hurried back to the rug with a wave. In the next break, he came straight to my easel. This time I didn't hide my drawings. Or my smile.

'So what books did your grandmother read you?'

My smile faded. 'My grandmother's a strict feminist,' I said. 'She wanted to protect me from patriarchal messages.'

It would have been easier to say my grandmother was in jail. No one outside Andrea's world admitted to feminism any more.

Feminists were hairy-legged, man-hating monsters, who were bitter because no one wanted to have sex with them.

'So she gave you … feminist books?' He sounded intrigued, not contemptuous.

I nodded. 'Feminist books, feminist plays. And absolutely nothing with advertising. No magazines, no commercial radio, no TV.'

'Wow,' said Ryan.

Wow? I searched his face to see if he was mocking me, but he looked awed.

'That means you haven't been exposed to mainstream culture.' His eyes were almost starry. 'Think of the art you could make!'

'*Art?*' I glanced at my easel.

'You won't need to steer clear of clichés, because you never learnt the clichés in the first place. Your perspective is *totally original!*'

Did Ryan actually envy me? I'd never been envied before. Then the sneers at Jess's party crept back into my mind, and the brief glow inside me winked out. 'That's not such a good thing.'

'How do you mean?'

'It's embarrassing,' I explained. 'There are all these things I'm just supposed to *know*, and I don't know what they are.'

He gave me a quizzical look. 'What things don't you know?'

'Slang. Fashion. *The Chronicles of Narnia.* Madonna songs. *Everything.*'

'Hmm.' His brow crinkled in concentration, like I was a puzzle he was trying to solve. 'You know what you need? A mentor. Someone who *just knows* those things, and can teach you what they are.'

Something wary stirred inside me. Was he about to volunteer for the post? Before I dared ask, Sally spoke.

'OK everyone,' she announced, 'time for the twenty-minute pose. We'll be doing this pose again for the next slot, so take your time.'

For half of the next break, Ryan sat on the podium while Sally marked the position of his limbs with masking tape. He spent the rest of the break talking to an artist who wanted to hire him, but once or twice he threw me a quick smile or glance to let me know I hadn't been forgotten.

When the timer rang for the last time, Ryan dressed in record time, came over and pressed something small into my palm. 'I have to run,' he said, 'but if you want to continue your education, give me a call.'

He scampered for the exit. I opened my hand and found a chic cream business card with *Ryan Prince* printed on it. Underneath his name it read *Artist, life model and art teacher*, with his phone number, URL and Instagram handle.

'So, Sage,' said Sally, a knowing smile on her lips, 'I smell success.'

My jaw tightened at her smirking, nudging tone. 'How do you mean, success?'

'A successful pick-up. Are you going to call him?'

My face flamed. 'It's not that,' I said, closing my fingers over the card. 'He's just … I don't know much about popular culture, and he's … offered to fill me in.'

Sally chuckled. 'Don't be shy, he's a lovely guy. If I was single, I'd have a crack at him myself. Give him a call. This was his last week, so you won't see him again unless you do.'

She winked and headed off. I slid the card into my pocket, rolled up my drawings and slunk out, pulsating with embarrassment.

Have a crack at Ryan? I'd never *had a crack* at anyone in my life. Picking up men was what other women did, women with painted faces and low-cut tops. I told myself this as I walked back to the Humanities building, but I also slipped my hand in my pocket every few steps, to make sure his card was still there.

Back at the office, I opened a new Word document and tried to think sensibly about research. Half an hour later, when I shut down my computer the document was still empty.

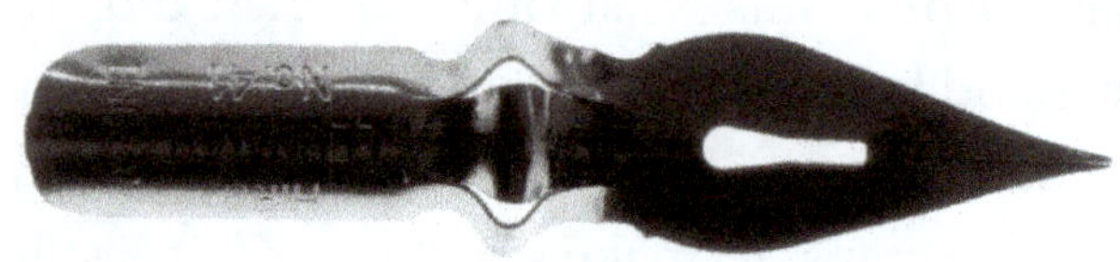

Chapter Five

Dated

My cursor hovered over the Send button and then retreated to the corner of the screen, as if trying to hide from what I'd written.

Dear Ryan,

I'm writing to thank you for our discussion on popular culture. Being home-schooled sometimes makes me feel alienated from mainstream society, and I've long wanted to learn more about media familiar to people my own age. I'd be delighted to discuss this further with you, and look forward to your email.

Kind regards,

Sage.

Two hours of redrafting, and it still sounded like a grant application. I made some adjustments, changed them back again, closed my eyes and pressed Send. Almost immediately, the office phone rang.

'Hello, Sage Rampion speaking.'

'Sage! It's Ryan, voice of the underworld. How's the view up there?'

Hairs rose on the back of my neck. 'How did you get this number?' I said, my voice shrill.

'Off the email you just sent me.'

'Oh.' Contact details came up automatically on the bottom of university emails. I knew that.

'Anyway,' he went on, 'I was ringing to see if you're free for lunch on Friday.'

Lunch. The word simmered in my ears. Did he mean just him and me? Was he asking me out on a *date?* The karaoke party heaved in my memory like a sinister whale. 'Um,' I said, 'you mean lunch with just you, or lunch with you and your friends?'

'Well, I thought just me, but you can bring Grandma to keep an eye on me, if you want.'

An appalled second later I realised he was joking. 'Um, no, that's OK, I … I'll come. By myself.'

'I *see.*' His voice was arch and playful. 'So you trust me now, do you?'

'So long as we eat in a public place,' I said. Never meet a strange man alone.

'Does *The Gentle Lentil* at twelve-thirty qualify?'

'Is it public?'

'Very. It's just outside the south gates of campus and it's always packed.'

My brain seized up in disbelief, but my mouth kept on speaking. 'See you there, then.'

'See you, Sage.'

I hung up, walked straight out the door and tottered down the hall to the mirror in the women's restroom. My wild-eyed reflection stared back. I no longer had butchmeister hair, but I was glamour-less and awkward, with clumpy shoes, shapeless clothes and ugly glasses.

Andrea had chosen these glasses for herself in the eighties. They were huge, roundish, and made from plastic, in a blotchy mix of purple and mustard yellow. When I'd first needed glasses she'd put my lenses in these frames as a virtuous nod to recycling.

The first payment of my doctoral grant came through yesterday. I could use this money to buy new glasses. But I had no idea what was fashionable, or how to pick frames that suited me. And even if I found out and bought some, Andrea would denounce me for vanity and waste as soon as she saw them.

Unless, of course, my current glasses met with an accident.

I took them off and was twisting them experimentally when Andrea walked in.

'Hi, hon.' She glanced at the glasses bent almost double in my hands, and I hastily cleaned them on my shirt. 'When did you last have your eyes checked?'

'A couple of years ago.' I shoved the glasses back on my reddening face and took a deep breath. 'Speaking of glasses,' I said, in my most casual voice, 'I was thinking of getting a spare pair. Just in case.' *Just in case I go on a date with the model from my life drawing class.*

'If you want,' said Andrea, locking herself into a cubicle. 'I've got plenty more old frames at home.'

The contents of Andrea's drawer of old frames leered into my memory. 'Actually,' I said, even more casually, 'I thought I might buy some new frames. Maybe.'

Behind Andrea's door, the toilet roll gave a disapproving rattle. 'Have you looked at the price of new frames?'

I flinched. 'Not really.'

'If you had, you might have considered the ethics of charging several hundred dollars for fifty cents' worth of metal and plastic. Which was probably made in a Third World sweatshop.' She flushed the toilet, as if condemning my idea to the sewer.

Shame bowed my head. One invitation from a man, and I was already placing sexual peacocking ahead of social justice. 'Sorry, Andrea. I didn't think.'

Andrea emerged. 'No,' she said, washing her hands, 'you didn't. Glasses are an optical aid, Sage, not an accessory. Leave fashion to the likes of Fran.' She held the door open and I scuttled through it, conscious of my disgrace.

'Speaking of Fran,' I said, keen to change the subject, 'I saw her yesterday in the staffroom.'

Andrea sniffed. 'My sympathies. Wanted to chat about Freya's breast implants, did she?'

Neither of us had seen Freya since the makeup and heels incident. By now, Andrea speculated, she was probably doing pole dancing and having plastic surgery.

'She wanted to congratulate me for starting a PhD,' I said. 'And disapprove of me sharing your office.'

Andrea gave a snort of contempt and stabbed the door with her key. 'Tell her to mind her own business. Speaking of business,' she added, 'I spoke to Hilda for you, and she's free at two on Friday.'

Hilda? Then I remembered. Last week, Andrea had asked what I planned to research, and I'd said the feminist art movement. Partly to give Andrea an answer, and partly as a cover story in case she discovered my drawings. Feminist art was Hilda's field, so Andrea had set up a meeting.

'Oh, good,' I said. 'Thanks.'

We went to our desks, and Andrea picked out a folder labelled *Gender Discrimination on Campus: A Symposium*. 'So how's progress? Drafted your proposal yet?'

I pressed Page Down to hide my two lone bullet points. 'Not really. I'm still at the exploratory stage.'

Her mouth thinned. 'Then I suggest you explore more quickly,' she said tartly. 'You know what Hilda's like.'

Everyone knew what Hilda was like. She published more articles than the rest of the department put together, and made collages from bras, contraceptives and sinister brown stains of what students swore was her own menstrual blood. But she was a good supervisor, who held her students to exacting standards of progress and punctuality.

Andrea left for a meeting, and I rolled my desk chair over to the window, glasses squatting on my nose like a toad. Hunched with insecurity and fear, I stared through the skylight at Studio 3.

Why would Ryan ask a woman like me on a date? Maybe he planned to mock me, like Caitlin and Kayla had. Maybe my ignorance made him feel superior. Maybe he thought I'd be an easy sexual target, because I was a plain, hairy feminist who couldn't catch a man. But if that was the case, why had he volunteered to be seen with me in public?

I straightened, reminding myself I was an intelligent adult, not a sex toy or piece of arm candy. Ryan knew how I looked when he asked me out. If it embarrassed him, therefore, that was his problem, not mine.

This thought sustained me until Friday, when I flung open my wardrobe with my head held high. I coiled my hair into its bun with less care than usual, stepped into my flattest shoes and pulled out clothes at random, to show how little I needed Ryan's approval. All the same, when I checked the mirror before leaving the house, I noticed that my hands had, quite on their own, selected the tightest pair of pants on the rail.

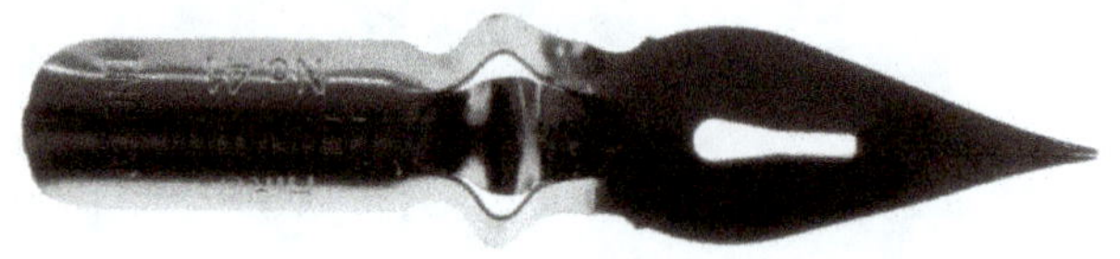

Chapter Six

Principality

I hadn't been to a cafe since my friendship with Jess. Since then, the streets south of the university had grown into a district, where bars and quirky cafes nestled among shops selling candles and brightly coloured clothing.

The Gentle Lentil's sign was made from actual lentils, arranged to form whimsical letters and glued to a piece of card. The entrance was obscured by dangling strands of broad beans threaded on brown string. With my stomach twisting like a kite, I parted the strands and stepped into air that smelled of soup and vegetarian curry.

'Sage!' called Ryan from a round green table. Behind him, a mosaic made from legumes covered the entire wall.

I took a seat opposite him, trying to look as though I went on dates every week.

'So,' said Ryan, 'rabbit food? Or rabbit?'

What? Then I realised he was asking if I was vegetarian. A tactical minefield opened up before me. Andrea's vegetarian friends considered eating meat a crime on a par with murder. Jess considered being vegetarian a perversion on a par with goat worship. Torn between murder and goat worship, I opted for the truth. 'Um, a bit of both. I eat meat, but only ethical, organic meat.' Andrea bought ours from a special supplier.

I tensed on the edge of my seat, not sure whether to expect diatribes on animal cruelty or ridicule for being a hippy wanker.

'Are you happy to eat vegetarian today?' he said, doing neither. 'Because we can go next door, if you want.'

My buttocks inched closer to the back of my chair. 'Rabbit food's fine.'

'Good move.' He slid a menu across the table. 'The cafe next door *say* their meat's organic, but I wouldn't bet my ethics on it.'

The menu was round, like the table. Dishes were listed in three columns, labelled Peckish, Hungry, and Starving, with symbols alongside to indicate whether they were vegetarian, vegan or gluten-free.

'What about you?' I said. 'Are you a vegetarian?'

'Nah, bring on the dead animals,' said Ryan. 'The mind is willing, but the flesh is too tasty.'

I chuckled and then stifled myself. Laughing at his joke made me feel like I was conceding too much ground.

A waitress arrived, and we put in our orders—a vegetarian pasta dish for me, a Thai tofu curry for Ryan. When she left, Ryan pushed back his chair a little, looking amused.

'Sage, Sage,' he said, shaking his head. 'I'm disappointed in you.'

My jaw dropped. I'd only been here five minutes. How had I disappointed him? By turning up in my normal clothes? By refusing to sexualise my body for his benefit? Outrage began to simmer in my guts. I shouldn't have accepted his invitation. I shouldn't have let myself chuckle. I should have … I should have …

'We've been here at least five minutes,' continued Ryan, 'and you haven't even *mentioned* my T-shirt of the day.'

He tweaked his T-shirt plaintively. It was pale green, with a bright green frog printed in the middle. The frog wore a crown and a doleful expression, and carried a golden ball in one flipper.

Confusion defused my outrage. '*The Frog Prince?*'

'Exactly!' said Ryan, looking pleased. 'So you do know fairy tales, at least?'

'Sort of.' Andrea had used fairy tales to teach me about hidden sexist messages. According to her, *The Frog Prince* taught girls that they'd be rewarded for submitting to men.

'Screen-printed last week,' said Ryan, with a hint of pride. 'My latest variation on the theme.'

Theme? Then I remembered his business card. 'Oh … your surname?'

He nodded ruefully. 'I hated it as a child. Prince Charming jokes. Prince of Darkness jokes. Prince songs sung tauntingly in school corridors. Then I got old enough to understand irony and decided to run with it.'

I considered his other T-shirts. '*The Frog Prince, Prince Caspian*… What was the one the other day? With the boy and the giant lemon?'

His face lit up. 'You noticed! It's an illustration from *The Little Prince*. French children's novel.'

'About giant lemons?'

'About a prince who visits lots of tiny planets. Carried through space by a flock of birds on strings.'

'Right,' I said, trying to get my head around this. 'So it's… science fiction?'

'Philosophy, really,' said Ryan. 'It's about how people lose sight of what matters as they grow up. One of my favourite books.' He looked at me with his quizzical face. 'You look stunned, Sage.'

'I am, a bit.' Though 'stunned' wasn't quite the right word.

'Why's that?'

Because a philosophical French novel about a prince that travels through space by bird is one of your favourite books. Because you screen print illustrations from children's novels on your T-shirts. 'I suppose I didn't expect you to like … that sort of book.'

His face fell. 'Why not? Because I'm too mainstream? Too conventional? Too … *banal?*'

'Not that. It's because … because you're …' *Because you're a man*, I thought unguardedly. Men wrote and read novels. Socrates and Confucius were men. Why was I so surprised?

'… I'm not sure,' I finished in a sheepish voice.

The waitress arrived with our meals, and Ryan scooped a spoonful of curry into his mouth and shrugged.

'Oh well,' he said, 'I suppose these things are subjective. Anyway … do you realise we've now had three conversations without asking each other the classic questions?'

'What are they?'

'Number one is "So, what do you do?"'

This time I didn't suppress my chuckle. 'So,' I said obligingly, 'what do you do?'

'I'm studying for my teaching diploma. Three years of trying to be an artist has convinced me I need a back-up plan. And you?'

'I've just started a PhD.' Would this intimidate him? According to Andrea, most men were threatened by clever women.

'Cool.' He didn't sound remotely threatened. 'What in?'

'Women's Studies,' I said in a small voice.

This time, surely, he'd react. Men found the very existence of Women's Studies disturbing. Most felt obliged to ridicule or discredit it, and the few who enrolled were often only there to pick up women. I twisted my fork in the pasta, waiting for his response.

'What's your thesis on?' said Ryan.

I cautiously lifted the pasta. 'I haven't decided yet. I was thinking about exploring the feminist art movement.'

'Really?' His eyes lit up. 'I went to a feminist art exhibition once. One artist did a series of paintings of pregnant women, all in bright acrylic colours. Quite beautiful. I've still got the brochure at home, if you want to see it.'

A strange ache swelled inside my ribs. 'Thanks.'

'Speaking of Women's Studies, isn't there a Professor Rampion somewhere on campus? Any relation?'

My spine stiffened against the back of the chair. Andrea was the sort of person most people at the university had heard of. 'She's my grandmother.'

Ryan nodded. 'She raised you, didn't she?' he said. 'Why was that?'

My mouthful of pasta turned cold and tasteless. I made myself swallow it. 'My parents were … they weren't able to raise me.'

'How come?'

I twisted the spaghetti round and round my fork as I assembled a reply.

'My mother got pregnant at sixteen,' I said at last, lifting a huge wad of pasta. 'She ran away when I was six months old and left me with my grandmother.'
The spaghetti unravelled and fell into my lap. Before I could do anything about it, the strange ache flooded up my throat and spilled down my face in an unexpected wash of tears.

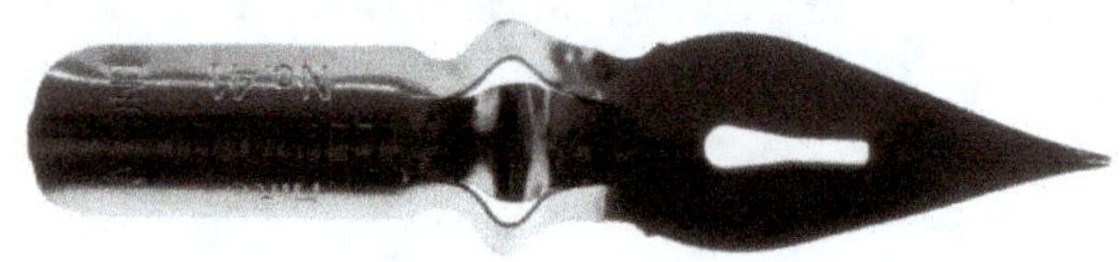

Chapter Seven

Motherlode

Ryan and the round green table blurred as tears poured down my cheeks into the bowl of pasta.

'Sage? My God, are you OK?'

'I'm fine,' I said, but the tears kept on coming, like beads from a broken necklace.

Ryan snatched a handful of napkins and passed them to me. I took off my glasses and clamped the napkins against my eyelids.

'Shit, I'm so sorry.' He sounded panicked and guilty, as though he was to blame. 'Do you want to go somewhere? Or do you want to be alone? I can go, if you want.'

I swallowed and shook my head, the sodden napkins turning to pulp in my fingers. Part of me was aghast to be crying in front of a man, like some cliché of a damsel in distress. Yet there was another, smothered part of me, deeper down, that definitely didn't want him to go.

He gave my hand a comforting squeeze. 'I'll just be a minute.'

When I looked up, I saw him standing at the cash register and realised he was paying the bill. I froze, horrified. I was an independent woman with the means to buy my own food. If I let Ryan pay, I might as well chuck in my career and wear an apron. Besides, what would he expect in return? *It's not lunch he's buying,* Andrea would thunder, *it's a sense of entitlement to your body.*

I almost broke the drawstring on my backpack in my haste to find my wallet. Just as I unearthed it, Ryan returned with another handful of napkins.

I opened my wallet. 'How much—'

'Let's just get out of here.'

I started to protest and realised that half the cafe was staring at my tear-stained face. Vowing I'd pay my share later, I got up and ducked past Ryan, as he swept aside the curtain of hanging beads.

Outside, the clouds had retreated, flooding the street with light. Squinting my puffy eyes against the sun, I walked with Ryan down the street to a large, landscaped park. He sat on the grass by a tree and spread his jacket out beside him, giving it a pat. 'Sit down.'

I hesitated. Andrea would have called this 'chauvinism dressed up as chivalry'. Weakened by my outpouring of emotion, I decided to call it 'comfortable' and sat. The lining of the jacket felt smooth and warm against my skin.

'Feeling better?' he asked.

'A bit.'

I hadn't cried this much about my mother since I was a child of five or six. Mothers were everywhere then, waggling fingers, wiping noses, making children eat their broccoli. Other children talked about their mothers all the time, and whenever I heard them, something grated inside me. Not a sharp pain, like a knife wound, but a slow, constant grating, like a stone wearing a raw spot into the wall of my stomach that could never completely heal.

'Do you want to talk about it?' Ryan's voice was wary, but gentle. 'We don't have to. If you want, we can change the subject to something safer. Like terrorism, or global warming.'

He half-smiled at me, and I half-smiled back. I'd never talked to anyone about my mother. A week ago, I would have been appalled at the thought of discussing my mother with someone I barely knew. With a man I barely knew. Now, though, sitting on Ryan's jacket, the worried grip of his fingers still warm on my hand, I looked into his earnest, bright-eyed face and realised I wanted to.

'I can talk about it,' I said. 'If you're interested.'

'I'm interested. If you're comfortable.'

'I'm comfortable.'

I leant back against the tree, hugged my knees to my chest, and began.

When I was about three, I noticed I was different from other children. They called the lady that looked after them 'Mummy', whereas mine answered only to 'Andrea'. I tried calling Andrea 'Mummy', but she went strange and stiff, and said I couldn't do that, because she was my grandmother, not my mother. At first I accepted this, as little children do. It wasn't until my friend Lauren's fifth birthday party that I started asking questions in earnest.

Lauren's house was full of boisterous little girls in ponytails and pink dresses. I felt shy and out of place with my short hair and overalls, so I retreated to the kitchen, where the food was.

There, among the plastic bowls of chips and candy, was the most magnificent cake I'd ever seen. It was shaped like a frog and covered in green frosting, with googly eyes and a stripe of five pink candles along its back.

When Lauren walked in with a gift wrapped in ballerina paper, she found me there, still staring.

'I like your frog cake,' I said.

'My mum made it for me,' she said, stashing the present under the table. 'It's cool, isn't it?'

I nodded, wide-eyed with awe.

'When's your birthday? Get your mum to make you one.'

The swell of joy from the cake deflated. 'I can't. I don't know where my mum is.'

Lauren looked astonished. 'Doesn't she live with you?'

I shook my head. 'I live with Andrea.'

'Who's Andrea?'

'My grandmother,' I said in a small voice.

'Then you shouldn't call her Andrea,' Lauren said sternly. 'You should call her Grandma. Or Nan.'

She grabbed a handful of chips and walked back into the living room full of girls in pink dresses. Girls who lived with their mothers and called them 'Mum'.

That evening, when Andrea was putting me to bed, I said 'Goodnight, Grandma,' for the first time. Andrea's lips pressed together, and she shook her head.

'I don't want you to call me Grandma, Sage,' she said, tucking me in. 'My name's Andrea.'

Much later, when I was a teenager, she explained that 'Grandma' defined her solely in terms of her relationship to me. She'd wanted to make clear she was a person in her own right, with a life and achievements of her own. But that night I was five, and all I understood was that I'd never have someone to call 'Grandma'. Or 'Mum'.

I burst into tears and asked question after question. *Why can't I call you Grandma? Why do I live with you and not my mum? Where's my mum now? Why doesn't she want to live with us?* Andrea tried to comfort me and respond as best she could, and over the next ten or fifteen years I pieced together the story.

My grandfather left Andrea when my mother, Emmeline, was three. After a nasty court battle, Andrea won the house and custody of her daughter, but found herself close to bankrupt. After four years off work she couldn't find a job in journalism, where she'd trained, so she took work as a typist, and put Emmeline into full-time care. In those days this was rare, and she was condemned by her neighbours, colleagues and family. To make matters worse, her manager began bullying and groping her at work. At the time there were no sexual harassment laws, and she needed the money too desperately to resign. Finally, after three demoralising years, she stumbled on a feminist article in defence of day care in the newspaper.

Inspired and reassured, Andrea enrolled in a Graduate Diploma in Women's Studies at night school. After topping the class, she enrolled in a Master's degree, and was awarded a prestigious scholarship to progress to a PhD. She began lecturing, volunteered at a women's refuge, fought for lesbians' rights to IVF treatment, and made a name for herself as a hard-hitting court support worker for victims of domestic violence and sexual assault. When she finished her thesis to rave reviews, the Department of Humanities promoted her to senior lecturer of Women's Studies, then to professor only a few years later.

Around this time, the problems with my mother became too serious to ignore. At fifteen, Emmeline was so embarrassed by

Andrea she refused to bring her friends home from school. Her marks were in freefall, and the teachers who'd once called her 'lazy but bright' started calling her 'disruptive and rebellious'. Worst of all, this didn't bother her. What mattered was looking pretty and being popular with boys, and at these things she excelled.

Andrea tried to interest her in feminism, but Emmeline sneered and laughed. Suspicious of her daughter's ever-growing wardrobe, Andrea tracked her discreetly and discovered she was cutting school to work. In the months of almighty battles that followed, it emerged that Emmeline had also fallen pregnant, to a married man she'd met through her job.

Andrea wanted to charge him with statutory rape, but Emmeline insisted that she was in love and wanted to have his baby. But she was only sixteen, and the pressures of a baby were too much. Six months after I was born, my mother walked out, leaving me in the sole care of Andrea.

I didn't look at Ryan while I told my story. I bowed my head and told it to my shoes. When I'd finished, there was a pause of several minutes before I dared to look up.

Ryan's normally animated face was still. 'Have you seen your mother since she left?'

I shook my head.

'But she calls you, doesn't she? Or … or emails, or something?'

Tears welled again. 'Andrea says she lives in the city somewhere, so they must be in touch, but I've never heard from her. I wouldn't even recognise her now. I've only seen photos of her as a teenager.'

My eyes overflowed, and I hugged my knees to my face. Something touched my hair. I reached up to brush off what I thought was an insect or leaf, and my hand found Ryan's. Shock crackled through me. I snatched my hand away as if his were electrified, but I didn't push him off. I just sat, my scalp tingling under his touch as his hand moved in long, soothing strokes down my hair. When the strokes lightened, as if he was about to stop, I unfolded my knees and shifted a little closer. He smelled of curry, and freshly laundered T-shirt tinged with tears.

After what seemed like a long time, Ryan spoke again, his hand coming to rest on my shoulder. 'I can't imagine growing up without my mum. Let alone having her … leave.'

My eyes filled again at the kindness in his voice.

'Are you going to be OK?'

I lifted my face from his shoulder and nodded, blotting the tears with the back of my hand. 'Sorry about all the crying,' I added, with a watery smile.

Ryan shook his head. 'Don't be.' He pulled out his phone. 'What's your number?'

'I don't have a mobile phone.'

'You don't have a *phone?*' He looked aghast.

'I've never had one.'

Jess had been as shocked as Ryan to learn I didn't have a mobile phone. She spent hours on hers every day, posting to social media, texting her friends, checking everything from celebrity news to weather, directions and the time. The only thing she didn't use her phone for was phoning people. We were friends for weeks before she grasped that the only ways to contact me were by email or ringing Andrea's house.

During our friendship, I'd screwed up my courage and asked Andrea if I could get a phone of my own. Emitting disapproval like static, Andrea told me I was an adult, and could make my own choices if I funded them myself. Before I'd come up with a way to earn the money, my friendship with Jess had ended.

'Shit.' Ryan ran a hand through his hair. 'OK, well, I've got a modelling gig in the mountains to get to, so we'll have to arrange things now.'

'Things?'

'That lesson in popular culture I promised you. When are you free?'

I discarded the idea of the weekend, when Andrea would ask where I was going. 'Do you have any afternoons off during the week?'

'How about Thursday afternoon?'

Andrea was attending a training program that day. 'Thursday suits me.'

'Outside the Humanities building at two?'

Where Andrea's staff and students might see me meeting a man? 'How about on the Library lawns instead?' The Library lawns were behind Fine Arts, invisible even from the top floors of the Humanities building.

'Done.'

We stood up, and Ryan stuffed the jacket into his bag. A few strands of my hair had come loose, so I redid my bun.

'See you next Thursday, Sage,' said Ryan.

Without warning, he leant forward and touched his lips lightly to my forehead. Then, with the same jaunty movement I'd seen in the studio, he slung his bag over his shoulder and dashed off, flourishing one hand over his head in farewell.

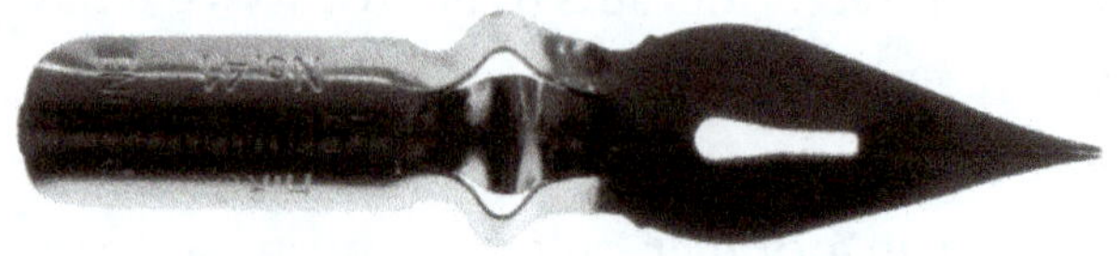

Chapter Eight

Brought to Book

I floated back to the office, as disconnected as a runaway balloon. I'd gone on a date. I'd cried in a crowded cafe. I'd told a man my life story, and he'd kissed me. This morning, I wouldn't have believed such things could happen, and yet here I was, just on the other side of them. I fumbled for my keys, and they felt strange to the touch, like something from another dimension.

The office door swung open.

'Sage,' said Andrea, and I knew at once that she was displeased. 'Hilda called.'

Hilda? Then I remembered the meeting. The one Andrea had set up for me at two o'clock. It was now a quarter to three. The balloon burst and plummeted to earth. 'When did she call?'

'At 2:02.'

Other staff would have waited until 2:15, but not Hilda. As far as she was concerned, you weren't on time for a meeting unless you arrived five minutes before it started. 'To live in this country is to be frustrated,' she would say. 'Everyone arrives two, five, ten minutes late, and by the end of the day you have lost *half an hour!* It is a disgrace. In Germany we have more respect for people's time.'

Horror drained through me. Being late for a meeting with Hilda was a serious offense. Forgetting one altogether was dire. 'I'm really sorry. I was … I was doing research in the library and lost track of time.'

'Why are you telling *me* this, Sage?'

I blanched. 'Sorry. I'll ring Hilda.' I slunk to my desk chair and turned on my computer.

'Now would be a good time,' Andrea said pointedly.

'Yes, I know, I was just …' *Just hoping I could make the call when you're not in the room.*

Andrea gave an exasperated sigh. 'How old are you, Sage?'

She knew exactly how old I was. 'Twenty-two.'

'Then act like it and call Hilda. Now.' She dumped the phone on my desk.

I dialled the number with a cowering finger.

'Hilda Ziehler speaking.'

'Um, hi, Professor Ziehler, it's Sage Rampion here. I'm just ringing to—'

'To waste more of my time? No. Already I put aside one hour for you this afternoon.'

'I'm so sorry, I was—'

'You still want me to consider you, you email an excellent proposal by this time next week.'

Hilda hung up. Avoiding Andrea's eye, I replaced the phone on her desk, and crept back to mine. When she left ten minutes later, I wheeled my chair to the window and sat looking at the skylight, touching the place where Ryan's lips had met my forehead.

The Library lawns were lined with bushy, gnarled trees that created lots of nooks for benches. Ryan was waiting on one of these, the leaves above him dappling his hair with shade.

'So,' he said as I approached, 'are you ready to begin your education in popular culture?'

I adjusted my glasses in a scholarly fashion and produced a ten-year-old black notebook with 'Social Studies' written down the spine.

Ryan grinned. 'Good. I can see you're taking this seriously. Now, before we start the lesson, what do we comment on first?'

'Your T-shirt of the day?'

'Excellent! Gold star for the lady with the notebook.'

Today his T-shirt was black, and featured a photograph of a man in a flowered fedora. He was holding a guitar with a circular body and a neck that ended in an arrow, and an odd cross-piece shaped like a J where the body joined the neck. Both man and guitar were orangey-gold.

'Should I know who he is?' I asked.

'Definitely. You don't, though, do you?'

'Not a clue. Something to do with princes?'

'This man,' said Ryan, plucking importantly at his T-shirt, '*is* Prince. The late and great. Spiritual son of James Brown, King of Funk. As a boy, I hated people singing his songs at me. As a man, I've come around.'

I opened my notebook. 'Why's his guitar that shape?'

'That's the symbol he changed his name to in the nineties.'

With this bizarre pronouncement, Ryan led me to the shopping strip that ran from the university to the skyscrapered realm of the city. Near campus, the windows wore gay-friendly rainbow stickers and the smell of Fairtrade coffee leaked from doorways. As we approached town, the rainbows gave way to boutique restaurants, beige and silver homewares, and a huge, glossy megastore selling books and music, where Ryan stopped.

'Welcome to your new School of Popular Culture!' he said, ushering me in with a grandiose sweep of his arms.

Inside was all bright lights and towering shelves filled with diet manuals and lurid-looking blockbusters. Ryan swept among these like an animated whirlwind, gathering an armload of books.

He pressed one into my hand. '*The Chronicles of Narnia*, printed as one volume.' Inside the cover was a hand-drawn map of a forested coast, with a sailing ship and compass just offshore.

'Everyone but *everyone* reads this as a kid,' said Ryan. 'They've made some of them into movies.' He held up a book with a photo on the cover of a woman's hands cupping an apple. 'And *this*,' he went on, placing it on top of Narnia, 'is *Twilight*. Vampire romance. Massive with teenage girls a few years ago.'

I skimmed the blurb, and picked up my pen. As I started to write notes, Ryan slapped *Harry Potter and the Philosopher's Stone* on top of *Twilight*. 'Now this, even you must have heard of. It's—'

'Ryan,' I interrupted.

'Mmm?'

'I'm not taking much in here.'

'You're not?'

'No. I need time to read at least the blurbs.'

'Oh.' He contemplated his armload of books. 'Would it help if I summarised the plots?'

'Yes, but that that would take forever.'

'Hmmm.' He looked wistfully up the escalator. 'And I haven't even *started* on movies and music yet.'

'We need to rethink this,' I said firmly. 'Do you own some of these books?'

'Some of them. Most of the hard copies are at Mum's, but I've got a few at my place.'

'How about lending me a couple a week? As a sort of homework assignment?'

His face lit up. 'Brilliant! My place it is. If we run, we might even catch the three-fifteen.'

Before I could explain I hadn't meant *now*, Ryan leaped up and charged toward the exit. Not knowing what else to do, I ran after him, and we pelted to catch the train, flopping onto our seats seconds before it pulled away. Only then did I register the momentous nature of what I was doing. Ryan was taking me back to his place. *His place.*

I eyed him, only half-listening to his animated summary of *Game of Thrones*. Why had he lured me to his house? Was I putting myself at risk? I searched for signs of his agenda, but I didn't know what to look for.

Three stops and a short walk later, I walked through a peeling, creaky gate into the front garden of Ryan's house.

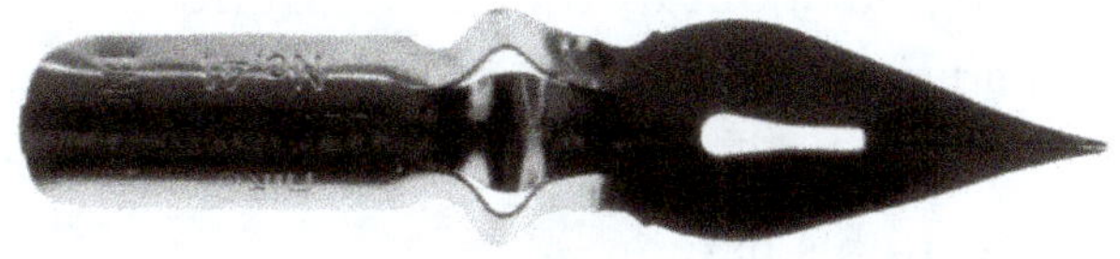

Chapter Nine

Meeting Mrs Jones

The path to the house was overgrown with feathery weeds. Ryan steered around the corduroy couch on the verandah and unlocked the door, releasing the scent of old furniture and herbal tea.

He led me to a sunroom at the back of the house, where a plump woman with ringlets sat in a beanbag in front of the TV, a small ginger cat in her lap. Behind her was an old-fashioned kitchen, with pastel green tiles and tarnished faucets. Scattered through both rooms was an assortment of chairs, one wooden and three vinyl with piping around the seats, all in different styles and colours.

'Hey, Shell,' said Ryan to the woman.

'Hey, Ryan,' said Shell. Her voice and eyes were drowsy, as though she was on the verge of falling asleep.

'Sage, my roommate, Shell. And Tango.'

'Hi,' I said, wondering if I should say 'hey' instead.

Shell lifted a limp hand. 'Hey, Sage. Nice to meet you.' In her lap, Tango gave a small, dismissive meow.

'Tea?' asked Ryan, opening a cupboard.

I accepted a mug of peppermint tea and sat on a lime green chair, scrutinising Shell out of the corner of my eye. Ryan hadn't told me he had a female housemate. Was she his girlfriend? Maybe our lunch was a friendly lunch, not a date. Maybe he was trying to add me to his harem.

Shell turned off the TV and clambered out of the beanbag, clutching her cat. 'I'm off to the vet,' she said. 'My little warrior's limping again. If Tom comes home, tell him I'll be back around five.'

'Sure,' said Ryan. 'See you.'

The front door closed. 'Tom?' I asked, trying to sound nonchalant.

'Her boyfriend. They share the other bedroom.'

She's not his girlfriend, then. So our lunch was a date. Probably. The muscles in my shoulders and jaw slackened; the ones around my stomach tightened.

I sipped my peppermint tea, at last understanding why Jess had spent hours recounting what men said and did: she was trying to figure out what they meant.

'Grab your drink,' said Ryan, heading back up the corridor.

He opened a door and I realised with a jolt that he was taking me to his bedroom. My mouth went dry. *What did you expect?* sneered Andrea's voice in my head. *That's what men think women are FOR. And as soon as you step into his bedroom, he'll assume he's entitled to sex.*

I froze on the threshold.

In my mind's eye men's bedrooms were dark and primeval, with shuttered windows and stained sheets, but this room was painted white and brightly lit. The window was curtained with a batik sarong, and shelves full of books, CDs and DVDs covered one walls. An old fireplace had been bricked over, and Ryan had blu-tacked postcard reproductions of surreal art—Miro, Kandinsky, Dali—to the chimney.

He was looking at me now with a puzzled frown. 'Are you coming in?'

Hovering just outside his door suddenly felt ludicrous. 'Sorry.' I stepped into the room, brandishing my mug of peppermint tea like a weapon. Which it could be, if he tried anything. It wasn't as though I was helpless, I reminded myself. I was an alert, empowered woman, and I'd studied women's self-defence since I was thirteen.

'So,' said Ryan, 'where do you want to start? Books? Music? Movies?'

Still gripping my mug, I scanned Ryan's shelves, his bed squatting balefully in my peripheral vision. It was a double futon mattress, resting on a layer of milk crates and draped in a quilt with a geometric design in cream and black. On top of it, two pillows kept watch, like a pair of squashy orange eyes.

'Um,' I said, trying to concentrate, 'how about … the singer on your T-shirt of the day?'

'Prince?' Ryan pulled out his phone and started typing something in. 'I've got a couple of albums on vinyl at Mum's place, but I'm pretty sure … Aha!' He plugged his phone into a pair of speakers and pressed a button. '1999. Most played song at parties on New Year's Eve 2000.'

The first few bars of the track sounded like something from a cabaret, with drums and a flashy synthesiser. 'Is this a dance song?'

'Yeah, I guess. Do you dance?'

A memory of Caitlin gyrating in the karaoke bar singed my brain. 'Definitely not.'

'Then it's time you did. Consider it part of your education.' He held out a hand and I shrank against the chimney, shaking my head so emphatically that I knocked a couple of postcards to the carpet. Entering his bedroom was bad enough, letting him *take my hand* was going way too far. Especially if it involved dancing.

'Come on, Sage! I promise I won't watch. In fact …' He opened one of the drawers in his desk, and took out a nylon eye mask with an airline logo on it. '… I'll make sure I *can't* watch.'

Ryan pulled the blindfold over his eyes and started dancing, in a prancing, energetic way that involved a lot of arm-flailing. *Keep your guard up*, Sage. Andrea's voice again, as if she'd installed herself in my head. Yet he looked so ridiculous dancing in his blindfold that my reservations dissolved into smiles. I dodged a particularly enthusiastic hand gesture, drank the last of my tea and placed the mug on his desk.

'So are you dancing yet?' he demanded, groping through the air in my direction. 'You're not, are you?'

'I am so!' I said, backing away from his hand. I even tried, feebly, to jig up and down to the music, reassured by the blindfold and the knowledge that I couldn't look sillier than he did.

'Let me check.'

Still dancing his ludicrous dance, he inched up his blindfold and I swiftly reached out to pull it down. As he pranced backwards to escape me, he tripped over the leg of his desk chair. He thrust out his arms to break his fall and caught me across the face, dislodging my glasses and knocking us both to the floor.

'Ow!' Ryan ripped off his blindfold. 'Shit, are you OK?

The song ended, and the room fell quiet. I sat up. Without my glasses, the outer edges of my vision were blurred and mellow, like a soft-focus photo. 'I think so. Are you?'

He rubbed a red mark on his shin. 'I'll live. My manly dignity mightn't, though. That was seriously stupid, wasn't it?'

'Dancing with a blindfold on? Um, yes.'

He released his leg and it fell so that it was touching mine, so slightly I wasn't sure he'd noticed. A tiny, forbidden sizzle went through my skin. Forbidden because this was his leg. And his bedroom. Tiny because the area of contact was so very small. *Sexual assault usually starts small,* said Andrea's voice. *And escalates slowly, so that when the victim gets uncomfortable she feels it's too late to object.*

'Did you dance, though?' His voice was innocent, but his leg was still touching mine, filling the room with a soundless hum.

'A bit.' I should nip this in the bud. Move my leg away and rebuke him. *Now.*

He grinned, a warm, generous grin that crinkled his face. 'Then it was stupidity well spent. You need to dance.'

'I do?' *Move your leg, Sage,* snapped Andrea, but my leg didn't move.

'Definitely.'

A pool of shared warmth was growing where my skin met his, dissolving all the words in my head. 'Why's that?' I managed to say.

'Because when I met you, you came across sort of … stiff. And scared. As if you needed to be on your guard all the time in case someone attacked you.'

A too-vivid memory of the first art class reared in my head. My leg stiffened away from his, and the warm pool evaporated. 'So what's that got to do with dancing?' I said, not looking at him.

'Dancing frees you up, and lets you express who you are.' He was focused and quiet, wanting me to understand. 'And I like who you are. I want you to feel safe, so you can let down your hair.'

I looked at Ryan again and suddenly he wasn't A Man any more, not the sort I'd read about, who wanted to keep women in their place. He was a person, a friend, someone who'd listened to me and comforted me and was trying to help. He hadn't coerced me into his room. I was here because I wanted to be. 'Like I did at the window?'

He smiled. 'Exactly!'

'That,' I said sternly, 'was an accident.'

'Serendipity. I take my luck where I find it.'

He reached across the room and retrieved my glasses. As he leant back, the entire length of his leg came to rest against mine. A huge, glittering wave swelled my veins, because this time I knew it was deliberate. And this time I didn't even pretend I wanted to move my leg away.

He looked at my glasses. 'Are these strong?'

'Pretty strong.' *What are you doing?* screamed my Inner Andrea.

'How well can you see me?'

'Maybe not the … finer details.' *This leg business is a SEXUAL ADVANCE, and you're allowing it!*

He folded up the glasses and leant so close I could hear the rapid rasp of his breathing. 'Is that better?'

I nodded, not trusting myself to speak. *Look at you, sitting on his bedroom floor like territory waiting to be conquered!*

Ryan shook his head with a wondering smile. 'This is one of those Miss Jones moments.'

Unable to hold his gaze any longer, I dropped my eyes to my locked, twisting fingers. 'Miss Jones?' *You've barely met this man!*

'Hollywood movie reference. The director hires a gorgeous actress, pulls back her hair and puts glasses on her to play the ugly duckling. Then, at the crucial Swan Moment, she takes off her glasses, undoes her hair, and the hero cries: "But Miss Jones—you're beautiful!"'

He's grooming you for seduction, Sage! Don't let him suck you in. Be assertive. Say something. DO something! 'Is that … does that really happen in Hollywood movies?' My voice sounded throaty and strange, as though everything lower than my mouth was underwater.

'More of them than you'd think.' He slid the glasses into my hand, and the brush of his fingers created a wave that broke in my stomach and washed Andrea away.

'So,' I said, my heart pounding so hard I could feel it in my eardrums, 'what happens after that?'

'Usually something like this.'

He kissed me on the mouth. For two or three shimmering seconds I let him. Then he tried to pull me closer and part my lips with his, and panic gripped me. I jerked back and Ryan whipped his leg away. He got to his feet and stumbled over to his desk, where he stood avoiding my eyes, clinging half-stooped to the back of his desk chair while the aftershocks of his kiss flickered through me like shooting stars.

Andrea clawed her way back into my head. *Good,* she said. *You finally stood up for yourself. For a moment I thought you were going to let him exploit you, like some passive sexual vessel with—*

NOW HANG ON, said a second, louder voice that I didn't recognise. *What about women's lust? What happened to women reclaiming their own sexuality?*

So following him meekly to his bedroom and sitting tongue-tied while he shoved his leg against yours and kissed you was 'reclaiming your own sexuality', was it?

Maybe it wasn't, said the second voice. *But this is.* As I got up and tiptoed over to Ryan, I realised that the second voice was mine.

'I'm sorry,' I said. 'I didn't mean to … I was … I was just startled.' *No one's ever kissed me on the mouth before.*

'Startled?' said Ryan to his desk.

Hot and cold with my own daring, I rose, walked over and laid my hand on his shoulder. He didn't move, but I felt his muscles relax a little. He lifted his head to look back at me, and this time I didn't look away. The shimmering, pounding feeling returned like a tide, and this time I admitted to myself it was desire.

'Also,' I added, 'you forgot something important.'

I plucked his hand from the desk chair and placed it on the bun at the back of my head. For a moment he didn't react. Then he turned to face me, slipped the hairnet off and tossed it onto the floor. The last thing I remember clearly before the world melted away was the tickle of his springy dark hair, and my own hair, pouring onto the futon like a sea of spilt champagne.

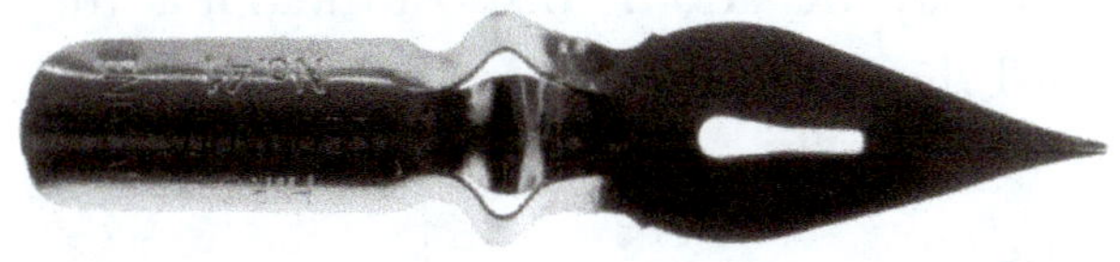

Chapter Ten

Turning the Tables

When I arrived home, the street lamps were on, filling the garden with spiky purple shadows. The garden and its shadows were as familiar to me as my face, yet tonight they looked different, as if the events of the afternoon had changed them as well.

I reached for my keys with a tingling hand. An hour ago, this same hand was on Ryan's skin, feeling the muscles of his back tense and shift, marvelling at the way his jaw changed from prickle to sleek. Standing in front of my childhood home, the afternoon's events seemed impossible. Only the salty tang of him on my lips, and the unfocused afterglow in my body, kept me trusting that my memories were real.

I took hold of the doorknob and it jerked from my grip. The door swung open, and light flooded the porch, cut in two by an Andrea-shaped shadow.

'It's nearly nine o'clock, Sage.'

A day ago, her pointed tone would have withered me, but not tonight. 'Sorry,' I said. 'I was just … at a friend's place.' Time to shelve the library excuse for something closer to the truth.

'This friend doesn't have a phone?'

I started to say 'he' and then substituted it at the last minute. 'They do, but I thought … I didn't think I'd be quite this late.'

Andrea's mouth thinned. 'You lost track of time again.'

'I suppose so.'

'I see you also lost track of what night it is.'

It was Tuesday. Andrea and I made dinner on alternate nights, and Tuesday was my night. A chink of guilt opened in my hazy golden mind. 'I'm so sorry, Andrea. I could … Would you like me to make you something now?'

'I made something for myself. At eight.'

The chink widened at the resentment in her voice. 'I'm so sorry. I honestly forgot.'

'Like the meeting with Hilda.'

Andrea advanced down the hallway and looked me over. Nervous and guilty, I tilted my head to hide the rash Ryan's chin had left around my mouth.

'Have you written your proposal for Hilda?'

'I've started it,' I lied.

Andrea gave an exasperated sigh. 'A month ago you were a responsible adult. What's happened, Sage?'

I groped around for a reason, but every thought I touched turned into mist. 'I think it's the transition to a PhD,' I said at last. 'I found it easier to get motivated when I had deadlines and exams.'

'Then we'll put together a timetable with deadlines. In the office, first thing tomorrow morning.'

Andrea partitioned her own time into half-hour blocks with labels like *Online Research, First Year Marking,* and *Conference Administration.* Something told me my version was unlikely to contain blocks labelled *Learn About Popular Culture* and *Have Sex With Ryan.* 'Could we make it Thursday? I'm … I've got a meeting with someone in the Art faculty.'

'At what time?'

Ryan had the morning off tomorrow, and I'd arranged to be at his place at ten. For more education in popular culture. Among other things. 'Ten o'clock.'

'Then we'll do it at nine.'

My shoulders slumped. There was no way I'd get to Ryan's place by ten. I'd have to find some way of calling him and letting him know I'd be late.

The midmorning sun shone directly through the sarong on Ryan's window, dappling our bodies with blurred batik patches of orange and green.

'So, Sage,' said Ryan, wriggling his arm out from under me, and propping himself on one elbow. 'What was this mysterious tryst this morning? Should I be jealous?'

I lifted my head, damp with a mixture of my sweat and his. 'Mysterious tryst?'

'The unexpected meeting at nine that made you late. You didn't ring until eight thirty, and it sounded like your hand was cupped around the phone.'

'Oh! That was just my grandmother,' I said, settling back onto the futon. 'She was helping me put together a schedule.'

'A *schedule*? For what?'

I dug the schedule from the puddle of clothes on the floor beside the bed. Andrea had printed three copies, one for me, one for her, and one to laminate and put on the fridge at home.

'Time management,' I said, handing it to Ryan. 'She wants to make sure I honour my PhD commitments.'

Ryan contemplated the schedule. 'And your catering commitments, I see,' he said gravely. 'Not to mention your hairdressing commitments. And oh! Today's ten o'clock appointment at the Art faculty.' He looked up, one ironic brow raised. 'Why didn't you tell her you were meeting your boyfriend?'

I shuddered at the thought. 'It's not the sort of thing I can tell her.'

'What, the truth?' Ryan started to laugh. 'Come on, Sage. You're not in high school any more.'

My throat constricted with shame. Normal twenty-two year olds plainly didn't lie about these things. Why had I? Because I was cowardly. Weak. Juvenile. 'I never went to high school, remember?' I said, forcing a smile.

He stopped laughing. 'You didn't miss much there,' he said, tossing the schedule to one side. I folded it and slid it back into the pocket of my pants.

'Anyway,' he said, as I climbed back onto the futon, 'tell me about your PhD.'

He extended a repentant arm and I settled into it, 'PhD' buzzing in my head like a fly. The PhD was part of Andrea's world. It didn't belong here, on the sun-dappled futon. 'What do you want to know?'

'Everything. What it's about. Why you chose to do it.'

So far my PhD proposal consisted of two bullet points: (1) *Something about feminist art and body image?* and (2) *What would Hilda like?* I decided to answer Ryan's second question. 'I suppose it just seemed logical.'

He looked incredulous. 'You started a *PhD* because it was *logical?*'

'Well, yes,' I said, unsettled by his amazement. 'I want to lecture in Women's Studies, so I need a PhD.'

For the first time, I pictured myself working as an academic. Writing journal articles. Going to conferences. Setting essays. Facing lecture theatres full of students like Jess. My heart withered a little.

'That was just what came next, huh?' Ryan shook his head—the slow, smiling shake of someone marvelling at what they've just heard. 'So,' he went on, 'are you planning to follow in Andrea's footsteps? Become the next Head of Women's Studies?'

Perhaps he didn't think I could do it. Perhaps he felt threatened by Women's Studies after all. I stiffened out of his hug and turned to face him, arms folded. 'You think there's something wrong with that?'

'Not wrong, exactly,' said Ryan, 'but it sounds to me like your career, not your calling.'

My arms slackened. 'What do you mean?'

'Your calling's your passion. Something you have to do because it's who you are. Your career's something you do to make money. Or fall into because your grandmother does it. Or because it's *logical.*'

Women's Studies is my passion. As a feminist nothing's more important to me than fighting for equality and women's rights. But I couldn't say it. The two bullet points on my screen stifled the words like a gag.

'So what about you?' I said, reversing the spotlight. 'What were you studying again?'

Ryan's mouth twisted, and he withdrew his arm. 'A Diploma of Education,' he said, in a colourless voice I hadn't heard before.

Curious and unsettled, I searched his face and he dropped his gaze to his hands. 'So why did you choose to do that?'

'You want the sensible answer or the honest one?'

'Both.'

Ryan slumped into the pillows and closed his eyes, as if the thought of answering me exhausted him. 'The sensible answer is *marketable skills*.' He spat the words like a wad of used gum. 'I need to support myself. Generate an income. Become a productive member of society.'

An uneasy twinge went through me. What were my marketable skills? Essay writing. Research and analysis. But I'd never tried to market them. Andrea owned the house where I lived, bought my food and clothes, and covered other expenses when I asked. My two grant payments this year were the first independent income I'd ever received.

'So what's the honest answer?' I asked.

'Failure,' he said, his eyes still closed.

Touched by the bitterness in his voice, I laced my fingers through his. His hand was limp. 'Failure?'

'I decided I wanted to be an artist when I was six,' he went on. 'By fourteen, I had this … *vision*. I'd start at the College of Visual Arts at eighteen and stun the place with my genius. By twenty-one, galleries would be lining up to exhibit my work. By twenty-five, I'd have it all—commissions to build public sculptures; celebrities clamouring for me to paint their portraits; moodily lit photos in front of my easel in The New Yorker; my own radio program: *Ryan, Prince of the Arts*.' He swept his free hand in a melodramatic circle.

'Well, you're only twenty-four now,' I said, trying to keep things light.

'I am. And how many galleries have exhibited my work? One. Two years ago. A student exhibition in the College gallery. And what did the reviewer say? In the *College newsletter?* His eyes flew open, blazing at me as if I was the reviewer. *'Prince's work shows technical skill,'* he quoted in scathing tones, *'but lacks the freshness and originality shown by some of his peers.'* I told myself he was full of shit. I told myself I couldn't let one review poison my calling. But after two years of trying to be an artist, I got sick of living off life modelling and enrolled in Education. So I could teach other people to be better artists than me.'

He threw my hand off, rolled off the futon and stalked naked down the corridor to the bathroom.

Alone in his bed, I lay on the edge of the warm shape left by his body. Part of me felt frightened by this new side of him, and bruised by my failure to comfort him the way he'd comforted me. Another part of me felt a pang of envy. He knew his calling at the age of six. All I had at twenty-two was two bullet points and a key to my grandmother's office.

I retrieved the schedule, scowling at the slots for Research, and tried to muster some passion. The words blurred together and I cast the page aside, curling in a small, troubled ball among the sheets as I waited for Ryan to return.

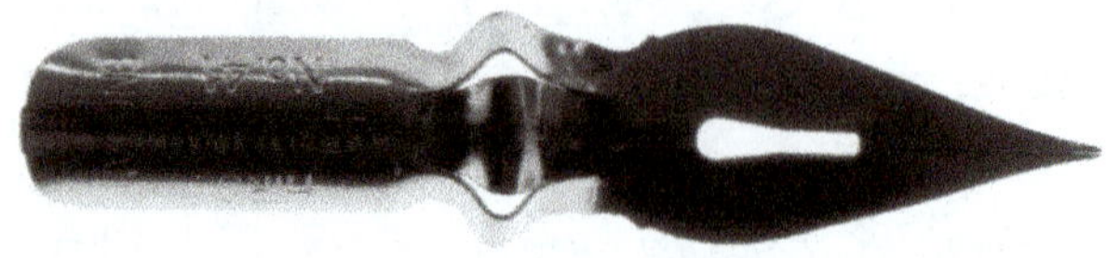

Chapter Eleven

Indecent Proposal

Only the Head of Women's Studies was entitled to a top-floor office. The rest of the staff lived on the dingier floors downstairs, where the uncarpeted corridor rang beneath the soles of my sandals. Offices on this floor didn't have engraved gold nameplates. They had metal brackets, into which their occupants slotted pieces of cardboard or paper. Hilda had typed her name in a chilly serif font, printed it on card and trimmed the card to fit the bracket perfectly.

My watch read 3:51. Four minutes to wait. Tucking my research proposal under one arm, I contemplated Hilda's door. Other staff blu-tacked whimsical cartoons to their doors; Hilda had installed a pinboard and planted a neat row of green, white and violet pins along the top. Her signature colours, standing for GWV—the old suffragette slogan 'Give Women the Vote'. At present there were two notices, one showing when she was available for consultation, and one detailing her appointments for the week. I was slightly troubled to note that the meeting I was about to have with her wasn't listed.

At 3:55, I applied punctual knuckles to the door, evoking a muffled *ffff* of exasperation, and the clomp of advancing Birkenstocks. Hilda favoured the clog style, in classic tan leather. In winter she wore these with lumpy socks she hand-knitted herself; in summer, she wore them barefoot, the hems of her linen pants flapping around her hairy white ankles as she cycled to the campus.

The door opened just wide enough for Hilda's face. The outline of a bike helmet was embossed on her greying blonde hair, and the sliver of doorway above it framed a glimpse of books sorted by spine colour.

'Yes?' said Hilda. Her voice implied that my knock had distracted her from something more important than me.

'Hi, Professor Ziehler.' Students were not permitted to address Hilda by her first name. 'I'm here for our four o'clock meeting.'

'I have no meeting at four,' said Hilda, without referring to the timetable on her door. Hilda always remembered her appointments. Which made it all the odder that she'd forgotten mine.

'We made it last week, remember?'

The creases on Hilda's forehead deepened into furrows. 'Last week we had a meeting and you did not attend. This week we have no meeting.'

My hand sprang up to catch the closing door. 'You said you'd consider supervising me,' I said hastily, 'if I gave you an excellent proposal at four today.' I brandished my proposal, tantalising her with its excellence.

'I did not say at four,' said Hilda, her voice curt and immovable as a Swiss Alp. 'I said by four. You sent no proposal, so I assumed there was no meeting.'

The proposal wavered in my hand. 'But … but I thought … I did write the proposal, and … and …'

'And now you want to watch me read it? No. That is not a meeting.'

'I could give it to you now,' I said in desperation, thrusting the proposal through the closing door, 'and when you—'

'When I supervise a PhD student,' said Hilda, snatching the pages from my fingers, 'she emails work two, three days before we discuss it. She confirms appointments with me the day before. And she comes to every one of them on time.'

She slapped the proposal into my palm and closed the door in my face. Her Birkenstocks clomped back to her desk and I sagged against the wall.

Tailoring my proposal to Hilda's tastes had taken a week of twelve-hour days. I'd put in references to articles she'd published, cited several of her favourite artists and writers, and attached a three-year plan with a weekly breakdown of tasks, colour-coded in green, white and violet. All of which meant it would need to be completely redrafted before I could offer it to another academic.

I limped back to the office and considered the three remaining supervisors who were available. Madhu Baghel specialised in South Asia. Maybe I could watch some Bollywood films, read up on Hindu temple paintings, compare their portrayals of women. Kate Cleaver-Murray's field was queer theory. Maybe I could read articles called *Why He Won't Commit* and *What He REALLY Thinks of Your Body* and study their heteronormative agenda. But either of those options would take work. Several weeks of work.

A little slug of sickness lodged in my gut. I didn't want to spend weeks revamping my research proposal. I wanted someone who'd supervise the project I'd already proposed, with as few changes as possible. Which meant I had one choice left. I picked up Andrea's phone, took a deep breath and dialled the extension for Fran Mackenzie.

Fran's office was less than half the size of the one I shared with Andrea. The furniture was on wheels, so it could be pushed aside to access the floor-to-ceiling shelves on every wall. Many of the offices on this floor felt cluttered, but Fran's looked organised and chic. She'd even found space for a watercolour either side of the window and a small potted plant on her desk.

'Sage,' said Fran. Her expression was cool and watchful, like a fox guarding its den. 'You're looking for someone to supervise your PhD research.'

In the eight years since Fran was ousted from our house, I'd had countless conversations with Andrea about her. Fran was our straw woman, our personal symbol of the decay of modern feminism. We'd sneered at her male apologist attitudes. We'd rolled our eyes at her irresponsible parenting. We'd engaged in hours of baleful speculation about Freya. The symbolic Fran was so potent in my head that the presence of the real Fran was deeply unsettling. Especially when I was asking her to supervise my PhD.

'I—yes.'

I had the uneasy feeling that she could see into my head and read every sneer and eyeroll Andrea and I had ever exchanged.

The symbolic Fran might have bristled and refused to consider supervising her enemy's granddaughter; the real one was far too professional for that.

I handed Fran my proposal and averted my eyes as she read. Apart from her laptop, there were only two things on her desk. One was a pot plant, a fern with pale green tendrils curling over the sides of its terracotta pot. The other was a framed photograph of a smiling young woman holding up a graduation certificate. A second or two later I recognised the woman as Freya.

Inside my head, Freya was frozen on our doorstep at fifteen, defiant in her mini-skirt and heels—the outfit that had ended Andrea's friendship with Fran, and launched a thousand dark predictions about Freya's future. Looking at the twenty-something Freya, in black pants and top, I struggled to reconcile her with the troubled teenager of my conversations with Andrea. She looked calm and happy. And proud. As Fran must have been, to keep a picture of her daughter's graduation day on her almost-empty desk. My throat tightened.

I crushed the thought of proud mothers underfoot and looked out the window. From this floor, the Studio 3 skylight was a stripe of metal just above the tiles. Had I been assigned a shared office on this floor, like other PhD students, Ryan and I would never have met.

Fran was leafing through my proposal with a raised eyebrow that told me subterfuge was useless. 'You wrote this for Hilda, didn't you?'

I hung my head. 'I could scale down the focus on classical art, if it helps,' I said in sheepish tones. 'Compare drawings of life models in present-day art classes with pictures of fashion models in ads.'

Fran mulled this over, tapping the desk with her pen. My fingernails bit deeper and deeper into the arms of her chair. If Fran wouldn't supervise me, it was back to Hindu temple paintings or articles called Flirt Your Way to The Top.

'It needs theory and tightening,' she said at last, 'but it's interesting. And your personal link to the industry will help.'

I froze. 'Personal link?' I said in a shrill voice. Did Fran mean Ryan? Did she know?

'Your mother. I don't know if Emmeline's still modelling herself, but she must know people in the fashion industry. Have you talked to her about your project?'

I felt a strange falling sensation, as if the floor was disintegrating beneath me. I heard a voice answering Fran's question, but it sounded like someone else. 'I didn't even know my mother was a fashion model. I was a baby when she walked out, and I haven't heard from her since.'

Several minutes passed before I registered that Fran was saying my name, at first gently, then loudly, loud enough to reach the part of me that was still there to hear. I lifted my face.

Fran was standing beside me, her own face oddly flushed. 'Are you OK?'

I nodded.

'Then let me say something strictly off the record. Something that's your family business, and none of mine. I haven't seen Emmeline for years, but I know her, and I know she wouldn't have left you behind without trying to contact you.'

I realised then that she was flushed because she was angry. Not at me, but for me, angry at how I'd been treated. 'Then why haven't I heard from her?'

Fran's face darkened. 'I don't know, but I have a tip for you. I wouldn't assume that Andrea's told you everything about

Emmeline. Or that everything Andrea's told you about Emmeline is true.'

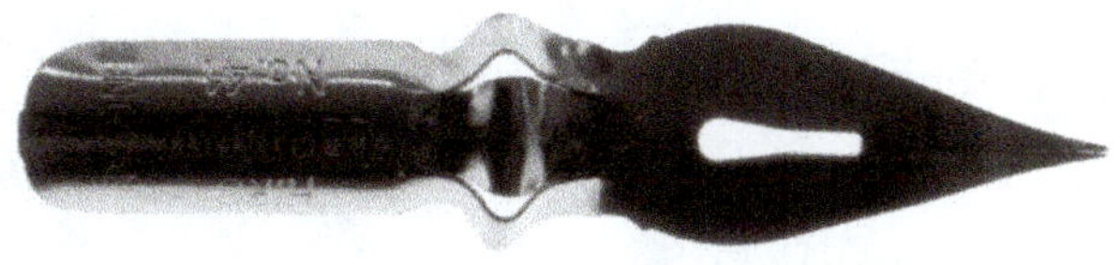

Chapter Twelve

Going Postal

I left Fran's office and stumbled for the lift through the avalanche of students pouring from Seminar Room 4, my mind a tangled blank.

I began asking Andrea about Emmeline when I was four years old. Her answers were fact sheets, framed and hung in my memory, pictures around which I'd built my life. And now Fran had torn them off the wall and thrown them overboard.

My feet kept on walking, down flights of stairs, through shadows cast by red-brick buildings, out iron gates into the street, where brick gave way to glass, and the shadows turned into people, flowing around me like a sea of faceless statues until an automatic door in front of me disgorged a thirty-something woman with a pram.

I jerked to a stop. The woman looked tired, and there were milky stains on her T-shirt. In the pram, batting at a dangling stuffed elephant, was her baby, dressed in pink, with a halo of wispy blonde hair. Hair even lighter than mine. Emmeline would be in her thirties by now. Had she pushed me around in a pram, before she left? Did she string toys above my cot, and coo when I threw up on her top?

'Excuse me,' said the woman, with a tight, weary smile.

Belatedly realising I was standing in her way, I stepped toward the closing glass doors. The doors opened again, revealing the inside of a post office.

The world came back into focus. Andrea and I still lived in the house where Emmeline grew up. I always checked the mail. If Emmeline had posted me anything in the last twenty-two years I would have found it. We received very little mail, because Andrea made a lot of enemies in her work, and didn't like to publicise our address. Just about everything went to her pigeonhole at the office.

I did an abrupt U-turn, my feet stomping the question into the pavement: *Had Emmeline ever sent me letters?* Maybe she had, and Andrea had thrown them out. Or hidden them in a filing cabinet, like the one at home where she kept the only photographs I'd seen of my mother.

Andrea didn't like photographs. Her colleagues put up pictures of their children and pets; she put up certificates and famous feminist quotes. I didn't even know she had photos of Emmeline until I was seven or so. Tired of telling me what my mother looked like, she'd unlocked her filing cabinet and produced three photos. A pigtailed pre-school Emmeline on a swing, her smile missing one front tooth. A serious Emmeline at ten, with Andrea's eyes glaring from a dainty, heart-shaped face. And the most recent one, of Emmeline at seventeen, a fortnight before she walked out.

Andrea said I could keep these, and locked the filing cabinet again. I'd wanted to know if there were more photos of Emmeline in there, but I didn't dare ask. For a year or two, I kept the pictures in the top drawer of the dresser by my bed, so I could look at them before I fell asleep. Later, when I grew old enough for an adult-sized wallet, I took out the picture of Emmeline at seventeen and slipped it between the dollar bills.

The door to the office was ajar. Inside, Andrea was scowling over a stack of essays, reading glasses perched like a bird of prey on her nose. In Fran's room, in the streets, the idea that Andrea had prevented my mother from contacting me had seemed probable and appalling. Here, in the office, it seemed ludicrous and far-fetched.

Andrea, lying to me? Andrea, hiding mail from my mother? Far more likely that this was Fran avenging herself on Andrea. For the Freya incident, for their disagreements about feminism, for the professorship Andrea had given to someone else.

Andrea looked up from her essays. 'I hear you've found a supervisor,' she said, in a curt voice that made me nervous.

'Yes,' I said, sidling into the room. 'I just thought that Fran would be … that she was …'

'The only person left after Hilda turned you down?'

My conscience squirmed. Everyone knew about Andrea's feud with Fran. When the word got around that Fran was supervising my PhD, all of Women's Studies would be abuzz. 'Is she … is that going to be a problem for you?'

Andrea picked up her pen. 'It's your PhD, Sage.' She scored an angry black line across the essay she was marking and turned the page with a flick.

I watched her deleting, considering, scrawling notes in margins, every cell of me screaming with the need to *know*.

Andrea never talked about Emmeline. It was always me who brought the subject up, asking questions, wanting photographs, wringing information from Andrea's reluctant mouth.

'Is my birth certificate at home somewhere?' I asked, in my most casual voice. Birth certificates had details about the child's parents. Their dates of birth. Their occupations.

Her pen froze mid-word. 'Why?'

I put on a grave, studious expression. 'I'm hoping to interview high school girls about body image, so I need ID for a police check.'

For a second, I thought I saw something odd in Andrea's face. Then she turned, unlocked one of her filing cabinets, and slid out a hanging file labelled P-Z. The plastic tab attached to it was angled away, and I couldn't read what it said.

Andrea flipped through the file with her usual briskness. 'Here.' She handed me a sheet of pale blue paper. I took it, but my gaze stayed on the file. What else was in there? Before I could ask, she replaced the file, locked the cabinet with a clunk and gathered up the notes for her five o'clock lecture.

'What time will you be home tonight?' she asked, opening the door. Still that odd expression—a sort of wary stiffness—on her face.

'Six or so,' I said.

'See you then.'

It was only twenty to five, but her receding footsteps sounded hurried, as though she was running late.

The sheet in my hand was printed with a grid and headed 'Birth Certificate (amended)'. *Why amended?* I wondered, but my eyes had already locked on the first box in the grid, which contained my place and date of birth, and my name: *RAMPION, Sage*. The second box contained *RAMPION, Emmeline*. Her occupation was listed as student. The third contained the details of the father who'd returned to Helsinki before I was born. *VIRTANEN, Matti. Occupation: Fashion photographer. Age: 36.* Twenty years older than my mother. My stomach twisted like someone was wringing a wet towel inside me.

Without details, my father had been hardly more than a sperm donor. A faceless commuter in a business suit, maybe, who seduced the teenage casual and went home to lie to his wife. As a fashion photographer, he had a face, and a scheme. He was a predator, a paedophile, who'd lured a teenage model to his bed. And he was my father.

My skin began to itch, as if I could feel his DNA crawling through my flesh. Matti had been married when I was conceived. Maybe he had children, other children, with his wife back in Finland. Maybe Emmeline had had more children since I was born. I was twenty-two years old and I didn't even know if I had brothers or sisters. All I had was Andrea, and the little she'd told me. And whatever she'd hidden in the bottom drawer of her filing cabinet.

The key to my own filing cabinet wouldn't turn in her lock, and none of the others would fit. After a failed experiment with a paperclip, I sneaked downstairs to Seminar Room 4 and peered through the window in the door. The room was filled with students taking notes in books and laptops. All were women, aged from late teens to middle age. Andrea was pacing and gesticulating at the front of the room, and beside her on the table, mere feet from the door, sat her keys.

A burst of commercial music erupted through the glass. In the far corner of the seminar room, a student jumped and scrabbled frantically through her bag for the offending phone. Andrea advanced toward her, rigid with anger. As she began a rant on the rudeness of leaving phones on in class, I slipped through the door, swiped the keys and sprinted for the stairs.

I opened the office door, my eardrums thumping with fear and guilt. The filing cabinets stood either side of Andrea's desk, brass keyholes trained on me like guns. I fumbled my way to a matching brass key, stabbed the left keyhole, and turned it with a satisfying *clunk*.

A third of the way through P–Z, I unearthed a slender file labelled *RAMPION, Sage*. I opened it, and the first page was the same blue as my birth certificate. The heading at the top read *Change of Name by Deed Poll*.

My stomach plunged like a stone through cold water. The name I'd used all my life was printed halfway down the page under *New Name*. Above it, in a box headed Former Name with my place and date of birth, was *VIRTANEN, Sadie Melissa*.

The contents of the file slithered to the floor. Letters, records, all labelled with the names of my parents and the name of someone listed as their daughter, who shared my birthplace and birthday. It was like looking into a mirror and seeing a stranger. Or seeing no one there at all.

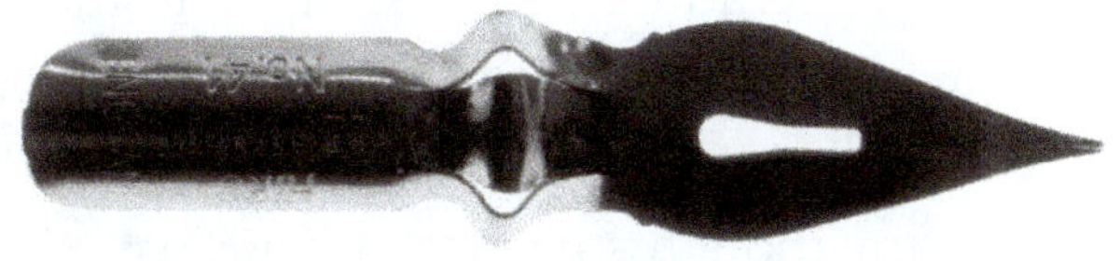

Chapter Thirteen

To the Letter

The first coherent thought that returned to me was a three-year-old conversation with Jess.

'So how come you're called Sage?' she'd asked, eyes wide and wondering. 'Is it a feminist thing?'

At the time I'd reassured her that 'Sage' had nothing to do with feminism. Now I knew it was Andrea who'd chosen my name, *amended* my name, I wondered if I'd been wrong. Andrea despised twee, childish girls' names. Maybe she thought Sage was stronger and more dignified than *Sadie Melissa*. Andrea also loathed it when women adopted their husband's surname. To her this symbolised submission, slavery, the surrender of a woman's identity to her new lord and master. Not that Matti had been Emmeline's husband. Why had my mother given me his surname?

The answer welled up as I reread the certificate. Because that was what Emmeline had wanted—to be my father's wife, with his legitimate child, instead of a single teenage mother, pining for her married lover. A bubble of grief for her burst inside me.

I retrieved the documents from the carpet and leafed through them. Most concerned my education: a letter from the government granting Andrea permission to home-school me, materials on how to do this. There were no personal letters. Biting back disappointment, I replaced the file and sat, *Sadie Melissa* beating in my thoughts like a moth against a light bulb.

Andrea's lecture ended at six. At five to six, I locked the filing cabinet and left for Seminar Room 4. Halfway to the stairs, a new possibility occurred to me. I rushed back to the filing cabinet and flipped through the files until I reached the letter V. And there, overshadowed by the three drawers above it, was a file labelled *VIRTANEN, Sadie*.

I yanked out the file with shaking hands. Its contents had been sorted into manila folders labelled by year. All except for a single envelope, postmarked about a month ago. An unopened letter, addressed in a round, feminine hand to Sadie Virtanen, care of Andrea's address on campus.

The envelope weighed in my palm like a planet. I desperately wanted to open it, but Andrea's lecture finished in two minutes, and I still hadn't put back her keys.

I jammed the file back in the cabinet, locked it and bolted for Seminar Room 4, letter in one hand, Andrea's keys in the other. Students were pouring out, and Andrea was fielding a short queue of people who'd come down to the front to ask questions. I ducked inside, dropped the keys on Andrea's notes and joined the crowds squeezing into the lift. When I reached the ground floor, I hugged the letter to my chest and ran all the way to the bench on the Library lawns where I'd met Ryan. Heart hammering, I slit open the envelope and took out one handwritten page and a birthday card with a pink gift card stuck inside. I opened the letter.

Hey Sadie,

Happy 22nd birthday! Hope you had a fab day. I didn't know what to buy you, as usual, so I got something close to every girl's heart. Spend it unwisely!

Your grandma tells me you've just graduated from university. Well done you!! Your brains must come from your dad, because I was never that great in school (as I expect your grandma's told you). I want to go back one day, though. Maybe I'll study psychology or something. Might be the only way I'll ever understand Dirk!

I know this sounds weird, but sometimes you're like my psychologist (or therapist or whatever). I open up and say all sorts of things to you because you don't judge me. Actually, you probably do judge me, but you never answer, so I don't know about it. I know why you never answer, and I know it's totally my fault, but it still hurts. I wish you'd drop me a line some time, even if it's just a one-line email. Even if it's just to tell me to get out of your life.

Anyway, enough from me. Look after yourself, and I'll write again soon, OK?

Lots of love,

Em.

I reread the letter until the words fused together on the page. Each time I read it, 'Sadie' stuck in my eyes like a piece of grit, as though I'd finally found my mother and she'd been stolen by someone else.

I opened my wallet and took out the photo. Emmeline stared out at me, curled like a cat in the armchair that still sat in our living room. A thin wrist hugged her knees to her chest, and long, rope-coloured hair draped around her like a shawl. She had Andrea's eyes, looking much larger in her young, heart-shaped face, but her lips must have come from her father. They were full, with a deep Cupid's bow, as if a fingertip had dented her top lip. Like mine. When I first saw this photo, I sat in front of the mirror for hours, fitting my fingertip into the lip that linked me to my mother. My mother the fashion model.

She probably wasn't a model any more, of course. By now Emmeline would be in her late thirties, and fashion models peaked at my age or younger. In my imagination I tried to age her, thickening her waist and jaw, carving crow's feet around her eyes, sprinkling grey through her hair, but the embellishments slid off her smooth young face like butter.

The return address appeared to be an apartment in a big block, somewhere among the city skyscrapers. Forty minutes away on foot, fifteen by bus, ten by train. I might have passed her in the street, or sat beside her on a bus. But I wouldn't have recognised her, because Andrea had locked away her letters and only given me a photo of how she looked at seventeen.

Something flared in my chest. I slung my bag over my shoulder and started walking, my feet pounding the ground, my mother's letter clenched in my hand like a dagger.

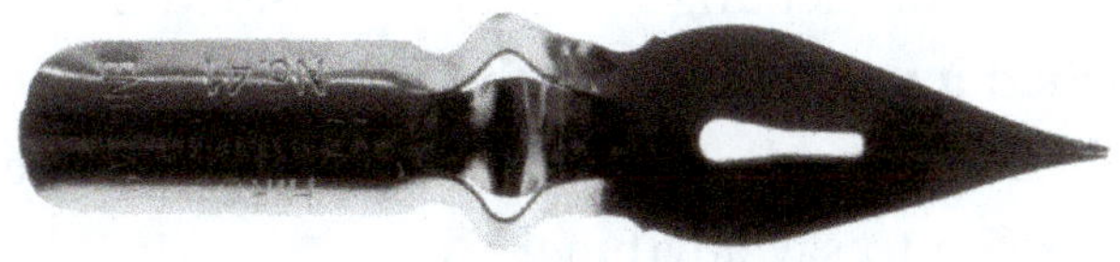

Chapter Fourteen

Bombshell

The house I shared with Andrea was dark and empty. All I could hear as I headed for the kitchen was the sinister drone of the fridge. I laid my mother's letter on the table and sat in front of it, as if I was at a formal dinner where I couldn't eat until the other guest arrived. Ten minutes later, the front door opened, and Andrea stalked past me, a batch of envelopes in one hand.

'Forgot the mail, I see.' Her sarcastic tone implied that this was only to be expected.

A week ago I would have apologised to her. But not today. 'So did you, it seems.'

Andrea looked up from her mail, her finger ripped halfway through an envelope. She opened her mouth to respond and her eye fell on the letter on the table. Her mouth stayed open.

'According to the postmark,' I said, in a cold, gritty voice, 'this letter arrived in your pigeonhole a month ago, but it seems you forgot to pass it on. And absent-mindedly locked it in your filing cabinet.'

The skin around Andrea's eyes tightened. I tensed for attack, but she said nothing. Her mouth closed, and her gaze returned to the gas bill without meeting mine. She unfolded the bill, checked it, and attached it to the fridge with a *Reclaim the Night* magnet.

I grabbed my mother's letter and thrust it under her face. 'Aren't you going to say anything?'

Andrea opened a second bill, still not meeting my eye. 'What do you want me to say?'

'My mother has been *trying to contact me*.' I spat the words like missiles. 'She sent me a letter and a birthday present, and you never gave them to me.'

'No. I didn't.'

Andrea attached the second bill to the fridge. It was a phone bill. Our phone number was silent, and she changed it regularly. She said she did this to protect us from the bullying men she fought each week at work. Had she actually done this to stop my mother ringing me?

I slapped the letter back on the kitchen table. 'This isn't the only letter she's sent me, is it?'

Andrea shrugged. 'She's sent a few.'

'And you've never passed them on to me.'

'No.'

She inserted her finger into the third bill, and I snatched it from her hands. '*Why not?*'

She looked at my blazing cheeks and trembling lips, and I recognised her expression. It was the one she wore in court, grim-jawed and merciless, the face that withered men in the dock.

'Because unlike you,' she said in blistering tones, 'I know Emmeline. Do you know what she did to you? When you were only six months old?'

'She abandoned me.' My voice began to teeter.

'Before that. She put you in a *beauty pageant.*' Andrea snatched back the bill and slapped it on the fridge. 'Baby girls too young to crawl, in makeup and tiny tiaras! I've never seen anything so grotesque. Then there was the business with your father.'

Unable to look at Andrea, I turned my gaze to the letter, imagining my mother's hand brushing across this envelope as she addressed it in round, careful writing. I didn't know Emmeline, but I'd grown up in what used to be her room, walking on carpet dented by her childhood furniture, lying in bed looking at the patches left by pictures she'd blu-tacked to the walls. It was her absence that haunted me, not the absence of the Finnish man who got her pregnant.

'She wanted to take you to see him. Hours on a plane to Helsinki with a baby. No plans, no place to stay at the other end. She figured once she arrived, Matti would sweep in and take her to happily ever after. Leaving behind his *two children and wife of ten years.*'

My stomach lurched. My mother was only sixteen when that happened. Sixteen, in love with the father of her baby, and too young to understand that love might not be enough.

'Then there was her obsession with her appearance,' Andrea went on. 'Leaving you to cry while she did sit-ups. Refusing to breastfeed because it might ruin how she looked in a bikini.'

My mother was a fashion model. Her looks were her career. I wanted to shout it, loud enough to drown out what she was telling me, but I couldn't get my lips to move.

'And no,' she said, 'I didn't want you in contact with her. Why? *Because I didn't want you growing up exposed to those values.*'

Years of submission dragged on me. But this time, the counterweight of years of betrayal was enough to strengthen my spine.

'I've grown up now, Andrea,' I said, wobbly but defiant. 'You should have let me choose for myself.'

She gave a contemptuous snort. 'You would have *chosen* to be exposed to those values?'

'Yes. I would.'

Andrea's face hardened. 'Oh, you would, would you? Why's that?'

'Because she's my mother.' My voice teetered again, and I had to look away.

Andrea made a sound between a scoff and a laugh. She turned her back, plonked a glass on the counter and filled it to the brim with pinot noir. 'Your mother's not the person who gave birth to you,' she said, in a rusty voice I hadn't heard before. 'She's the person who looks after you, and reads you stories and makes sure you're safe. Emmeline's not your mother, Sage. I am. I'm the only mother you've ever known.'

She corked the bottle, picked up her glass and headed toward her room.

The door closed behind her, and I sat without moving with the letter in my hands, listening to the drone of the fridge. My grip had left new creases in the envelope. As I smoothed it out, the thought I'd been avoiding pinched like a buried splinter. Emmeline had grown up in this house, and she didn't live that far away. If she'd really wanted to see me, she could have demanded to be let in, or tapped on my window in the night even. But she hadn't. She'd posted off letters and presents, as if we were on opposite sides of the world. And Andrea had destroyed or hidden all of them, to make sure she didn't corrupt me.

I picked up the letter and retreated to my room. The last of the sunset had drained away, but the curtains were ajar, letting in an apricot glow from the street lamp outside. Hugging my mother's letter like a teddy bear, I climbed into bed and lay staring at the rectangles her posters had left on the wall.

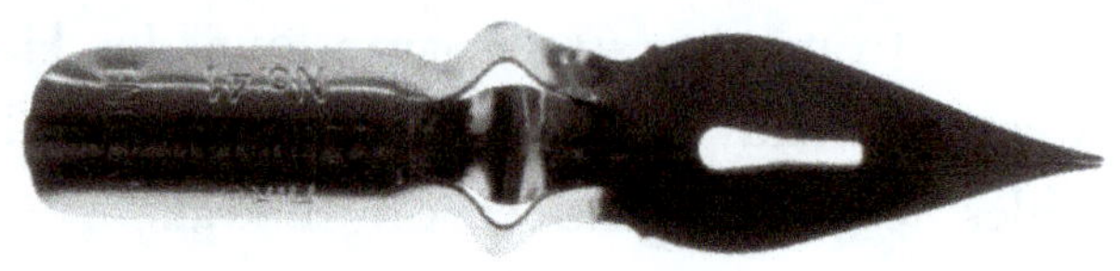

Chapter Fifteen

Eye for an Eye

Ryan's arms engulfed me. 'Why didn't you *call?*'

He sounded both horrified and hurt, hurt that my natural reaction to crisis hadn't been to ring him for comfort and support. I flattened my face into his shoulder. Underneath the warmth of his arms, I felt cold and bruised, as if I'd been in a car crash.

Ringing Ryan hadn't occurred to me. He wasn't part of the disintegrating world I shared with Andrea. He belonged to a different, magical place where I danced and lay on a futon with my legs tangled round his naked body.

'There you were,' he went on, 'having a major life crisis, and where was I? In the kitchen drinking Shell's vile homebrew! I would have *welcomed* a crisis call! You weren't scared of waking me, were you?'

'Not exactly, but—'

'Call my mobile! Call at four if you have to!'

I smiled into his shoulder. 'I'm sorry. Next time I have a major life crisis, I'll call you straightaway.'

'I should think so!'

He laid his cheek against my hair and held me without speaking until my cold, bruised heart began to thaw. My eyes flickered open and fell on his quirky retro clock. 'When are your lectures on today?'

'Twelve and three.'

It was a quarter to twelve. He was missing his lecture to comfort me. I felt as though I'd swallowed something too big for my throat. Wanting in some clumsy way to thank him, I pulled my mother's letter from my bag and held it out.

He hesitated. 'Are you sure it's OK for me to read this?'

I nodded. He took the letter and his eyes widened. '*Sadie Virtanen?*'

'Andrea changed my name when she became my legal guardian.'

'To Sage Rampion.'

'Yes.'

Ryan turned the envelope over. 'This is an address in town. We could get on a train and be there in twenty minutes.'

I smiled bitterly. 'We could, but she wouldn't be there. I looked it up. It's a hotel.'

His face fell. 'She wrote to you when she was on holiday here?'

'Looks like it. Nice of her to drop by.'

'Oh, Sage.' He gathered me close again, and hot tears striped my face.

'You know the worst thing?' I said into his chest. 'There were more letters in there. At least I think they were letters. Lots of them, sorted into manila folders. She can't have written all of them on holiday. And I just left them there. I stole Andrea's keys, and I was running out of time to put them back and I panicked.' I lifted my head to look at him. 'Why didn't I grab the lot?'

'We'll get them out, Sage,' said Ryan, taking my hands. 'I'll break into her filing cabinet and get them for you. Tell me when and I'll do it.'

I sank my face back onto his shoulder and wept.

I would have answered your letters, Mum. I would have. I always wanted you in my life, I never wanted to punish you. And it's not totally your fault, it's Andrea's. It's Andrea's.

When I raised my head, Ryan was reading the letter. 'Andrea's told her you're doing a PhD.' He looked up, and his eyes were like bullets. 'That means they're in touch. Probably by email. We should hack Andrea's computer, too. Search her hard drive. Check her browsing history. Crack the passwords for her email accounts.'

I shivered at the vicious note in his voice. People didn't talk about Andrea like this. Not her colleagues, not her students. Even the men she brought to justice through her work—men who would have stuck a knife in her and jeered while she bled—cursed her name with a measure of respect. My flesh shrivelled at the thought of what she'd do if someone hacked her computer. 'Isn't that… unethical?'

'Compared with twenty years of lying to you and hiding your mother's letters? Frankly, I'd call it divine justice.' He shoved the letter back in its envelope and noticed the gift card. 'What about this?'

I took the card. One side was lollipop pink, with *Bradenfield Gift Card $300* on it in curly silver letters; the other had a signature panel and a magnetic strip. *I got something close to every girl's heart,* my mother had written. Meaning shopping. Not going out to buy something I needed, but shopping as a pastime. Hours of browsing the unnecessary stuff sold to women to decorate their bodies. Andrea thought that sort of thing was disgusting and exploitative. But apparently she was fine with lying, hiding letters and making a child think her mother didn't love her.

Gripping the card, I took Ryan's hand and stood up. 'You hate your three o'clock lecture, don't you?'

'God, yes. ATC. Advanced Teaching Curriculum, also known as A Total Crock. Why?'

'Because I thought you might like to skip it and come shopping with me.'

I ducked into a corridor labelled 'Centre Management', gasping as if I'd been swimming underwater. Ryan joined me, looking unfazed.

'Are shopping malls always like this?' I had to repeat the question twice before he could hear me over the noise.

His eyebrows drew together. 'Like what?'

'This!' I waved a weak hand at the hordes of people, stomping among garish shops, dangling glossy bags, shouting into mobile phones, wielding their prams like bulldozers through an endless, mixed blare of music. Andrea called shopping malls temples to greed. To me, this was more like a crowd scene from a play set in Hell.

'Busy, you mean? Depends on the time of year. This is quiet. Just before Christmas everything stays open until ten and there are five times as many people.'

My imagination tried to cram five times as many people into the escalators and aisles, and it fractured. I sank onto a bench, clutching the store directory like a shield.

Ryan took the directory from my hands. 'So how do you want to spend your gift card?'

He unfolded the directory and a massive list of shops swam before me. I forced my eyes to focus, and the words 'Eyewear and Optical Accessories' floated to the surface. Two escalators later, I was blinking at a mirror while Ryan perused the racks of frames.

Ryan plucked a pink frame from the wall. 'Try these!' The lenses were shaped like cat's eyes, with diamantes and odd pointy bits near the browline. 'Funky and cutting edge? Or Bride of Elton?'

I put them on. 'Bride of who?'

'Elton John. Ageing gay singer with a taste for mad specs. I'll borrow a CD from my mum for you.'

I peered at the price tag and nearly fell off my stool. '*Four hundred and eighty dollars?* Just for the frames?'

Ryan shrugged. 'Funky doesn't come cheap. When did you last buy new glasses?'

'I've never bought new glasses.'

'Where are those from, then?'

I handed him the Bride of Elton frames, a worm of embarrassment coiling in my stomach. 'They're Andrea's old frames. She had my prescription put in them.'

Ryan's mouth hardened. 'So,' he said, folding up the frames, 'Andrea's devoted her professional life to empowering women.' He replaced them in the rack with a *click*. 'Makes it kind of ironic,' he went on, 'that's she's devoted her personal life to oppressing one.'

For a second, I couldn't process what I'd heard. Ignoring the contribution of women to history was oppression. Penalising women for childbearing was oppression. Sexualising six-year-old girls was oppression. 'How is Andrea supposed to have oppressed me? By making me wear her old glasses?'

The idea was laughable. Ludicrous. Disrespectful to genuine victims of oppression. I started to say so, but Ryan's grim, troubled face made me stop.

'My mother was a fashion model,' I said, turning to the mirror and reaching for the dent in my lip. 'She got pregnant at sixteen to a married man. Andrea didn't want me to turn out like her. She shouldn't have kept the letters from me, but I understand why she did. She wanted to protect me.'

I glanced up at Ryan's face above mine in the mirror. He didn't look appeased.

'Why are you defending her, Sage?'

'I don't know.' I felt uneasy, like I was covering for a bully. A criminal. An *oppressor.* 'I'm sorry,' I said at last, not sure what I was sorry for.

Ryan shook his head. 'It's Andrea that should be sorry, not you.' He selected another pair of frames. 'Try these.'

I looked down at the frames. They were narrower and squarer than the previous pair, in mingled shades of iridescent blue. The label read *I-Wair Paua Shell, $180.*

I put them on and looked in the mirror. Not at myself, but at Ryan again, whose face showed plainly that he liked what he saw.

'What do you think?' asked Ryan.

'I'll take them.'

I paid for the frames, and the sales assistant gave me their email address so that I could send through my optical prescription. I pocketed the business card, pondering the question I hadn't answered. Why *had* I defended the woman who'd cut me off from my mother?

The answer came to me piece by piece as we set off through the crowd. Because Andrea was the only family I had. Because I wanted to believe she'd been protecting me, not oppressing me. Because even if Andrea's world was oppressive, it was the only world I knew.

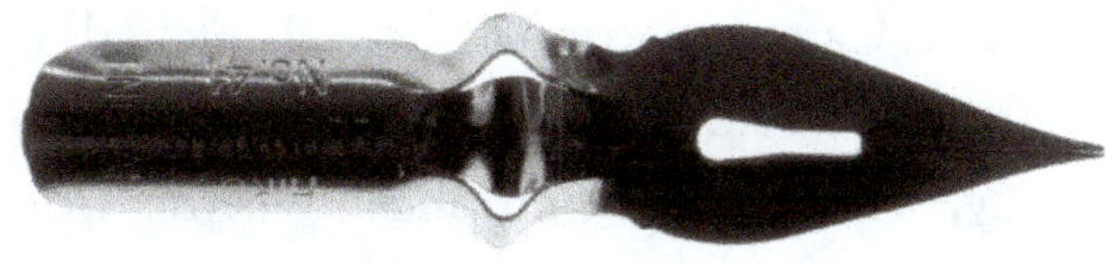

Chapter Sixteen

Framed

In the days that followed I avoided Andrea as much as possible. I left the house early and filled my time in the library or with Ryan, going in to the university only when I had supervision meetings with Fran. My path crossed Andrea's only in the evenings, when we exchanged stilted questions about work. Neither of us mentioned Emmeline.

A week later, Ryan and I went back to the mall to pick up my new glasses. They sat lightly on my nose, like a friendly butterfly. Ryan loved them, and his compliments buoyed me up as I made my way back to university.

Only when I stepped into the Humanities building did the buoyancy start to fade. As the lift rose, the butterfly grew heavier and heavier, turning into a target for Andrea's scorn. Walking down the top floor corridor, I was tempted to swap the glasses for my old pair, but I reminded myself of the lies and the letters and made myself open the door.

Andrea was sitting at her desk, looking through a folder.

'Hi, Andrea,' I said, walking to my desk with a forced, jerky nonchalance. 'What are you working on?'

'Organising next month's conference on women in fiction.' I could feel her eyes raking my face. 'You've been busy too, I see.'

'Yes,' I said. Calm, matter-of-fact. 'I picked up the new glasses I bought last week. With the gift card my mother gave me for my birthday.' I put a slight emphasis on the word 'mother', and was pleased to see Andrea twitch.

'And that took all morning, did it?'

Her sarcasm pinched well-worn nerves, but I shook it off. 'Yes. It did.'

'I expect you'll be working late tonight on your proposal, then.'

Fran was expecting a revised proposal and preliminary overview of the field by next Thursday, neither of which I'd started. My shoulders wilted, and I was about to mumble assent when the second voice, *my* voice, took over. *Why are you submitting to this woman? She hid your mother's mail. She lied to you and tried to control everything you saw and read! You're not in high school any more, Sage.*

I lifted my chin. 'I think I'll... I can decide for myself what I'm doing tonight. Thanks.' The words sounded rushed rather than cool and assertive, but at least I managed to get them out.

'I see,' said Andrea in a dry voice. 'What's brought on this sudden rudeness?'

Several replies competed in my head, but I picked the most inflammatory one and threw it at her. 'I'm tired of being oppressed.'

A flash of outrage lit Andrea's face. '*Oppressed? By me*, you mean?'

I quaked, but stood my ground.

'Don't make me laugh.' Her tone was withering. 'You're educated, Western and white, and you grew up in a comfortable, middle-class home free of sexism. You're one of the most privileged women on this earth, thanks to me. That you have the gall to suggest that I was *oppressing* you is one of the most naïve and hurtful things I've ever heard.'

The assertive new Sage crumpled as her own bomb blew up in her face. I felt like a petulant child, pouting at the hand that fed her.

Is that what I am? Shaky and depleted, I tried to regroup. 'I have a mother who wants to be in touch with me, and you hid her from me.'

'You think you'd have been better off with a single teenage fashion model? *She* left *you*.' Andrea slammed her folder on the desk, marched over to me and stood, arms folded. 'You never answered my earlier question, Sage. Where's all this coming from?'

I bowed my head, refusing to look at her.

'Something you learnt at the *library*, is it?'

My head jerked up as if she'd yanked my hair. 'The library?'

Andrea's expression was knowing, icy. 'The place where you spend most of your time, despite getting no work done on your thesis. The place which seems to leave a nasty rash around your mouth.'

My bones turned to water. She knew. She *knew*.

'So where did you meet this man, Sage?'

'I … he … he was the model at my life drawing class.'

She looked appalled. 'The one *exposing* himself under the skylight?'

'He wasn't exposing himself!' I shouted, hot and cold with shame. 'He didn't know anyone outside the class could see him, he was—'

'And is he, by any chance, the person who said I've been oppressing you?'

I wanted to deny this, to hurl Andrea's assumptions back in her face, but my voice failed. Because it *was* Ryan who'd said it first.

Andrea's lips curled. 'I see. So as well as trying to sabotage your PhD, he's—'

'*Sabotage my PhD?*' This was beyond outrageous. 'Ryan's never tried to sabotage my PhD. He supports me.'

'Oh, so monopolising your time when you're being paid to work on your doctoral research is *supporting* you, is it? Does he know it's in Women's Studies?'

'*Yes.* And it doesn't bother him. He respects feminism.'

'He does, does he?' Her scorn would have melted steel. 'That would explain why he took you to get a makeover.'

'*Makeover?*' The idea was laughable. 'We went shopping. *Once.* To spend the gift card from my mother that *you* didn't pass on to me. It was *me* who chose to spend it on new glasses, not him.'

'Did he choose the frames, or you?' Andrea said with a wintry smile.

I hesitated. 'Well, he did, but—'

She made a sound between a laugh and a snort, as if to rest her case. I shoved my chair back and stood, fists clenched with frustration. 'You haven't even met him!'

She ambled back to her desk and picked up her folder. 'No,' she said, 'because you've never mentioned him before. Telling, that.'

'What do you mean, telling?'

Andrea took out an itinerary and studied it, her chilly calm restored. 'So far, I know that Ryan is an exhibitionist who's threatened by your PhD in Women's Studies, grooming you as eye candy and accusing *me* of oppressing *you*.'

'*Exhibitionist?*'

'If I were you,' continued Andrea as if I hadn't spoken, 'I wouldn't mention him to my feminist grandmother either. Now, if you'll excuse me,' she said, replacing the itinerary and picking up her keys, 'I have a lecture to give on Gender Politics.'

The door closed behind her. I wanted to kick her laptop through the window and take to her filing cabinets with an axe, but I made myself sit at my desk and breathe deeply. The angry fog receded, leaving Andrea's accusations in plain sight.

I tackled them one by one. Ryan hadn't been 'exposing himself', that was just ridiculous. And I was pretty sure Women's Studies didn't faze him. But he had picked out my glasses. And accused me of pursuing a career for which I had no passion. Maybe he was ashamed of how I looked, and intimidated by my PhD. Maybe he was plotting to make me quit my course and remake me as a vapid bimbo.

Was that likely? I sifted through the memories from my month of knowing Ryan. The kind, thoughtful way he'd listened to my story. His clever, quirky T-shirts and hatred of the mainstream. How he'd missed two lectures to comfort me, and promised to help me find my mother. Ryan wasn't the person trying to crush and control me. It was Andrea, undermining my trust in my boyfriend because she sensed he was helping me outgrow her.

The angry fog returned. I stomped over to Andrea's desk and punched Ryan's number into her phone.

'Hey, sagacious girl. What's up?'

'Andrea's on a conference over the semester break.' I consulted the detailed schedule on her wall and stabbed my finger at the block labelled *Mid-Semester Conference*. 'Remember how you said you could hack her computer and break into her filing cabinet?'

'Uh, yes.'

'Her flight leaves at five on the 30th. I'm booking you in.'

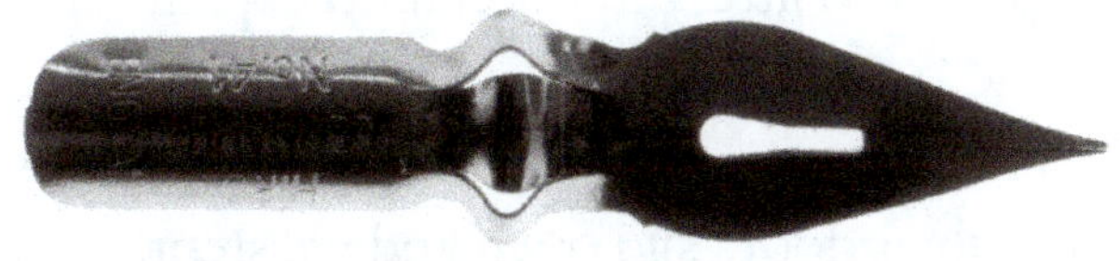

Chapter Seventeen

Desktop

The ground floor of the Humanities building was shiny with wet footprints. Outside, the sky was so dark it looked like dusk instead of late afternoon. A skewer of lightning pierced the foyer, splashing silver over me and the squashy vinyl couch where I sat.

The clock above the lifts read 4:56. Andrea's flight was leaving in four minutes, and she wouldn't be back until the middle of next week. Ryan and I would have five clear days to ransack the office and house for information on Emmeline. Since the day I got my glasses, sharing Andrea's house and office had felt like living in a war zone. I'd expected relief when she left for her conference, but I still felt shivery and sick.

A second skewer of lightning lit up Ryan, climbing the steps under a giant umbrella printed with koi fish. I leapt up to open the door as he closed his umbrella. He was dressed all in black and his lips tasted of rain.

'Who is it today?' I said, looking down at his T-shirt. A cloaked man with lank hair and a sullen, hook-nosed face was printed on the front.

'Severus Snape. Anti-hero of the Harry Potter series.'

I let this pass, too jittery to ask him to explain the connection to princes.

Ryan stabbed the button for the lift with the point of his umbrella. The silver doors slid open and we stepped inside. Heart pounding with guilt, I pressed the button for the top floor.

The offices were silent behind their gold nameplates. On the Friday before semester break, even senior academics left early to sip wine at the Staff Club. I unlocked Andrea's office door and Ryan walked in.

'Check out the *view!* He grabbed the ledge and stared spellbound through the rain-spattered window. 'Hey, is that the skylight where you saw me?'

I nodded, struck silent by the enormity of what I was doing. Bringing Ryan here was worse than a betrayal of Andrea, it was a violation. And I was about to violate her further.

'So where do you want to start?' he said, plonking himself on Andrea's leather chair with an irreverence that made me wince.

For a moment I wanted to drop the whole thing, go back to his place, spend the next five nights in his arms. But then what? Could I go on with my PhD, and forget about the mother Andrea had kept away from me? Let Emmeline keep writing letters I'd never get to see? *I know why you never answer,* she'd written, *and I know that it's totally my fault, but it still hurts.*

My jaw turned to granite. 'Start with the filing cabinet,' I said.

Ryan trundled Andrea's chair over to the filing cabinet and laid out a selection of paperclips, small keys, bent nails and other implements, like a surgeon about to perform a caesarean section. Breaking open my grandmother to pull my mother out.

'Have you googled "Emmeline Rampion"?' he said, picking up a paperclip.

'Lots of times.'

'No luck?'

'None,' I said, turning on my computer. 'But I haven't tried "Emmeline Virtanen". Or "Emmeline fashion model".'

'Excellent. Try those. You track, I'll crack. And then hack.'

'Virtanen' turned out to be the Finnish equivalent of 'Smith', and there were no Virtanens called Emmeline. There were models called Emmeline, but none of their photos looked like the slender teenage girl in the photo. Maybe she'd modelled under a pseudonym. Or had stopped modelling so long ago she didn't have a profile online.

Ryan was working his way through his lock-picking tools, with a series of clunks and curses. After a particularly sharp clunk, I glanced over and saw him sucking his knuckles. 'Are you OK?'

'Cut myself,' he said with a grimace.

His bent nail had left a scar in the lock, a bright gold comma against the dull gold of the brass. I imagined Andrea's eyes on it and winced. 'No luck, then?'

'None.' He laid the bent nail next to the other implements. 'Do they have master keys at reception?'

'Not for filing cabinets. I asked.'

He pinched his chin thoughtfully. 'How about a locksmith? Could you say you need to access it and Andrea forgot to leave you a key?'

I shook my head. 'Not without her authorisation.'

'Bugger.' He sat in Andrea's desk chair, clutching at his springy hair. 'Find anything on your mother?'

'Nothing.'

'OK then, total fail on the cracking and tracking. That leaves the hacking.'

He took out his mobile phone and pressed the power button on Andrea's computer. The sound of it booting up sent a quiver down my spine. No one touched Andrea's computer. Even the IT manager signed a privacy agreement before he laid a finger on her mouse. And here was Ryan, turning it on like it was a desk lamp.

'Did you install the keylogger program?' he said, consulting something on his phone.

I nodded. The very mention of the keylogger program made me queasy. The USB Ryan had given me spent the first ten days in a sock in my bedroom before I'd dared to bring it into the office, and three days in a drawer wrapped up like a drug stash, before I mustered the courage to stick it in a port under the desk at the back of Andrea's computer. Apparently what it did was record everything she typed, including the passwords to her email accounts.

'You're *sure* she won't be able to tell?'

'Positive.' A few minutes later, Ryan announced 'I'm in!'

My heart leaped into my mouth. He did a search for 'Emmeline', and results flooded onto the screen.

He clicked on a random document. 'Emmeline Pankhurst! Might your mother have married a Mr Pankhurst?'

I shook my head. 'Emmeline Pankhurst was the first suffragette. Andrea named my mother after her. Try Emmeline Rampion.'

No search results returned.

'Damn.' He thumped the mouse pad. 'Before we look for hidden files, let's crack her email.' He went back to work.

Unable to watch, I looked at Ryan instead. His brow was furrowed and his springy hair quivered as he tinkered and clicked, doing his illegal best to find out what he could about my mother.

Sensing my gaze, he looked up at me, and emotion swelled my throat. I took off my glasses, climbed into his lap and kissed him. A long moment later, I withdrew my lips and laid my forehead against his, our lashes touching as we blinked.

'Thank you,' I whispered.

He smiled. 'You're welcome.'

I leant in to kiss him again and knocked something heavy to the floor with a clunk that made us both jump. A heavy book called *The Phallocentric Imperative* lay open on the floor. Ryan and I looked at each other and started to laugh.

'Mood killer,' said Ryan, pointing at the book with an accusing finger.

The open page had angry black notes on it in Andrea's writing. I imagined her seeing what was going on in her office, but instead of my usual clench of fear I felt a raw and almost sacrilegious glee.

'What are you grinning about?' asked Ryan, looking amused.

My grin widened. 'How Andrea would feel if she knew what was going on in her office.'

He chuckled. 'It does look like it could do with a man's touch.'

I slid into his lap until my body was pressed against the unyielding pillar of the patriarchy. 'Definitely.'

My hands slid up his T-shirt. Underneath Severus Snape's sullen face, Ryan's heartbeat was starting to accelerate. I pulled the T-shirt off and pressed my face into his chest, breathing him in and feeling his muscles flex and shift as he unbuttoned my shirt.

'Is this authorised?' he said, reaching around to unhook my bra.

I shrugged off my shirt. 'Is what authorised?'

'This!' He brandished the bra at me. 'Why hasn't Andrea burnt it yet?'

'Feminists,' I said, unbuckling his belt and pulling it, 'did not actually go around burning bras.' The belt slithered through the loops on his jeans like a flat leather snake.

'*What?*' He undid the button on my pants. 'My boyhood fantasies, in tatters!' He tossed the bra onto Andrea's keyboard, turned me side on and yanked off my pants with a jerk that took my shoes and socks with them.

'There was one bra,' I said in soothing tones, undoing the button of his jeans. 'At a protest against the Miss America pageant.' I unzipped his fly, so slowly that he shoved my hand aside and wrenched off his jeans himself.

He pulled me to him. 'So,' he said, 'what did they do to it? Were there flamethrowers?' His lips were half an inch from mine, and his voice was heavy and breathless.

I shook my head sadly. 'They threw it in a trash can.'

'A *trash can?*' he said, sounding so outraged that I started to shake with laughter. He scooped me from the floor and plonked my naked body on the end of Andrea's desk.

'What were you hoping for?' I said, trying to straighten my face. 'Bra-less feminists, dancing around a—'

He silenced me with his tongue. The rest of my sentence dissolved in a wave of heat. On some distant plane, I heard the flutter of papers falling, but I didn't realise it was my twisting limbs that had knocked them off the desk, until the wave of heat juddered and broke. Ryan was standing at the end of the desk, the curls on his chest shivering as he breathed heavily in and out.

Thunder rattled the window panes. I hooked my leg around Ryan's hips to pull him in, but he resisted, looking down at me with a soft expression.

'What are you thinking about?' I asked.

'How beautiful you are.' He ran a gentle finger along my hairline. An ache rose in the back of my throat. 'What about you?'

A voice inside my head said *How much I love you*, but my lips wouldn't say it. I made them smile, swallowing the ache, pretending to be light-hearted. 'How we'll never, ever manage to put Andrea's desk back the way we found it.'

His smile lit the room. 'And how do you feel about that?'

'Liberated.'

This time he didn't resist when I pulled him in. The wave gathered force again, swelling and swelling until a *ding* from the lift made it crash.

My body went rigid, but Ryan was too close to orgasm to notice. Footsteps were approaching down the corridor, accompanied by the trundle of a suitcase on wheels.

'Ryan,' I said urgently, but he was tense and panting on the brink. When keys jangled right outside the door I screamed his name again as the key plunged into the door at the same time as his final, shuddering thrust.

His limp, gasping weight pinned me to the desk. I struggled in terror, begging him to get off, get *off*, but it was too late. Andrea charged in, tore his body away from mine and blasted him in the eyes with a handbag-sized can of Mace.

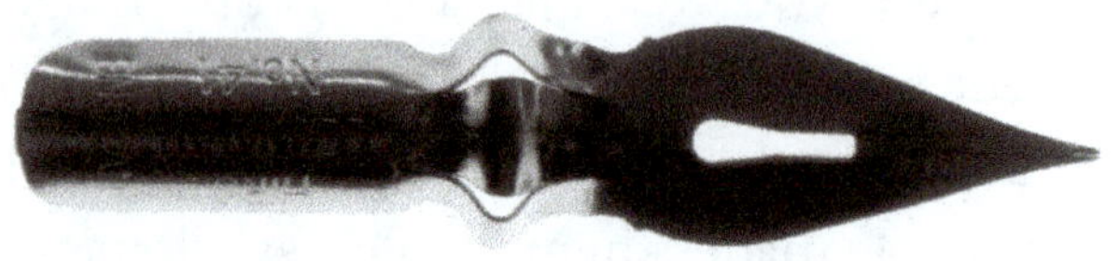

Chapter Eighteen

Washout

Ryan's harrowing scream splintered the room.

'Get off her!' shrieked Andrea, and as I jumped down from the desk, the scream cut off abruptly with the whipcrack sound of her belting him across the face.

'Get *off* her!'

Crack.

'Get off her!'

Crack.

He crashed to the floor, coughing violently and clutching his eyes, and I seized Andrea's arm before she belted him again.

'Stop it!' I screamed, as she wrenched her arm from my grip. *'Stop it!'* I grabbed her shirt and yanked her away from him. *'Andrea!'*

She stopped then, twisting my hands off her shirt and turning around to seize my shoulders in a brutal grip. 'Don't go near him, Sage. Don't go near him.'

Her white-ringed eyes raised goosebumps on my back. 'He *wasn't raping me.'*

Behind her, Ryan's coughing subsided into a hideous wet rasping. I tried to break free, but her grip on my shoulders tightened until I squirmed with pain.

'You were screaming,' said Andrea, a furious tremor in her voice. 'I heard you through the door. "Get off, get off"!'

'That was because I *heard you coming!*

Her grip slackened. I wrenched myself free, and crouched beside Ryan. He was curled in a ball now, trembling and twitching like a dying spider. His hands were clamped over his eyes, and blood-tinged mucus was dribbling from his nose and both corners of his open, wheezing mouth.

My stomach contracted with horror. Every muscle in me wanted to hold him and soothe him, but he was in so much pain all I dared do was kneel and stroke his shoulder with my fingertips. 'Are you OK?' I said, my voice breaking, knowing he wasn't, but not knowing what else to say. The Mace on him made my eyes sting.

He shook his head, and I glimpsed the reddening evidence of Andrea's blows between his fingers. 'I can't see,' he said, in a fractured voice so unlike his own it made me shiver. The voice of an artist who'd lost his sight.

'It's just Mace,' I said, trying to sound calm. 'I'll get some water and wash it out.'

As I got up, I saw Andrea was on the phone. She lowered her voice and cupped the receiver as I rummaged in my bag for a bottle of water. I gathered some of our fallen clothes and knelt beside Ryan again, putting on my shirt. 'I've got the water.'

He nodded and peeled his hands off his face. My heart shrank. The skin around his eyes was puffy and raw, and a thin fluid was oozing from his lashes. His cheeks were blotchy, and blood was seeping from his left nostril into the saliva dripping from his mouth.

I poured a shaky trickle across his eyelids. 'Is that better?'

'A bit,' he said, his eyes still pinched shut.

'I'll get you a doctor.'

I draped his T-shirt and jeans over his shivering body and got up again, retrieving my pants and pulling them on before I hurried across to the phone. Andrea had finished her call, and she was standing by the window.

'Who was that you called? An ambulance?'

She didn't answer. I called an ambulance myself and gave them directions to the office. When I hung up, Andrea turned to me, her eyes unfocused. As if I were transparent and she was staring through my face at someone else.

'We thought you'd left,' I said, pulling on my pants, not sure she could hear me. 'For the conference.'

'I see,' said Andrea, in a stilted voice. 'So you thought you'd have a quick fuck on my desk.'

The word 'fuck' punctured me, leaving a black hole that drained the magic from everything. Ryan kissing me in the desk chair, telling me I was beautiful, helping me find my mother.

'Actually, no,' I said with tremulous defiance. 'He came here to help me find out more about my mother. The information you *hid* from me.'

Andrea gave a brief, bitter laugh. 'That's what he told you, was it?'

The sneering note in her voice unsettled me. 'What do you mean?'

Andrea gave me a bleak, cynical smile. 'How well do you know this man, Sage? Any father or brother I might have met in court?'

Court? My jaw dropped. 'You think Ryan seduced me to get to *you?* To avenge someone?'

Another *ding* from the lift outside made adrenalin spike in my blood. Heavy footsteps started down the corridor, and I heard the crackle of a two-way radio. Someone rapped on the wall outside the door.

'Security,' said a brusque male voice.

'In here,' said Andrea.

The owner of the voice entered the room, short and stocky in a pale blue shirt. 'Evening ma'am,' he said to Andrea, looking around. His gaze fell on Ryan.

'I've called an ambulance,' I said, in a low, trembling voice. 'He's been assaulted. By her.' My hand flicked at Andrea as if hurling a brick. 'She *maced* him, and she *hit* him, and she—'

'Miss!' The security guard held up a hand. 'I need you to calm down.' He turned to Andrea. 'Now, ma'am. When you called, you said—'

'What did you tell him?' I started towards Andrea and the security guard stepped across to block me.

'Miss—'

'Did you tell him Ryan raped me?'

I tried to shove past, but the security guard grabbed me by the wrist. 'Miss—'

'You did, didn't you?'

'Miss!' He yanked me away from Andrea, and his cool, firm voice broke through my rage. 'I need you to calm down and listen. The police are on their way, and it's their job to go into

exactly who did what. Until then, sit down and stay calm. Can you do that for me?'

I nodded. The guard released my wrist and I made my way back to Ryan. The twitching of his limbs had eased, but his breath was shallow and rasping, and his hands were still clamped over his eyes. I sat on the floor beside him and very gently stroked his hair.

The third ding of the night rang down the corridor. The security guard went to look out the door, and I judged from his nod that the footsteps clomping towards us belonged to the police.

I glanced around the office. Andrea was standing by the window looking out, her face unreadable. Torn articles and books lay scattered over and around her desk. The keylogger was still in her computer. Her filing cabinet had an obvious gash in its lock and lockpicking tools lined on top. I felt suddenly cold, as if the rain beating on the windows was running down my back.

Two policemen arrived at the doorway and took in the scene. One pulled out a notebook and started making notes.

'Evening, everyone,' said the other officer, who was older and stouter than his colleague. He looked down at Ryan.

'Mace,' said the security guard.

The older officer nodded. 'There's an ambulance waiting downstairs. Could you go down and tell them to come up?'

The security guard nodded and headed for the lift.

'Now,' said the older officer. 'I need to ask a few questions. Which of you is Professor Rampion?'

'I am,' said Andrea, her voice flat and ungracious. She didn't like policemen.

'Got some photo ID for me, Professor?'

She pulled her wallet from the pocket on the front of her suitcase and tossed her staff card on the desk.

'Thanks, Professor. Now. About fifteen minutes ago, we received an urgent call from university security. Can you tell me what happened? In your own words?'

'I was meant to be on a five o'clock flight,' she said, shoving her card into her wallet, 'but it was cancelled because of the storm.'

'What happened then?'

'I caught a cab here from the airport to get some notes I'd forgotten.'

The other policeman scribbled in his notebook. 'What time would that have been?'

'About six.'

About six. I bowed my head over Ryan and closed my eyes, as if my eyelids could make everything that had happened since then vanish.

'And then?'

'As I walked towards my office, I heard my granddaughter screaming, so I—'

I lifted my head. 'Don't you dare say he was raping me.'

Andrea raised her voice. 'I took out the—'

I rose to my feet. 'Don't you *dare*,' I said through gritted teeth, and this time she stopped. I swung around to face the policemen. 'There was no sexual assault. We were—'

'Miss,' interrupted the older policeman, 'settle down.'

As he spoke, another *ding* from the lift rang down the corridor. This time the footsteps were joined by the rattling squeak of a trolley.

The policeman glanced at his watch. 'Look, ladies, how about we chat about this at the station? The one a few blocks from here. You OK to get there?'

Two paramedics wheeled a hospital trolley into the office, followed by the security guard carrying a bucket of water.

Andrea shrugged. 'We can walk.'

The policemen exchanged glances, and the older one nodded. 'How about I take you there in the car?' he said. 'These guys won't be long.'

'Stand back please,' said one of the paramedics.

I backed away, and the paramedic crouched down beside Ryan. 'How are you doing, sir? Can you tell me what happened?'

'Mace,' said Ryan through his hands.

'We need to wash your eyes and face,' said the paramedic. 'Can you sit up for me?'

Ryan peeled his hands away and my guts plunged again at the sight of his swollen, oozing face. The paramedic set Ryan with his back against the wall, and started rinsing his eyes with a spray bottle.

The younger policeman approached me. 'Could I check some ID, Miss?'

I tore my eyes from Ryan, fumbled in my bag and pulled out my wallet. As I handed over my student ID, I heard a sharp gasp from Ryan.

'*What are you doing?*'

I rushed towards him, and the paramedic held up his hand to stall me. 'We just put disinfectant on one of his cuts, ma'am. Gave him a shock.'

'I'm OK, Sage,' said Ryan, in a weak, scratchy voice that chilled me. He groped for my hand and held it while the paramedics dabbed him dry.

'You OK to get dressed?' asked one of the paramedics.

Ryan nodded, and I grabbed his jeans and T-shirt and helped him to his feet. As he struggled into his clothes, the younger policeman approached him.

'Could I have your name please, sir?'

'Ryan Prince.'

He dug out his wallet and handed it over. The policeman took out his driver's license, wrote down the details and handed the wallet back. Ryan tucked it back in his pocket, and the paramedics helped him onto the stretcher.

Panic stirred again. 'Where are you taking him?'

I directed my question at the paramedics, but it was the younger policeman who replied. 'To hospital. Those injuries need to be looked at. I'll be accompanying him.' He gathered up the rest of Ryan's clothes and placed them on the foot of the stretcher.

'Can I come?'

The policeman hesitated, and then shook his head firmly. 'He'll be fine. Make your statement, go home and get some rest. You can come and see him in the morning.'

I stepped back to let the paramedics wheel him out, and something snapped under my foot. As they trundled out the door, Ryan lifted his swollen face and tried to make it smile. 'I'll be OK, Sage.'

The rasp in his voice tore my heart. As the gurney receded down the corridor, I looked down and saw I'd trodden on my paua shell glasses. They were broken in two places on the spreading dark stain where Ryan had been lying on the carpet.

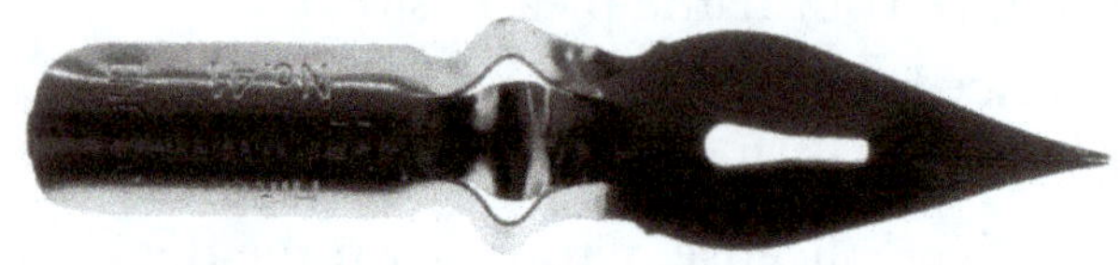

Chapter Nineteen

Making a Statement

The ceiling of the police station foyer was lined with fluorescent tubes. As I waited to give my statement, one of them malfunctioned and buzzed above my head like a wasp. Everything was the colour of concrete, from the grille on the front of the empty reception desk to the two benches bolted to the floor.

The door to my left swung open with a *thunk* that jolted my bones. Andrea emerged, her face closed and grim, still pulling her black wheelie suitcase. I braced myself for battle, but she stalked past my bench to a rack of community pamphlets.

The older policeman nodded at me from the doorway. 'Miss Rampion? Come on through.'

He led me to a small, shabby interview room, where we sat on plastic chairs at a desk. Not opposite each other, as I would have expected, but side by side in front of a computer. Next to the mouse pad was a little sign that read Officer Ross Murray.

'Now,' he said, opening a new document headed *Witness Statement*, 'let's begin with you telling me what happened.'

In the clinical cool of the police station, the events of the night seemed barely plausible. Like a story that had happened to someone else. The only memory that felt like mine was Ryan's battered, oozing face, lodged in me like a hot coal.

'I don't know where to start.'

Officer Murray tapped a finger on the desk, looking thoughtful. 'How about you start with the older lady, Professor Rampion.'

My jaw tightened. 'She's my grandmother.'

'Tell me about her.'

My feelings about Andrea were so warped by anger that I struggled to frame a response. After several false starts, I gave him an account of Andrea's role in my life until the day I began my PhD. Not the naked, weepy account I'd given Ryan, but a stilted summary of the facts.

Officer Murray nodded solemnly, typing a series of bullet points on his computer. 'What about the young man?' He consulted his notebook. 'Ryan Prince.'

Image of his body receding on the stretcher filled my mind, so vivid I could almost smell the Mace in his eyes. 'He's my boyfriend.'

'How did you meet him?'

'I met him at a drawing class.'

I'd never told anyone about Ryan before, but once I'd begun, the story poured from me, faltering only when I reached the point where I'd let him into Andrea's office to break into her computer and filing cabinet.

My gaze dropped to the desk. 'That's illegal, isn't it? Hacking. Violation of privacy.'

Officer Murray hesitated. 'Look,' he said at length, 'just tell me what happened. Don't stress about those things now.'

I nodded, but his expression told me that the time to stress about those things would come.

When I finished my story, he scrolled back to the top of his document. 'OK. Let's convert this into a statement.'

About ten minutes later, he printed off three pages and laid them on the desk in front of me.

My name is Sage Rampion, and I am 22 years old. I have been in a sexual relationship with Ryan Prince for two and a half months. I was raised from the age of six months by my grandmother, Professor Andrea Rampion. She has been hiding mail sent to me by my mother, Emmeline Rampion. This is why Ryan and I decided to search the filing cabinet and computer in Andrea's office...'

The last few months of my life, boiled down into short, bald sentences, on paper still warm from the laser printer. I read through the statement a couple of times and looked up at Officer Murray.

'Anything you want to change?' he said.

I shook my head and he handed me a pen. 'What about Ryan?' I said after I'd signed the statement.

'Depends on the doctors,' he said, adding his own signature. 'He was in a bad way. They might keep him in hospital overnight.'

'Which hospital?'

'I'll have to check. Probably the William Wilde.'

He led me down the corridor and paused by the door to the foyer, looking at me kindly. 'He'll be fine. Go home and get some rest.'

Andrea was sitting on one of the benches. She was writing on a pamphlet called *Women and Safety,* with the expression she wore when marking a really bad essay. The sight of her twisted my stomach with a mix of mutiny and fear.

'Let's go,' she snapped, voice tight. She shoved the pamphlet in her suitcase, and stood. Our eyes locked for the first time since we'd left her office.

'What,' I said, in a quiet voice, 'did you tell the police?'

'Police statements are confidential.' Her words were cold, but she averted her eyes as she said them.

Fury simmered. 'Did you lay charges against Ryan?'

She strode out the door without answering and I marched after her. It was dark outside, and the rain had stopped, leaving dripping windowsills and rushing gutters that sprayed and splashed under the wheels of passing cars.

Andrea reached the corner and lifted her hand. A taxi pulled over, sluicing dirty water onto the footpath. The driver jumped out and reached for her suitcase, but she waved him away and heaved it into the boot by herself. She banged it shut and yanked open the back door.

'*Get in,*' she said, in the caustic tones she reserved for traitors to feminism.

A day ago, I would have hung my head and hopped in obediently. Tonight I stood on the pavement and stared her down. 'Did you charge Ryan with sexual assault?'

'Get in.'

I pulled out my keyring, yanked off the keys to her office and house, and held them out.

Andrea stared at them as if I was offering her a dead body. 'What are you doing?' Her tone was shrill now, balanced on the edge between anger and panic.

'Going.' I turned my hand over. The keys made a tinny metallic ring as they bounced and came to rest on the pavement.

Andrea stared at them for a moment, then grabbed my wrist and tried to haul me towards the door. 'Get in the fucking cab.'

I twisted free with a self-defence move she'd taught me herself, and stepped back, hands up to fend her off if she tried to grab me again.

Her arms fell to her sides, a patchy flush rising in her cheeks. 'Where are you going, Sage? To *Ryan?*' She uttered his name with a savagery that would have raised blisters on steel.

'Ryan's in hospital.' I hitched my backpack onto my shoulder.

'So what'll he do when he gets out? Give you a diamond ring, make you his little princess?'

Her voice was trembling, but I felt disconnected, as if I was listening through glass. 'That's our business,' I said, looking out into the cold, wet streets.

'And what if he doesn't?'

I turned and saw with a shock that Andrea's face was streaked with tears.

'How long have you known this man?' she demanded. 'Two months?'

'I—'

'You haven't learnt *anything*, have you?' She was shouting now, the muscles of her face contorted into a rigid, blotchy mask that disturbed me more deeply than her anger. 'Twenty-two years of feminist education and you've learnt *nothing!* What happens after the fairy tale, Sage? What happens then? How are you going support yourself? *Sell your body?*'

'Now you're being ridiculous.'

'I'll tell you what happens.' She seized my arm again with an urgent, paralysing grip, and this time I didn't pull away. 'He'll run off with someone younger, leaving you to be the mother and the maid and the breadwinner all by yourself. And people will sympathise with *him*. Because you nagged him, or didn't fuck him enough, or let yourself go. He'll *shaft* you, Sage. That's men. That's what they do.' Her grip tightened. 'Now get in the cab, Sage. Please.'

Her voice was hushed, desperate. It wasn't only Andrea's husband who'd left her. Her daughter left too, fourteen years later. And now me. I was the third person in Andrea's life to walk out.

Something broke in me. I looked into Andrea's wild eyes and took a half-step toward her. For a brief, awful moment, a flicker of hope crossed her features. Then I noticed the taxi driver, thumb on his meter, using the sudden silence to catch my eye.

Andrea glanced at him, and the wildness vanished from her face. She released my arm and smeared a hand across her cheeks, as though her tears offended her. 'Yes, turn it on,' she snapped. She swiped the keys from the ground, and climbed into the taxi. 'Are you coming?'

She waited for my answer, her face still and tense, but her tears had beaten all the words out of me. My arm was still hanging mid-air, palm open, but the rest of me didn't budge. I had to look away before I shook my head.

'Fine, then,' she sneered. 'Run away. Try living in a world ruled by men. And when you're weeping on my doorstep in a month's time, don't say I didn't warn you.'

The door slammed, trapping the corner of her coat and leaving a dangling grey flag that fluttered as the engine rumbled to life. I watched it jerk and flap as the taxi pulled away through a puddle, splintering the air with drops like the fragments of a shattering glass jar.

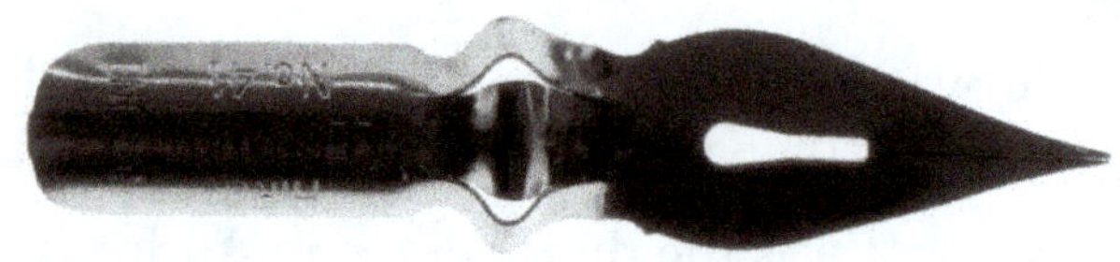

Part Two – The Golden Tower

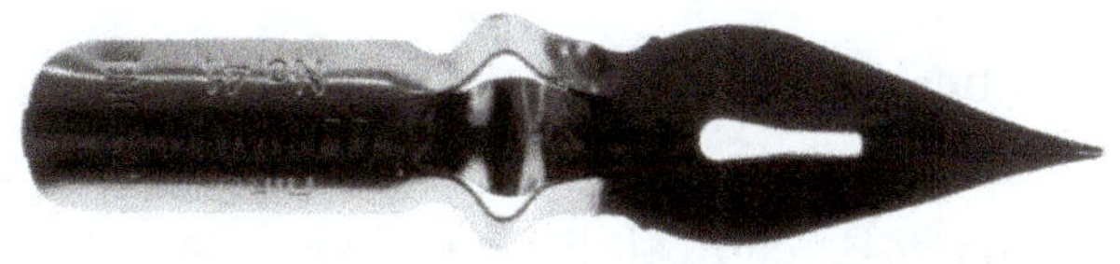

Chapter Twenty

Cutting Edge

The exhaust fumes from the taxi took a long time to fade. An icy wind fluttered the sleeves of my thin linen shirt. I shivered and folded my arms across my chest, wondering what to do next. Go home and get some rest, the policeman had said, but the place I'd known as home belonged to Andrea, and I'd just handed back my key. My stomach grumbled loudly, reminding me I hadn't eaten since midday. Down the road was a lighted retail strip, so I headed there in search of somewhere to eat.

The cafés and shops were starting to close, and people dressed for dinner were spilling out and heading for their cars. I saw a small café still half-full of people, and ducked inside, relishing the sudden sense of warmth.

A ponytailed girl of about sixteen leaped up, pen poised. 'Table for one?'

'Yes, thanks.'

I followed her swishing ponytail among tables of emptying plates to a glass case full of cakes.

'Our kitchen's just closed,' she said, 'but you're welcome to *anything* in our dessert cabinet. Pay at the counter, and I'll bring it straight over.'

I thanked her again and selected a random dessert.

'The apple cake? Ooh, good *choice*,' she said, with perky conviction. 'That'll be eight dollars, please.'

I reached into my bag for my wallet and my fingers hit the bottom. Pulse rising, I peered inside, wormed my hand through the maze of books and papers, and then upended my bag onto a table, producing two journal articles, my mother's letter, a textbook on feminist art and a battered copy of my optical prescription.

With sudden, sickening clarity I remembered the last time I'd seen my wallet. I'd opened it to get out my student ID a second or two before the paramedics disinfected Ryan's face. When I ran to him, I must have left my wallet on the desk, or dropped it on the floor.

My pulse pounded until I felt it in my eardrums. 'I'm really sorry,' I said, 'but I think I've left my wallet in the office.'

The girl's dimples faded. 'Oh.' She glanced nervously at the man behind the till, but he was serving a customer. 'How close is your office? Could you go back and get it?'

It wasn't far, maybe fifteen minutes' walk. But to enter the Humanities building at this hour I'd need the swipe card in my wallet. And the key I'd given back to Andrea.

My mouth went dry. 'Um, not really,' I said, cramming my things back into my bag. 'Thanks anyway.' I hoisted my bag on my shoulder and fled, crashing into two tables on my way out.

I sank onto the doorstep of the shop next door and rested my forehead on the window. A patch of fog grew and shrank on the glass, growing larger as my problem unfolded. Semester break had started, which meant swipe card-only access to the building for the next two weeks. With ID, university security might let me in, but all my ID was in my wallet, as was the card I needed to access my bank account.

A bubble of panic formed under my ribs. Trying to swallow it, I closed my eyes. Andrea's tearstained cheeks filled my head like a terrible ghost. By now she'd be home, organising another flight. With her own swipe card safe in her wallet, and the key to her office on her big jingly keyring. *When you're weeping on my doorstep in a month's time, don't say I didn't warn you.* If I went to her now, my bid for independence would have lasted barely an hour.

I pushed the image of her face away, but her voice wouldn't stop. *So where are you going, Sage? To Ryan?* Ryan was in hospital. Shell might take me in, but I didn't have the train fare and I didn't know how to get to his place on foot. And at night, the university and surrounds had the highest rates of assault and rape in the city. Andrea quoted the statistics in her Women's Self-Defence class.

The bubble in my chest began to expand, crushing the air from my lungs. A passing man glanced at me, and I shrank further into the doorway, dislodging a stand of business cards. I picked one up. *Roy's Wigs*, it read, in a flourishing typeface. *Quality wigs, extensions and hairpieces in every style and colour. We use only real human hair.*

Still holding the card, I rose and peeped through the window of Roy's Wigs, tapping my bun of waist-length real human hair. Inside, a man in velvet trousers lounged on a stool beside the open cash register, chewing something as he counted the day's takings. The wall behind him had two rows of shelves, on which sat blank wooden heads wearing wigs. The sign on the door read *Open.*

How are you going to support yourself? Andrea had sneered. *Sell your body?*

I pushed the door, and antique bells jangled over my head.

The man looked up, and I caught a whiff of fennel. 'Sorry, darl,' he said in a drawling voice, 'I'm closed.' He took a pinch of colourful seeds from a bowl on the counter and popped it in his mouth.

My stomach somersaulted, but my body didn't move. 'Your sign says you're still open.'

With a world-weary sigh, he plonked the sheaf of bills on the counter, swept past me and turned the sign over to *Closed.* 'Ten o'clock tomorrow,' he said, pointing out at the street.

He tried to close the door but I caught it. 'I want to sell my hair.' I yanked the hairnet off my bun and shook my head to uncoil it. Thick, silky hair fanned over my back.

He stalled, and my heart gave a hiccup of hope. He scanned my hair from root to tip, his pupils dilating. Long seconds passed. Then, with a single, lofty gesture, he swivelled the sign back to *Open* and beckoned me inside.

'Roy of Roy's Wigs,' said the man. He issued a limp handshake, returned to his stool and crossed one languid leg over the other. 'You sure you want to do this, darl?'

Was I? Images battered the inside of my skull. Ryan twitching on the carpet, Andrea's face streaked with tears. The dark streets outside, filled with rapists and muggers.

I squared my shoulders. 'Yes.'

'Then I'll ask you some direct questions, if you don't mind.'

His fingers delved again into the tiny bowl of seeds. An Indian restaurant I visited with Ryan had a bowl like that on the counter, for cleansing the palate after meals. I turned my attention back to Roy and realised he was waiting, none too patiently, for my response.

'OK. That's fine.' I flattened out the creased Roy's Wigs card in my hand to dodge his eye.

'Do you take drugs?'

The card clattered to the floor. 'Pardon?'

'Drugs.' His fingers ran through a series of gestures, indicating smoking, snorting, shooting up and dabbing a tab on his tongue. 'Weed, coke, MDMA. They leave traces in the hair.'

'Oh.' Jess took things sometimes, and some of Andrea's friends smoked weed, but I'd never tried anything myself. 'Uh, no.'

Roy looked as though he doubted this, but he let it pass. 'How often has it been washed?'

My scalp tingled. He was speaking about my hair in the past tense, as if it no longer belonged to me. 'A couple of times a week.'

'What products have you used?'

Andrea bought organic shampoo from the local co-operative, where she decanted it from a vat into recycled bottles. When I explained this to Roy, he stared as if unicorns were sprouting from my head.

'No other products? Wax, spray, colouring?'

'No.'

'How often have you heat-styled it?'

'Heat styled?'

'Blow-drying, straightening, hot rollers.'

'Oh.' I flushed at my ignorance. 'I… I've never heat-styled it.'

Roy lifted a long, pale hand. 'May I?' Without waiting for an answer, he took a lock and rubbed it between his fingertips as if it were a sample of fine fabric.

'Looked after it, haven't you?' His drawling tones were tempered with a faint hint of awe. 'Most girls come in split to the ears from straighteners and spray.' He looked up at me. 'What's the rush?'

'The rush?'

'You're pushing in at two minutes to nine. You want a quote tonight, don't you?'

A *quote?* The streets loomed up again, waiting to devour me. I looked back at Roy. He was ogling my hair again, and the gleam in his eyes woke a calculating hip pocket nerve. Roy *wanted* to buy my hair. All I had to do was state my terms. I set my jaw. 'No. I don't want a quote. I want to sell it now. For cash.'

For the first time since I'd entered his shop, Roy's poise faltered. *'Tonight?'*

I fixed him with an unwavering eye. 'How much can you give me for it?'

He ran a clawed hand through his own wavy hair. 'Look, darl,' he said at last, 'I'm happy to buy your hair, but I don't do cuts here. If you want me to recommend a stylist, I—'

'How much?'

He hesitated, fingers still hooked through his hair. 'Six hundred dollars. Without seeing it in daylight.'

'Fine.' I didn't know whether this was fine or not, but it was enough. 'Do you have a pair of sharp scissors?'

Roy gaped. 'You mean—'

I held out my hand. Taut with horror, Roy opened a drawer and took out scissors and a sheet of paper headed *Disclaimer.* I reached for the scissors, and he whipped them away. 'If you're going to do this to yourself, darl, you sign first, OK?'

I skimmed the disclaimer, signed, and held out my hand again. With the expression of a first-time executioner, Roy handed me the scissors and produced a hairband and ziplock bag. 'Tie it back and cut it just below the band.' He averted his eyes.

I scraped my hair into a ponytail, remembering with a pang how Ryan had stroked it in the park, and made a sunburst on the futon round my head. Growing my hair had been the first thing I'd done in defiance of Andrea's wishes. It seemed ironic to sever it on the day I severed my ties with her. Gathering my hair and my courage, I twisted it into a rope, placed it in the jaws of the scissors, and cut.

Roy took the zip-locked bag of hair, counted six hundred dollars into my palm and showed me out. Jagged ends tickled my neck and chin. I felt light, as though a weight of more than hair had come off, leaving me unburdened and clear on what to do. I pocketed the money, dug out my mother's letter and raised my hand to flag a taxi.

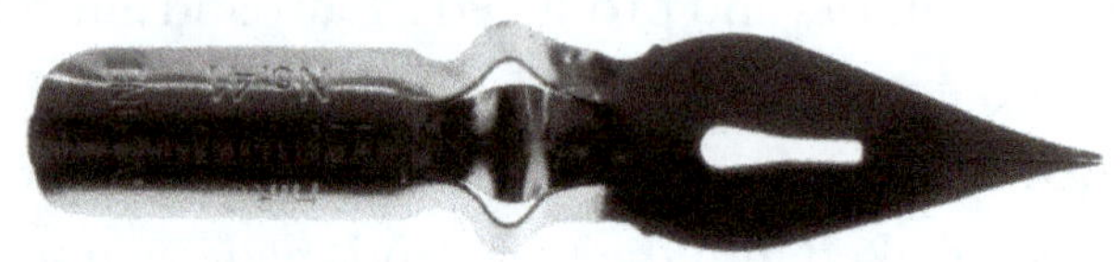

Chapter Twenty-One

Winging it

In the glow of the street lamps, the hotel had a lustre, as if built from blocks of gold. The driver pulled into the curved driveway, joining the line of taxis and limousines approaching the entrance. I sat and stared as uniformed staff ushered guests in lush coats through shimmering glass doors into a lobby the size of a ballroom. The ceilings inside were hung with giant chandeliers, glittering like galaxies through windows ten feet high.

Unease shrank my guts to the size of a fist. Had my mother really stayed *here*? Or had she put down this address to pretend—to me, to Andrea—that she had the life of those opulent women in the foyer?

I tilted the envelope into the light and checked the address one more time. Weeks of being carried in my bag and re-read had creased and softened the paper. This was definitely the place. Hotels always asked guests for their contact details at check-in.

Maybe, just maybe, if I showed them this letter, they might give me a forwarding address.

The driver looked over his shoulder. 'Cash or card, Miss?'

I peeled a note from my fennel-scented wad and slipped the change into my pocket.

As I stepped out of the taxi, I noticed a large muddy splash on my pants. I gazed down at my wrinkled, rain-spattered shirt and then back at the glamorous guests. No staff at this hotel would give me anything looking like this. I turned to call the taxi back, but it was already driving away.

The clarity that had struck as I left Roy's Wigs crumbled into exhaustion. I limped up the street, away from the entrance, and sank onto a nearby bench. Hugging my shivering body, I bullied my half-starved brain into weighing up options. Hail another cab. Find somewhere to eat. Look for somewhere cheap to stay the night.

A woman clacked past, swipe card in hand. She carried a briefcase, and her face looked tired and harassed. She opened a glass door at the side of the hotel, so close that a puff of warmth stroked my knees. Behind the door was a small lobby, with palm trees in pots either side of a lift.

The woman turned left and took out a key. Only when she re-emerged with a sheaf of envelopes did I register the grid of locked private mailboxes covering both sides of the foyer.

Adrenalin spiked in my blood. I jumped up and scanned the numbers on the boxes, my breath fogging the thick glass wall. Then, with a twinge like a key turning inside me, my gaze fell on the number on the back of the envelope. It wasn't the number of my mother's hotel room, as I'd thought. There were permanent apartments in the building, and this number was the one where she lived.

I thumped on the glass, hoping the woman would let me in, but she ignored me and swept into the lift. As the doors closed, I saw the sign in the middle of the foyer: *Guests of residents please enter through main foyer. Note that appropriate dress standards are expected in the hotel at all times.*

Appropriate? My stomach buckled with dismay, but my feet headed straight for the entrance. While my letter wasn't enough to get details out of staff, it might well get me through to that lift.

Holding the letter like a security pass, I strode through the shimmering doors. Two steps into the foyer, a man in red and gold uniform appeared in front of me, appraising my attire with a smile that managed to be both apologetic and condescending. He opened his mouth to speak and I thrust the letter under his nose.

'Excuse me,' I said, in a professor voice, 'could you tell me how to get to this apartment?'

Caught off-guard, the man took the letter, and the condescension faded from his smile. 'That's a suite in our residential wing, ma'am. Are you visiting one of our residents?'

'My mother.' The word 'mother' sent a shockwave through my veins.

'Right this way, ma'am.' He gestured me through a door with an unfurled hand. On this side of the glass, the world outside was hidden by the dazzle of the lighting. The palm trees and central heating made the room feel artificial, as though the designer had tried to recreate the tropics in plastic.

Wobbly with fear and hope, I crept to the keypad on the wall beside the lift. It was silver, with a tiny camera peeping from the top and a button embossed with a bell in one corner. As I read the instructions on how to call a guest, the lift opened and an expensively dressed elderly couple stepped out. Their conversation stopped mid-sentence. *Who let in this scruffy pauper?* said their faces. *Should we call Security? What's the point of dress standards if they don't enforce them?*

As they hurried out, I saw my reflection in the window and almost turned myself in to Security. There was a spider web of creases and wet patches on my linen shirt and pants, patches which grew progressively muddier from collar to hem. My hair was an inch longer on the right side of my head, but there were two stray strands that straggled almost to my shoulders on the left, and a strange dip behind my right ear where the hair was much shorter. Andrea's 1980s spectacle frames hid most of my face. I looked homeless and half-crazed. And my mother was a fashion model.

Clammy with fear, I scuttled to the other side of the palm tree to hide from the camera's pitiless eye. My mother was chic and sophisticated, even at seventeen. What was she like now? How could she afford to live here? Maybe her modelling career had been massively successful. Maybe she'd become a famous actress. Maybe she'd gone into business and made a fortune. She was a multi-millionaire high flyer, and what was I? A half-hearted PhD student, on a grant that paid less than the minimum wage. A nobody.

On the verge of walking out, I looked back at the envelope and remembered the last time I'd despaired at my reflection. The day Ryan had asked me out, and I'd stood in front of the mirror in the toilets, looking at the loser Caitlin had mocked in the karaoke bar. But I'd gone anyway, dressed much as I was now, and he'd bought me lunch, listened the way no one had listened to me before, and stroked my hair when I cried. And, just this afternoon, he told me I was beautiful.

The memory infused me with warmth. Then an image of him clutching his face filled my mind. Was he OK? By now he'd be in hospital, having Mace flushed from his eyes. I pushed the image away, telling myself he'd be fine, and that I'd talk to him in the morning.

I returned to the keypad and punched in the number of my mother's suite. Then, with a shaky but decisive finger, I pressed the button embossed with a tiny black bell. The keypad made a gentle *brr-brr* and I waited, heart pounding.

'Hi-iii!' said the speaker in the keypad.

A woman's voice, with a chirpy quality that turned the word into a two-note song. The sort of voice used to advertise pantyhose and small pink cars. I gaped at the keypad, my mind a total blank.

'This is Suite 451, babe. Were you after someone else?'

There's a camera above you, Sage. You're gaping on her screen. Say something. Say something!

'I … I … yes. No. I was … I'm looking for Emmeline. Emmeline Rampion.'

The speaker fell silent for so long I wondered if she'd gone. I was double-checking the suite number when the voice returned, the chirpiness replaced with a wary cool.

'No one calls me that any more.'

My stomach lurched. It *was* my mother. I was listening to my *mother's voice*. And if I didn't convince her of who I was soon, I might never hear it again. I perched onto my toes, peering at the lens as if I could climb through it into her suite.

'I'm sorry I called you that, I just … I wasn't sure what—'

'Did my *mother* send you here?' The chirp was gone now, replaced by a tight, icy tone that filled me with panic.

What could I tell her? What? 'Andrea didn't send me; I came myself.' As soon as Andrea's name left my mouth I realised I'd made a terrible mistake. 'I mean, it's got nothing to do with her, I—'

'Oh, it *hasn't*, has it?' The voice was blistering now. In a few seconds she was going to slam down her intercom phone. I suddenly knew what I had to say.

'Well,' she snapped, 'seeing you seem to be on *first-name terms*, you can—'

'I'm *Sadie*.'

Her speech stopped as if cut off by a guillotine. The tiny metallic hum of the intercom filled my ears. 'Sadie?' she said at last, in a hushed, shaken voice.

'Your daughter.' Somewhere in our conversation, my hand had crushed her letter. I smoothed out the creases as best I could and held it up to the camera.

'Oh my God.'

Behind the hum of the intercom I heard shallow, shivery breathing, somewhere between the breathlessness of shock and the shuddering that comes after grief. I stared intently at the camera as if she might leave if I blinked.

'Oh my God,' she said again, her voice cracking. 'Oh my God. I'm just … I don't know what to say.'

Did she not want to see me? 'I'm sorry,' I said, fresh tears erupting down my cheeks. 'I should've warned you. Should I … do you want me to leave?'

The words hung in the air. Then, striving to restore her earlier chirpiness, she said, 'Oh *babe*, I wouldn't do that to you! Come on up. Door number one on the forty-fifth floor.'

The lift doors glided open. Inside, the walls were mirrored, with soft golden lighting that reminded me of candlelight. Beside each button was a description of what was on that floor. I skimmed past the restaurant and retail levels, bypassed the gym and swimming pool and followed the unmarked numbers to number 45. Beside it were the words *Penthouse Level*.

Heart-shaped hot tubs and weird erotic sculptures pinwheeled through my mind. I pressed the button and tried to think sensibly as the round lights by the floor numbers lit up one by one, as if a golden coin of light was climbing the mirrored wall. Penthouse wasn't just a magazine. It meant top-floor luxury apartment. In a hotel like this, one of those would cost seven figures. Maybe even eight.

The golden coin rose higher and higher, and my spirits sank lower and lower. The doorman and residents didn't think I was good enough for the lobby, let alone the penthouse. The thought of my mother looking at me with that same condescension and distrust made me sick. The lift reached the top with a gentle *toong*, and I held down the *Close Door* button. When I'd pushed the sick feeling a little further away, I released the button, and the doors glided open again, filling the lift with the smell of exotic flowers.

I stepped out onto dense cream carpet, and the lift closed behind me. On ornate tables either side of the lift sat porcelain vases filled with orchids and lilies and fronds of fern. The ceiling was high and domed, like the ceiling of a cathedral, and the arched windows opposite were big enough to fall through. From here, the city was a console of tiny, winking lights that seemed far more remote than their backdrop of star-peppered sky.

The doors to the penthouse were opposite. The one on the right was closed and bore a gold number '2'. The one on the left was ajar.

Heart pounding so hard I could feel it behind my eyes, I approached the left door, the carpet swallowing my footfalls. As

I raised a hand to knock, it swung slowly inward. And there in the entry hall, with her hand on the doorknob, stood my mother.

157

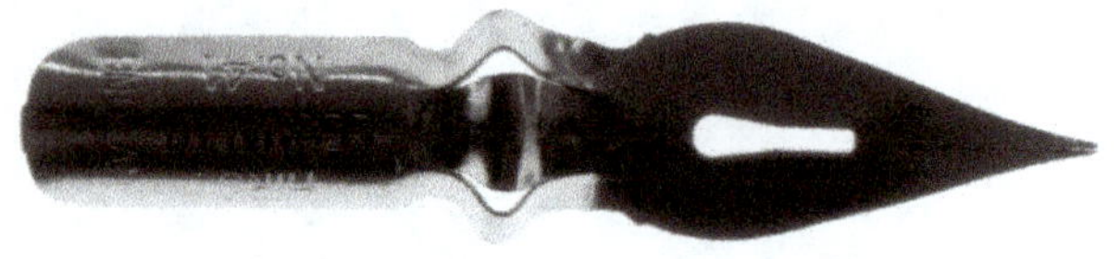

Chapter Twenty-Two

Mother of Pearl

Had I passed my mother in the street, I would have guessed her in her late twenties. She looked older than my photo of her, but not in the clumsy ways I'd imagined. Her face was unlined and still heart-shaped; her flowing caramel pants hugged hips barely wider than they'd been at seventeen. Her asymmetrical black top left both arms bare, and her hair had been lightened to a streaky gold that could almost have developed naturally on the beach. She might have been posing in her entry hall for *Vogue*, were it not for her left hand, which was gripping the doorknob beside her so tightly her knuckles had turned white.

My face seemed paralysed, so she smiled for both of us—a careful, charming smile that didn't reach her eyes.

'Sadie?'

I nodded.

'Oh my God,' she whispered, her face twisting as if she was trying not to cry. 'Look at *you!*' She released the doorknob, half-leant toward me and then jerked herself back.

A mortified wave swept through me. I *had* looked at me. Downstairs, in the foyer window. The memory of my lopsided hair and crumpled, muddy clothes made me hot with shame. I wanted to apologise for my appearance, but my mouth felt like it was made of rubber.

Tears spilled from her eyes like drops of black ink. They'd almost reached her chin before I realised that the blackness was mascara, and the strange jerk was her being too afraid to hug me.

She turned her head to hide her tears, and I put my arms around her in a weak, awkward embrace where only our shoulders touched. Her body felt like a sapling in clothes, and she smelled of perfume and makeup. She placed her forehead on my shoulder, and I remembered how Ryan had stroked my hair and listened until my tears ran dry. By now he might be home, eyes flushed free of Mace, curling up alone on his milk crate futon. Or being treated in hospital, waiting for me to call when he was discharged in the morning.

I laid a nervous hand on my mother's glossy hair, but before I could stroke it she lifted her face. 'I'm sorry, babe,' she said, detaching herself and trying to restore her charming smile. 'Come on in.' She ushered me over the threshold.

The inside of the suite was like a beachfront mansion facing an ocean of murmuring city lights. The deep cream carpet of the foyer flowed down a short corridor into a vast rectangular room, lit by a constellation of downlights. A television the size of a car was mounted on the wall, bracketed by a semi-circle of black leather couches. On its screen, wafer-thin women prowled along a catwalk to dance music, their outfits the only splashes of colour in the otherwise monochrome decor. Beyond the couches, a floor-to-ceiling window ran the length of the room.

Caramel fabric rippled around my mother's legs, revealing glimpses of black suede boots. Her heels must have been over three inches high, yet she crossed the room with the effortless grace of a yacht in light wind. Flat-footed in lace-ups, I followed, feeling more graceless and awkward with every step. She gestured me into a leather armchair. 'Take a seat,' she said. 'I won't be a minute.'

She hurried away down a hallway, leaving me with the television and the view. In the background, I heard tissues being pulled from a box, followed by a metallic clinking, and the sound of a drawer being opened. I stared out the window, blood thumping in my ears. I had just met my mother. I was *in my mother's apartment.* It was as if a character from a childhood story had come to life and hugged me in her doorway.

Other children had imaginary friends, I had an imaginary mother; a patchwork stitched together from mothers I'd met and read about. Until I reached nine or so, she was just *there*, like a guardian angel, baking me frog-shaped cakes. As I approached puberty, though, she started being *out there somewhere*, a real person I was one day going to meet. Even then, I knew she wouldn't be what I'd imagined, but I convinced myself meeting her would change everything. That she'd fill the hollow, kiss my bruises better, heal the wound her absence left behind. Yet now that I was sitting on my real mother's couch, I felt lost and out of place.

Down the corridor, the drawer closed, and my mother re-emerged, lashes curled, inky streaks erased from her cheeks. As our eyes met, her smile returned, flashing just the right amount of pearly teeth, as if she'd been practising her smile for the camera. Which, as a fashion model, she probably had.

Looking at that smile, I felt more disconnected than ever. *Smile back, Sage. Talk to her. She's your mother*, I told myself, but I didn't believe it. My mother was the patchwork figure I carried in my head, not this glamorous stranger who'd stolen her face.

She gave a self-conscious eye-roll. 'Sorry about that,' she said, switching off the television and beckoning me into the kitchen, which was divided from the lounge by a marble-topped bar lined with stools. The double-door fridge, cupboards and bench tops were stainless steel, and everything else was a sleek, shiny black.

'So what can I get you, babe?' She opened one of the fridge doors to reveal a dizzying array of cans and bottles. 'Juice? Coffee? *Wine?*' Her eyebrows and lips gave a mischievous waggle, as if we shared a naughty secret.

'Thanks, but I … A glass of water's fine.' My stomach was empty, and I didn't want it full of wine for our first conversation.

'*Water?* Oh, come *on*.' She slid two glasses from the rack above her head and laid them in front of me. 'Red or white?'

'Seriously,' I said, 'I haven't eaten since one, so I—'

'You *what?*' Her mouth made an appalled O. 'You mean you skipped dinner?'

'Not skipped, exactly, I just—'

She held up a manicured hand. 'Say no more, babe. We've all been there. We know we shouldn't, but we've been there. OK, then.' She took a gold-embossed leather folder from behind the bar. 'Pick something from room service. On me.'

I turned to the section labelled *Room Service* and saw the prices. My watering mouth went dry. 'Actually, don't order anything, I'll just have something from the fridge.' *Do people who live in penthouses even keep food in the fridge?*

'Are you *sure?*' Even her concerned expression looked rehearsed. She opened the other fridge door and frowned at the contents. 'There's this,' she said, pulling out what looked like an entree platter for a corporate lunch. 'I was going to throw it out, but—'

My stomach wailed with hunger. 'I'm fine with that. Really.'

She slid the platter onto the bar, and I fell on it like a famished dog. Halfway through the smoked salmon and cheese I realised that she was watching me, wine glass cradled in both hands. Her wide-eyed smile returned, as if I'd flipped a switch. The last of my appetite evaporated. I wanted to grab my bag and run back to a world where my imaginary patchwork mother was all there was.

'I wish I'd known you were coming, babe.' Her voice was quieter now, the sing-song note extinguished. 'I could've … I don't know, ordered champagne or something. Why didn't you call me?'

A piece of cracker stabbed the roof of my mouth. 'I don't have your number.'

She gave a short, brittle laugh. 'Sorry, honey, you don't get off that easy. I gave you the number of this place the day I moved in, remember? And you also have my email and my mobile, because I put my card in at least two letters last year.'

She drained her glass. I stared at her fixed smile, her flawless makeup, realisation starting to build. She thought I'd come without warning on purpose. To catch her off guard. To punish her for abandoning me.

'I never got those letters,' I said, suddenly desperate to explain.

She put down the bottle with a *clunk*. 'So what about the one you showed me downstairs, honey?' Her smile was steely now, guarding her face like a shield.

'That's the only one I *got*.' Sudden tears fought their way to the surface. 'I didn't even know you were sending me letters. Andrea didn't pass them on.' The tears broke free, falling so fast I could taste them in my mouth as I spoke. 'I only found it because I broke into her filing cabinet.'

Her face paled. 'You're shitting me.'

Unable to speak, I shook my head.

'I must have sent you hundreds. Presents, photos, postcards … you didn't get any of them?'

I shook my head again.

'You thought I'd just … walked out and … Fuck. *Fuck.*' She staggered across the room to the window, resting her forehead against the glass and breathing as if she were about to drown. A halo of condensation formed around her, fogging the view.

I slid off my stool and tiptoed toward her. 'Emmeline?' I said, not knowing what else to call her.

Her head whipped up, eyes blazing, tears pouring out of them unchecked. 'Why are you here, Sadie?' Her ragged voice frightened me. I took a step backwards, and she grabbed my shoulders, as if trying to force her question into my skin. 'Why?'

'Because I walked out on Andrea tonight,' I said, taking her hands, 'and thought it was time I met my mother.'

She bowed her head. 'You don't hate me?'

I shook my head. With her first genuine smile of the night, my mother lifted her face and hugged me, a proper, crushing hug that made me feel like I'd come home.

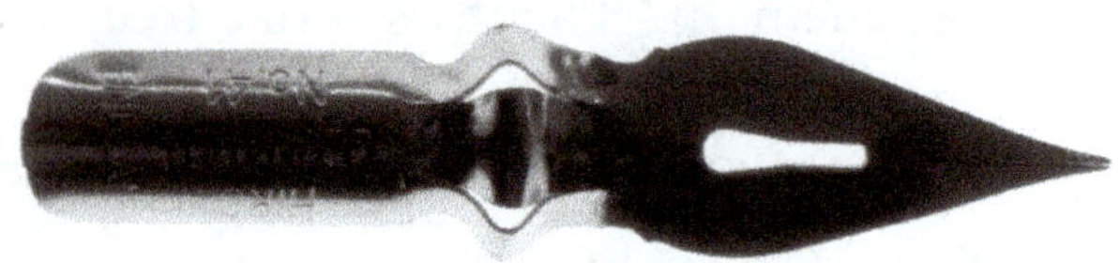

Chapter Twenty-Three

Missionary Position

I woke to a sea of white. Everything around me was white: the walls, the furniture, the fine, silky bedclothes. It was like floating in a bath of warm milk. After a brief, disoriented moment, memories of talking to my mother for the first time ever trickled back. We hadn't touched on what drove me to find her, or why she left me with Andrea, but now we had the rest of our lives to get there.

I sat up and looked around me. My mother's guest room had the impersonal look of a hotel; there was even a paper-wrapped soap on a pile of white towels at the end of the bed. I twisted the rod attached to the vertical blinds. They tilted open, casting pencils of light across the carpet, and falling on a wall-mounted phone.

The memory of Andrea belting Ryan's face crashed through my warm, sleepy glow. The clock by the bed said 8:15 am. Surely he'd be awake by now. I wrenched back the covers, opened the laptop Emmeline had lent me and googled the hotel I was in. When I'd tracked down the number for reception, I swiped the receiver from the wall and punched in Ryan's number.

'Hi, you've just failed to reach Ryan Prince.' My heart swelled at the sound of his voice. 'If you want to talk to the man, not the message, let my voicemail know.' An electronic beep and then silence, humming as it waited for my message.

'It's me.' The words wobbled out, jerky with fear and concern. 'Just ringing to … to see how you are. Whether your eyes are better, and … everything.' I swallowed. 'Are you still at the hospital? I'm in a hotel.' I read out the numbers for the hotel reception and Emmeline's suite. 'Give me a call when you can, OK?' The words I couldn't say in the office—*I love you*—teetered on my lips, but I still couldn't bring myself to say them. Not now. Not over the phone. 'Take care,' I said instead.

I hung up, googled the William Wilde Hospital and dialled the general number on its web page.

'William Wilde Hospital,' said a cheerful female voice. 'How may I direct your call?'

'Um, hi,' I said, feeling self-conscious. 'I'm trying to contact a patient called Ryan Prince. He would have been admitted last night.'

'Let me have a look for you.' Her keyboard clattered. 'Ryan Prince, admitted 7:35 pm yesterday, Ward 2 East. I'll put you through.'

My heart leapt. It felt like weeks, not hours, since I'd seen him. 'Thank you.'

The next female voice sounded impatient and distracted. 'Ward 2 East.'

'Hi, I was hoping to speak with Ryan Prince.'

'Just a moment.' She put me on hold. 'He's asleep,' she said, after a few bars of *Für Elise*. 'Call back in an hour or two.'

My heart fell again. 'Is he going to be discharged this morning?'

'Can't tell you, sorry,' she said, and hung up.

Annoyed and disappointed, I swiped a towel from the pile, and padded into the bathroom to take a shower. After glimpsing my face, I avoided the mirror until the sight of my butchered hair was blurred by steam.

When I emerged, the clothes I'd arrived in were wrapped in plastic and draped over a chair. A receipt was taped to the hangers: *Thank you for using our professional one-hour dry-cleaning service. Ladies' pants, 1 pair; ladies' blouses, 1; ladies' underwear, 2 pieces; ladies' socks, 1 pair.* The total at the bottom made me wince as I tore open the plastic. My clothes smelled of chemicals, and knife edge pleats had been ironed into my pants. I put them on and tiptoed down the hall.

By daylight, the living room looked more like a place where real people lived. The carpet had four dents from a former coffee table, and there was an empty wine bottle next to the bin. Cushions were haphazardly scattered on the couches, and a handbag sat open on one of the bar stools.

Emmeline was outside on the terrace, already dressed and reclining on a sunlounge. She put her coffee down on the table beside her and pushed her sunglasses onto her head with a manicured finger. Her hair had been twisted into a chignon, and her long oval nails wore a hint of translucent gold.

'Morning, babe.' She gave me a smile, a little shy but real, and for the first time I saw lines: starbursts around her eyes, creases running up from the corners of her mouth. Humanised by sunlight, like her living room.

With a shy smile of my own, I clambered onto an identical sunlounge on the other side of the table. Emmeline poured me a coffee, and I sipped it, looking over the railings at the view.

All that remained of the previous night's rainstorm were a few feathers of cloud, as far above us as the bustling city was below. By day, it looked like an anthill, swarming with tiny cars and people, making a distant roar studded with car horns.

'Amazing, isn't it?' said Emmeline. She handed me the room service menu. 'So what do you feel like to eat?'

I turned to *Breakfast*. The only thing under thirty dollars was fruit salad. 'I'll have the fruit salad, thanks.'

'*Fruit salad?*' She rolled her eyes. Her makeup was so expertly applied that only the lip-prints on her mug gave away that she was wearing any. 'Oh, come *on*. You don't need to get fruit salad, babe. I mean, *look* at you!'

I glanced down at myself, confused. Emmeline had on a tight black sweater and jeans tucked into knee-high suede boots. My shoulders hunched, as if to hide what I was wearing.

Emmeline grabbed back the menu. 'Here, get the Eggs Florentine. You won't regret it, I swear. Or the blueberry and cream cheese pancakes, if you want fruit. Bad, but *divine*.'

Bad? Then I realised she meant *fattening*. An evil temptation that might sneak in and ruin my figure. Feminist alarm bells jangled in my head. 'I'm happy with fruit salad. Honestly.'

'Are you sure? Oh, you *are* good. No wonder you're so slim.' She picked up the phone and rang through my order.

Good. Eating fruit salad made me *good*, because I was putting my looks above my taste buds. I drowned a sermon on body-shaming with a gulp of coffee and pulled out my wad of fennel-scented bills. *Emmeline was a fashion model,* I reminded myself, as I counted out twenty-eight dollars. *That sort of 'thindoctrination' takes years to shake off.*

Emmeline hung up. 'What are you doing, babe?'

I held out the money. 'For the fruit salad.'

'Babe!' She pushed my hand away. 'While you're with me, you don't pay for anything, OK? It's on me.'

I stood my ground. 'I can't just let you pay for everything. It's—'

'Honey. Does it *look* like buying you a fruit salad would put me out?' She gestured at her luxurious quarters.

'No, but—'

'Put the money away.'

My hand retreated to my pocket. Emmeline sipped her coffee, and I surveyed the penthouse. 'How did you come to be living here?'

Emmeline gave a small smile. 'How did I get rich enough, you mean?'

'Well, yes.'

'It's not actually my place. It's Dirk's.'

'Your husband?'

'My boyfriend. Although,' she added, with an arch sideways glance, 'I am hoping for an upgrade.'

Another alarm bell went off. My mother was a *trophy girlfriend.* Playing ornament and sex toy to a wealthy man, in exchange for the perks of his cash. Hoping for a ring to seal the deal.

This time even coffee couldn't subdue the feminist missionary. 'Don't you find that a bit …' I swallowed the word 'demeaning', '… dependent? Not earning your own money?'

Emmeline's eyes hardened under their curled lashes. 'Are you judging me, honey?'

'Not judging you, I—'

'Just because I'm not employed doesn't mean I don't work. Look at me, Sadie. I look good, don't I?'

I hugged my knees against my badly dressed body. 'Yes.'

'This,' she said, swishing a hand at her figure, 'is my work. Dirk's a marketing executive. In his business, image is everything. I maintain my looks. I take care of him when he comes home tired and stressed. I accompany him to work functions and make conversation with his colleagues. It's not always fun, but the rewards'—she indicated the penthouse and terrace—'are pretty impressive.'

The intercom buzzed and she went inside, the heels of her boots snapping resentfully across the tiles. I drank the last of my coffee, the feminist still shrieking inside me. *Live in his house and off his money, and you give him total power! What will you put up with to hang on to your lifestyle? What if he cheats or abuses you? What will you do if he loses his money or your relationship breaks down?*

Emmeline returned bearing a tray and a carefully restored smile. 'I've never ordered the fruit salad before.' She lay the tray on the table and lifted the lid, revealing a beautifully assembled tower built from chunks of mango and melon and berries. I added some cream from a side dish and started to eat.

'So,' she said, swiping a strawberry, 'how about *your* love life, Sadie? Are you seeing anyone?'

I swallowed a too-big mouthful of fruit. 'I am, actually.' A faint flush toasted my cheeks.

'*So?*' said Emmeline in a meaningful voice, climbing back onto her sunlounge.

I was baffled. 'So?'

'So tell me about him! What's his name? What does he do?'

He dances with a blindfold on to make me feel comfortable. He misses classes to take me shopping for new glasses. He hacks into computers for me and tells me I'm beautiful.

'Ryan. He's studying to be an art teacher.' Had he got my message? I bit my lip, half-wanting to run back to the phone and ring and ring until he answered.

'How old is he?'

'Twenty-four.'

'And he's still *studying?*' She sounded as though she'd never heard of such a thing. 'What does he live off?'

I stiffened. 'He does life modelling.' *And twenty-four's not old to be studying!* I added in silent affront. His bitter words that day on the futon trickled back into my head. *I had a vision. By twenty-one, galleries would be lining up to exhibit my work. By twenty-five, I'd have it all.* I gripped the handle of my fork and promised myself that I'd give Ryan back his vision.

Emmeline's face lit up. 'He's a model?'

'A life model. He poses for artists.'

Her eyes widened. 'You mean *naked?*'

'Well, yes, but it's not—' *About sex*, I was going to say, but Emmeline interrupted with a hysterical laugh.

'My God, a *nude model!* Don't you get jealous of other women seeing him naked?'

'No. They're art students.' *And nudity doesn't equal sex*, I added to myself, stabbing a chunk of pineapple with my fork.

'Yeah, right.' Emmeline settled back onto her sunlounge. 'All I can say is, don't give Dirk ideas. Not that anyone would paint Dirk at the moment. Too much office, not enough gym. So your Ryan's pretty buff then, huh? Muscles, six pack …'

'Life models don't have to be buff. He's sort of … lean.'

Ryan's bright-eyed face welled up in my mind's eye again. Was he still in hospital? Maybe by now his phone would be back on. I should try to ring him again.

'How did you meet him?'

'I kind of saw him out my office window, and wanted to meet him,' I said, glossing over the fact that he'd been life modelling at the time.

'So what was it about him?'

I thought of the day when he'd looked up through the skylight. How he'd watched until I'd freed my head from the window, and then grinned and waved, as if we were friends.

'I mean,' said Emmeline, still waiting for my answer, 'I can see what he saw in you.'

'What do you mean?'

'He sees this gorgeous blonde looking down from a window—'

I swung my legs over the edge of the sunlounge and strode to the railing. She was mocking me. Or, worse still, humouring me to try and make me feel better about myself. Emmeline approached from behind, but I ignored her, staring down at the traffic.

'What's the matter, babe?' She sounded puzzled.

'Don't call me gorgeous.'

'Why not?'

'Because I'm not gorgeous, and you know it. I'm a freak, with bad hair, bad glasses and bad clothes.'

'Oh, Sadie.' She laid a hand on my shoulder, and its warmth was like balm on my long-open wound. 'I was a model, remember? I can see past that stuff. What counts is height and bone structure, and let me tell you, babe, you have both. In spades.'

I looked up, wanting to believe her.

'As for clothes, you should have seen some of the things I wore on the catwalk. There was one $2000 number that looked like a clown costume made from curtains. The point isn't your outfit, it's *working* your outfit.'

'Working?'

'Put it this way,' said Emmeline, guiding me back to the table. 'You could have walked out this morning like you had on chic retro glasses, a mussed choppy cut and the latest in slouchy weekend wear by Kate Sylvester. But you didn't. You walked out like your clothes made you feel self-conscious. You know what that tells me?'

My hand gripped the back of the chair. 'What?'

'That you're not comfortable with your look.'

I released the chair and sat, thinking about the karaoke night, and what happened afterward. How the world had filled suddenly with mocking, sneering faces. How I'd left university to study from home. How I'd started growing my hair. 'I suppose you're right,' I said slowly, picking up my fruit salad.

'Of course I'm right,' declared Emmeline, swinging gracefully onto her sunlounge. 'And you know what else that tells me?'

'What?'

'That it's time for our first mother-daughter shopping trip!'

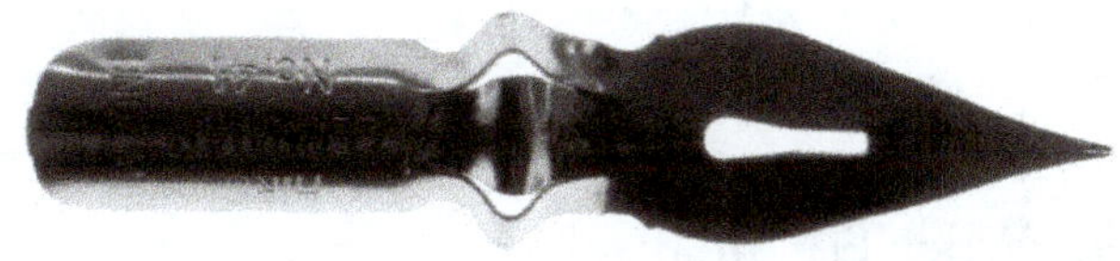

Chapter Twenty-Four

The Road to Brazil

Twenty-five minutes into my mother-daughter shopping trip, and I still hadn't got the first dress off its hanger. For some bizarre reason, it seemed to be tied on with a pair of thin black ribbons.

'So, have you got it on?' Emmeline called through the door.

'Not yet,' I said.

Embarrassed and desperate, I yanked out the ribbons with my teeth, took the hanger out and pulled the dress over my head. It was snug and steel-blue, with three-quarter sleeves, and it fell to an inch above my knees.

Emmeline peeked in, looking me up and down with a professional eye. 'Check out that figure! So what do you think?'

From the neck up, the woman in the mirror looked like me, with my jagged hair, small chin and 1980s glasses. From the neck down, I looked like a stranger. My bare calves were long and graceful, and the snug wrap of the dress shrank my waist to a handspan between neat, rounded buttocks and breasts. The only familiar thing was the beige bra sticking out of the neckline.

'Do you like it?' said Emmeline, hanging another dress on the back of the door.

'It looks good, but it … it doesn't look like *me*.' I poked the exposed bra undercover, and it sprang out again.

'That's definitely you in there, babe. And take it from me, you look *fan*-tastic. Try the black one.'

She unhooked the thin black ribbons from the hanger with two deft flicks, handed me the black dress and stood back, plainly intending to stay while I put it on.

'Um,' I said, feeling like a prude and a coward, 'could you maybe wait outside while I change?'

'Oh!' Emmeline seemed taken aback. 'Sorry, babe.' She retreated outside and closed the door. 'When I go shopping with a girlfriend we share a cubicle when we try things on. More fun, less lining up.'

I peeled off the blue dress and put on the black one, which was so tight it showed every seam in my underpants. This time more than half of my bra was on show.

'How's the black?'

I hastily stripped it off before she asked to see it. 'Not as good.'

'Let's just take the blue, then.'

I put my own clothes back on and we joined the line for the checkout.

'So where do you shop, babe?' said Emmeline, and I sensed that she meant clothes, not groceries.

Embarrassment squeezed my throat. The one time I'd gone shopping, I'd been so overwhelmed that I'd taken refuge with Ryan in a corridor. 'Um, I don't. Not really.'

She frowned. 'How do you mean, you don't?'

'When my clothes wear out, Andrea goes through her old stuff, and if there isn't anything that fits me she asks her friends or goes to a charity shop.' *Where you could buy two or three dresses for the price of one fruit salad.*

My stomach dropped as her features took on a terrible, familiar expression. The saucer-eyed horror of Jess and Sumeet, on the face of my long-lost mother. The world clouded over. Somewhere through the clouds the sales assistant spoke, but her words sounded faint and far away.

Emmeline took out a Visa card, and the sight of it cut through the fog. I pulled the wad of notes from my pocket, and she pushed my hand aside. 'Put it away, babe.'

'That'll be $380,' said the sales assistant, folding the dress into tissue paper.

Three hundred and eighty dollars for *one dress?*

'Christ,' said Emmeline in a shaky voice as we headed for the exit. 'Tell me you're joking.' It took me a second or two to realise she meant Andrea, not the price of the dress. 'She never bought you *anything* new?'

I shook my head. 'Not if she could help it. Buying new things is mindless consumerism.'

Emmeline shook her head as if she couldn't take this in. 'She was pretty bad when I lived with her, but that's just … just … it's *child abuse.* Oh babe, I'm so sorry.'

Child abuse? Once, everyone grew up wearing hand-me-downs, and people mended old clothes instead of buying more. Now children in the third world suffered genuine abuse to make cheap clothes for Westerners.

Had Jess suggested that not having new clothes was *child abuse,* I might have said these things out loud; now they sounded smug and self-righteous, even in my head. This was my mother, and I knew it wasn't my clothes that upset her, not really. She meant my life, the life she'd abandoned me to when she handed me to Andrea and left. Part of me wanted to hug and reassure her, but my fingers closed tight around the money I'd offered and replaced it in my pocket.

We stepped onto an escalator, and our silence lasted the whole way down.

'Can I ask you something?' said Emmeline, as we stepped off. 'Why do you call her Andrea? She's your grandmother.'

I shrugged. 'Because she's her own person, not just my grandmother.'

'Oh, for fuck's sake.' She rolled her eyes. 'She tried that one on me, when she had her femmo epiphany. "*No more Mum*", she said, and spun some crap about not defining women by their relationships. Don't buy into it, babe. Call her what she is. *Grandma.*' She said the word with a kind of vicious relish. 'Or *Granny*. Or better still, *Nanna*. Call her *Nanna*.'

She flashed a smile, as if we were two naughty schoolgirls, but her eyes were bitter. Envying Emmeline her spirit, I looked away, remembering the one time I'd called Andrea *Grandma*.

'What about you?' I said lightly, as if it didn't matter. 'What should I call you?'

'What do you want to call me?'

Mum. 'What you want to be called. Your real name.'

'My real name's Emily. Andrea changed it to Emmeline when I was ten.'

'After Emmeline Pankhurst, the first suffragette.'

'Something like that.' She steered me into a lingerie shop. 'I changed it back when I turned eighteen. Just call me Emily. Or Em, if you like.'

Swallowing a lump of disappointment, I followed her to a section called *Exclusive*. 'She changed my name to Sage, actually. I didn't even know you called me Sadie.'

'She called you *Sage?*' said Emmeline, incredulous. 'What? Oh, hang on. The blessingway ritual.'

'The *blessingway ritual?*'

'Some hippy shit where they rub sage leaves on you. She wanted me to do it after you were born, and I told her to shove it.' She glanced at my chest, and picked out four sets of luxurious lingerie.

I shut myself in a cubicle and checked my watch again. Forty-five minutes now since the nurse in Ryan's ward said to call him again in an hour or two.

The topmost set of lingerie was turquoise with gold embroidery. I put on the bra, trying and failing to imagine Andrea naming me after the herb in a blessingway ritual. Or being told to 'shove it' by a child. By anyone. What had she been like, before her 'femmo epiphany'?

The matching brief was a G-string. Emmeline had warned me to try it on over my own underpants, but even through them the string felt like a cheese wire dissecting me.

Emmeline peeked through the curtains, and I covered myself with my arms. 'So how's the—' She cut off with a gasp and whipped her head out, overlapping the curtains behind her. 'Oh, babe,' she said, in a hushed voice, 'I'm *so sorry*. You should have just *told* me!'

Confusion tightened my arms around my body. 'Told you what?'

She peeked in again, dropping her voice to a stage whisper. 'That you were shy because you hadn't been to Brazil.'

'*Brazil?*' I said, bewildered.

'To mow your … lady garden.'

Mow my … oh. I looked down. Either side of the underpants hung a fringe of dark gold curls. My skin began to prickle. I'd written an essay in second year on how razor manufacturers doubled their market by convincing women their body hair was ugly and unhygienic. In my essay, I'd called this 'shameless profiteering'; now, with my overgrown 'lady garden' in full view of Emmeline, I felt repulsive and ashamed.

'When did you last have it done?' she asked, in an understanding whisper.

I was tempted to feign girlish embarrassment for letting things get out of hand, but her gaze had moved on to the fuzz on my legs, and the thickets of curls in my armpits. *Her pants have to be that baggy to hold in all the feral pubes and leg hair.* My cheeks flamed, and I clamped my arms to my sides. 'Actually, I … I've never had it done. Any of it.'

'*Never?*' gasped Emmeline, in the tone she'd used for the words *child abuse*. 'But what about Ryan?'

Her eyes were like headlights, flooding me with shame. I wanted to put a paper bag on my head and rip out every hair on my body. '*Ryan?* How do you mean?'

'When you guys … you know.'

Her coy smile opened up a new, humiliating vista of possibility. I'd never considered how my body hair looked to Ryan. The first time he'd seen it I'd been too distracted to remember most young women waxed it off.

'He didn't care. At least, I don't think he did.'

'Oh, babe,' said Emmeline, worldly and kind. 'Of course he cared. They all care. But he didn't say so, and that's the main thing. It means you've found yourself a gentleman.'

She gathered the lingerie strewn around the cubicle, oblivious to the terrible pit opening in my stomach. Maybe Ryan had been secretly revolted by my body hair. But then I remembered lying on Andrea's desk, and the softness in his face when he'd told me I was beautiful.

Longing for him seized me. Why hadn't I left a message with the ward? He might be awake now, eating breakfast, getting ready to go home.

'I'm sure some men don't mind hair,' I said, almost sure I believed it. Almost.

Emmeline gave a small, jaded laugh. 'Yeah, OK, so you get weirdos who like hairy women and huge women and whatever, but I'm talking about normal men. And normal men like their women hairless.' She stooped to pick up the last bra and hung it over one arm. 'Trust me on this one. It's what they grow up with on internet porn.'

She closed the curtain, her words wearing down the wall I'd built between Ryan and Other Men. Other Men learnt about sex from internet porn, and expected real women to look and act like tanned waxed actors with implants. *Ryan's not like that*, I told myself, but even in my head I sounded hopelessly naïve.

Emmeline was waiting by the exit, a glossy bag of lingerie in one hand. 'Now for the hair.' She didn't specify *which* hair.

We boarded the escalator, my heart sinking faster than the steps. The mirror by the handrail convinced me my ragged blonde head needed professional help, but that was quite different from letting someone rip out my pubic hair.

We steered into a salon called Klever Kutz. The name reassured me a little. Had it been Wylee Waxes I would have fled for the carpark. Inside, the air was filled with droning dryers and a spectrum of chemical smells.

'Hi-ii!' chirped Emmeline at the woman behind the counter. 'Is anyone free to do a Combo Deal 2 and a wash, cut and blow-dry?'

The woman consulted her schedule. She looked barely out of her teens, and had gum wedged in her cheek. 'For both of you?'

'Just for Sadie, here.'

I smiled weakly, pretending I knew exactly what a Combo Deal 2 was and ordered one every month. 'Um, yeah,' she said, 'should be no problem. Shona! You free to do a Combo Deal 2?'

A second teenager looked up from a head covered in tabs of aluminium foil. 'Sure,' she said, glancing at a timer on the bench among her arsenal of scissors and bottles. 'Come on through.'

We headed to a small room out the back, with what looked like a stretcher bed resting against one wall, by a machine full of bubbling pink gel which I assumed was some kind of styling product.

Shona took out a plastic spatula and what looked like short white bandages. 'I'll do your legs first,' she said. 'Pants off.' Only then did I realise the bubbling pink gel was liquid wax.

Tingling with horror, I backed toward the door. 'I never said I wanted to be waxed,' I squeaked.

'Come on, babe,' said Emmeline. 'It doesn't hurt. Not *that* much, anyway.'

I shook my head emphatically. 'It's not the pain,' I lied, 'it's that I'm not … I don't actually believe in it. Waxing, I mean.'

Shona looked bewildered. 'You don't *believe* in it?'

But Emmeline's eyes narrowed. 'This is a *Nanna* thing, isn't it? What's the femmo line on waxing again?'

'It infantilises the body,' I said in a small voice. 'Makes women look like pre-pubescent girls.'

Emmeline sighed and raised her eyes to the ceiling. 'What a crock. So that's why men shave and wax their backs, is it? Fuck that. People have been doing things to make themselves look good forever. In caveman days, we stuck bones in our hair; these days we wax and get plastic surgery.'

In a tutorial or essay, I would have argued and ranted; here in the waxing room, I couldn't seem to speak.

Emmeline draped an arm around my shoulders. 'You're twenty-two years old, Sadie. Cut the apron strings. Most girls your age have been waxing for years.'

Shona looked more bewildered than ever. 'So are you having it done, or what?'

'Come on, babe,' coaxed Emmeline. 'Think of it as a present for Ryan.'

Ryan. His voice filled my mind, telling me I was beautiful, even though I had ugly glasses and bad clothes and hair on places other than my head. Maybe Emmeline was right. Maybe he secretly wished I waxed, like a normal woman, but was too polite to say so. Maybe he'd love it.

I mustered a feeble smile, and undid the button on my pants.

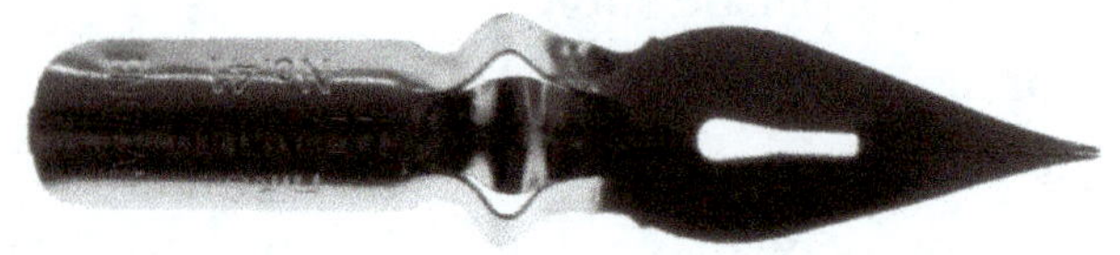

Chapter Twenty-Five

An Object Lesson

Forty painful and humiliating minutes later, I hobbled out for my haircut. Another woman eased my neck into a big porcelain horseshoe and sluiced my ragged hair with warm water. 'So what did you get up to last night?' she said.

As I struggled for an answer, Emmeline stepped in. Slumped in blessed silence, I listened as she chattered and advised, from the very first snip until the straightening tongs slid through a sleek chin-length bob.

By the time we left the salon, it was over two hours since I made the call to the hospital. Definitely time to get back to the penthouse and call the ward again. We took escalators down to the floor where we'd come in, and I strode towards the doors.

'In here, babe,' Emmeline called from somewhere behind me.

I turned and saw to my alarm that she was standing outside an optometrist's.

'You hate those old glasses of Andrea's, don't you?' she said, with an understanding smile. 'Let's chuck them out, and upgrade your look for your new, post-Nanna life.' Her knowing, conspiratorial smile faltered as she picked up that something was wrong. 'You OK, babe?'

I reminded myself that this was Emmeline, not Andrea, and it was safe to tell her the truth. 'It's just that … I was hoping to get back to the penthouse soon and call Ryan.'

She looked mystified. 'Why from the penthouse, babe? Did you leave your phone there?'

I swallowed. 'I don't actually have a mobile phone.'

'You *what?*' Emmeline gasped the way people always reacted to this news—as if I'd told her I lived in a cave. Then her expression became cynical. 'Hang on. This is another Nanna thing, right?'

I nodded and she shook her head with a sigh of disgust. 'We'll get you a phone. For now, you can use mine.' She pulled out her pink smartphone. The wallpaper picture was of herself in a plunging floral dress, smiling seductively over one shoulder. 'You know his number, don't you?' she said, unlocking it.

I nodded again, took the phone and dialled.

'Hi, you've just failed to reach—'

My hopes deflated. I hung up, not wanting to leave him another message in front of my mother. I considered calling the hospital, but then she'd want to know why he was there. The thought of explaining everything that had happened, here in a shopping mall, made me edgy and self-conscious. And then I'd be speaking to that cranky ward sister, with Emmeline listening in.

I gave her back the phone. Ryan would know I'd been trying to call him. I'd called twice and left a message. By now he'd probably got it and left me a voicemail at the penthouse.

'Didn't pick up?' said Emmeline, in sympathetic tones. 'Just text him, and try again later. And in the meantime …' With a flourish of a manicured hand she waved me into the optometrist's.

Memories of Ryan from the day we bought my new glasses welled inside me. I studied the racks of frames, only half-listening to the conversation Emmeline was having at the counter.

'So,' Emmeline was saying, with a wheedling, winsome smile, 'she can get contact lenses straight after her eye test?'

'Depends on her prescription,' said the man behind the counter, turning faintly pink.

'Do you need my optical prescription?' I said, digging in my bag. 'Because I've got it in my bag.' I handed the battered slip of paper to the man.

'Yep,' he said, studying it, 'we'll have those in stock for you. Come on through and we'll measure you up. '

Two and a half hours after I'd called the hospital, we finally got back to the penthouse. I half-ran to the guest room, checked the voicemails (none), and dialled the hospital again. I was put through to the impatient woman in Ward 2 East.

'He's been discharged,' she said, her tone making it clear that I was keeping her from more important things.

My heart stalled, caught between delight that he was better and a creeping sense of unease. Why hadn't he called me? Did he get my message? Then it hit me: his phone was probably flat.

'So he's gone home?' I pictured him plugging his phone in the recharger and sitting down to drink tea with Shell.

'We don't release that information.'

'Oh. OK, then. Sorry.'

She said an abrupt 'Goodbye,' and hung up.

I sat on the bed, pondering the news. Ryan's place was only twenty minutes from the hospital by train. How long ago did he get out? Could he still be on his way? Maybe he'd dropped his phone in Andrea's office, and it was still locked up inside, along with my wallet. Ryan and Shell didn't have a landline, but they both had their own computers. Whatever had happened to his phone, he'd be able to access his emails once he got home.

I grabbed the laptop, logged in to my email account, and started composing my message. Without going into too much detail, I told him I'd cut my ties with Andrea, and had tracked down my mother at last. I added Emmeline's number and address, said I was missing him and wanted to hear from him as soon as possible.

After three deleted attempts to type 'I love you', I signed off 'Love, Sage' and pressed Send. Minutes later, Emmeline poked her head around the door.

'Hey, babe,' she said, her eyes bright. 'Are you ready to try on your new clothes?'

'Sure,' I said, closing the laptop and following her down the hall to her bedroom.

The bedclothes on the king-sized bed were a dazzling white. On it were the three glossy bags that held our purchases for the morning. A door off to one side was open, and the bathroom beyond was gigantic, tiled in black marble, with a double shower, a spa and shiny twin sinks.

'I'll just be in here,' Emmeline said, slipping into the bathroom with a wink and closing the door behind her.

I put on a new set of lingerie and donned the steel-blue dress. When I said I was ready, Emmeline returned and sat me down at her vast dressing table. She slid off my glasses and made up my face with sponges and feathery brushes. Then, in a final flourish, she washed her hands and opened the box of contact lenses.

'Hold still.' She pulled back my eyelids, one at a time, and inserted the lenses. 'How do those feel?'

I felt like I had grit in both eyes and a film of grease on my face. After a few minutes of blinking repeatedly, I managed to open my eyes properly. Everything looked vivid and sharp, and much brighter. 'Not too bad. I can still feel them, though.'

'They take a bit of getting used to.' Emmeline crossed the room and opened the doors to a giant walk-in wardrobe. One entire wall was lined with little shelves on which sat rows and rows of fancy high-heeled shoes. 'What size are your feet?'

'Size 8.'

'Perfect!' She sounded exultant. 'Same as mine. Let's pick you a pair of shoes.'

My mother surveyed the little shelves with an expert eye, and selected a pair the colour of a Band-Aid, with alarmingly high, spindly heels.

'Nude pumps. Classic and discreet, like you.'

She laid them by my feet, then opened a drawer and tossed me a pair of pantyhose. With a jittery smile, I put both items on and rose unsteadily to my feet.

'My God,' said Emmeline, in a hushed, awed voice, looking me up and down. 'You are stunning, babe. I'm taking a photo right now and sending it to Ryan. He is going to *die* when he sees you.'

She pulled out her smartphone, took three shots from different angles, and went through her call history to find Ryan. Before I could protest, she'd texted them through, her face beaming like the midsummer sun.

I watched her toss her phone in her bag, wondering what Ryan would make of those photos. Still beaming, Emmeline linked her arm through mine and led me to the mirror.

The reflection in the changing room had looked like a stranger, but with my head grafted on top. This time the reflection was a total stranger, from the sleek golden bob to the four-inch heels. My face was heart-shaped, like Emmeline's, with a small, shapely mouth, but my eyes were now a brilliant, cornflower blue.

'So what do you think?' said Emmeline, letting go my arm and stepping back. 'Better than the look *Nanna* picked out?'

I stared, and the woman in the mirror stared back. 'That's not me.'

'You mean, that *wasn't* you. That's you now, babe. And you are *smokin'*.'

I took a step closer to the mirror, and almost toppled off my pumps. 'How do women *walk* in these?'

'Practice, babe.' She linked her arm through mine again. 'Lots of practice. You'll be fine. Let's head back out.'

'Like *this?*' The eyes and mouth of the stranger in the mirror dropped open in dismay.

'Of course!'

She steered me through the door, and I tottered at her side through the penthouse and out to the lift.

'Where are we going?' I said, as we descended.

'To get you some shoes of your own,' she said, with a winning, girlish smile. 'And a couple of tops, and a jacket, and some jeans. We hardly got started this morning!'

We stepped into the ground floor lobby, and Emmeline opened the glass door. 'And don't stress about Ryan,' she added. 'You can use my phone any time you want.'

Out in the street, two chatting teenage girls stopped mid-sentence to look me up and down. I shied behind my mother, feeling exposed and self-conscious, silently wishing them away. The girls exchanged a glance and walked on, but a few yards later they peered over their shoulders for a second head-to-toe scan.

Emmeline glanced my face. 'What's the matter, babe?'

'Those girls were staring at me.' *Check out the hairy dyke pretending to be a beauty queen. What a try-hard.*

Emmeline nodded wisely. 'They were. And you know why?'

'Why?'

'Because they were trying to find flaws in your appearance.'

'*Flaws?*' I looked at my reflection in the window. 'Why?'

'To prove to themselves that you're not as great as you think you are,' said Emmeline, as if confiding something weighty and profound.

I gaped at her. 'But I don't think I'm great!'

She threw back her head with a silvery laugh. 'That's not the point, babe. The point is you look gorgeous. Too gorgeous. And when a woman looks too gorgeous, other women feel threatened. They make themselves feel better by finding some cellulite, or telling themselves you're arrogant. Or stupid. Rise above it, babe. Now, let's find you some shoes.'

She led me down the street. I hobbled and wobbled, but gradually my strides grew steady. When at last I felt brave enough to look up from my feet, I found myself surrounded by staring faces. Women, contemplating me with furtive resentment. Men, less furtive, staring at my figure and face with appreciative disbelief. One of them even crashed into a bollard as I passed.

'Welcome to the world of being beautiful, babe,' said Emmeline with a grin. 'How does it feel?'

Part of me wanted to run away and hide. But another, newer part of me was sparkling with triumph, because I wasn't a loser any more. I was stylish and stunning, the centre of attention, an object of jealousy and lust.

'You know what?' I said. 'It feels great.'

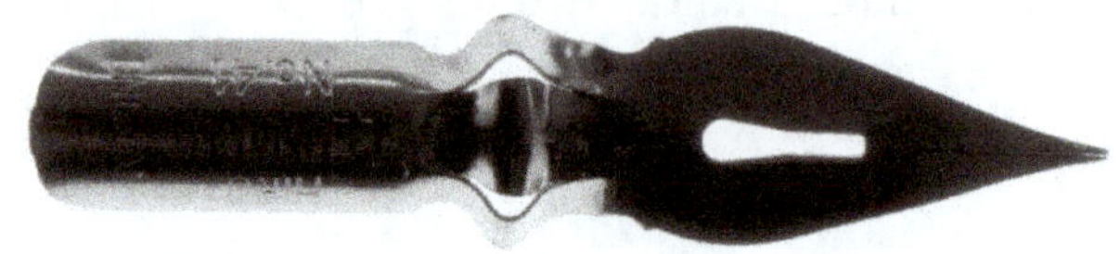

Chapter Twenty-Six

Homecoming King

By the time I returned to the penthouse, my triumph had dwindled into something small and bittersweet. For a while, in the streets, buoyed by crowds of gaping people, I'd relished the new me. Alone in the guest room, it felt like an ill-fitting costume I wanted to take off. A costume my mother had assembled to win the approval of what Ryan called 'the mainstream'.

Still no voicemails. I tossed my garish collection of shopping bags in a corner, my disappointment flavoured faintly with relief. If Ryan's phone was out of action, at least that meant he wouldn't have seen those photos Emmeline had texted him.

The thought of him seeing me decked out like this made me shudder with embarrassment. Ryan asked me out and called me beautiful when I was wearing Andrea's cast-offs, and he prided himself on being offbeat and original. He'd probably see dressing like this as a sign I'd 'sold out'. Like an artist designing corporate logos.

I opened the laptop and logged on. Still no emails. I checked Ryan's Twitter feed and his Instagram. No updates for months. One whole day since the chaos in Andrea's office, and not a single word. Ryan always left his phone on. Even during lectures and modelling jobs he switched it to silent and checked it whenever there was a lull. In two-and-a-half months, he'd never taken more than a few hours to respond if I called. And today I'd called three times and sent an email. And three texts, if you included the photos from Emmeline.

The possibility I'd been trying to quash clawed its way into my mind. Maybe after everything that had happened, he didn't want to be with me any more. Maybe he'd decided to find someone with sane, friendly parents instead of a crazed grandmother who maced and bashed men, and reported them to the police.

A new and terrible thought made sweat break out on my back. *The police.* Technically Ryan and I were guilty of hacking and vandalism and who knew what else. Maybe he hadn't rung because he'd been released into police custody to be interviewed and charged. I googled the number of the police station where I'd given my statement and dialled it with a shaking finger.

'Gothel Police Station,' said a deep female voice.

'Hi. My name's Sage Rampion. I came in last night, and gave a statement about an incident at the university.'

'Who was the officer you gave your statement to?'

'Officer Murray.' Who'd looked sombre, and changed the subject when I asked him what the hacking and vandalism might mean for Ryan.

'He's not in today. Is there something I can help you with?'

I gripped the phone, trying to stay calm. 'I was just wondering about my boyfriend, Ryan Prince. He went to the hospital with a policeman after the incident, and I thought maybe he … someone at the station might have … spoken to him? Or something.'

'Let me have a look.' I heard the rattling of a keyboard. 'Yes, Ryan Prince came in today for an interview at eleven, and he left at half past one.'

'Do you know where he went?' Home? *Jail?*

'That's all I can tell you, I'm afraid.'

'Thank you,' I said, my entire body thumping to the panicky rhythm of my pulse.

I hung up and dialled Ryan's number for the fourth time since I'd woken this morning. My heart no longer swelled at the sound of his recorded voice; it contracted, as if someone was squeezing it.

'Hi, Ryan, it's me again. Where are you? What happened with the police? Please call me. I'm getting really worried.' I shut my eyes, wishing that I'd told him I loved him when everything was OK. Still unable to say it, I said, 'Please call me' again, hung up and curled into a ball on the bed. A long time passed before I composed myself enough to creep out and get a drink.

Emmeline was on the couch in the living room, reading a magazine. She'd re-applied her makeup and changed into a sleek black dress and strappy heels.

'Dirk likes me dressed up,' she said, with a self-conscious flutter I hadn't seen before. 'Some men go for vamp, some go for innocence. Dirk is *definitely* a vamp man.'

I attempted a smile and hurried past her to the kitchen, where I poured myself a glass of orange juice.

'You're wondering what kind of man Ryan is, aren't you?' Her eyes were mischievous. 'Ryan is an innocence man. Take it from me.'

The cold of the juice in my mouth cleared my head enough to bristle a little at this comment. What was that supposed to mean? That only an 'innocence man' would want someone like me?

Before I could frame a reply, the front door opened and a man walked in. It had to be Dirk. He was half a head shorter than Emmeline in heels, and looked ten or fifteen years older. His dark hair was receding at the temples, and though his face was affable enough, everything from his walk to the tilt of his double chin had the air of a man who was very, very pleased with himself.

Emmeline flurried over and deposited a showy kiss on his mouth. 'So, how'd it go, babe?' she said, helping him out of his coat and hanging it in the hallway. 'Did you win the contract?'

Resentment flared inside me. Directed at Dirk, the breezy ring of 'babe' was cheapened into something false and twee.

'Pipped at the post,' said Dirk with a rueful sigh.

Emmeline carried his briefcase to the lounge and trotted to the kitchen. 'Who by?'

'Leo Burnett. Again.' He strode into the living room like he was surveying his kingdom, and his eyes alighted on me. With a faint, lofty smile, he crooked a finger in greeting as he sprawled on the largest leather couch. 'I see you've got company.'

'I have, babe.' She poured a measure of single malt whiskey and popped an ice-cube out of a tray. 'This is Sadie. Sadie, Dirk.'

I forced a smile. 'Hi.'

He smiled back, as if he found me mildly amusing. 'Sit down, love,' he said with a lazy beckoning movement. 'I promise I won't bite.'

I sat on the couch furthest away from him. He looked me up and down in an idle, appraising way, as if inspecting a yacht up for auction. 'Em's playing model mentor, is she?'

A twinge of astonishment. He'd taken one look and assumed I was a model? 'Actually, I'm—'

'We haven't really got to that yet,' said Emmeline, intercepting so adeptly it felt more like a baton change than an interruption. Evading my eye, she glided over to Dirk and placed his whiskey on the coffee table. 'For the moment I'm playing style consultant.' As she joined him on the couch, she flashed me a warning look to clarify that she *didn't want Dirk to know I was her daughter.*

Dirk placed a hand on her thigh, and I recoiled. As if I was the mother, and Emmeline was the teenage daughter, pretending we weren't related because I embarrassed her. And wanting me to vanish so some ham-fisted man could feel her up on the couch.

'Yeah?' He looked me up and down again with an approving nod. 'Well, when you want to shoot your portfolio, love, just let me know.'

'Fabian de Carlo's one of Dirk's major clients,' said Emmeline, in proud, proprietary tones that had no problem claiming ownership of her boyfriend's success while denying her daughter's existence. 'He's just *amazing*, isn't he, Dirk?'

'He's the best.'

Unable to bear any more, I stood up. 'Anyway,' I said, as brightly as I could, 'I'm feeling nauseous, so I might go and rest for a while.' I turned and stalked down the hall.

'Are you OK, babe?' said Emmeline to my back. 'Can I get you anything?'

'I'll be fine,' I snapped, without turning around. *You go fawn on your sugar daddy in peace.*

I shut myself into the guest room and checked my email again. No new messages. The stirrings of terror began again inside me, but I shoved them away. I googled 'trophy wife', and the list of links that appeared included one titled *Mogul's moll: The new prostitution*. I clicked on it and made myself read every word, pitting my anger at Emmeline's betrayal against my fear that Ryan had abandoned me.

Half an hour later, I heard a tentative knock at the door. 'Babe?'

When I didn't answer, Emmeline opened the door and peeped in. Her expression was guilty.

I pressed page up, making sure the heading *Gilded cage: The trophy wife trap* was visible on the screen. 'So,' I said, 'you don't want Dirk to know that I'm your daughter.'

'Babe, he's just had a major deal fall through. It's—'

'Does he even know you've had a child?' *Or did you cut that out of your CV? Not a real selling point, a teenage pregnancy. Not a great conversation starter at the yacht club.*

Emmeline bit her lip. 'Look, until last night I thought you wanted nothing to do with me. I'd been sending you letters all your life, and as far as I knew you just didn't want to answer.'

Anger and hurt fermented inside me. 'So what have you told him?'

'What he guessed. That I'm helping you get started on a modelling career. And that you're having some problems with accommodation, so I invited you to stay.'

Anger triumphed over hurt. 'Well, you can tell him I'm leaving tomorrow morning, then.'

'For Ryan's place? Has he got back to you?'

'Not yet, but he'll be home by now. And now *Dirk's* back,' I added, with heavy sarcasm, 'I shouldn't be intruding on my *style consultant.*'

Her face fell, and I immediately regretted what I'd said. I wanted Ryan, but didn't want to leave my mother, not like this. I wanted her to love me, and be proud of me, and tell everyone in the world that her daughter had finally come back to her.

'I'll get you a bag for the clothes,' she said at last.

'Thanks,' I said. *I'm sorry, Mum.*

She hovered for a moment, as if she wanted to say more, then closed the door softly behind her.

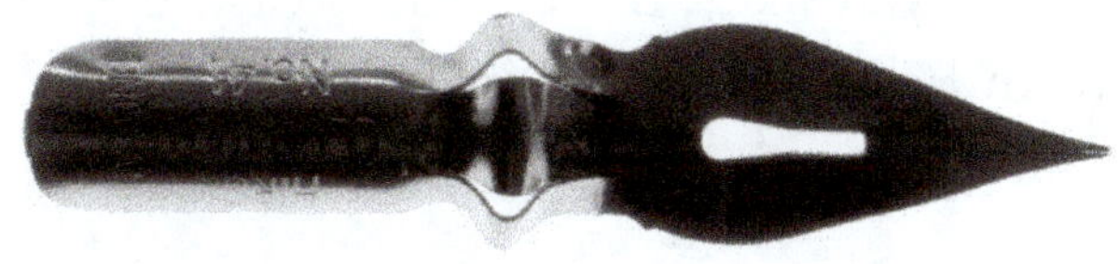

Chapter Twenty-Seven

Crying Jag

When I woke the next morning, Ryan hadn't answered my email. I rang his phone and hung up when the recorded message began. A hollow of insecurity opened in my ribcage, echoing with soft, eroding whispers.

He doesn't want you any more. You were a charity case, a damsel in distress he could rescue to get sex. Now you're a homeless sell-out with a psycho grandmother. You'll probably never hear from him again.

I shoved clothes brutally into Emmeline's weekend bag, as if the whispers were coming from its unzipped mouth. Then I emptied them all out again, because I had to find something to wear.

My old clothes looked shapeless and drab beside the figure-hugging glamor of yesterday's purchases. At the height of my rage, I'd planned to leave the new clothes behind and march out in the old, to show Emmeline I couldn't be bought. This morning, I looked at my baggy shirt and pants and saw the frumpy loser from the karaoke bar. And even though Ryan had embraced me as I was, I couldn't bring myself to put them on.

After fifteen minutes of fretting and discarding, I put on my old shirt, but with new jeans, jacket and boots. Low-key enough not to look to Ryan like I'd sold out; stylish enough to avoid comment from Emmeline and Dirk. It took me another fifteen minutes to insert the contact lenses before I headed out to the living room.

The sky was a blanket of ominous grey. It was too cold to breakfast on the terrace, so we ate around the shiny glass dining table, Emmeline and Dirk on one side, me on the other, counting the seconds before I could leave.

'So,' said Dirk, contemplating me over the rim of his coffee mug, 'where does Loverboy live?'

Please don't call him Loverboy. 'Kingsley Park. Near the station.'

Dirk glanced at his watch. 'I'll run you there after breakfast.'

God, no. 'Thanks, but I wouldn't want to put you out. I can catch the train.'

Dirk made a sound between a snort and a laugh. 'Kingsley Park's not putting me out, love. On a Sunday, that's fifteen minutes. Max.'

'It wouldn't put us out at all, babe,' added Emmeline. 'I'd *love* to meet Ryan. Maybe we can all go out to lunch. Have a little double date!'

The hairs on my neck stood on end. I was just about to insist that I liked taking the train, that I wanted to see Ryan alone, anything to quash this dreadful idea, when I noticed the pleading look in Emmeline's eyes. She wanted me to accept the lift because she wanted to do something for me. To apologise for not telling Dirk who I was. To make up for last night.

'Well, OK then,' I said, trying to sound grateful. 'But no double date. I need to speak to him alone.'

We caught the lift to the residents' carpark, and a uniformed valet arrived in a gleaming silver car. Dirk held open the car doors for Emmeline and me, and then slid behind the wheel. Eight or ten speakers poured pulsing rock music into the car.

'Just like being there, isn't it?' he said, steering the Jag through the carpark.

'It's fantastic, babe!' gushed Emmeline. 'Did the sound system come with the car, or did you have it put in?'

'Came with the car, believe it or not.'

'Dirk only bought this car last week,' said Emmeline, glancing at me.

'Latest model Jag,' said Dirk, in a smug tone.

'So what does Ryan drive, babe?' asked Emmeline.

I steeled myself. 'Ryan doesn't have a car,' I said airily, in a tone that suggested he was above owning a car.

'He doesn't have a *car?* How *old* is this guy?' Dirk exclaimed.

'Twenty-four,' I said, trying to sound offhand.

'*Twenty-four?* I owned two properties by the time I was twenty-four.'

Well, hooray for you, you smug bastard. Fortunately, Emmeline stepped in before I said this out loud.

'He's studying to be an *art teacher*, babe. He's probably not interested in cars and things.'

Dirk gave a cynical grunt. 'Well, that explains why he didn't come and pick you up, then.'

Emmeline glanced at my seething face, and steered the conversation back to Dirk's business. By the time we turned into Ryan's street my rage had dwindled to a simmer. The rusted wire fence came into sight.

'Just here,' I said.

Dirk and Emmeline stared at the overgrown garden as if I'd directed them to a slum. I shouldered my bags, daring them to say something, but they sat without speaking on their black leather seats, rock music washing around them. I opened the door and stepped out onto the curb.

Emmeline jumped out and half-tripped in her haste to get to me. 'It's been really great meeting you, babe,' she said, her voice quavering a little. 'Have you got my card?'

I nodded. She hugged me, and I laid my head on her shoulder, an ache growing somewhere between my stomach and my throat.

'Stay in touch.' She released me, and smeared a tear into her hairline. 'We'll wait in the car until you're in, OK?'

I nodded, the ache blending with anticipation at the thought of seeing Ryan again at last. Pulse rising, I waded through the feathery weeds and rapped on the front door. No one answered. I knocked harder. Still nothing.

On the other side of the wire fence, the Jag's motor was running. I knocked a third time, as loudly as I could, and followed up with a couple of bangs on the window. To my relief, a human figure appeared, blurred by the frosted glass. The door opened to reveal Shell in a bathrobe, smelling of weed, cheeks flushed and ringlets askew. Disappointment clamped my throat. *Where was Ryan?*

'Hiiii,' said Shell, in a vague, breathless voice with no hint of recognition. 'Sorry, I was just … in the middle of something. Can I help you?'

'Shell, it's me.' She blinked. 'Sage. Ryan's girlfriend.' It struck me that the 'something' she was in the middle of was having sex. I felt my face start to blush. 'I'm looking for Ryan. Is he home?'

'Ohhhh, you're Sage! God. I didn't recognise you.' She exhaled, and ran a hand through her tangled curls. 'Look, um, Ryan's not in. You know he got *maced*? He had to go to hospital and everything.'

'*Yes*, I know,' I said, trying not to sound impatient. 'Do you know where he is?'

Shell pondered this. 'I think he's staying at his mum's place. They picked up some stuff yesterday, and he looked totally shattered. Hasn't he called you?'

'No.' The morning's Eggs Florentine turned over in my stomach. 'Did he leave his mum's address? Or a number or something?'

She shook her head. 'Sorry.' A faint glimmer lit her hazy eyes. 'Have you, like, texted him, or left a message on his voicemail?'

I resisted the urge to strangle her with one of her stupid ringlets. 'Yes, Shell.'

'Oh good. Anyway, I'd better get back to what I was doing, so …'

'Bye, Shell.'

She closed the door and I rested my forehead against it, suddenly feeling limp. The wood was cool against my skin. Why hadn't Ryan called me to say where he was? Could I invite myself in and wait until he came back? As I steeled myself to summon the annoying Shell again, Emmeline pushed open the gate.

'What's happening, babe?' She hurried through the weeds. 'Where's Ryan?'

A great mound of tears heaved inside me. 'He's gone to his mum's place.'

'Oh, Sadie.' Emmeline put an arm around my shoulders. 'Come back to the car. There's a great Greek restaurant near here. We'll treat you to lunch.'

She propelled me to the Jag, and successfully steered the conversation away from Ryan until halfway through our chargrilled seafood platter.

'Can I ask you something, love?' said Dirk, helping himself to more octopus. I sensed at once what he wanted to ask me about, and my body went rigid. 'How long is it since this guy called you?'

My stomach gave a sickening lurch. 'I saw him on Friday night.'

'That's only a day and a half,' said Emmeline.

'It's long enough when he's been ignoring all her messages.' Dirk swallowed a tentacle and turned back to me. 'Have you read that book *He's Just Not That Into You*?'

'*Babe*,' said Emmeline in gentle reproof.

'No, Em, let me finish. Let me tell you something, love. If a guy is twenty-four, living in a dump with no car, and doesn't even answer your calls, you don't make excuses for him. You lose him. You're a beautiful young girl, and you could do a lot better for yourself. A *lot*.'

I shoved away my plate and stood up, swallowing down a fresh wave of nausea. 'What,' I said, my voice shaking with anger, 'a smug, rich bastard like *you*, you mean?'

Dirk gave a squawk of laughter. 'Exactly!'
He started to say something else, but the contents of my stomach lurched so violently I only just reached the bathroom before the next heave sent them spurting from my mouth

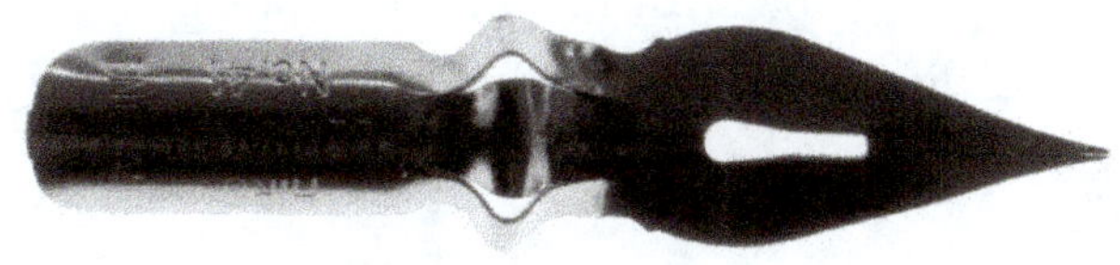

Chapter Twenty-Eight

Picture Perfect

A timid knock sounded through the guest room door. 'Are you OK, babe?'

I gargled and spat a glass of water by way of reply. I'd drunk two and gargled three since returning to the penthouse, but the sour taste wouldn't wash away.

Four calls to Ryan's mobile. Two calls to the hospital, one to the cops. Three texts and one email. A day and a half and he'd left me to find out where he'd gone from *Shell*. If he'd really decided to dump me, wouldn't he at least have sent a text?

Maybe not, said a sinister voice in my head. *He paid a high price for agreeing to help you find your mother. He's been maced, and bashed, and taken to hospital, and he'll be facing criminal charges. Not calling you back is probably his way of saying your relationship is over.*

I turned my back on the sinister voice, telling myself there must be some other reason. But the voice was still there, lurking just behind me and casting an ominous shadow.

Emmeline peeked in, looking tentative and fretful. 'Dirk's gone out to drinks with some friends.'

Dirk. My body stiffened with dislike. Dislike all the more intense because I was now terrified that he'd been right about Ryan dumping me. 'Oh, Dirk has *friends*, does he?'

Emmeline flinched. 'Please don't say things like that, babe. Dirk's a self-made man, and he's … he speaks his mind, sometimes.'

A twinge of guilt reminded me that this was Dirk's house. And at the moment, I was as much his kept woman as Emmeline.

'Dirk's really sorry he upset you,' said Emmeline. 'He is, honestly. He even rang Fabian de Carlo and got him to squeeze in a portfolio shoot tomorrow. I don't know what you think about modelling, but you could try it. Do you have a job?'

'I have a PhD scholarship.' Remembering this lifted my spirits. My grant payments weren't much, but they were an income. Maybe if I staked out the Humanities building on Monday, someone who knew me might let me in to get my wallet.

'You're doing a *PhD*, and you got a *scholarship?*' She drew back, as if I might explode in a shower of IQ points. 'My God, you must be *so smart*, babe. I bet that pays a lot.'

'Not exactly.' The scholarship paid me the minimum wage, and payments were contingent on satisfactory progress. The reassuring thought of my grant sprang a leak. My level of progress would be judged by my Department. Which was headed by Professor Andrea Rampion.

'So what happens when you get your PhD? Do you become a professor?'

'You look for a lecturing position.'

The leak widened into a torrent. Lectureships in Women's Studies were rare and competitive. With Andrea's fame and contacts I might well have secured one; as things stood now, she might even sabotage me. And before I could even apply for a position, I'd have to finish my PhD. In her department. *Sharing her office.*

Emmeline nodded, attentive and respectful. 'And *then* you earn heaps?'

'Not heaps. Most people start with sessional work. If you manage to get an entry-level lectureship, you start at about $50,000.'

The torrent grew to a freezing ocean closing over my head. By cutting off Andrea, I'd killed my academic career. And while Ryan had been right to say academia wasn't my calling, it looked like he'd abandoned me too. All I had left was Emmeline, and a room in her sugar daddy's penthouse.

Emmeline looked flabbergasted. 'Fifty thousand dollars after all that studying? A model can make more than that in a *day!*'

My turn to be flabbergasted. 'Fifty thousand dollars in *one day?*'

'A top model,' she amended. 'I never made anything like that much. My best one was a wedding dress shoot, where I got about eighteen thousand dollars.'

Eighteen thousand dollars. The freezing ocean receded a little.

'But look, babe, it's not just about money. If being a lecturer's your dream, you go for it.'

Being a lecturer wasn't my dream. Ryan had seen that within days of meeting me. My dreams had centred around my long-lost mother. Who'd earned almost a third of a junior lecturer's salary in one day for posing in a big white dress. And while I found this appalling and wrong, I could no longer afford to stand on principle.

I took a deep breath. 'What time's Fabian de Carlo free?'

'Two thirty tomorrow. So you'll do it?'

I nodded.

'You're going to be *great!*' She crushed me in an exuberant hug. 'Let's find you some outfits.'

We filled a Gucci suitcase with clothing and swimsuits, and I trundled it back to the guest room. The suitcase was small, but it felt heavy, as though it held a new life. As if I were emigrating to a country where my looks were a saleable asset. I sat and gripped the handle as hard as I could to keep my fears about Ryan in check. Telling myself that whether or not he got back to me, I was going to need a new career.

When I returned to the living room, Emmeline was sitting at the dining table. 'Hi, babe.' Her face was a little shy. 'Now you've decided to do the photo shoot, I thought I'd show you something.'

She opened a daisy-printed photo album to a picture of a blonde, dark-eyed baby in a terry-towelling jumpsuit. And even though I'd always longed to learn more about her life, now that I was about to, I didn't feel ready. There was no room inside me for her past. Realising that Ryan might have dumped me was more than enough to deal with for one day.

Before I could stop her, she turned the page to a toddler, standing unsteadily, with her hands above her head in the clutch of a tall, skinny man. He had collar-length fair hair and his face crinkled with laughter. My grandfather.

Andrea had told me almost nothing about her ex-husband. I'd begged to know more about Emmeline, but my mother was my business, whereas even as a child I'd sensed that my grandfather wasn't. He was Andrea's business, a no-go zone, a closed, forbidden book. And now Emmeline was sitting beside me, her album gaping open like a blouse.

'What do you know about Dad?' she said.

'Almost nothing.'

'He was a Geography lecturer,' she said, as if this summed him up. 'I barely remember him. He left with one of his graduate students when I was three. I think he's living in Vancouver now.'

On the opposite page, a slightly older Emmeline was sitting in the lap of a dark-haired woman in her twenties. My heart jolted when I realised this was Andrea.

Twenty-something Andrea had shoulder-length hair, and her cheeks were round and smooth, with a rosy tinge that had long since faded. Her eyes were softer and wider, and her smile showed no hint of the cynical twist it had now. I reminded myself of the reasons why I'd left her, but looking at that open-hearted face all I remembered was her flicker of hope when she'd thought I might join her in the taxi.

'That's the only photo of her I have now. I think it was taken a month or so before Dad left. I had more, but I burnt them when I left home.' She flashed me a wry smile. 'I was kind of pissed off with her.'

Had Andrea known what was happening when this photo was taken? That her husband was cheating and plotting his escape? When I'd been hiding my relationship with Ryan, I'd told her I was studying late, working in the library, attending fictional meetings. Perhaps she'd recognised those lies. Perhaps they were the ones her husband had told her in the months before he left. Had she believed them then? Looking at her unsuspicious face in the picture, I felt certain that she had. Or she'd tried to.

'What was Andrea like when you were little?' I asked, wondering how that wide-eyed woman had turned into the Andrea I knew.

'Angry. I hardly saw her and when I did she yelled at me. The other kids at crèche used to cry when their mothers dropped them off; I cried when mine came to take me home.'

Emmeline tried to smile, as if this was a joke, but the corners of her mouth were unsteady. As if she were four years old, and Andrea had just arrived to pick her up from crèche. I watched her mouth, biting the inside of my own. She wanted me to unite against Andrea in a weepy embrace, but I just sat, pinned to her luxury leather dining chair by a small but powerful hand. The hand of another small girl raised by Andrea, whose mother walked out and never came back.

Emmeline's smile faded, and her gaze retreated to the album, as if seeking firmer ground. 'I understand now that she was miserable because Dad left her, and we had no money, and she was getting hassled at work. But all I saw then was that my mother told me off all the time, and that I couldn't seem to please her no matter what I did.'

Her mouth pinched shut, and she pressed her forefingers into the corners of her eyes for a moment. Then she turned the page to a spread of four photos of herself, aged three or four.

The pre-school Emmeline was impossibly pretty, a Christmas card cherub under plastic. Her hair was long, and she wore frilly dresses that Andrea didn't yet disapprove of. Stripped of years and makeup, her face looked eerily like my own. As a child, people often said I looked like my mother. Andrea would smile tightly and change the subject, but I was always thrilled, as if my face were a secret message from the mother I didn't remember. Now that resemblance was on a page in front of me, the thrill was colder, mixed with fear.

'Me in the park,' said Emmeline, indicating the first photo. She was on the high end of the see-saw, ponytail dancing in the sunshine. On the low end was a stocky little girl with a determined expression that reminded me of Fran. An odd expression for a four-year-old face. The daughter of one of Andrea's colleagues? A friend from kindergarten?

'Who's the other little girl on the see-saw?'

Emmeline shrugged. 'Can't remember. Someone I played with in the park that day.'

If you only met once, why put her picture in your album? But before I could say it she went on.

'Me in kindergarten.' In one she was peeking through a tyre swing; in another she wore a paint-daubed smock, and stood pointing at a lurid purple finger painting. 'Me and Santa.' She was patting his giant, fake beard and peering back over one shoulder.

I wanted to know what it was like going to kindergarten, whether she kept on painting, who took these photos, and countless other things, but she told me nothing more, as if the pictures said enough.

In the next spread she was primary-school age, every shot so picture-perfect she could have been posing for a catalogue. Once again, she gave each photo the barest of factual captions—*me playing the recorder, me on school sports day*—and it occurred to me that a catalogue was exactly what this was. These photos were a montage called 'Scenes from my childhood', assembled not from the pictures most important to her life, but from the pictures where she looked her best.

'Who took these photos?'

'Mum, mostly,' said Emmeline, with a jerky shrug. 'She just put them in a box somewhere. I picked out the ones I liked when I got this album.' She turned the page quickly, as if closing the door to an untidy room. 'Oh *God*, the corduroy era.'

Four more pictures of Emmeline, aged eight or nine. Her hair had been cut short, and the dresses had been replaced by shirts, and corduroy pants in shades of brown and green. The sort of clothes I'd always worn. In fact, when I looked closer, many of them were the actual clothes I'd worn.

'I wore some of these.' Had I known they were hers, I would have treasured those hand-me-downs, and searched the pockets for a pebble or coin she might have left behind. But Andrea hadn't told me, and for a brief, blistering moment this was as deep a betrayal as the letters.

Emmeline grimaced. 'Poor you. I hated them. Mum tried to make me wear brown boys' cords to a party once, and I was so upset I cut them up.'

Whereas I'd turned up to Jess's party in baggy men's clothes without even realising how this would look to her friends. But then, I was born into Andrea's world, whereas Emmeline watched it being built. I was an insider; she was an inmate, wearing her short hair and sensible clothes like a prison uniform. And yet, looking at the album, I realised I preferred these photos to the earlier ones. In drab, shapeless clothing Emmeline looked less like a catalogue model and more like a child in a family snapshot. More like someone's mother.

'At first I quite liked it when she started femmo night school. She didn't yell at me as much, I got babysat by someone I liked. Then one night she came home and went ballistic. She threw out my Barbie dolls and nail polish, gave my books and toys to a charity shop, and said she didn't want me wearing dresses and skirts any more, because they stopped me from romping and getting dirty. The next day she cut my hair and started dressing me like *this*.' She waved an appalled hand at the album.

'Then she started making all these weird new friends. Yoga teachers whose houses stank of incense. Tattooed lesbian couples who did tarot readings. Hairy vegans who ranted about bee slavery when I asked for honey on toast. Worse still, she got them to *collect me from school!* It was a nightmare. I was terrified that the kids at school would see with me those freaks. I told her I had sport or detention after school to make sure no one saw them. I mean, God, check out Ravenwitch.'

She indicated a sullen Emmeline of about eleven, clamped to the side of a doughy, grinning woman with red dreadlocks, a ring through her left eyebrow and a voluminous green dress printed with giraffes. I recognised a younger version of a loud, flamboyant woman who used to babysit me when Andrea went on conferences. These days she had a shaven head and called herself Zirconia.

'Ravenwitch was the absolute worst,' she said, rolling her eyes. 'There was this awful day in Grade Six when I was walking toward the gates, and saw Ravenwitch in this hideous hot pink kaftan. I pretended I didn't know her, but she yelled my name and waved, so practically the whole school knew she was waiting for *me*. I wanted to die. It was the most embarrassing moment of my life. People were still hassling me about it four years later.'

Before the karaoke night, I wouldn't have understood. Zirconia had never embarrassed me. But now I knew the cost of being a 'freak', and I felt Emmeline's embarrassment like a blowtorch. Because in the mainstream world, I was the freak, as shaming for Jess as Ravenwitch had been for Emmeline.

'The next time I saw her at the gate, I ran away and hid at a friend's house. Ravenwitch called the police. When I turned up home safe that night, Mum went *psycho*.'

We exchanged a rueful smile, Andrea's white-ringed eyes burning holes in our memories. She didn't specify what she meant by 'went psycho', but I remembered the whip crack of Andrea's hand hitting Ryan, and didn't dare to ask.

'After that, I'd had enough,' said Emmeline. 'Enough of the femmo preaching, enough of the freak show friends, enough of doing anything she told me. I was out to embarrass her as much as I could. I wore heels and makeup, bought beauty magazines, put boy band posters on my walls and hitched up the skirt on my school uniform until you could see my undies flash when I walked. She hated it, and I loved that she hated it.'

She smiled again, lipstick half-bitten from her lips. Her spirit shamed me. My mother waged war on Andrea's regime at twelve; I didn't defy her until the night I refused to let her cut my hair, aged eighteen. But then, Emmeline had grown up in the mainstream world, watching television, attending school, learning what was 'normal' and how to rebel. I'd had none of those influences. Just Andrea, and the world she created.

The next spread was a collage of pictures cut from catalogues and magazines. Emmeline at the start of her modelling career, in jeans and brief, bright dresses. Long-ago versions of the outfits that made Andrea cast Freya from our house.

'It started when I was in a department store one day,' Emmeline went on. 'I was fifteen, and this woman came up and gave me her card, asking if I was interested in modelling. I said absolutely, because what little girl *doesn't* dream of being a model?'

A little girl like me, I answered silently. *And look what I'm doing tomorrow.*

Looking at the modelling photos animated Emmeline in a way the earlier shots hadn't. Her face brightened, and she lingered over each page, telling me details of the shoots and the clothing in the way I'd hoped she'd talk about herself.

Something significant occurred to me. 'Don't you need your parents' permission to model if you're under eighteen?'

Emmeline waved a dismissive hand. 'I forged Mum's signature and got a friend's unemployed older sister to come to jobs with me. I needed a guardian, she loved the shoots, it was a win-win. By then Mum was so busy with her femmo stuff she didn't suspect anything for ages. A few months later, I met Matti.'

Emmeline turned a page and I found myself staring at my father. The man who provided half my genes. The photographer. The paedophile. The sight of him sucked the air from my lungs, as if I'd been locked in a cage with a monster.

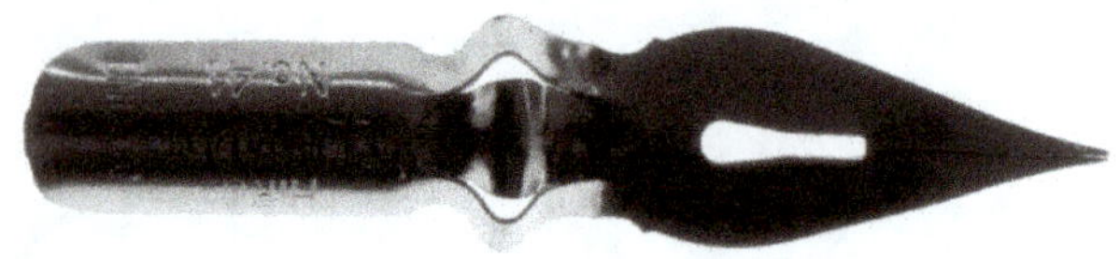

Chapter Twenty-Nine

Fatherland

My father was sitting on a low stool, with a camera in his lap and a lit cigarette, held in the European way between thumb and forefinger. His face was lean, almost gaunt, with sideburns and pale blond hair that trailed over one eyebrow in an angled, silky sheet. His cheekbones were high, and his eyes were blue but angular, like Asian eyes. Like my eyes.

Emmeline was looking at Matti, her beautiful face as still as a waxwork. It was as though she didn't know whether she wanted to tear the photo up or crawl inside it and live there forever. Feeling my gaze, she flashed a camera-ready smile and turned to another page of modelling shots.

'He wasn't rude or sleazy, like some of the other photographers.' Her voice was hushed, as if telling the story of someone who'd died. 'I thought he was the most beautiful man in the world. He was older, and wiser, with amazing blue eyes and this sexy Finnish accent. I knew he had a wife, but he said he'd divorce her, and I wanted to be with him more than anything in the world. When he went back to Finland I cried for weeks. I was so devastated that I missed three periods before I realised I was pregnant.'

My heart contracted. Pregnant. With *me*. Accidental product of an affair between a teenage fashion model and a married photographer. Twenty-three years ago, I was *growing in the stomach* of the glamorous woman beside me.

'I was so scared.' Emmeline's face buckled. She pulled out two tissues, scrunched them into balls, and rammed them into her eye sockets as if staunching a wound. 'I didn't dare tell anyone, especially not Mum. When it got obvious, she confronted me, and when she found out that I'd been modelling behind her back and sleeping with a married man, it was like a bomb went off. Screaming, slamming doors, smashing crockery. Trying to make me get an abortion, trying to come up something to charge Matti with. Abuse of power, sexual assault, statutory rape, anything she could think of. Which was just *stupid*.'

She ripped out two more tissues. 'I was over the age of consent, for a start, and it's not like I was a virgin or anything. And there was no way I was aborting Matti's child. I knew men hardly ever leave their wives, but we were so in love, and I was so young and beautiful, I couldn't believe he'd stay with her when he had a child with me.'

She rammed more tissues into her eyes, and they turned at once to mulch. I handed her two more, compassion and bitterness at silent war inside me. Had she been a vain, naïve teenage stranger, compassion would have won. But Emmeline was my mother, and I was the child she'd kept as her ticket to happily ever after.

'Then I had you. I thought I'd just pop you in a cot and go back to normal, but babies don't work that way. I was getting up every two hours for *months*. Cleaning up vomit, changing your nappies and sheets, making bottles, begging you to sleep while you screamed in my arms. All with Mum standing by, criticising everything, like I was the worst mother in the world.'

She yanked a fresh handful of tissues from the box, and tossed the drenched ones at the bin in the kitchen. One landed on the lid; the other one slid in slow motion to the floor.

'You'd think she could've cut me some slack. I was *sixteen*, for Christ's sake! But no. Everything I did was wrong, bottle-feeding, using disposable nappies, dressing you in pink, saying you were pretty. Putting you to bed too late, or not enough, or too much. Wanting time out to exercise and see my friends. Not that I had much fun when I did. It was like they were still kids and I was an adult who might give them Teenage Mother disease. As for exercise, we're talking a couple of times a week. The way Mum went on you'd think I was locking you all day in a cupboard so I could get my nails done.

'Well, *fuck her*. I cared about how I looked, and I looked like shit, which made me feel like shit. I was terrified that if I didn't get my looks back, I'd never model again and Matti might not want me any more. And I wanted him so desperately. He wrote to me sometimes, and sometimes those letters were all I had to live for.'

She hugged her knees to her heaving chest in a gesture so like mine that it pierced through my bitterness into a deep well of grief. I pushed back my chair and put my arms around her, but she kept on weeping like I wasn't there.

I released her and sat until her sobs petered out. With a shuddering breath, she reached out and turned to the final page. And there, beneath a smooth sheet of plastic, was the picture of Emmeline I carried in my wallet. The final square that connected the real-life patchwork to the fantasy one in my head. A shiver went through my bones.

'Mum took this photo,' said Emmeline. Her face was bare and puffy, and her voice sounded flat, as if all her emotions had been wrung out. 'I left a week later.' She turned away, not wanting to look her teenage self in the eye.

'Because she stopped you from taking me to Helsinki.' My words came out rusty.

'Not quite.' She picked up the second album, small and pink with 'Little Angels' embossed on it in silver. 'The argument that made me leave was about this.'

She opened the second album. Inside the cover was a pudgy-cheeked baby, with white-blonde hair and a winsome gummy smile. The photo was oval, and the edges misted into a soft pink background. Me, aged six months.

Something huge and messy shifted inside me. I'd never seen a photo of myself as a baby. If Andrea had any, she'd thrown them out or locked them away in her filing cabinet. Just like she'd locked me away.

A series of photos in costume followed. In one I was lying on my tummy in a denim skirt and fur-edged jacket; in another I was sitting on a throne with a tiny tiara studded with heart-shaped pink jewels. In a way, it was grotesque, as Andrea had said. Yet looking at myself in those twee little outfits, I also saw something Andrea hadn't wanted to see: that these photos were teenage Emmeline's way of being proud of her daughter, and wanting to show her off.

I looked up from the last photo. Emmeline was watching with a nervous expression, as if awaiting my verdict.

'Your first portfolio,' she said, half-joking, half in earnest. 'You were the cutest baby ever. I entered you in the Little Angels beauty contest and you won. Part of the prize was being signed by an agency to model kids' clothes. I was so proud I was stupid enough to show Mum.'

I gaped. 'You showed *Andrea* this album?'

She bit her lip and nodded.

We shared a pained grimace at her youthful naiveté, briefly on the same side once more. 'She didn't rip it off you and burn it?'

'She tried to. But I snatched it back and barricaded myself in my room while she banged on my door and told me I was exploiting my baby. That I was shallow and disgusting and unfit to be a mother. You'd think I'd put makeup on my six year old and taught her lap dancing. OK, so it was a bit trashy, but you were *six months old!* You wouldn't have remembered a thing! But she preached and screamed until I just couldn't cope. I said "Fine, if I'm so crap and you're so perfect, you fucking raise her." And I left.' Her eyes overflowed again, and she drew her knees back to her chest. 'I'm so sorry, babe. I'm so sorry.'

This time I didn't try to hug her. I looked out the window at tatters of cloud, drifting across the sky like the fragments of a torn curtain.

A long time passed before she lifted her ravaged face. 'Anyway,' she said, 'I used the last of my modelling money to fly to Helsinki and stayed in a cheap hotel for three nights, ringing and ringing Matti's number. He finally called back, and we met in a park on the edge of town. When he arrived, I flung myself into his arms and he shook me off, looking around like there were spies in every tree. Then he said he wasn't leaving his wife, gave me five thousand dollars, and told me to go home on the next plane.'

Grief of my own began stirring at last, somewhere too deep inside me to see clearly.

'So I did. I stayed for a few weeks with friends, but I could feel their parents thinking I was this fallen woman they didn't want near their daughters. Eventually I ran into this guy I knew through modelling who had his own place, and we had this kind of live-in relationship while I got back in shape for modelling. So everything was … everything from then was OK.'

Emmeline shoved back her chair and walked out, balled fists against her eyelids, hunched over as if walking against a strong wind. I didn't follow. When her bedroom door closed, I leafed through the Little Angels album again, empty and dry-eyed. I stared at the pictures until the reddening sky turned dark, trying to shove my mother's story into bookshelves already jammed too tight.

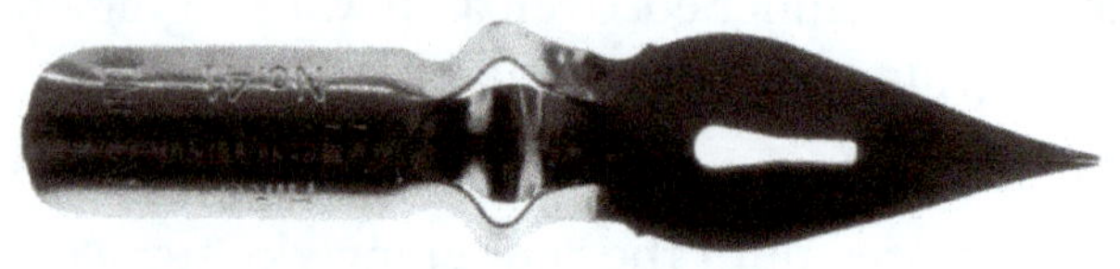

Chapter Thirty

In Camera

Fabian de Carlo's studio was built in an old warehouse. The ceiling was high and barred with iron girders, and the floor was divided into areas by curtains and black scaffolding. The shoot took place among these, on a small white stage, where I posed on stools and podiums, slick with sweat from the blazing studio lights. Even though all I was wearing was Emmeline's bikini, I somehow felt less self-conscious than I'd felt fully-clothed on campus.

'Can you lift your chin for me, bella?' called Fabian from behind the lens. 'A bit more. A bit more. Ah! Now you are perfect.' *Clickclickclick*. 'Now look over your left shoulder. Bring the shoulder closer. Closer. *Beautiful.*'

Clickclickclickclick.

Beautiful. The word rang in my ears, thrilling yet somehow unearned. Coming from Ryan, *beautiful* had been a private gift. Coming from Fabian, it felt like something valuable I'd been given by mistake. Something intended for Sadie, the chic young model Emmeline had created.

Fabian consulted the gold watch on his perma-tanned wrist. 'OK, my bellas. I love you and leave you. But I tell you,' he said to Emmeline, 'she has something special. I show these to Peter at La Carina, and I promise you, he will use this girl for his Birds of Paradise collection. *Ciao ciao*!'

Something special. Once again the strange, detached sense of thrill, as though the compliments belonged to someone else.

A flock of assistants descended to prepare the stage for the next client, and Emmeline ushered me back to the changing area. 'Oh my God, babe,' she whispered, 'he's sending your pictures to La Carina!'

'La Carina?' I said, shutting the curtain between us.

'Exclusive lingerie company, based in Italy. They must be shooting in town. So are you excited?' she said. 'You could be the next Gigi Hadid!'

'The next who?' I said, levering my aching breasts into one of my new bras. Despite being bought only a couple of days ago, it already felt a bit tight.

'Gigi Hadid. Blonde American girl. 2016 international model of the year.'

I emerged as Emmeline was taking out her Visa card, and for the first time I saw that the name on it was Dirk Rusden. I choked on my glass of water. Emmeline was buying me clothes and waxing on *Dirk's* credit card?

'Technically, you're a bit old to start modelling now,' she said, handing the card to one of Fabian's assistants, 'but you look young. Tell them you're eighteen. I did for years.'

My transformation had already cost several thousand dollars. I'd stopped protesting about this, figuring this was the least she owed me for growing up without her. Except that now I owed

Dirk. Not just for my haircut and wardrobe, but for the food I ate, the clothes I wore, and the glamorous roof over my head. Just like she did.

'Do you … not work at all any more?' *Are you completely dependent on Dirk?*

The assistant returned with a USB. 'Not really,' said Emmeline, signing the terrifying bill. 'Most of the high-paid interesting stuff is for younger girls, like you. I could still look for catalogue work and ads if I wanted, but why bother?' She swept up her designer bag and led me outside to the taxi rank.

Why bother? Why work if you've caught a man rich enough to keep you in luxury? You *and* the daughter you're pretending is an aspiring model you met through a friend?

Because it leaves you one break-up away from destitution. Because trophies lose their shine and get replaced. Which is why most models' careers are over by the time they turn twenty-five. Or earlier. And I was already twenty-two.

'How much would a model make for a La Carina shoot?' I asked, climbing into the taxi.

'Oh, it depends on lots of things.' She checked her lipstick in a tiny hand mirror. 'How experienced you are, how long the shoot goes for, how many of your photos they use. But a few grand, at least.'

My spirits lifted a little. If I could get semi-regular modelling work at that rate, I could rent my own place and model for a year or two while I built myself an alternative career.

But in what? Everything I thought of was haunted by Ryan, telling me I had yet to find my calling.

Still no calls. Still no emails. Still no answer when I rang his mobile phone. I'd checked his social media, but nothing had been touched for days. It was as if he'd vanished, leaving nothing but a message and that awful, humming silence that sucked in my messages and turned them into poisonous whispers.

How many messages do you plan to leave? Twenty? Fifty? You look desperate and pathetic. He's ignoring them, or deleting them, because he's over you. Move on. Find someone else. The way you look now, you'll be fighting off offers! And even if the offers would be for Sadie, not me, at least I wouldn't be sneered at.

I shoved the whispers away. 'So what do I have to do to get modelling jobs?'

'There's a few ways. If you register with an agency, clients contact them and pick models from their books. If you're freelance, you find work yourself. In this case, Fabian's going to send your photos direct to La Carina.'

When we arrived at the penthouse it was ten to five. I hurried to the guest room and opened the laptop to check my email. *Invalid username and/or password.* I entered my details a second time, then a third, and a fourth, but the same message came up every time. I'd got into my email just that morning—was the university server down?

Suddenly convinced my inbox was full of messages from Ryan, I clicked on *IT help*. Maybe there was something wrong with his email account, or he couldn't access it from his mother's place. Maybe now it was Monday he'd gone in to the university to sort things out. Academic departments locked their doors over the semester break, but the IT help desk stayed open. It was too late to ring today, but I could get them to reset my password first thing tomorrow.

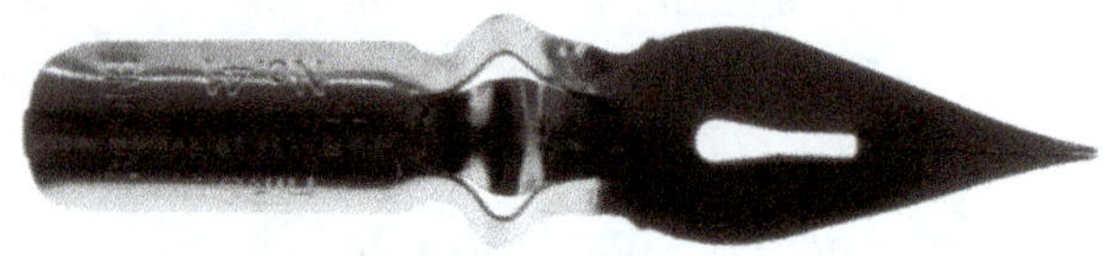

Chapter Thirty-One

Suspended Animation

I stepped off the bus, and crammed the Styrofoam container from my breakfast in a bin. Student Administration was about ten minutes' walk from the bus stop. I got there in four minutes and took the stairs three at a time to IT.

The barriers set up to make students line up were empty, and only one of the three counters was attended. The soft-bodied man in headphones behind it was transfixed by the dragon on his screen. He wore a T-shirt printed with a cartoon character and a name tag that read 'Alan'.

'Um, hi,' said Alan, hastily restoring the IT home page and plucking the headphone from one ear. 'Can I …' The words *help you?* died in his mouth. His eyes skated over me, furtive and shifty, as if I'd caught him doing something wrong.

'Hi,' I said. 'I haven't been able to access my email.'

Alan looked me up and down again, lips still parted, headphone dangling like a round white spider. My shoulders hunched instinctively to shield me from contempt, but his gaze came to rest on my top. Only then did I recognise the distraction on his face: Alan wasn't sneering, he was leering.

I folded my arms over my breasts, feeling more uncomfortable than I had at the studio, where I'd chosen to be on display. 'Um, don't you need my student number?'

Alan straightened and ran a hand over his head. 'Um, yeah. Sorry. What was it again?'

I recited the number, thinking of Emmeline, who'd always been beautiful. Her coy smiles, her perfect grooming, the way she smoothed her hair. The preening of someone who knows that a beautiful woman is always on display.

'Your candidature's been suspended.'

My thoughts derailed. '*Suspended?*'

'That's what it says.' His eyes slid down to my legs. 'Have you taken leave from your degree?'

'No,' I said, tightening my arms around me. 'I only started a few months ago.' As you would see on your screen, if you stopped staring at my breasts.

Say it out loud, Sage, snarled my inner Andrea, springing back to life. *You're not his private peep show. Humiliate him. Say it. SAY IT.*

'How about misconduct?' His eyes darted up again, and then dodged away from my thunderous face. 'I had one guy who couldn't log in because his department had suspended him for plagiarism.'

Misconduct? A new thought landed in my head like a lighted match. My department. Andrea's department. Andrea's office, hacked and vandalised by Ryan and me. Had Andrea suspended me?

I ducked under the barricade, grabbed the internal phone and dialled Andrea's office. 'You've reached Professor Andrea Rampion, Head of Women's Studies.' Her sharp, resentful voice buzzed through me like a drill. 'I'm away on a conference until the fifth. If your query is urgent—'

I hung up, pelted downstairs to the payphone in the lobby and rang her home number. Another answering machine. I rang Ryan, and got his voicemail yet again. My head was spinning and my breasts were aching, as if Alan's stare had hit them like a hammer. I staggered to a squashy vinyl couch and sat.

The dizziness dwindled into a little slug of sickness, lodged where my throat met my gut. Ryan had been nagging me to get my own phone, but I'd been too scared of how Andrea might react. All my life, doing things and not doing things out of fear of Andrea. And now my scholarship payments would stop, my academic career was collapsing, and Ryan was gone, and I didn't know where to look for him. Or whether he wanted to be found.

I wanted to go to his place, but the thought of him being gone and facing Shell again made me queasy. Instead, I clutched my stomach and shuffled out the gates to catch a bus back to the hotel.

Emmeline had given me a card for the front door. I swiped it through the reader and half-fell into the penthouse.

My mother came rushing over, eyes bright. 'Hi babe, I've been looking at … my *God*, are you OK? You look awful!'

She half-carried me to the bathroom, and I hung retching over the toilet while she fetched me a glass of water. 'Drink this. Did you eat breakfast?'

'I bought some from the cafe on the corner.' I took the glass and sipped it gratefully. 'Maybe the eggs were off. Or the bacon.'

'It's not just today, though, is it? You've been sick a few times.' She took back the glass, her face troubled. 'Babe, can I ask you something? It was a big, fried breakfast, wasn't it?'

Confusion knotted my brows. 'Well, yes, but what—'

'Oh, babe,' she said, a pained, understanding note in her voice. 'Listen, I want to you trust me, OK? You look *beautiful*. You're naturally *very slim*. You don't need to do this to yourself.'

I closed the toilet and sank on to the lid, completely baffled. 'Do what to myself? Eat a big fried breakfast?'

'It's nothing to be ashamed of. When I was modelling, everyone went there at least once. All that living off coffee and salad: of course you sometimes crack and eat a cheesecake. But seriously, this isn't the way to fix it. It wrecks your teeth, for one thing.'

Oh God, she thinks I am bulimic. 'Em, I'm not making myself throw up on purpose. Really I'm not.'

She gave me a sceptical smile. 'Look, babe, how about I make you an appointment with the hotel doctor? He's on the third floor, and he really knows his stuff.'

Too weak to object, I nodded, and she made an appointment for the following morning.

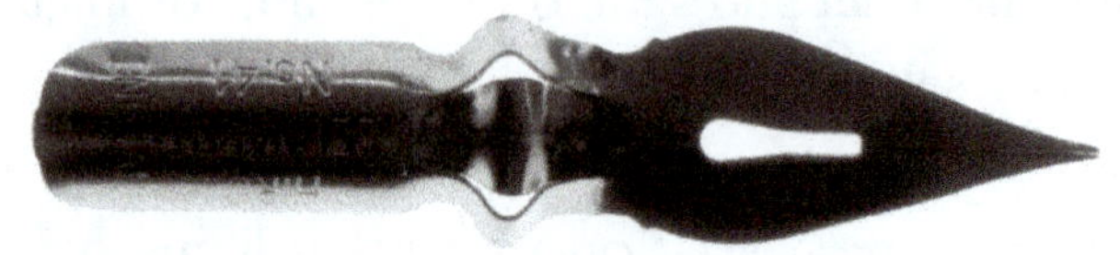

Chapter Thirty-Two

The Thin Pink Line

Dr Clarke was in his fifties, with gingery brows that disappeared behind his rectangular glasses when he frowned. As he led me to his office I lagged behind, eyeing him as if he were an unpredictable dog. I'd never been treated by a male doctor before.

He installed himself behind the desk. 'Take a seat,' he said, opening a new patient file.

I sat in the seat closest to the door. Before Ryan, I'd been invisible or contemptible to men. Now everyone stared like I was walking in a spotlight. If I put on my old clothes and glasses again, I might be able to escape it. But now I'd had a taste of being attractive, being *acceptable*, I didn't think I could bring myself to go back.

'So,' said Dr Clarke, 'what can I do for you today?'

I shifted uneasily under his tired, pouchy eyes, remembering Alan, and Dirk, and the men in the streets. *This man is a doctor*, I reminded myself. Not that that guaranteed anything. Andrea once led a class action against a male doctor accused of harassing female patients. His favourite trick was telling them they needed a breast inspection, to give him an excuse to feel them up.

'Just a check-up,' I said. 'I've been having bouts of vomiting and dizziness, so I thought I'd make sure nothing's wrong.'

Dr Clarke made a note on his file. I settled back, perversely reassured by his dourness. He seemed too jaded to ogle anyone. 'How long have you been having these bouts?'

'A few days.' I hadn't actually vomited until the Greek restaurant, but my stomach had felt on edge before that. It hadn't been quite right since Andrea had revealed that she knew about Ryan.

Dr Clarke made another note. There was a drug company logo on the side of his pen. 'Been eating anything suspect? Something refrozen, or left out of the fridge?'

'Not that I know of.'

'Health otherwise good?'

'Yes.'

'Hmmm.' His brows knotted and sank from sight. 'How do your breasts feel?'

My arms locked round my body, like armour. 'My *breasts?* I said, my voice shrill. Did he mean how my breasts felt, or how they ... *felt?*

'Yes,' said Dr Clarke, as if he were referring to my earlobes. 'Any swelling or soreness?'

Soreness? Was this his way of bringing up my breasts and making it sound medical? My arms tightened, and then hastily loosened, because my breasts *were* sore. And had been for a few days now. 'A bit. I've just started wearing underwire bras, though, so it's probably that.'

Did I just describe my *underwear* to this man? My cheeks flamed. Perhaps this was his trick. Raising the topic of breasts with young female patients, getting them to talk about their bras. And I'd fallen for it. I wasn't falling for any more, though. Any more inappropriate questions, and I'd report him to the Medical Ombudsman.

Dr Clarke opened a drawer in his desk. 'Ms Rampion,' he said, extracting a small box, 'have you had unprotected intercourse in the last couple of months?'

I shoved back my chair and stood up. 'Excuse me,' I said, blazing with righteous anger, 'I'm consulting you about nausea and dizziness. My sex life is none of your business. If you—'

Dr Clarke tossed the box onto his desk. *Matrisure*, it read. *Your reliable early stage pregnancy test.* The rest of my sentence withered. My mouth fell open and my head started hammering, as if my heart was trying to break into my skull.

He opened the box and handed me a flat white tube with a cap on one end, like a pen lid. 'There's a toilet next to the waiting room. Take off the lid, pee on the tab and bring it back.'

The hammering grew louder, and the room began to mist over. 'But … but I get the nausea around the middle of the day,' I said, my voice shaky and high-pitched. 'And in the evening, sometimes.'

'Morning sickness is a colloquial term. The nausea can happen at any time of day. Or all day.'

He dropped the tube and instructions into my cringing hand, and I slunk out, holding them at arm's length, as if they might infect me. When I crept back into the office, Dr Clarke placed the test in a plastic tray. A minute or two passed before I could bring myself to look.

The first pink line that meant the test was working was already showing in the clear plastic window on the side. And beside it, in the spot marked *Pregnant*, a second line was forming, pale but unmistakable.

'So,' said Dr Clarke, his mouth forming a vindicated line. 'When was your last period?'

My numb mouth took two or three attempts to form an answer. 'I … I don't know.' A memory from a disconnected time surfaced through the mist. A memory of laughing with Ryan as I squatted by the futon, extracting a condom left inside after sex. I'd meant to take the morning-after pill. I'd meant to. But had I? The memory melted away and the thin pink answer took its place.

'Then we'd better get an estimate of when you conceived. Hop up.'

He strode to the corner and pulled back a curtain to reveal a narrow stretcher bed. A no-frills version of the bed at the beauty salon, when the worst I had to fear down there was wax.

'I doubt that you're more than eight weeks pregnant, so you may need an internal ultrasound, which I can't do here.'

I tottered over and climbed up. 'Internal?'

He snapped on a pair of latex gloves. 'Vaginal.'

My knees slammed together. Shivery with dread, I watched as he opened a tiny fridge, took out a tube, and switched on the screen mounted in the corner. His fingers looked like knobbly white grubs beneath the latex.

Dr Clarke yanked back my top as if it were a curtain, and squeezed a worm of cold blue gel below my navel. Ignoring the way I cringed from his hands, he smeared the gel across my skin and picked up a plastic device that looked like a hand-held supermarket scanner. I expected him to glide it over my skin, but he gouged as if the scanner was an ice-cream scoop, so deep in my flesh that it hurt. Then I looked at the screen, and pain gave way to wonder.

The mist drained away, leaving a hyper-real sharpness, like a film had been peeled off my eyes. I'd imagined just-conceived babies as shapeless flesh jellybeans, but my child was already recognisably human, its outsize head bent in prayer on lizard-leg arms. The image was black and white, but translucent, allowing me to see through the rib cage to the tiny, pulsing dimple of its heart.

I felt a flutter inside, as though something warm had taken wing. 'How pregnant am I?'

Dr Clarke zoomed in, took some measurements, dug in the scanner a bit further, and then withdrew it. The image skidded to one side and vanished.

'About seven weeks.' His ginger brows knotted. 'Let me look again. I thought I saw something.'

Something? I held my breath, already afraid something was wrong with my child. He gouged in the scanner and the praying foetus reappeared, tiny legs wiggling like the limbs of a frog.

'Is she … he … all right?' I asked, dreading the answer.

'Too early to say,' he said. 'But it's late enough to say something else. You see that bump on the left side of the screen?'

'Yes.' It was a grey lobe, smaller than the baby's head.

'Watch.'

He inched the scanner across my stomach and the lobe became a curve, attached to a tiny back knobbled with vertebrae. Just inside the vertebrae was another pulsing dimple, slightly out of sync with the heart of its twin.

I arrived at Ryan's house three-quarters of an hour later. When no one answered the door, I sat on the doorstep and opened my bag of pregnancy pamphlets. The initial shock had dwindled into the unnatural calm of the eye of a storm. Sometime soon the tornado of *pregnant with TWINS* was going to hit again, but while the calm lasted I might as well prepare myself.

Twenty minutes later, Shell's ancient orange Ford rumbled around the corner and double-parked across the road. A man got out of the passenger side, not Shell's boyfriend, Tom, but a stranger of maybe twenty, with skin-tight jeans and asymmetrical hair.

Shell wound down the window, and he stooped to take something from her, his angled hair sliding into his eyes. He wore heavy-framed glasses not dissimilar to mine, but with a self-conscious irony that made them what Emmeline called statement geek chic glasses.

'… but whenever, OK? Any time from tonight,' Shell was saying.

The man adjusted his hair with a long, pale hand. 'Yah, sure thing.' His voice was self-conscious, too, as if he were acting a part and wasn't sure of his lines. 'I'll call when I decide, yeah? Later.'

The orange Ford rumbled away and the man opened the gate. I shoved *How having a baby can affect your relationship* back in the bag, and struggled to my feet with a tentative smile. 'Uh, hi.'

'Hi,' said the man, giving me a once-over. Then a slower twice-over. 'Um, can I help you with anything? Because, like, I'm here to see the house, so …'

'I'm waiting for Ryan. You don't know when he might be back, do you?'

'No, I don't, sorry,' he said, not sounding terribly sorry.

I gripped my bag of brochures, containing my panic. 'Is it OK if I wait inside for him? I've been trying to find him since Saturday, and it's really, really urgent.'

'Um, sorry,' said the young man, pushing at his hair again, 'but I can't just let you in. It's not my house, and like, I don't actually *know* you, so …'

'Shell knows me,' I said quickly. 'I'm Sage. Ryan's girlfriend.' Or at least, I was the last time I saw him.

'Sorry.' He gave me a tight, unyielding smile. 'Could you let me pass, please?'

For a brief, gritted moment, I wouldn't budge. *No, I couldn't. Hand over the keys, or I'll bash you unconscious with this bag of pregnancy brochures.* But then he'd call the police, and being charged with assault would hardly improve my situation. What I needed was Ryan. And Shell wouldn't need to lend this annoying man her keys if she expected Ryan to be home. Maybe he was spending the week at his mother's. Or maybe he was avoiding this house, hoping his ex with the crazed feminist grandmother would give up and go away. His hairy, frumpy, stalking ex, now pregnant with twins. *Pregnant with TWINS.*

I stepped aside, and the young man unlocked the door. The lock went clack behind him and I deflated like a collapsed balloon. Suddenly exhausted, I stumbled out the gate, the whisper of insecurity swelling into a roar.

The lift doors trapped me in a glowing, mirrored womb. As the golden coin climbed the wall I sank to the floor, composing a voicemail message in my head. *Hi, Ryan, it's me. Are you getting these messages? I just saw a doctor, and he … there's something really important I want to … we've got a serious … a serious …*

The doors opened. I stuck one foot out to stop them closing and cradled my head against the wall. The lift in the neighbouring shaft rose and fell away, over and over like waves on a beach. After a long time, I got up and stepped out into the foyer, and my lift descended with an electronic hum. I swiped Emmeline's spare card through the reader, opened the penthouse door, and limped down the hall.

'Babe!' cried Emmeline, leaping up from one of the leather couches. 'Guess who called?'

Fireworks of relief burst inside me. '*Ryan!* When?'

Her face fell, taking my still-queasy stomach with it. 'Oh babe, I'm so sorry. It wasn't Ryan. But it *was* someone exciting. It was Peter. From La Carina. He wants to hire you for this Friday's Birds of Paradise shoot!'

'Great!' I said, trying to sound excited instead of shattered.

'He wants long hair, so I've made an appointment tomorrow with my stylist for a full head of hair extensions. It's her afternoon off, but I made her an offer she couldn't refuse. You're going to be a La Carina model!' She ran forward to hug me, and I whipped the bag of brochures behind my back.

'So what did the doctor say?' she added.

My whole body went cold. I had to tell her. I had to tell her. 'He, uh … he asked me some questions about the nausea, and he, uh …'

'Did he run any tests?'

The handles of the plastic bag burned my hand. 'Uh, yes, he ran … one.'

'And?'

'And he said that I'm … I'm …' I couldn't tell her. I couldn't. '… that my health is fine.'

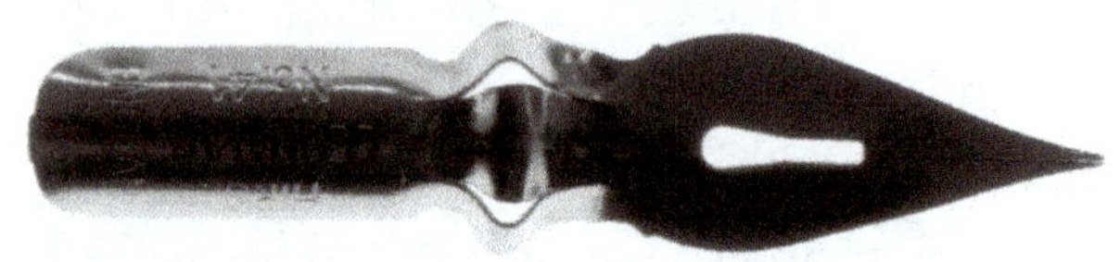

Chapter Thirty-Three

By Extension

The dryers in the hotel salon hummed softly instead of droning, and the staff had sleek updos full of highlights and spray.

'You OK, babe?' said Emmeline, in the quiet tone people use at a sick bed.

The knots in my stomach winched tighter. Since seeing Dr Clarke, I'd barely been able to assemble a sentence. Emmeline thought I was being nervous about my modelling job, and I hadn't told her otherwise. I nodded.

She gave me a one-armed squeeze. 'Don't stress so much. They'll love you, I promise. Now take a seat and let me handle everything, OK?'

Emmeline went to the counter, and I sleepwalked to the couch, my secret pounding on the walls of my womb. The spotlight that had followed me since I'd become beautiful was now a giant arrow suspended over my head that read *Single, Homeless and Pregnant with TWINS.*

Desperate to distract myself, I leafed through a glossy magazine from the nearby coffee table. *Hollywood's latest baby bumps. The truth about your post-birth body. Jessica's baby joy: pregnant at last!*

'Feeling clucky, are we?' said a world-weary drawl over my head.

I slapped the magazine shut on an article titled *My biggest role yet: Being a mum.* 'No, no,' I said, my voice higher than usual. 'I was just … flicking through.'

The owner of the drawl gave me a knowing smile. She was a chic forty-five or so, with a caramel chignon and a uniform that matched the salon decor. 'Don't worry, angel. It'll happen for you. Probably sooner than you think.'

I gave her a watery smile, and followed her to the sinks.

'My name's Monique,' added the woman, lowering my head into a porcelain horseshoe, 'and I'll be your stylist for today.'

A soothing stream of water sluiced over my scalp. Beneath it, my mind whirled like a hamster wheel. Ryan vanished. Suspended from my PhD. Starting work as a fashion model. Living with Dirk. Emmeline not telling him I was her daughter. Pregnant with TWINS.

'You're *such* a lucky girl,' said Monique, rubbing shampoo into my hair. 'I'd *die* to be a natural platinum blonde. Are you Swedish?'

'Half-Finnish.'

Matti's lean face floated across my memory, staring into the distance through a coiling wisp of smoke. The platinum hair which won me this modelling contract was his only contribution to my life. Platinum hair and five thousand dollars.

'Lucky thing.' She massaged in conditioner. 'I might have to tint it to match the extensions, but I'll do a temporary colour. Wouldn't mess with natural colour like this.'

Emmeline was chatting with the woman at the counter, looking too young and glamorous to be anyone's mother. Yet twenty-three years ago she'd been more or less where I was now. Young, pregnant, single. With a career that required her to look thin and beautiful. Almost anyone in her position, in my position, would get an abortion. Yet she hadn't. Because she thought having her lover's child would convince him to leave his wife.

Monique tilted my head back and rinsed my hair with warm water. I stared at the ceiling, breathing in the bitter smell of hair products. I owed both my conception and my birth to Emmeline's naivety. Or to her love for Matti, if I was feeling charitable. And seeing I was living off her charity at the moment, the least I could do was offer her mine.

Monique squeezed out the moisture with a tiny plush towel, and showed me to a leather swivel chair. Protected from small talk by the blow-dryer, I swallowed my bitterness and tried to figure out what to do.

I'd always believed in abortion on demand. Yet every time I thought about clinics and procedures, I saw Emmeline, pregnant at sixteen with me. And the two tiny heads floating inside me, bowed as if waiting for the guillotine to fall.

'You found some long blonde extensions in time, then?' said Emmeline, as Monique blow-dried my hair. 'Did you have to courier them in from interstate?'

'Found them locally, would you believe. Little place north of the city. Natural light blonde, real human hair, enough for a full head. Rare as rocking horse doodoo, and he knew it. It'll cost you, I'm afraid.'

Emmeline gave an easy shrug. 'That's fine.'

Chalk up another debt to Dirk's Visa card. Did he even check what Emmeline spent his money on? Maybe he was too rich to care. But surely even the richest man would notice if a bill from an abortion clinic appeared on his statement. Or two babies appeared in his penthouse.

My womb heaved and capsized, a ship with two stowaways on board. Could I handle this without Emmeline? If I earned enough through modelling to pay for an abortion, she wouldn't even need to know I'd been pregnant.

Monique took a lock of long, straight blonde hair from the box of extensions, and laid it against my bob. '*God*, Em, look at that. Perfect match.'

Emmeline gaped. 'It's like you grew them yourself, babe!'

Suspicion narrowed my eyes. The hair extensions were sitting on a trolley. I peered in the box, and caught a faint but distinct whiff of fennel. Emmeline left to see her personal trainer, and Monique started re-attaching the hair I'd sold to Roy.

My chair was well-padded, yet somehow I couldn't get comfortable. I shifted and squirmed so much under Monique's fingers that she asked if I needed the toilet. The second time she asked, I said that I did, mostly to escape from her small talk.

The face in the bathroom mirror was whiter than the sink. White as mother's milk and freshly laundered nappies. White as the bones of a two-month-old foetus. I felt like a murderer-in-waiting. One pregnancy and my mind was waving pictures from a pro-life picket line.

I washed and washed my hands, trying to remember what my position had been last week—when fashion modelling was an appalling profession that objectified women, instead of the career I hoped would liberate me from my mother's sugar daddy. When women's reproductive rights were something I wrote essays about, instead of something I needed to exercise.

Pro-choice doesn't have to mean abortion, I reminded myself. I could continue the pregnancy. But what would we live off? And where? The thought of begging charity from Dirk—or crawling back to Andrea—made me want to claw my face off. But unless I came up with an alternative plan to support and house myself and two newborn babies, they were the only people I had to ask. And it was very possible that both would say no.

Without warning, a floodgate broke and Ryan tumbled in. Stroking my hair, teaching me to dance, hacking Andrea's computer. Being wheeled away to hospital. And then deserting me, disappearing so completely it was like he'd died. I shut my eyes and pain poured in like tar, shutting down my thoughts and turning everything black.

By the time the last extension was bonded and styled, it was past six, and I'd inhaled enough hairspray to lacquer my lungs. My head was aching, and the hamster wheel had spun on for hours without solving my problems.

Monique picked up a huge hand mirror and angled it to show me the back of my head. 'All done. Stand up and take a look.'

I stood, and the mirror reflected my still-flat stomach. My hands sprang up to cover it, as if muffling two tiny heartbeats.

'So what do you think, angel?' drawled Monique.

My hair hung to the middle of my back—five or six inches shorter than it was before I sold it to Roy—and Monique had layered it, to disguise where the extensions began. To my surprise, the overall effect looked natural, as though all of it was still growing from my scalp.

'It's beautiful,' I said. And it *was* beautiful, sleek and swishy in a way it had never been before. Beautiful, but foreign. Whatever Roy had done to turn my hair into extensions had made it feel like a wig.

Emmeline appeared in the doorway, pink-cheeked in Lycra. 'My God, babe,' she gasped, 'look at *you!*'

'Scrubs up well, doesn't she?' said Monique, looking at me as if she'd made a particularly fine sculpture.

'She looks like a fairy princess!' Emmeline circled me, open-mouthed. 'Are you happy with them?'

I wasn't sure, but I nodded. My new hair rippled like a sheet of golden water.

'Wash and style them like your own hair,' said Monique, producing the bill. 'When they need touching up, or you want to take them out, just give us a bell.'

Emmeline paid, thanked Monique for fitting me in, and led me to the lift. 'So how are you feeling? A bit more confident?'

She looked so earnest and concerned I longed to tell her the truth so I didn't have to carry it alone. 'A bit,' I lied.

'Oh, *babe*,' said Emmeline, with a one-armed squeeze. 'You're going to be fabulous, I swear. You are *gorgeous*. The way you look with long hair, you'll be on the cover of Vogue before you know it.'

We stepped out on the second floor and into a restaurant called Dominique's. A tuxedoed waiter handed us leather-bound menus and took us to a table marked *Reserved*. 'Anything to start, ladies?' he said, pouring us glasses of water.

'An antipasto platter for two, thanks,' said Emmeline. 'That OK with you, babe?'

'Sounds great.'

The swirly words on the menu swam under my eyes. Emmeline was trying so hard—to groom me, to reassure me—and here was I, weeks away from being too pregnant to model and too scared to tell her. I felt like a coward and a liar, but I still couldn't tell her.

'What happened to *your* modelling career, Em?' I said. She'd managed to model after having a baby, so it was possible. Or possible so long as you handed the baby to your mother to bring up. I pictured Emmeline, raising my twins while I modelled, fitting them in around her beautician and personal trainer, changing nappies with her manicured hands. The idea was laughable. But if not her, who else? A nanny? How much did that cost? The freezing ocean returned, icier than ever, sucking me deeper and deeper.

'Well, I didn't make the cover of Vogue.' She gave me a wry smile. 'But I did pretty well. Before I had you, I got lots of work. It got tricky, coming up with new reasons why I wasn't at school. In the end I forged a note from Mum saying I had glandular fever.'

The antipasto platter arrived. It looked like an illustration from Dr Clarke's *Foods to Avoid during Pregnancy* brochure. Smoked salmon. Uncooked fish, which might carry salmonella (foetal damage). Camembert and fetta. Unpasteurised cheeses, which could harbour listeria (risk of miscarriage). Salami, chorizo and prosciutto. Preserved meats, which contained nitrites (potentially carcinogenic for unborn babies).

Emmeline looked at my untouched fork. 'Aren't you having any, babe? Have some cherry tomatoes. Only a calorie or two each.'

Raw vegetables (risk of toxoplasmosis if improperly washed). And now Emmeline was back to thinking I had an eating disorder. I scanned the platter and located some cheddar. Hard, pasteurised cheese. Risk of cross-contamination from other foods, but otherwise safe.

I ate the cheddar as slowly as I could, searching for a main course that didn't break the rules. 'What about after having me?' I said, trying to sound casual. 'How long was it before you could model again?'

'Nearly a year. Having babies is really tough on your body. I didn't get stretch marks, but my tummy went to squish, and I put on *masses* of weight.'

The delicate, leggy teenager in the photo from my wallet flitted uneasily across my mind. How thin had she been *before* she got pregnant? How thin would I be expected to be? How had I gone from articles about the evils of modelling to preparing for a photo shoot in the space of a week?

'So what did you do?' *Live off cherry tomatoes?*

'Oh, my tummy sprang back in a month or two,' she said, beckoning to the waiter. 'No personal trainer, nothing. I was only seventeen, remember. And I was so miserable the weight just fell off. There was no saving my boobs, though.'

Something about the way she said *saving* troubled me. It was like her body was a building, and her breasts were an awning too damaged to repair. 'How do you mean?'

'They were awful. Sad and saggy and under an A cup. Like someone stuck a nail in a tyre.'

She spoke as if those sad saggy breasts no longer belonged to her. As if she'd had that damaged awning removed. Or … renovated.

My stomach bunched up. Her breasts were about the same size as mine, but they sat a little higher, and were round as half-grapefruits. 'You mean you … you had a … a …'

Emmeline gave me a weary smile, as if I were impossibly innocent. 'Babe, I had to. My clothes looked like shit, and every time I saw a girl with cleavage, I wanted to cry.'

My bunched-up stomach plunged toward my feet. Cosmetic surgery. My mother had paid a surgeon to cut open her breasts and put in a bag of chemicals. Going under the knife, not because she was sick, but to make her *clothes* look better. *She was a model, Sage,* I told myself. *Making clothes look good was her job.* 'Isn't that … expensive?'

'Absolutely. Especially if you get a good surgeon. And you don't trust your body to a cheap one. But hey,' she said, with a conspiratorial twinkle, 'it doesn't cost five thousand dollars to fly home from Finland.'

Her matter-of-factness disturbed me. *Babe, I had to.* Looking good was compulsory, and having a baby didn't entitle her to time off. Any lapse in standards made her body an enemy that had to be bullied into line. 'But you were *homeless!*'

The twinkle turned flinty. 'Excuse me, honey, are you judging me? For having a boob job?'

'I was just—'

'This is *Nanna* stuff, isn't it?' Her voice was scathing. 'What was I meant to do, donate the money to a women's shelter?'

I bit my lip, already wishing I hadn't brought it up. 'I just thought you would have spent it on somewhere to live. Setting yourself up. Instead of your … looks.'

Emmeline's eyes blazed. 'I *was* setting myself up, honey. You think I would have got any more modelling work with flat, saggy tits? You think I'd be living in a luxury penthouse with Dirk?'

Flat, saggy tits. Ugly words, brandished in my face like a broken bottle. 'You could have started a different career,' I said in a small voice. 'And found a man who didn't care about your breasts.'

She laughed, a diamond-hard laugh with no humour. 'Don't give me that inner beauty shit. All men care. And all women care, too. Everyone wants to be pretty. I would have got a boob job even if I *wasn't* modelling.'

'Something to drink, ladies?' said the waiter, peeking wryly at Emmeline's cleavage.

'A bottle of the Moet, thanks.' She flashed her camera-ready smile and turned back to me. 'So what about you, Sadie? You're modelling now. Are you saying you'd never have plastic surgery? Not even if you had a baby?'

I coughed on a stuck lump of cheddar. 'I hope not.' *But ask me again in seven months.*

'Here you are, ma'am,' said the waiter, filling Emmeline's wineglass with something golden and bubbly.

'You *hope not*,' Emmeline scoffed. 'Get off your high horse, honey. Look at you, picking at your entrée like it might poison you. What, dieting's OK but plastic surgery isn't?'

I straightened up indignantly. 'I'm not *dieting*. I'm just … just …' My mouth stifled the word *pregnant* as my eye fell on the bottle approaching my glass. Alcohol. Number one on the *Foods to Avoid during Pregnancy* list.

'And for you, ma'am?' said the waiter.

'No, thank you,' I said in a feeble voice. The wine I'd drunk a few nights ago with Emmeline lurched against my conscience. Had I already given my babies foetal alcohol syndrome?

Emmeline gave a gasp of outrage. 'What, and now you're not *drinking?* It's champagne! To celebrate your first modelling job! What's wrong, scared of being hungover tomorrow?'

'It's not that,' I said, and then kicked myself, hard. *She offered you a perfect excuse, Sage! Why didn't you take it? Why?* 'It's that I … I don't really feel like it tonight.'

She studied me, brow crinkling with concern. 'Are you OK, babe? You look stressed. Are you feeling sick again?'

My skin tightened, as if scared she might see her grandchildren through it. 'A bit.'

'Was Dr Clarke sure there was nothing wrong? Maybe you should get a second opinion.' She got out her phone and started scrolling through her contacts list. 'There's this doctor on the south side of town—'

The effort of maintaining the dance of evasion was abruptly too much to bear. 'Em, it's OK. I know why I'm sick.' I took a deep breath and threw the truth on the table. 'It's because I'm seven weeks' pregnant. With twins.'

Emmeline's face went very still. Seconds stretched into minutes, her forefinger stalled on the screen of her phone. My pulse grew louder in my ears as I waited. For the hug and cries of 'Babe!' I realised I'd been expecting. For sympathy. Shock. *Anything.* I was just about to repeat what I'd said, in case she hadn't heard me, when she spoke.

'To Ryan?' Her flat, quiet voice made my pulse beat still louder.

Of course to Ryan! Who else would I be pregnant to, Dirk?

I nodded, not trusting myself to speak.

'Oh my God,' she said. No babe, no sympathy, not a trace of her gushy italics. 'And you've just got your first job, too.' Belatedly, she reached across the table and squeezed my hand. Her fingers were cool.

Something tore, as if she'd ripped the dressing off an old internal wound. 'Why's my job the first thing you thought of?' My voice was tense and trembling. 'You think I should get an abortion, so I can keep modelling?'

'Babe, I—'

I snatched my hand away and stood up, my chair shrieking on the floor. 'Is that what you wish you'd done to *me?*'

'*No,* I—'

I bolted for the exit, crashing blindly into chairs, pounding the lift button until Emmeline caught up.

'Sadie?' She put a nervous hand on my shoulder and I shoved it off. 'Please don't think I didn't want you. I did, I swear. I wanted to have you more than anything.'

What you wanted was Matti. You kept me because you hoped I'd clinch the deal and it was too late to abort. And when he dumped you, you dumped me on Andrea and left. But the words stuck in my throat, as though saying them would confirm beyond doubt that they were true.

Emmeline put her hand on my shoulder again, and this time I let her hug me. She clutched my body as if I were a doll, stroking the grafted-on hair. 'It's OK, babe. You can model maternity wear. And I know great trainers and surgeons to get you back in shape. We'll work something out, OK? Now let's go up and get ready for tomorrow's shoot.'
The lift doors slid open, like the jaws of a shiny steel trap. She steered me inside and I watched over her shoulder as the gold coin crawled slowly up the wall.

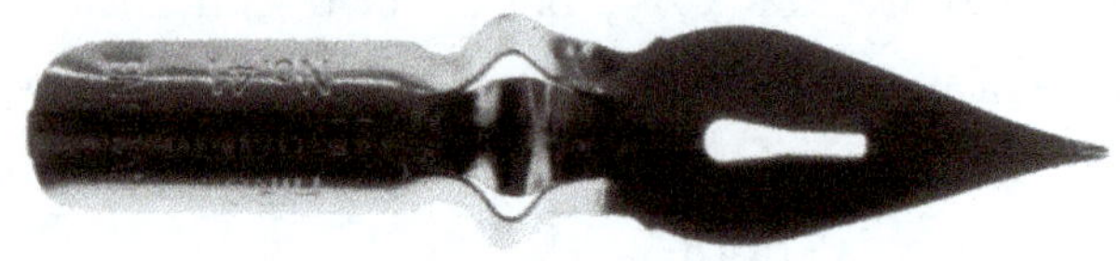

Chapter Thirty-Four

Just Shoot Me

The La Carina shoot was on a country estate two hours out of town, in a section of the grounds styled as ornamental jungle. The tropical plants looked as uncomfortable in the autumn morning chill as the shivering models did in their bathrobes.

My fellow birds of paradise disturbed me. The six of us were so similar in shape, height and colouring we looked like a matching set of dolls. The one or two who'd tried to chat to me had hastily retreated, sensing that while I looked like them, I was really an intruder in camouflage.

Six days after my transformation, the woman in the mirror was still a stranger. I hadn't grown into the costume Emmeline designed for me. Instead I seemed to be shrinking, as if the real me was standing inside her on tiptoe, peering out through her blue-tinted eyeholes.

Last night's conversation pulsed inside me like a pair of tiny heartbeats. When I'd told Emmeline I was pregnant, her first reaction was *To Ryan?* Not *Are you OK?* or *What are you going to do?*

The response of a trophy girlfriend. Maybe if Ryan were wealthy she'd see these babies as a meal ticket, instead of a burden that would ruin my body and my chances of catching someone richer. Though in one sense, she was right to think of him first. These children were also Ryan's responsibility. He needed to know they existed, even if he didn't want me or them. Even if he'd rather bribe me five thousand dollars to abort them and stay out of his life.

The photographer's irritated voice jolted me from my thoughts. '*Come on*, lovely, chop chop.'

How long had he been trying to get my attention? 'Sorry, Peter.' I hopped up from my chair and wavered, a cornered rabbit unsure of where to run.

His mouth was a disapproving crescent. 'You didn't get any of that, did you?'

Any of *what?* Everyone was staring. My eyes skittered from face to face, as if hoping to find Peter's instructions. 'I …'

'In front of the hibiscus bush. *Now*.'

I scurried across the lawn and installed myself in front of it.

'We're selling lingerie, not bathrobes.'

Hot with embarrassment, I stripped off my robe and bunched it up. I threw it to one side and it unravelled mid-air and knocked over somebody's coffee mug. Peter kicked it out of shot and plunked the empty mug upright. As he stumped back to his camera, a man holding a big reflecting shield caught my eye and winked. I twitched, as if a scorpion had landed on my skin.

'OK,' said Peter, his voice heavy with impatience. 'Pluck a flower and tuck it behind your ear. Leave your hands there and raise your left shoulder. A bit more. Hold it there.' *Clickclickclick.*

I followed Peter's instructions, uneasily aware of the man with the reflector. He was good-looking—early thirties, muscular, artfully mussed hair—but his wink unsettled me in a way other men's ogling hadn't. It was breezy, entitled; the wink of a man who'd seduced several models and was confident of doing so again. The sort of wink Matti might have used to seduce my mother.

Goosebumps surfaced along my limbs, partly from the thought of Matti, partly from the icy wind buffeting my barely-clad body. According to *Symptoms of Pregnancy: A Guide*, increased blood supply was meant to make me feel warmer. I prayed that my body would get the message soon.

'OK, lovelies, that's a wrap. Grab some lunch and be back here by two.'

I put down the hibiscus and stretched my numb legs. The man with the reflector held up my bathrobe, like a high-class waiter with a coat. 'First job?'

Matti's ghost breathed down my neck. I plucked the robe from his hands. 'Thanks,' I said, slipping it on and tying it tightly over my lingerie. A coffee stain covered most of the left sleeve.

His face broke into a lazy, sophisticated smile. 'Looks like you owe me a coffee, cutie. Want to join me for lunch?' His gaze trailed over me like the point of a needle.

I wanted to escape, but the need to be professional welded my feet to the ground. 'No thanks.'

His smile broadened, as if he found my refusal amusing. 'That's OK. Don't sweat it.' He took out a business card. 'There's a big swimwear job going next month. Let me know if you're interested.'

He slipped the card in my pocket and sauntered off. Feeling vulnerable and faintly unclean, I fished it out. *Owen Welford, Professional Photographer.* With a mobile number and web address. I scrunched it up, walked to the bin and hesitated. *What if this was the only offer I got before my pregnancy started to show?* I wavered, flattened out the card and tucked it back in my pocket.

One other bird of paradise was still on a folding chair, absorbed in her phone. The others had flown, presumably to get lunch. I picked up my clothes and headed for the mansion to get changed.

The bathrooms were at the side of a roped-off function room being prepared for a wedding. Everything was cream, gold and red, from the napkins and flower arrangements to the seating plans next to the door. I ducked into the powder room, which had a red and cream flower arrangement and a full-length mirror framed in gold. In front of this stood Chloe. She was the youngest of the models, with a quivering strawberry of a mouth and giant blue eyes that made her look like a china doll.

I changed in the toilets, and when I emerged she was still there, twisting fingers in her shiny flaxen hair. 'Are you OK?' I asked.

She shook her head. 'Peter said I looked *fat*.' Huge tears poured down her cheeks as she said that fatal word.

'*Fat?*' I glanced at Chloe's delicate body in disbelief.

'He gave me the negligee because I have a *roll* on my stomach.' With a fresh deluge of tears, Chloe opened her robe and pulled at the tiny bulge below her navel, as if she wanted to cut it off with a knife. 'He said it was totally unprofessional, and that I should get my trainer to iron it out, but I *already* train two hours a day! I'd get lipo, but I'm not eighteen for another year and a half and by then I'll be *history*.'

I put an arm around her heaving shoulders. *Everyone wants to be pretty*, Emmeline had said, but trying to be pretty was like chasing a rainbow. Even those who seemed to have the pot of gold never felt pretty *enough*. Because they compared themselves to the beautiful, not the envious. Because the more beautiful they were, the more the standards they aimed for retreated out of reach.

Chloe gave a tremulous sniff, and I handed her a tissue, searching for something reassuring to say.

'Chloe,' I said, 'you look beautiful. You're naturally *very slim.*' I almost called her 'babe'. With a final flourish I added: 'Don't let what Peter says make you feel bad about yourself.'

Chloe blew her nose and nodded. 'Thanks,' she said with a watery smile. 'Want a rice cracker?' She pulled a Tupperware box from her handbag. Inside were five or six crackers dusted with spice, and half a Lebanese cucumber. I hesitated, and she added: 'Don't worry, they're less than five calories each.'

My stomach stirred uneasily. Was that meant to be a meal? 'Didn't you get your lunch allowance from Peter?'

'Yeah, but I just keep those and bring my own lunch. I save heaps. So you don't want one?'

'No, no,' I said, trying not to show my dismay, 'they're your lunch. You eat them.'

Chloe looked scandalised. 'I'm not eating them after *that!* OK then, if you don't want them ...' She emptied the contents into the bin.

A flicker of horror. 'You're not eating *anything?*'

'I'll fill up on water. Thanks for that. I'd better get my makeup fixed.'

As she walked out, my hands cupped my stomach, as if to shield my womb from what I'd heard. I might have a daughter in there. I might have *two* daughters.

Chloe's crackers and half-cucumber stared up from the bin like a distorted face. When I was sixteen, I barely thought about my looks. But Andrea had achieved this by locking me away, which left me vulnerable, ignorant, and out of touch with society. I didn't want that for my daughters. But neither did I want them to spend their lives fretting that they weren't pretty enough. Or being told they weren't by a bullying employer.

A slow-burning anger built inside me. I didn't have Andrea's ferocity, or her watertight knowledge of bullying and workplace laws. But something she'd passed down to me drove me out into the grounds. I stomped toward the table where Peter sat with Owen. Both men had a mug of coffee in one hand and a cigarette in the other. Did all photographers smoke?

As I approached, Owen gave me another lazy smile. 'Hey, cutie,' he said, 'take a seat. How do you have your coffee?'

'Excuse me,' I said rudely to the side of Peter's head, 'why did you call Chloe fat?'

Peter glanced over his shoulder. 'Because she's a model, lovely. Like you. Being thin's your job, remember?'

I rankled at the condescension in his voice. 'She was crying in the bathroom over that. And she threw out her lunch.'

He shrugged and tapped a nub of ash into the ashtray. 'Good for her. Maybe it'll help.'

My foot itched to kick him in his overhanging gut. 'No,' I snapped, 'it won't help. It'll distress her into an eating disorder. If she doesn't already have one.'

Peter took an indifferent drag on his cigarette. 'Anything else you want to share?' he said, blowing a smoke ring past my ear.

'Actually, yes,' I said. 'It was less than fifteen degrees this morning. And you were making models pose outside. In *lingerie.*'

He gave a short laugh. 'Didn't arrange the right weather, huh?' Peter sipped his coffee and threw Owen a look. 'I'll have a word to God for you. Now, if you don't mind—'

Blood boiled behind my eyes. 'Actually, I do mind. I'm raising serious issues, and you're patronising me.'

Peter put down his coffee, finally goaded into irritation. 'Look, sweetheart, I don't have time for this.'

'Then I'm not selling you any more of *my* time. I quit.'

I dumped the stained bathrobe on the table, tossed the lingerie on top and left. My body was tingling with shock, but I no longer felt like a fraud in a costume. I felt like an angry and defiant version of me.

When I reached the railway station, the two o'clock train was pulling out. I bought sandwiches and a USB and found the local library, where I downloaded everything I could find on girls and body image. When the three o'clock train came, I boarded and made notes in the margins of my La Carina information pack. By the time I reached the city every page was black with scrawl and I wondered if I might have found my passion.

As I stepped out of the train, I noticed I was no longer panicking. I was still single, homeless and pregnant, but the hamster wheel had dwindled into a bulleted To Do list. Go to penthouse. Shower, change, pack. Go to Ryan's place. Sit on futon until he comes home. Beyond that, everything was dark, as if behind a closed door. I didn't need to go through that door yet. Time enough to unlock it tomorrow.

I strode through the city, leers bouncing off me as though my blue-grey dress was armour-plated. When I entered the hotel, the uniformed ushers said, 'Good evening ma'am', and showed me through with obsequious smiles. My reflection in the lift's mirrored walls looked like a fashion model eager to be home. I looked like I belonged.

The arched top floor windows framed a sunset sky the colour of hot coals. I slashed my card through the reader and opened the door.

'… few days to find her feet, but it's been nearly a week.'

Dirk's voice, coming from the leather couches in the living room. The fire in me abruptly went out.

'I know, babe, but she's had a really rough time. I just thought—'

'This isn't part of the hotel, Em. It's my home. And I didn't give you that credit card to spend *six thousand dollars* on someone else's career.'

My fingers were still around the doorknob, clinging as though it were all that stood between me and the city forty-five floors below. Had I honestly felt I belonged? I'd never belonged here. I was a gatecrasher, piggybacking on Emmeline's lifestyle, trying on the career she'd wanted for herself.

'Babe, it's La Carina. It's a once-in-a-lifetime opportunity! She'll make back that money in a day.'

My hand slipped off the doorknob and fell to my side. The La Carina job. My big break. My chance at finding an agent and building a modelling career. And I'd quit.

'Look, it's not like I *can't* support this girl's career. What I want to know is *why*. You've never even mentioned her before, and now she's living in my guest room. And pregnant with *twins*. How's she supposed to keep modelling now she's pregnant? Is she planning to keep them?'

My clammy palm found its way to my stomach. The skin underneath it felt warm, as if my babies were radiating heat. And I knew in that moment that the answer to Dirk's question was *yes*.

'She doesn't know yet, babe. But if she does, it doesn't mean she can't model. She can do maternity wear jobs.'

Silent as a cat, I crept toward them, hidden by the dim of the hallway. Dirk was sprawled on his favourite couch, holding what looked like a bank statement, and Emmeline was beside him on the edge of an armchair. Neither had seen me.

'And then what? Hire a nanny and turn my home into a nursery?'

'Of course not, babe. We can—'

'*We?* Doesn't this girl have friends or family to go to? Why exactly is she *our* problem?'

I set my jaw and stepped into the light, startling them both. 'Because,' I said in a defiant tone, 'I'm her daughter.'

Emmeline's face went ashen. She looked from me to Dirk, mouth open like she wanted to say something, but nothing came out. For once, Dirk also seemed lost for words. He looked from Emmeline's face to mine.

'It's true, isn't it?' he said at last to Emmeline, who averted her eyes. 'How old were you when you had her?'

'Sixteen,' she whispered.

'Why didn't you tell me you had a daughter?'

Her lips were trembling. 'Because I … I didn't think you'd …'

Dirk's face darkened. 'You didn't think I'd what?'

Frightened by what I'd done, I stepped in, trying to smooth things over. 'We weren't in touch. My grandmother—'

'*Honey!* Emmeline's voice lashed me like a whip. 'Dirk and I need to talk. Alone. Please go.'

Still reeling, I stumbled out on shaking legs and poked the button for the lift. When it reached the ground floor, I ran to the station, as if something monstrous was chasing me.

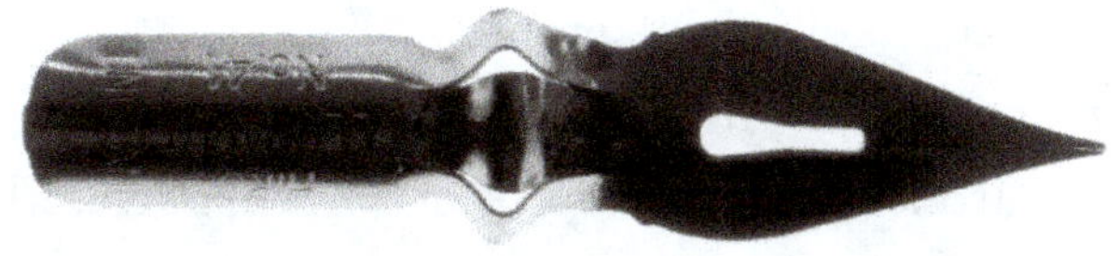

Chapter Thirty-Five

House Cooling

Blurred music wafted along Ryan's street. Everything looked menacing and vivid, as though the houses and fences had been sharpened. I focused on the pavement squares under my boots until my jolting heart ebbed to a slow thump of dread.

Had Ryan really abandoned me, less than a week after cracking Andrea's files and calling me beautiful? Surely his phone was just broken or lost, his emails to me bouncing for some reason. Surely he'd be home now, designing a T-shirt in the room where we'd danced and made love.

The music grew louder as I approached Ryan's gate, where someone had tied two balloons. They head butted each other as I opened it and waded through the feathery weeds to the door. I rapped the knocker, first lightly, and then with all the strength I could muster.

The door opened, and a loud wave of music poured out around a woman of about nineteen. She had dreadlocks, and a ring through her lip as well as several on her fingers, which were wrapped around a plastic cup of punch.

'Hiiiii,' she said. 'Welcome to the party. I'm Ange, and *you*,' she pointed at me, 'are one of Felix's friends.'

My body stiffened. I didn't want to tell Ryan I was pregnant in a house full of half-drunk guests. 'Uh, actually I'm not. I'm looking for Ryan, Shell's housemate.'

'Oh, *are you?*' said Ange, as if this was the most interesting thing she'd heard all night. 'I don't know him, sorry. I'll find Shell for you and see if he's here.'

I followed Ange's swaying dreadlocks down the hall, which smelled of strangers and smoke and spilled wine. Ryan's door was closed, and an unfamiliar Buster Keaton poster had been blu-tacked to it. An ominous chill lodged inside me.

The kitchen lights were off, but the windowsill and shelves were lined with tea-light candles. In their wavering light, I saw the annoying man from the doorstep, now in a velvet tuxedo, accompanied by a man with a straggly beard and very tight jeans. Installed in the beanbag was a woman in a 1960s mini-dress. Her voice was loud, and she spoke every syllable with a languid, husky precision. As I entered the room, her elaborate gestures narrowly missed my thigh.

'Hiiiii.' Ange issued a limp wave. 'Do you know where Shell is?'

The men glanced my way and did a gaping double-take that made me wish I'd changed out of my figure-hugging dress. The annoying one showed no sign of recognising me now I had long hair and full model makeup.

Conscious that her audience was distracted, the woman looked over and did her own double-take. Her scarlet lip curled a little. 'I think she's outside,' she said, turning back with a toss of her sculpted retro curls.

Ange and I steered around a bathtub full of drinks and melting ice and opened the sagging back door. Twenty or so guests were sitting on stumps and mismatched chairs around a fire built inside an old oil drum. As we stepped outside, they peered through the wood smoke and all did the same double-take.

Shell was lolling by the fire, a joint in one hand and a marshmallow on a stick in the other. She stared for a moment and then blinked with recognition. 'Sage! Sorry, I'm just a bit … spun out by your new look.' Her marshmallow caught fire, and she shook it into the coals with a puff of burning caramel.

The small woman next to Shell gave a wide, false smile. 'You must be one of Felix's friends.'

The ominous shadow darkened, tinted with a sense of unreality. *Where was Ryan, and who on earth was Felix?*

'Nah, she's Ryan's girlfriend,' said Shell. 'You know, the guy who used to live in Felix's room.'

My body went cold, and the crackle from the fire turned suddenly loud, as if someone had turned up the volume. 'Shell,' I said, 'can I talk to you alone for a minute?'

'Sure.'

She handed her joint to the woman with the false smile and I led her inside to a quiet spot near the front door.

'Shell, where's Ryan?' I said, clutching her sleeve. 'He's not answering my texts, and I need to see him. Urgently.'

Shell gazed at me with stoned, earnest eyes. 'Have you guys like … broken up or something?'

'No,' I said, a bit louder than I'd intended. 'Why?'

'Because Ryan's moved out. He got his stuff on Tuesday, and Felix moved in Thursday night. You know, the guy in the tux.'

Her words rang in my head. Across the hall, Buster Keaton stared down, his face a baleful blank. 'Did … did Ryan tell you where he was going? Or leave a number?'

Shell's expression turned from nonplussed to shifty. 'Yeah, I think so.'

'What do you mean you *think* so?'

She pinched her lip uneasily. 'He gave me a bit of paper,' she said, 'but I forgot to put the stuff on it into my phone.'

I wanted to kill her. Why hadn't I thought to leave *Ryan* a note here instead of relying on this idiot? *Why?* 'Can you *find* the bit of paper, then? *Please?*'

Shell's brow crinkled, as if I'd asked her to move a piano single-handedly. 'Can't it wait? It's Felix's housewarming party tonight, and—'

'No, it *can't fucking wait.*' I'd never said the word 'fucking' before. It spilled from my mouth, spiky and unexpected.

With a long-suffering sigh, Shell trudged into her room and started rustling about. Nausea reared up, and I bolted for the toilet. I retched and retched until the sickness subsided, then sat and cupped my forehead in my hands. A couple of feet above me, glass louvres let in cold air and conversation.

'My *God*, Felix, you have all the taste of a *footballer*,' said the voice of the languid woman in the mini-dress.

'I didn't say I'd want to *be* with her,' Felix protested. 'I just said she was striking. In a commercial sort of way.'

'She looks like a Barbie doll,' said the woman with the false smile who'd asked if I was Felix's friend. 'Skinny, blonde and plastic.'

Cold sweat broke out all over my body. Suddenly I was eighteen again, huddled in the toilets of the karaoke bar with Caitlin and Kayla at the mirrors.

'You think she's had work done?' Felix sounded fascinated.

'*Darling.*' I could almost see those languid eyes rolling. 'Most women who look like that have had work done. Nose jobs, boob jobs. Two hours a day with a personal trainer and a lettuce leaf for lunch. Personally, I'd rather drink *cask wine* than walk on a treadmill.'

Hooting laughter, like a trio of hyenas. I curled into a ball like a hunted animal.

'Actually,' said False Smile, who'd stopped hooting first, 'we shouldn't laugh. Did you see her Fendi clutch?'

Emmeline had lent me a handbag for the shoot. Its rectangular clasp was made from two long Fs, and it didn't have a strap, so one hand was always occupied with holding it.

'Those,' went on False Smile, 'are *eight hundred dollars*. Of which the sweatshop worker probably got fifty cents. It's criminal.'

The clutch fell to the floor with a *clunk*. When I walked out on Andrea, I thought I'd claimed my independence. Instead I'd just gone from being Andrea's puppet to being Emmeline's. From a sheltered, frumpy loser doing a PhD she hated, to an overdressed doll who'd walked out on her first job as a model. And still, *still* I was being sneered at behind my back. My brain clouded over.

'*Personally*,' said Languid in a portentous tone, 'I just feel sorry for women like that. This dress cost me twelve dollars in a charity shop. And it's *authentic sixties*.'

I'd heard those opinions before. From the mouths of eighteen year olds in first year Women's Studies, full of sophisticated airs. And themselves. Indulged by arty middle-class parents and thinking themselves superior to everyone. What would they know about me?

I slammed down the toilet lid so hard it sounded like a gunshot, and marched out into the kitchen, taking grim pleasure in seeing the shock on their faces. For a long, cool moment I stood, arms folded, staring them down. Then I turned my back and strode into Shell's room, where she was lounging on her bed sending a text.

'You didn't find Ryan's note, did you?' My voice was so harsh that she dropped her phone.

'Ohhh, um, no, I didn't, sorry. Give me your number and I'll text when I find it.'

Another silent, violent curse at myself for being too scared to get my own phone. 'Forget it,' I said in disgust. 'I'll find him some other way.'

I stomped out, slamming first Shell's door, then the front door behind me.

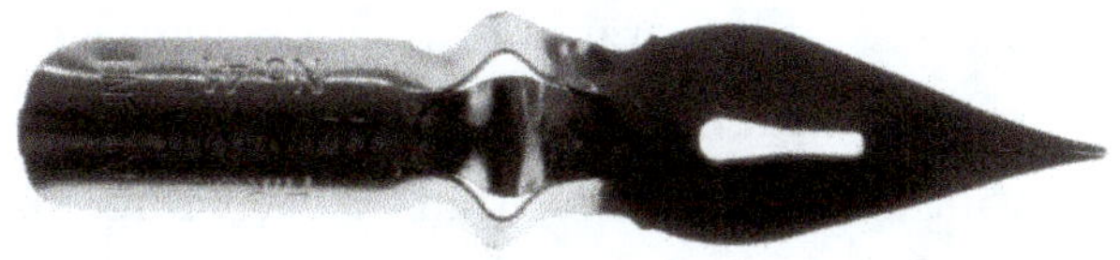

Chapter Thirty-Six

Retractions

The penthouse was unnaturally dark and silent. The living room lights were off, and the leather couches were hunched like ogres against a tapestry of stars.

My eyes found a needle of light under the master bedroom door. I padded toward it and knocked, very softly. When there was no response I opened the door a crack and peeked inside. The covers and pillows on the king-sized mattress lay tangled on the carpet around it. Facedown in the middle of the bed was Emmeline, streaky blonde hair strewn round her head like a broken halo.

I stood in the doorway, afraid to come closer. 'Em?'

She didn't answer. I crept among the covers to the side of the bed. 'Em? Emmeline?' I laid a tentative hand on her shoulder. '*Mum?*'

She shoved my hand away and sat up. Her face shocked me. When she'd cried before, her features had been delicate and controlled, as if crying for a scene in a movie. Now she was broken and blistering, with eyes like black holes.

'Why,' she said in a tear-ravaged voice, 'did you tell Dirk you were my daughter?'

I backed away, and she grabbed my wrist with a bruising grip. 'Because … so he'd understand why you—'

'Spent money on you? Is that why?' She shoved past, grabbed the heavy quilt with both hands and began wrenching it back onto the bed. 'For Christ's sake, honey, a few thousand is nothing to Dirk. He has millions of dollars. *Millions.*'

I bent to help her, shaking so hard I could barely grip. 'Is he … might you two split up?'

Emmeline yanked the quilt from my hands and dumped it on the bed. 'Why yes, Sadie,' she said with vicious sarcasm, 'we might.'

A lightning bolt of horror crackled through me. '*Why? Because of me?*'

'Like I said,' she hurled a pillow onto the bed, 'image is everything to a man like Dirk.' She grabbed another pillow and hurled it so hard it knocked over a bedside lamp. 'Before he had this perfect girlfriend. Now he's going out with a single mother with a pregnant daughter.'

Her words hit my guts like a club. 'But …' *But you aren't a single mother. You're a woman who gave up her child. This week is the only time in your life you've had to look after me.*

'And don't even think about telling me I'll find someone else. I'm thirty-eight. Thirty-*eight*.' She plonked the lamp on the bedside table, and turned to me, fighting for composure. 'So, how was the shoot?'

My heart turned to quicksand. 'I … I quit.'

'*Quit?*

'I was … it was the photographer. He made us pose in lingerie in the cold, and abused this sixteen-year-old girl about being fat, so I—'

'Oh, for fuck's *sake!*' She dropped face-first onto the bed again, her shoulders heaving. I stood by the bed, a pillow dangling from one hand. Finally she raised her face. 'Yes, Sadie. Sometimes it's cold. Sometimes photographers are pricks. But if you want to be a model, you smile, suck it up and deal. Especially when it's a client as big as La Carina.'

'Then I won't take jobs with big clients,' I said, my hand closing on the pillowcase. 'I'll only work with—'

'You won't be offered any more work, honey.'

The pillow I was holding fell to the floor.

Emmeline gave a small, bitter smile. 'Once word gets around that *Fabian de Carlo* got you a job with *La Carina* and you quit, no agent will take you on. Ever. You've fucked up. You've fucked everything up. My life, your life, Fabian's reputation.'

I wanted to say something, but no words came.

Emmeline climbed off the bed again, and began straightening the covers. 'I'm sorry, honey,' she said, turning so her back was facing me, 'but I can't have you staying here any more. Not after what you've done.'

Something in my stomach began to tremble. *What I'd done?* I'd stood up for better working conditions for models. I'd tried to protect a young girl from a bullying employer. 'But I haven't got anywhere to go. And I'm pregnant.'

'That's not my fault.' She placed the pillow I'd dropped at the head of the bed.

Two hot tears poured down my face. 'But you're my mother!'

'My mother threw me out when I was seventeen. Stay with a friend.'

She didn't throw you out. You walked. 'But I don't have any friends.' My voice cracked with the shame of this confession.

'Then go back to *Nanna*.'

The tears were rivers now. 'I can't go back to Andrea. You know I can't.'

'You think she'll turn you away? She wouldn't dare.'

'But—'

'Look, I don't *care* where you go, OK?' Her face was contorted with fury and grief, and she flicked a hand at the window as if telling me to jump through it. 'Just *GO!*

The world turned to ash. The person my feet carried to the guest room wasn't me. It was the ghost left behind while the rest of me broke apart and fell through the city air like splinters.

A knock at the door. 'Sadie?'

Dirk's voice. He'd never addressed me by name before. The room resurfaced. The Fendi clutch on the floor. The suede high-heeled boots, one by the door, one by the bed. The makeup smudged on my knees. I didn't know whether hours or minutes had passed.

A second knock. 'Sadie? Are you still there?'

Hatred flamed. I got up, planning to rip open the door, attack him, blame him, but it opened just as I was reaching for the handle.

Dirk's face was curiously neutral. I stood in front of him, blazing hostility, and he looked past me at my clothes, old and new, hanging in the half-open wardrobe. His gaze returned to me, cautious and cool. 'Are you leaving tonight?'

Another blaze of hatred. 'Yes. As soon as I can.' I wasn't beholden to this man any more. I could be as rude as I liked. 'I wouldn't want to live off a man so shallow he'd dump a woman for having a daughter.'

Dirk's lips thinned. 'That's what Em told you, is it?'

'She did. And if you think—'

'I have two daughters, Sadie.'

The rest of my sentence collapsed.

'They live with their mother in Hong Kong. I fly there to see them once a month.' His eyes wandered to the window, as if looking through the glass into a former life. 'Did Em see you when you were growing up?'

'She … she wrote me letters.' I tried to imagine my life with those letters and drew a total blank. 'I didn't get them, though. My grandmother hid them.'

'But she didn't check? Or visit you?'

'No.' The tears were gone now. Everything had been emptied out.

'Not even once?'

I shook my head, and Dirk's face darkened. He slid a slip of paper out of his breast pocket and took out a slim silver pen.

'So why not? You were living in the same city.' As he wrote I noticed the faintest of stripes on his left ring finger. How long had he been divorced? Had he still been married when he started seeing my mother?

'Probably because she didn't want to see Andrea. Her mother. She hates her. Thinks she's twisted and abusive.'

'I see.' He finished with a sharp, jabbing full stop. 'So she gave you to her twisted, abusive mother to bring up. And pretended she'd never had a child. Nice.'

My skin prickled. I hadn't put things so baldly to myself before.

Dirk looked up from his writing. 'What's your surname? It's not Rae.'

Emmeline had modelled as Emily Rae. 'My real name's Sage. Sage Rampion.'

He asked me to spell it, wrote something more on the slip of paper and held it out. It was a cheque for ten thousand dollars. 'To tide you over. I'll book you a hotel room while you sort yourself out. Give my name to Reception.'

I backed away, my mind full of Matti, paying off his teenage lover and going home to his wife.

'Go on, just take it.'

He tossed it on the bedside table and walked out. The zeroes on the cheque stared up at me like the eyes of a venomous spider.

I turned on the computer, googled 'removing extensions' and found a website with video instructions. I stripped off the outfit I'd worn to the shoot, wrapped myself in a towel, found tweezers in the bathroom cupboard and started pulling out the hair extensions. When the last one was out, I tied them in a disembodied ponytail, left them on the bed and went to wash my hair and remove my makeup. After my shower, I hung everything bought with Dirk's money in the wardrobe. Last of all, I took out the contact lenses, donned my glasses and went back to face the cheque.

Ten thousand dollars. With that much money and a room in this hotel, I could afford to take my time. Find a job and a place to live, track down Ryan, figure out what to do about being pregnant. Andrea and Emmeline would never know.

But I'd know.

I shouldered my bag, picked up the cheque and walked down the hall to the lounge. Dirk lowered *Business Review Monthly*, startled by my appearance, but I lifted my chin, strode over and placed his cheque on the coffee table.

'I can't accept this.' I plunked his whiskey glass on the spider eye row of zeroes.

'Don't be silly,' he said, pushing off the glass. 'What about your babies?'

He tried to give it back to me, and I stepped out of reach. 'I'll manage.'

'Look,' said Dirk, 'you're not being realistic. If you—'

'I'm not taking your money, Dirk.' I'd never addressed him by name before either.

'Why not?' He sounded genuinely bewildered.

'Because I don't want to be a kept woman like my mother.'

He hesitated for a moment, cheque still in his hand, and then replaced it carefully on the coffee table. 'Well,' he said, a bemused expression on his face, 'in that case, good luck. Let me know if you change your mind.'

'Thanks,' I said. 'I won't.'

For the last time, I walked down the hall to the door with the gold number 1 screwed in the centre. 'Bye, Dirk.'

'Bye, Sadie.'

As I left, he lifted a hand in farewell, with an expression that looked almost like respect.

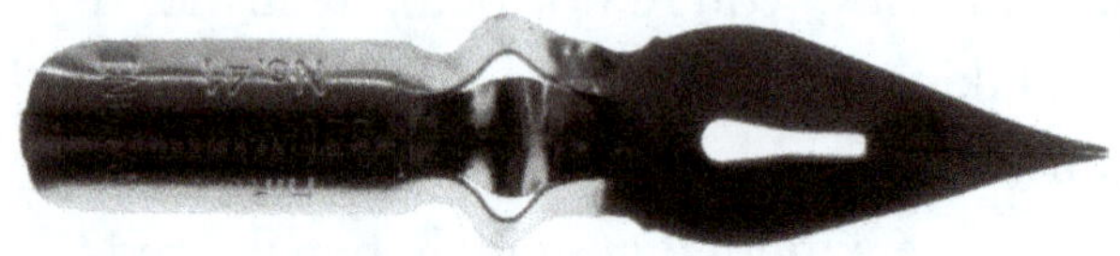

Part Three – The Wilderness

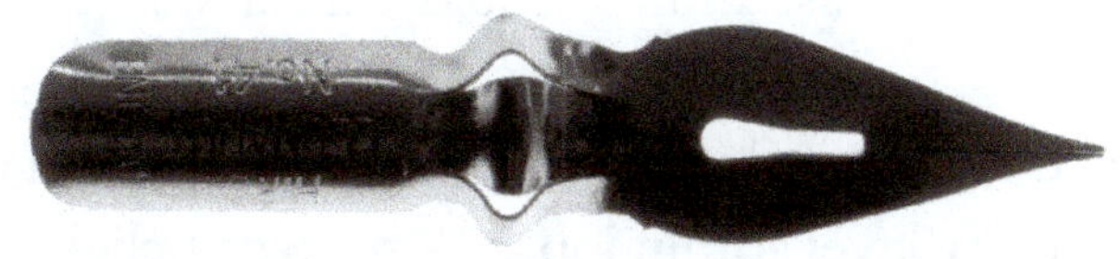

Chapter Thirty-Seven

Bag Lady

The keyboards at the internet cafe were grey with grime, and the keys felt warm, as though the fingertips that soiled them had just left. The warmth was repulsive but grounding, anchoring me to the mouse rolling under my hand and the desk chair underneath me. Inside me, everything was vacant, as if my heart and brain had been unplugged and locked away.

I googled for accommodation in the centre of town and scanned the results, sorting them by price. Backpacker hostels, hotels, Airbnb. I clicked randomly on some of the cheapest options, and windows and online forms began popping up, all demanding details I didn't have. *Email address. Mobile number. Current address. Credit card details.* A trickle of fear began in my chest. I could set up a new email account on the spot. I had enough money to buy a cheap mobile phone. But I had no fixed address, my credit card was in the wallet I'd left in Andrea's office, and by now anywhere that sold phones would be closed.

The wad of fennel-scented money was in the inside pocket of my backpack. I pulled it out and started counting. Four hundred and thirty-two dollars and a handful of change. Out of which had to come a phone and enough food and accommodation to last until I could find a way to earn some more.

I opened another tab, went to a job-hunting website and did a search for entry level admin jobs. As soon as I clicked on a link, another registration form popped up, wanting my name and contact details. The trickle of fear widened into a waterfall.

Back to the list of accommodation options. Who might accept cash? Not a hotel, not Airbnb. But a hostel might. Fingers rubbery with fear, I opened more tabs, typed in the names of the cheapest hostels, and searched their websites until I found one with what I was looking for: online chat.

Hi there! I'm Sam from City Limits Hostel. How can I help you today?

Hi Sam. Do you have any rooms free for tonight?

Sure do! For how many people?

Just me. Do you accept cash?

Yes, cash is fine. Reception closes at 11, so you'll have to hurry!

Limp with relief, I gave him my name, promised to get there soon, and logged out of chat. As I entered the hostel address into Google Maps, I realised I was being watched. Behind my left shoulder, two teenage boys with their hair in waxy spikes were exchanging low-voiced commentary. When they saw I'd noticed them, they sniggered.

'So,' said the shorter one, 'do you come here often?' His smirk stretched the pimples on his chin.

The taller one bent over in his swivel chair, shaking with voiceless laughter. My toes curled inside my shoes. Pretending I hadn't heard, I hitched my chair closer to the screen, unsettled and a bit confused by their attention. Before, I'd been invisible to men in these glasses and hand-me-down clothes. Why were these boys staring?

The shorter boy lounged against the desk beside me, and I turned my screen to block his view. He ambled to my other side and I stiffened as he draped his arm on the back of my chair. 'Looking for somewhere to stay, huh?' His breath smelled of Coke and cheap pizza. 'You're welcome to stay at my place.'

His friend doubled over again, and I jerked my chair free of his arm.

'Excuse me,' I said, stony-faced and impregnable, 'could you stop reading my screen?'

The boy widened his eyes. 'Sorry, am I hassling you?' He turned back to his friend. 'Am I hassling her?'

'No,' said his friend. 'You're offering to help her out.'

The first boy turned back to me. 'Not very grateful, are you? Where's your manners, gorgeous?'

Gorgeous. Beautiful. Now I was homeless, pregnant and desperate, the thrill had faded from these words. They felt sticky and unwholesome, like cobwebs that spread more and more when I tried to brush them off.

I pressed *Print*, shut down the browser, and strode to the printer. When my map printout emerged, I swiped it, paid at the desk, and walked straight out the door.

'Hey, where are you going?' called the boy as I yanked it shut behind me.

The streets were dry and cool, and the pavements were teeming with people. I set out for the hostel, which was about half an hour's walk away. As the blocks wore on, the crowds grew louder and drunker. A car horn honked a few feet from my ear. I jumped, and heard a volley of laughs and whistles from an old car with four youngish men hanging out the windows.

'Hey, hot stuff!' one shouted.

Head down, heart thumping, I walked faster and faster, and the car kept pace along the gutter. Andrea's voice returned to my head, reciting advice from her classes in self-defence. *Men hassle women in the streets for a reaction, to feel powerful, and score points in front of their friends. Be boring, and most will just give up.*

'Love the glasses. What's your number?'

If they persist, double back, or cross the road so they can't drive beside you. I did an about-face, ducked into the crowd and walked in the opposite direction. The car made a tire-screeching U-turn and kept pace with me on the other side of the street.

'Hey, hot stuff, where ya going?'

Never lead them straight to your destination, especially if there's no one there to meet you.

'Are you running away from us?'

I turned up a one-way street, and the car screeched away with a shout of 'Show us ya tits!'

Wobbling like a broken chair, I took refuge in a doorway. When my limbs steadied, I returned to the road and walked on, facing oncoming traffic until I came to a big T-junction. On the building opposite was a woman on a billboard, with her forearms crossed over huge, naked breasts. I checked the map and realised my hostel was in a lane off the main street that ran through the red light district.

Locking my hand around the straps of my bag, I crossed the road and turned right into a streetscape of yellow-painted windows and flashing neon signs. The names of the shops and venues were tawdrier than I remembered, and the women on the billboards had bigger breasts and lips, and more garish fake tans.

Below them, the pedestrians were almost all men, some furtive, some brash, some blasé.

More shouts and car horns floated my way, from cars and men passing in the street. Several admired my glasses and asked, 'What time's your shift?', presuming I was on my way to work. Eyes on the pavement, I walked at normal speed, and survived the first block intact.

Ten paces later, a venue called French Kiss disgorged a group of men in their thirties. Something about their belligerent, self-conscious swagger put me on guard. They lingered just ahead of me, blocking my path and exchanging sniggering commentary on the show they'd just seen. I edged past, planning to cross the road, and a hand grabbed the straps of my bag. Beads of sweat broke out on my back.

"Scuse me, princess,' said the owner of the hand, in a voice that smelled of lager and steak. He was wearing a business suit, with an off-centre tie and a gravy smudge on his right lapel. A circle of male eyes slithered over my cowering body. 'You work around here?'

'Let go of my bag.' I tried to sound firm, but the words came out in a quaver.

If someone grabs your bag, don't pull it back, they expect that. Shove it toward them, and they'll often lose their grip in surprise. If they do, snatch it back and run. If they don't, sacrifice the bag. Nothing in it is worth getting assaulted for.

'Me and my mates are looking for a good time.' He peered down my shirt, and I slammed the bag into him. Knocked off-balance, he released the bag, but another of his friends grabbed the strap. I let the bag go, dodged a lunging hand, stomped on an instep and bolted as they swore and gave chase. I steered through random laneways, dived through an open door and crashed into a woman in a shiny black dress.

'Settle down,' said the woman. She was sitting on a stool, stockinged legs crossed, jaw rotating around a wad of gum. Her hair was black and shiny too, a dyed blue-black that matched the heavy pencil round her eyes. 'Got lost, didja?' She sounded wry and knowing, as if she'd been expecting someone some time ago.

I stared at her, blood and breath pulsing behind my eyes.

The woman waved me at a chair and sauntered to a velvet-draped desk to consult a list. 'Sandi, right?'

'Sadie,' I corrected, playing for time. *Who was Sandi?*

Still listening for my pursuers, I sat. Long seconds passed. As my breathing slowed, I scanned my new surroundings. Black tiles speckled with silver. Low lights, red walls. Piles of shiny flyers that read WILD THING: OPENING NIGHT SPECIALS. A huge suited man with a number in his buttonhole and a neck the same width as his head.

'I'm Dana,' said the woman, writing something in a clipboard and checking her leopard print watch. 'So what happened, girlfriend? It's twenty to eleven.'

Her plucked brows were arched, and her voice was disapproving.

'Sorry, I was just … some men stole my bag, and I … I was …'

Dana's face changed from disapproval to outrage. 'You got *mugged?* Jesus! Have you told the cops?'

'No, not yet, I was just—'

'Watch the door for a sec, Jay.'

The huge man nodded, and she beckoned me through a door into an office that smelled of new furniture. The small sense of security this provided cleared my head.

'Jesus,' repeated Dana, shaking her head. 'Sit down. You OK?'

'I'm fine.' Except for having no home, no money, and nothing but the clothes I stood up in. With the bag had gone the last of my money and saleable goods, so I now couldn't pay for the hostel. Or even a meal to nourish me and the two tiny babies in my womb.

'Still wanna do your shift? I can put you on from eleven to three.'

Shift? A poster on the wall caught my eye. *WANTED*, it read. *Performers, bar staff and waitresses for new adult venue. Industry experience preferred but not essential. Apply in person.*

The sweat on my body turned cold. 'Actually,' I said, in an unsteady voice, 'I'm not Sandi. I'm not here to work.'

Dana's rotating jaw went still. 'Then what …'

'I was running away from the men who stole my bag, and I just … ducked in.'

Dana's plucked brows descended, and her scarlet lips tightened. 'Look, girlfriend, I'm sorry you got mugged, but this is a club, not a refuge, OK? Patrons and workers only. The cop shop's a few blocks that way.'

She pointed into the night with a long scarlet fingernail. My legs turned to putty. If I didn't leave, she'd throw me out. With no money, no home and those men still out there, angry and looking for revenge.

I groped for my voice and found a high-pitched squeak. 'What if I … took the shift?'

Dana looked at me suspiciously. 'You looking for work?'

'Yes.' Somewhere inside me, Andrea was screaming, but I fought her off with logic. *It's only for one night. I'll earn money, with security guards to protect me, and by the end it'll be four hours nearer daylight.*

'Stand up.'

I stood, and Dana appraised me. 'You've got a good look.' She licked a taloned fingertip and took out a form. 'Young, classy, nice rack. Any experience in the industry?'

The industry. The words had a sinister ring. 'Experience?'

'Stripping, pole dancing, burlesque.' Dana waved a hand, as if to indicate other things too obvious to mention.

Writing essays about pornography? I swallowed a bubble of brittle laughter. A week ago I was living in a middle-class home with my grandmother. Sharing her luxury office. Doing a PhD in Women's Studies. How could I be applying for a job in a strip club? It was ridiculous. Impossible. In a minute or ten I'd wake on the futon, and tell Ryan my dream so he'd laugh.

'I did a lingerie shoot once.' It occurred to me that the lingerie shoot had been today. *Today.* It felt like it had happened in another world.

'No performance work?'

'No.'

'Have to put you on tables, then.' She made a note.

Tables. Waitressing, presumably. Four hours of waiting on tables in a strip club. I could handle that. Although … 'Um, what do I wear? When I'm working?'

'Costumes are provided.'

Costumes. Not topless, then. Surely if it was topless she would have said so.

Dana handed me a pen and an Employee Registration Form. My first job. I remembered Andrea, sneering that Fran's irresponsible parenting would end in Freya working as a pole dancer. *Half her luck,* I thought. *All your parenting got me was a waitressing job. Pole dancers probably get more.* 'What's the pay rate?'

'Twenty-five bucks an hour for table work. Plus tips. Is that cool?'

A hundred dollars. Enough for a cheap phone and a meal or two. 'That's fine.'

I entered my name as *Sadie Rusden*, with a made-up mobile number and a random address in Ryan's suburb. At the thought of Ryan, something lumpy and painful rose up in my chest, but I managed to flatten it again.

The next item asked for my banking details. 'Um, sorry, but … I don't have my banking details on me. They were in my wallet, but …'

'Sorry, that's right, you got mugged.' Dana clicked her tongue and drummed on the desk with her scarlet nails. 'Look,' she said, 'how about I pay you in cash? Keep it quiet, though. We're not meant to.'

'Thanks.' My voice squeaked again, this time with relief.

'No problem. The changing room's the last door on the right. Get yourself a costume from the railing at the back, and I'll be down to fill everyone in.'

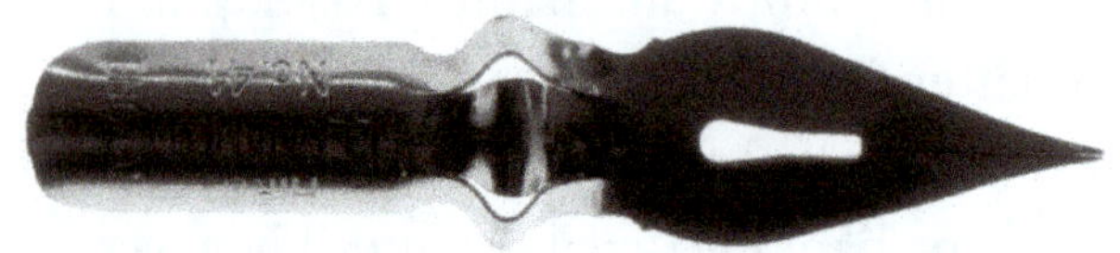

Chapter Thirty-Eight

Finger Food

The black vinyl bustiers provided by the club left a gap an inch wide above the cleavage. The criss-crossing laces that straddled this gap dug into my sore, swollen breasts. I tugged at them, conscious that *What to Wear during Pregnancy* said to avoid bras with underwires, which could press on the milk ducts, and lead to a disease called mastitis. The brochure didn't mention lace-up bondage gear.

Dana strode into the change room. 'OK girls, six minutes until you're on.'

Five other women were starting on my shift, and all but one sounded middle-class and educated. One or two had smiled and attempted to chat, but my face was too numb to respond. The others had arrived dressed in track pants and hooded tops, as baggy as my hand-me-downs from Andrea. Small wonder the honking men on the streets had been convinced I was on my way to work. Which, as it turned out, I had been.

I went to join the others by the door. Dana surveyed us, and when she got to me, her plucked brows drew together. 'No glasses on the floor.'

Suddenly my lenses seemed essential protection, like the transparent barriers in taxis designed to protect drivers from attack. 'But … but I need them.'

'You can see enough to get around, can't you?'

'Yes, but—'

'Get 'em back at the end of your shift.' She held out her hand.

I gave her my glasses and the world contracted to a puddle ten or twelve feet wide. Beyond it, the world was a soft-focus fuzz, where I felt as vulnerable as a half-blind baby bird.

Our job, explained Dana, was to mingle with the patrons and hand out complimentary finger food. 'Now for those who haven't worked in the industry before,' she went on, 'remember we're a club, *not* a licensed sex venue. Patrons can perve all they want, but they're *not allowed to touch*, OK? Most guys know, but you always get a couple of assholes. Tips go in the pockets on the sides of your hot pants, *not* down the front of them and *not* in your cleavage. If a patron tries to feel you up, back away and report them to Security. Whatever you do, don't hit 'em. Girl at a venue where I worked last year got charged with assault. And let me tell you, girls like us never win in court.'

Girls like us. Working girls. Women in adult entertainment. Ladies of the night. The floor was dropping beneath me like a lift.

Dana opened the door and music flooded in, with a drum track like the throb of an evil red heart. My own heart hammering, my toes cramped by patent stilettos, I headed down a ramp to a shadowy function room, with wine-and-gold paper on the walls. Mounted on these were electric candelabras, dimmed to a menacing glow. The new smells of sawdust and paint were receding behind a creeping tide of beer and male sweat.

The room was dotted with round, black tables, at which patrons sat on stools. In the middle was a larger, kidney-shaped table, skewered by a long, brass pole. On this, lit up by the chandelier above her, a woman was rotating like a lamb on a spit. She wore lacy red lingerie and a chunky silver watch, which she checked now and then, looking bored. In two of the chairs at her table sat two leering patrons in their fifties, balancing beer cans on their paunches.

The flesh contracted around my bones with dread as Dana led us through the room to the kitchen. The only men who studied us in detail were the pair at the pole dancer's table. Some clutched their drinks and shot self-conscious glances; others appraised us briefly with superior cool while talking to their friends.

The stilted conversations I heard between patrons were about real estate and sport, and other matters not linked to sex. The chats between patrons and waitresses could have come from an ordinary party or bar. It occurred to me that this was why many men came: for food and attention from attractive young women who'd normally snub or mock them.

We filed into the kitchen through swinging doors that shut out the club's throbbing dark. I retreated to a corner and slumped against a bench, breathing in the smell of frying meat. Three or four lungfuls of oily air later, a woman with an Irish accent addressed me.

'You OK there?'

A pale, pretty redhead was standing in front of me, ample bosom showcased by a low-cut white blouse. Behind her, on a trestle table, sat about fifteen oval platters with a range of deep-fried snacks. In the centre of these sat ramekins of sauce that made the platters look like giant, greasy eyes.

Sympathetic dimples dented the redhead's cheeks. 'First time working in one of these places?' Her accent had an Irish lilt.

I nodded. The last of my fellow waitresses banged out the door as the kitchen staff clattered and fried.

'You get used to it,' she said, in a voice that reminded me of my own, addressing Chloe at the modelling shoot. 'Any time you need a break, pop in here and catch your breath.' She winked and headed out.

Scraping together the last of my grit, I picked up a platter, shouldered through the doors, and made myself walk to a table.

'Spring roll?' I said with a rigid smile to a moon-faced man in a suit.

He cast an eye through the laces of my top, with a flick of his fat pink tongue. 'That depends,' he said, with a jowly chortle. 'Are your spring rolls better than hers?'

In the shadows on the other side of the table was another waitress carrying a platter of spring rolls. She squeezed out a weak laugh. Heat flooded my face, but before I could apologise a low buzz behind us drew attention to the kidney-shaped table. The woman in red lingerie was tucking a twenty-dollar note into her giant perspex shoe.

A worm of fascinated revulsion coiled in my gut. One of the men at her table must have paid her for a lap dance. Which presumably meant she was about to sit in his lap and 'dance' against his erection. I shuddered, but like the unheeding crowd at an accident, I couldn't make myself look away.

Back against the pole, she slid to her haunches, mesmerisingly slow, her shoulders undulating. Even the men who'd affected lazy cool fell silent and turned to watch. Her thumbs slid under her bra straps, plucked them twice and slipped them off. As they fell into the creases of her elbows, she peeled back the cups and inhaled so her nipples lurched in his face. They were large and pale, with a ring through the left one, on breasts the size and shape of half-cantaloupes.

I recoiled, but the men leant forward, as did she, jiggling and squeezing them together. Above them, her face was detached, as if her breasts were just tools of her trade. She lowered her buttocks to the table and undid her G-string, which seemed to be attached at one side. As *Nudity for twenty dollars?* flashed across my brain, she pointed her toes and slid her legs onto his shoulders one by one.

My platter hit the table with a *clunk*. Through the melting ice of shock, I watched her legs flex and kick, his head in between them like a censor's round ink blot. I briefly glimpsed her fully waxed genitals bucking in his face before I blinkered my eyes with two cupped hands and bolted for the kitchen.

I crashed through the doors and collided with someone who caught me by the wrists. For a brief, crazed moment I thought it was the man at the pole-dancing table, but the hands on my wrists were female, and the voice saying, 'Hey. Hey. *Hey!*' had an Irish accent.

The Irish barmaid steered me to a chair, where I hunched, my brain a kaleidoscope of fragments from things I'd read. *Legitimate performance art. Degrading and misogynist. Empowering and liberating. Symptom of a patriarchal society. Women's right to choose the work they want. Men buying a window of power over women. Women exercising erotic power over men. Raunch culture. Slut-shaming. #MeToo.* And behind these, the dancer's naked labia kept convulsing inside my head, in a ceaseless, grotesque parody of intimacy.

After a long time, maybe two minutes, maybe twenty, the kaleidoscope slowed and the image began to fade. I opened my eyes. The Irish barmaid's dimples had vanished, and her brow was creased with concern. 'You OK there? Maybe you should go home. Should I tell Dana you're feeling poorly?'

I swallowed and shook my head. My skin felt pinched and clammy under the black vinyl, and I could taste vomit in the back of my throat. But I had no home to go to, and I desperately needed the money.

'You sure?'

I nodded. After two failed attempts, I rose and picked up another platter of spring rolls. With a last, worried look, she held the swinging doors open. As I tottered through the door I heard a raucous laugh that turned my bones to wire. The man from the streets who'd stolen my bag had just arrived with his sleazy group of friends.

Dana was surveying the room from the ramp, like a football coach watching her team. Clutching my plate, I half-ran to her, almost losing one of my stilettos.

She frowned. 'What's up, girlfriend?'

'The men that just came in.' I hadn't run far, but my voice was breathless and wavering. 'They're the ones from the street. The ones that stole my bag.'

Dana's chewing jaws stilled. 'The ones that mugged you?'

'*Yes.*'

She squinted across the room, one scarlet fingernail tapping the railing. 'Look. You haven't got your glasses on, and if I'm ringing the cops, I need you to be sure. Can you get a bit closer, see if they've still got your bag?'

I bit my trembling lip, and her face softened.

'Don't stress, girlfriend, they won't recognise you. I'll get Mo to watch your back.' She indicated a doorway-sized man with the number fourteen pinned to his jacket, and he gave me an unsmiling nod. 'Now walk tall, OK?'

I crept toward the men, the world contracting further until all that remained was the platter of spring rolls. Before I could retreat, one beckoned me over. Turned to concrete with fear, I hobbled closer, and they started dunking spring rolls in sauce.

None of them recognised me with makeup and no glasses, but they were definitely the same men. The one with the gravy stain looked me up and down, his wet mouth open. As I turned my head from his sour, beery breath, he deliberately elbowed my platter. Spring rolls tumbled to the floor.

'Oops,' said Gravy Stain, mocking and wide-eyed. 'Better pick 'em up, princess.'

His friends chuckled, waiting for me to bend over in my too-tight hot pants.

Panicking, I looked around for Mo, and to my relief he was heading my way, arms like folded iron girders on his chest. The men withdrew a little as his unsmiling bulk arrived.

'What's happening here?' Mo's gruff, grim monotone sent a nervous ripple through the table.

Gravy Stain raised both his hands as if to protest innocence. 'She dropped stuff off her tray.' He attempted a matey half-smile.

Mo's granite face didn't move. 'Any more shit and you're out, understand?' He escorted me back to Dana, who dispatched someone to clean up the mess.

Minutes later, a shriek drew a bevy of guards to the bar. Before they closed in, I glimpsed the Irish barmaid, yanking a man's hand from her shirt.

Someone tapped my plate from behind. 'Hey,' said a male voice. 'Can you come here for a sec? My mate Jim wants to apologise.'

Hairs rose on the back of my neck. I snatched my platter out of reach and hurried off, but the footsteps followed. Two sets of footsteps. 'Hey,' said the voice again. Beer in hand, Jim of the Gravy Stain overtook me and blocked my way. A fresh film of sweat formed under my vinyl costume.

'Hi, princess,' said Jim, his wet mouth closed and mock-repentant. 'I wanted to say sorry about the spring rolls.'

'Excuse me.' Heart battering my ribs, I tried to steer around him, but his friend moved across to stop me.

I caught the eye of an unoccupied bouncer, who started sauntering over.

'Before I let you go,' continued Jim, 'I want to show you my appreciation.'

Leisurely as a leopard toying with its prey, he took out a fifty-dollar note. Eyes on mine, he rolled it into a cylinder and inched his tongue along the edge, as if sealing a roll-up cigarette. He hooked open the pocket on the side of my hot pants, and sniggered as I shrank from his touch. He thrust the rolled note in and slid it in and out, to the gleeful guffaws of his friends.

His eyes rolled back with a theatrical moan, and my brain whited out. Honed by years of self-defence, my muscles took over. I slammed my elbow into the back of his flushed neck so his head hit my knee in a bone-jarring thud.

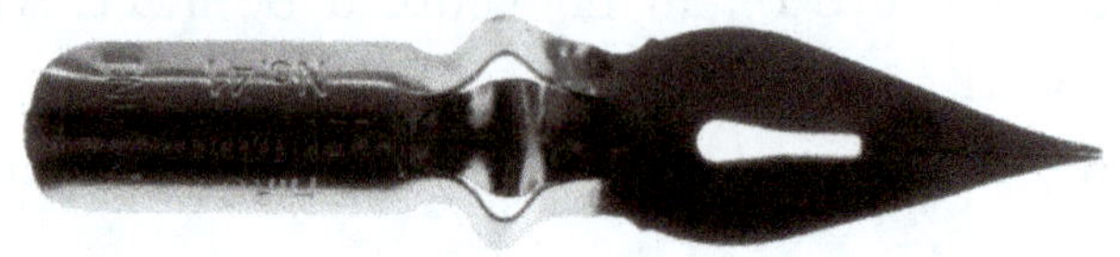

Chapter Thirty-Nine

Frequent Flyer

Jim doubled over, making strangled, staccato noises as if someone was choking him. For a few long seconds, the room went so still I could hear his beer fizzing on the floor. Then everything imploded. The bouncer charged, Jim's friend lunged at me swearing, and I kicked off my stilettos and bolted.

I reached the exit, fended off a patron with an arm twist, and dodged past the startled security guard in the foyer. Like a panicking rabbit, I pelted into the streets, skirting crowds and turning corners at random. Like a criminal on the run.

Girls like us never win.

Something tangled my legs and the pavement flew up to meet me with a shattering thud. The world turned to fireworks and then to concrete, gritty and cold against my burning skin. I lay motionless, and the pounding of my eardrums filled the sky. Time trickled back and with it came pain, first my palms and feet, then my shivering limbs, still caught in a torn plastic bag. I was in an empty laneway, where a skip half-shaded me from the glow of a single street lamp. The only other light was a convenience store sign, flashing where the lane met the street.

I sat up, and the shreds of my fishnet stockings flapped around my calves, like the lingering dregs of a nightmare. The nightmare was over, but I'd woken in a parallel universe, where I was trapped with no way home. A quiet, tearless whimpering was dribbling from my mouth. It wouldn't stop, so I ignored it and focused on retrieving the feisty new Sage from before. The one who slept with Ryan, and refused Dirk's patronage, and stood up for fashion models' rights. I searched and searched, but she seemed to have abandoned me, together with the last of my pride. And I knew that if I could, I'd take anyone's charity now. Live off Dirk, be Emmeline's proxy, bite my tongue at shoots, even go back to Andrea. But I was lost after midnight in the red light district, half-blind in a torn bondage outfit. All I could do now was hide and sit tight, hoping I survived until daybreak.

A gust of wind blew down the lane, stirring debris from an overturned bin. Apart from the odd chip packet or condom wrapper, most of the rubbish was paper. Tickets to X-rated shows, burger wrappers, and a range of glossy flyers. And among all the photos of pouting naked women was a familiar trifold flyer with green-and-purple print.

The whimpering sound stopped as if I'd turned off a tap. I jumped to my feet, chased it and swiped it from the air. The details were updated, but the layout hadn't changed in the ten years since Andrea handed one out the car window. The paper was wrinkled with a sinister yellow stain, but beneath it the numbers were still legible. The women's crisis centre Andrea had founded on a shoestring budget was based in the city. She'd made sure the centre had a toll-free number and a car to fetch women in trouble.

Clutching the flyer so tightly it cut, I hobbled down the lane to the convenience store and peered through the window. Inside, a lone young man was slouching at the counter, watching soccer on a wall-mounted television. I looked down. At my bustier, my hot pants, my torn fishnet stockings. But as I stiffened with shame, I felt a former self stirring, one who'd marched into a luxury hotel bedraggled but unbowed, brandishing a letter like a backstage pass. I squared my shoulders, raised the flyer like a sword, and strode through the door to the counter.

'Excuse me,' I said, in my best professor's voice, 'could I borrow your phone for a minute? I've been mugged, and I need to make a call.'

The man tore his eyes from the screen and looked me up and down. 'Sure,' he said, with no worse than a twitch of the lips. Working here, he'd long since seen it all. I pointed at the number on the flyer, and he dialled it and handed me his phone.

A woman picked up on the second ring. 'Bodleigh House. Is it safe for you to talk?'

A cheer from the TV seized the man's full attention.

'Yes,' I said in a low voice.

'Can I have your exact location?'

I looked hopefully at the sales assistant, but he was riveted by the screen. 'I … I'm not sure. I'm in a convenience store. In the red light district.' I gave her the name of the store, told her it was on a corner and described what I could see out the windows.

'I know the one.' The woman sounded calm and staunch. 'Is it safe to stay where you are?'

'Yes.'

'We'll send round an unmarked white car. The driver will be a plainclothes female security guard, and she'll wait in the car directly outside the door. When you see it, go out and she'll let you in.'

About ten minutes later, a white car pulled up in a No Standing zone out the front. I limped out, and a hefty, freckled woman in a polo shirt wound the window down. 'You for Bodleigh House?'

I nodded, and she let me in. A few blocks away, the driver pulled over by a nondescript building and keyed in a security code. A door clicked open, revealing a narrow flight of worn wooden steps. A strange sound rose and fell like a faltering motor. *Uh-uh-uh-uh. Uh-uh-uh-uh.*

As I climbed the stairs my footfalls sounded hollow, and the stuttering sound grew louder. The foyer at the top smelled of musty furniture, and had balding mustard carpet that felt greasy against my soles. The reception desk was like a bank counter: glassed-in, with a chute for passing small objects. There was a coffee table flanked on three sides by pea-green couches, yellow foam showing through the threadbare fabric. Blu-tacked to the fake wood-panelled walls were dog-eared posters with pictures of bruised women and children, and slogans like *No one ever asks for this.*

At first I thought their haunted faces were the room's only occupants. Then the *uh-uh-uh-uh* sound, less echoey up here, drew my eye to a photo booth-sized room off the side. Beside it, near a sign reading *Needle Exchange,* crouched two women. One was cringing like a beaten dog, clawing at her matted greying hair. The insides of her arms were marked with straight, raised scars. Sensing my white-eyed stare, she looked up. Her left eye was half-closed beneath a bruise, and her lips dangled open, forming an oozing, red-rimmed hole that grew and shrank, grew and shrank. *Uh-uh-uh-uh. Uh-uh-uh-uh.*

Goosebumps spread across my back. I looked away, not wanting to imagine what reduced her to this.

'Please don't blame yourself, Jenny,' the other woman was saying, and her voice made me look back. It reminded me of a long-ago universe, one where I was warm, and safe.

She took Jenny's hands, and Jenny wrung them as if they were a towel that wouldn't dry. From the back, all I could see was neat red hair, and a familiar small frame in olive pants. 'You're safe now,' said the red-haired woman, and this time I was sure.

Pulse thundering, I stood by the stairs until my half-naked body caught her eye. She raised her head and I found myself looking at the shrewd, oval face of Fran Mackenzie.

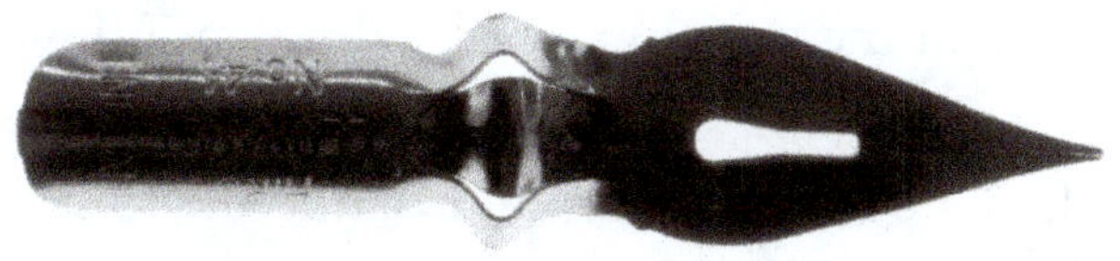

Chapter Forty

Oyster

Fran frowned, as if trying to remember something. Churning with shame and relief, I met her eyes until they widened in horrified recognition. Talking to Jenny in a reassuring murmur, she pressed a call button on the desk. The door behind us opened, letting in a low, troubled buzz of female voices. A woman stepped through, younger than Fran, with a heavy tread and a wide, suspicious mouth. She glanced from me to Jenny and then back at Fran.

'There's no rooms left,' she said. 'Not even to share.'

'Put an air mattress on the floor of the tearoom,' said Fran, with the same cool authority she used to enforce due dates for assignments. She turned back to Jenny. 'Val's here to look after you. She'll get you a cup of tea and somewhere to sleep. Are you OK to get up now?'

Jenny nodded, her good eye bloodshot and vacant. Fran helped her to her feet and guided her to Val, who ushered her away. The door closed, smothering the voices into something just short of silence.

I swayed by the couch. 'Hi, Fran.' My voice buckled.

'Sage.' Fran took in my chin-length bob and makeup, my black vinyl outfit, my blistered, bleeding feet. 'Take a seat,' she added, like I'd arrived at her office for a meeting. 'Do you want a drink?'

For the first time in hours I realised my mouth was parched. 'Yes, please.'

Fran filled a glass of water and handed it to me. Then she collected a towel, a face washer, and a cheap tracksuit covered with lint. 'The bathroom's inside, on the right. Take a shower and get changed.' She added a pair of flip-flops to my pile and pointed me at the door.

The bathroom tiles were the same dingy brown as the laminate on the coffee table. I locked myself in, drank the water and undressed. The bustier and hot pants had left furrows on my body. I scoured off the makeup and let the shower wash off the residue of lecherous male eyes. When I finally felt clean, I dressed and went back to the foyer.

'I heard from Andrea last Monday,' said Fran, who was back at the desk. 'She rang from the conference to say you'd been suspended from your PhD. I emailed you, but your account had already been shut down.'

She took out Band-Aids, cotton wool and antiseptic lotion, placed them on the coffee table and seated herself on the other couch. I unscrewed the bottle and started dabbing the wounds on my feet.

'I tried to track you down,' Fran went on, 'but I don't have your number and you weren't answering at home.'

'No,' I said, applying a Band-Aid. 'I'm not living with Andrea any more.'

Fran glanced at the lace-up bustier and hot pants beside me on the couch. 'Yes. I'd guessed that.' We exchanged a rueful smile, and she added, 'Good for you,' in a voice so warm and emphatic I sensed she meant it. Despite my arrival at a women's crisis centre. Despite the lace-up bustier.

'I would have kept looking,' Fran said, 'but it's been a hectic week. Someone broke into the building last Friday. Vandalised Andrea's office, tried to hack into her computer.'

I adjusted my Band-Aid with great concentration. 'Um, yeah, I … heard about that.'

'So,' said Fran, getting me another glass of water, 'what's been happening with you?'

Her face was a cool, pale oval, like a mirror. I extracted a second Band-Aid, wondering where to begin. 'It's quite a long story,' I said at last.

'Well,' she said, glancing at the clock, 'you've got an hour and a half. My shift ends at three.'

I took a bracing sip of water, and began. Meeting Ryan. Finding out about Emmeline's letters. Having sex on Andrea's desk. The police station, the taxi. My week in the penthouse with Emmeline. My short-lived stint as a waitress in a strip club. Fran listened without interrupting as the story poured out, barely a ripple on her cool mirror face.

'Quite a week,' she said when I'd finished.

'Yes.'

'So you're pregnant. Have you looked at your options?'

A spasm went through my womb. In the frenzy of the last few hours I'd managed to forget that I had a serious decision to make. 'A bit.'

'And?'

'I think I want to keep them. But I need to find Ryan first. Before I make a final decision.'

The thought of Ryan rose up like a mountain, making everything fracture and shift. I bit my lip.

'The university might give us his parents' address. We can check.' A teaspoon of warmth swirled through me at the word *we*. 'What do you want to do in the meantime?'

The warmth dissolved into a despair so crushing I could barely breathe. 'I don't know.' I sank my forehead into my palms. 'It feels like I've ruined everything.'

Fran leant across the coffee table and took my hands in hers, in the same way that she'd taken Jenny's. 'You're more resilient than you think, Sage.'

I closed my eyes, clinging to her hands and words as if they were all I had left.

'And besides,' said Fran, ironic and wry, 'you weren't that devoted to your PhD, were you?'

I smiled, between anguish and laughter. 'No. Not really.'

'I could talk to the board for you. Say you were unfairly dismissed, make a case. But to be honest,' she said, 'you'd be better off finding a career you're more passionate about. As for a place to live, let me make a quick call to Freya.' She squeezed my hands, released them and picked up the office phone.

My eyes widened. 'But it's the middle of the night!'

Fran shrugged, starting to dial. 'Freya and Brett aren't usually in bed until past one. They'll cope.'

She sat in the desk chair, a faint *brr-brr* coming from the receiver. Someone picked up. 'Hey, Frey,' said Fran. 'Were you asleep? Oh, good. Listen, we've got a crisis here, and I was hoping you could help.'

Her voice was relaxed and natural, speaking with an intimacy that clenched my guts like a fist. Fran didn't gush or use terms of endearment, but I could feel the love and trust between her and her daughter. I turned my face to the wall, unable to listen, the layers of dressings on my long-open wound peeling away.

Fran put down the phone. 'I'll book you an Uber to Freya's place,' she said. 'She lives with her partner Brett these days, up in the mountains. They've been looking for a housemate for ages.' She started writing something on a small scrap of paper. 'You can stay as long as you want. She said you can do her housework until you find a job.'

I tried to muster a smile. 'Thanks so much, Fran.'

'My pleasure. Freya always liked you.'

Surprise made the grief retreat a little. 'Freya liked me?' The fifteen-year-old Freya I remembered was feisty and tough, the sort of person who'd look down on someone as meek as me.

'She did. She missed you after the falling-out with Andrea.'

Missed me? Andrea's version of Fran flooded my memory. The irresponsible mother whose daughter would end up working in a strip club.

'What happened with Andrea?' I said, curious to hear Fran's point of view.

She handed me Freya's address and numbers. 'Andrea's a 1970s feminist warrior,' she said. 'Angry, principled, bitingly clever. She wanted to bring you up completely cut off from sexist influences. No imposed beauty ideals, no gender stereotypes, no fairy tales where marriage means happily ever after.'

My childhood flashed past like an empty train. No television, no shopping, no stories she hadn't vetted for sexist content. At the time this hadn't bothered me. But back when I met Jess I realised I'd missed out on a world other people took for granted. A world I fled, because my upbringing made me feel like a loser and a freak. Until Ryan made me believe I could face that world again. Until he made me feel like someone who mattered. I tried to push Ryan from my mind again, but the grief had grown too vast to shift. Tears gathered inside me, rows and rows of them filling me like pearls.

'As you grew older,' Fran said, 'Andrea and I disagreed more and more. I taught Freya about feminism, but I sent her to a normal school and let her do normal things: date boys, watch TV, make her own choices. Andrea thought I was mad. I told her the battlefield had changed since the seventies, that being out of touch with the world makes it hard for you to change it.'

I'd heard some of this from Andrea, repeating Fran's words with a sarcasm so scathing it carried me with it.

'She called me a deluded traitor and cut me off. At the time I was furious, but I realise now it was fear. She couldn't bear the thought of you turning out like Emmeline.'

Pain welled again, like hot liquid poison trickling down the walls of my stomach. In the blank space between them, Emmeline's hand flicked at the window, as if to say I might as well jump through. I curled into a ball, trying to blot the image out.

Fran's arm circled my shoulders. 'Should I say something to Andrea? I won't tell her where you are, but she'll want to know that you're OK.'

'Will she?' The words came out broken.

'Yes.' She touched my hair, just briefly, and memories of Ryan flared. 'Andrea's trained herself to be tough and cold, but in her own way she loves you very much. You're about the only person left she does love.'

What about Emmeline? Does she love Emmeline? Does Emmeline love me? Does Ryan? The questions poured through my head like acid, but my heart didn't want to know. The pearls were everywhere now, pressing against my lungs and gut and throat. If I opened my mouth, they'd gush out in a humiliating flood.

Fran took out her phone and the spell broke, pushing the pearls to where I could hold them for just a little longer.

'I've booked the Uber,' said Fran, rising to her feet. 'Let's head down.'

She guided me down the echoing steps to where the car was waiting. She spoke briefly to the driver, and then turned back to me.

'Will you be OK?' she said, and I wondered if I would be.

'I think so.'

She opened the rear door, and I climbed in, wanting to say more. How grateful I was. How I wished I'd thought of calling her when everything fell apart. How jealous I was of Freya, for having her as a mother. But I couldn't say those things. It was easier to ask her something that didn't really count. 'Where did you meet Andrea?'

Fran handed me a Post-It note with Freya's number on it. 'At this refuge, actually. About fifteen years ago. She founded it.'

I closed the door and wound down the window. 'So you met when you worked here together?'

Fran said nothing for a long time. Then she shook her head. 'That was a few years later.' A shadow crossed her face and she looked away, filling me with questions I couldn't ask. When she looked back, her face was impenetrable once more. 'You OK to go?'

I nodded. 'Thanks Fran. Take care.'

We said our goodbyes and the Uber pulled away and left her standing, small and pale, beside the grey refuge door.

'There's a bottle of water in the console,' said the Uber driver, turning right onto the freeway. 'Do you need anything else?'

I shook my head. By the time I realised he couldn't see me, it was too late to say anything. Still, thanks to Fran, I did have what I needed, at least on some levels. I had a place to stay, which meant I could find a job, look for Ryan, plan for my babies. I could relax. I was safe. My future was restored. Yet somehow, now that everything was going to be all right, everything that was wrong was suddenly far too much to bear.

Something dislodged inside me, and the loss and grief of the last week came crashing down, forcing out the tears in deep, gouging sobs. Unable to contain them, I curled up on the back seat and cried, fitting my finger into the dimple in my lip.

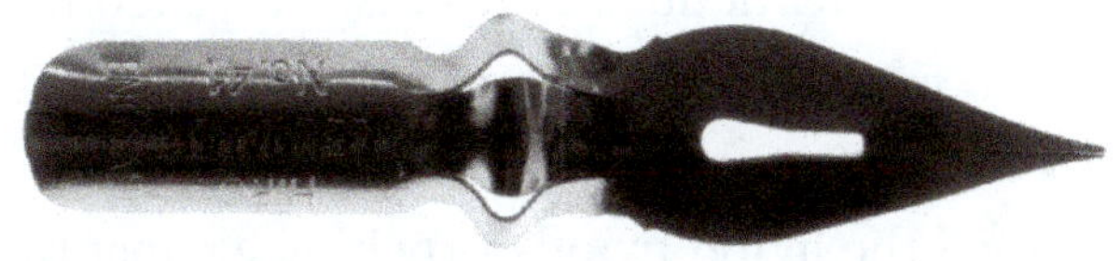

Chapter Forty-One

Thin Air

The Uber purred off, leaving me in Freya's front garden. The fresh, biting air smelled of moss and wet wood. A trail of cobblestones wound among ferns and trees to a lamp lit on the porch. Empty and dry as a long-dead moth, I headed for the light.

A bungalow emerged piece by piece through the garden, made from the same stones as the path. An old-style lantern hung from a bracket by the front door, beside a brass bell that made a deep and resonant *dongggg* when I rang it. Through a yellow glass panel I saw a light go on, and then the approaching shape of Freya.

At ten, Freya overtook Fran in height, and kept on growing, developing heavy breasts and broad hips and shoulders. Her hair was Fran's colour, and when I'd last seen her it was shoulder-length and straightened with tongs. Now it was wavy, and so long and thick it looked like a big auburn rug. Her face was rounder than her mother's, but she had the same unhurried gait and shrewd, composed eyes.

'Hi, Sage.' Her voice was matter-of-fact, as if I'd come to borrow a book. 'Come in.'

I stepped onto a colourful rug on a floor tiled in slate. To my right, through an arch, was a cosy living room with a piano and shelves filled with ornaments and books. Freya led me further to a large bedroom with a built-in wardrobe and a creamy sheepskin rug. The duvet on the queen-sized bed was printed with green ferns that echoed the living fronds brushing against the windows.

'I hung some clothes in the wardrobe,' said Freya. 'Too small for me, too big for you, but they'll do for a week or two. Brett can give you some shifts at the café until you find a job.'

I laid my flip-flops at the foot of the bed. On one of the two red pillows sat a toothbrush still in its wrapper and a folded pair of flannel pyjamas. 'Café?'

'Brett owns a gallery café called Molehill. I teach drawing in the studio upstairs and we exhibit the work of local artists in the café.'

I imagined myself living here among the ferns with Freya and Brett. Doing housework, waiting on tables in a gallery café, looking for a more stable job. For the first time in weeks, the muscles slackened round my bones, like elastic stretched too far.

'The bathroom's just next door,' said Freya, glancing at the clock. 'Anything else you need?'

I realised with a start that I was keeping Freya up. 'Sorry, Freya. This is great. There's nothing else I need. Thanks so much for putting me up.'

Freya smiled. 'Not a problem. Great to have you here. Good night, Sage.'

'Good night.'

She left for her room. I turned off the light, and slid beneath the covers fully dressed. Cradling a pillow against my unborn children, I fell into a deep, dreamless sleep.

When I woke, mid-morning, a sun shower was making the fronds by my window bob and dance. Inside me, all was quiet, as if a storm had passed. I waded to the wardrobe across the sheepskin rug, and chose a dress made from violet crushed velvet which was probably knee-length on Freya. On me it hung like an oversized smock, and swirled around my calves like a soft purple ocean.

Down the hallway, sunlight streamed into the kitchen through red-and-white checked curtains. Terracotta herb pots lined the windowsill, giving a fresh, leafy scent to the air. The table was made from pale, knobbled driftwood, and on it, propped on the fruit bowl, was a key and a note saying *Help yourself to breakfast*. At the bottom was Freya's mobile number and a hand-drawn map showing the route to Brett's gallery café.

I helped myself to juice and a bowl of organic muesli, and then rang Ryan's phone to leave him one last message. I wanted to say I had important news, and if he didn't want to talk to me, he could contact Dr Fran Mackenzie. His phone rang on and on without switching to voicemail, and eventually the line disconnected. I hung up, with a click that felt like breaking a bridge. For a few long minutes I sat and stared at a knot in the tabletop. Then I limped back to bed and pulled the fern-printed covers over my head.

The next time I woke, the rain had stopped, and drops clung to the ferns like crystal beads. I put on some tights, donned a much-too-big jacket, and stuffed toilet paper into Freya's shoes until they fit.

Outside, chill, bright air sparkled in my lungs. The tree ferns looked like lacy green parasols, and a bird was singing what sounded like a single note, repeated on a flute. I followed the cobblestones, feeling empty but clean, as if the rain had rinsed everything away.

The café was about fifteen minutes' walk from the house, down a path like a ribbon of bare earth beside the road. My healing feet began to hurt again, but it was a bearable, tingling hurt that lessened as I walked. The path ended at a much wider country road, with a strip of little shops.

Molehill stood two storeys high between a nursery and a secondhand bookshop. From a pole above the entrance, a square wooden sign swung gently. On it was a mole with a paintbrush in one paw, standing on a stylised green hill.

Inside, the walls were exposed stone, with a fireplace at one end and windows that opened onto forest. One side was lined with benches, currently half-full of customers reading or talking over coffee and cake. The other side had couches, sculptures on pedestals, and racks of bright clothing. On the walls were a mixture of framed art and shelves, on which sat pottery, glassware and books, with titles like *Nurturing your Organic Garden* and *Reiki for your Animal Companion*.

I was thumbing through *Painless Childbirth: A Guide for the Goddess Within* when a thin, loose-limbed man in a mole-printed apron approached me. 'Are you Sage?' When I looked surprised, he added, 'I recognised Freya's dress. Hand-made by Karen, one of our local dressmakers. I'm Brett, by the way.'

He held out a hand and I shook it, touched by the way he'd said 'our' local dressmaker, as if mountain folk were all a big family. He looked older than Freya, maybe late thirties. His hair was in a ponytail, and he wore loose cotton pants and an unbleached kurta with yin-yang symbols embroidered around the neckline.

'I was just about to have a chai,' he said. 'Want to join?'

'Sure. Thanks.'

Brett settled me at a bench and brought out a teapot and two cups. He sat opposite me, his posture upright yet relaxed.

I sipped my spicy drink, conscious of how much I owed Brett. Opening his house to a stranger, offering her a job, giving her free chai. 'Let me know when you want me to start work,' I said.

'Here, you mean? No rush.' He waved at the tables, as if to say they mostly looked after themselves. 'Take it easy for a week or two. Do some tai chi. I run a class upstairs on Mondays, and you're welcome to come.' He waved his other hand at a spiral staircase. At its foot was another wooden sign, with a mole holding an arrow that read *Studio*.

I glanced around the room. 'Is all this art done upstairs?'

'Some of it. The life drawings are.' He checked the clock. 'Freya's running a life drawing class there now, actually.'

My heart gave an enormous thump. Ryan had once mentioned modelling in the mountains. Might he be up there now, wearing his robe, spreading his scarlet blanket on the floor? 'Do you think Freya would mind if I went to her class?'

'Not at all. Do you draw?'

I hesitated. 'A bit.' I gulped my chai. 'Thanks for the tea. And … everything.'

'My pleasure.'

I ran up the stairs to a bright, airy studio. One corner was filled with equipment—pottery wheels, jars of brushes, paint-spattered easels—and the other had a pinboard covered with flyers that flickered in the breeze from the heater. The artists were arranged around a white wooden stool that held a bowl containing grapes and two red apples.

Freya looked up. 'Sage,' she said. 'Welcome. Get yourself an easel.'

'Brett said this was a life drawing class,' I said, deflated.

'It is.' She set a timer with an irritated click. 'The model hasn't shown yet, so we're doing still life and hoping she turns up.'

She. My heart dropped another notch. 'When was she meant to be here?'

'Half an hour ago.' Her voice was disgusted but resigned, as if this had happened before. 'If she's not here in the next five minutes I'm cancelling the class.'

I picked up an easel and joined the circle. My fellow artists ranged from late teens to late seventies, and their faces looked focused and calm.

The timer beeped. 'OK everyone,' announced Freya, 'looks like she's not coming. Let's just pack up.'

They started packing up, with discontented murmurs that made me wish there was a way to help them out. My mouth sprang open of its own accord. 'Would you like me to model for the class?'

The room went still. Heads swivelled from me to Freya, whose brows had risen to her hairline.

'I've done life drawing,' I said, my words stumbling over each other, 'and if you'd like me to, I think I can do it.'

Freya's brows descended, and her eyes turned cautious. 'Are you sure? I thought you'd probably had enough of …' She paused delicately. '… that kind of thing.'

That kind of thing. Exposing my body to strangers? Being looked at while naked, or half-naked? I thought about my brief stint at Wild Thing dressed in the black vinyl bustier. And my job with La Carina in hot pink lingerie, shivering in front of Owen and Peter. Or even my walk through the city at night, plagued by whistles, lewd comments and car horns.

I looked around the studio. Classical music was playing, and an urn was simmering on a table by the door. Beside it were two platters, one with scones and cupcakes, the other with crackers, fruit and cheese. Next to the podium, warm air poured from a heater, riffling the hair of fourteen artists. Five were men—two young and dressed like Brett, one middle-aged, and two older, one with a jaunty fisherman's cap, and one with a Santa Claus beard. All fourteen artists were looking me up and down, but not in a way that made me uncomfortable. The model was off-limits, and they all knew to mute signs of sexual appreciation.

'I'm sure,' I said finally. 'Whereabouts do I change?'

Freya indicated an area fenced off by bamboo screens. Minutes later, I slipped out and sat on the podium, naked under Freya's purple dress.

'Four five-minute poses,' said Freya, setting her timer.

I pulled off the dress, and sat on the stool, cupping the fruit bowl and twisting a little to the left. The breeze from the heater made the hair on my neck tickle, but I breathed deep and managed to stay still.

'Lovely!' said a fiftyish woman in a smock, picking up a smeary box of pastels.

When the tea break began, she offered to fetch me a scone and a cup of tea. At the end of the class, three more artists came up and invited me to model for their classes.

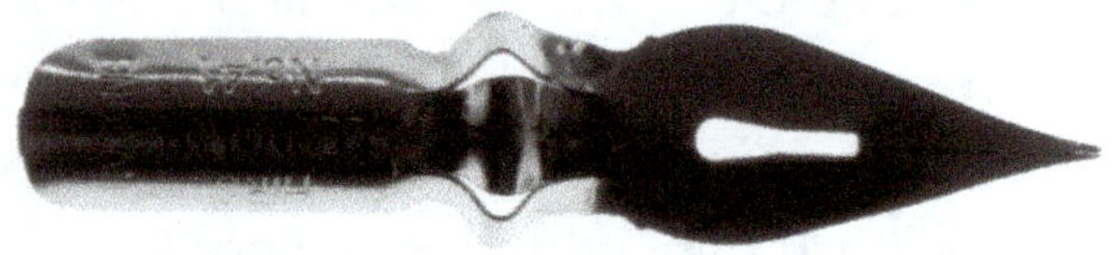

Chapter Forty-Two

Watershed

The beige bricks of the community centre provided little insulation from the heat. A ceiling fan blew heavy, humid air among the artists, their faces smudged with charcoal where they'd swabbed their sweaty brows. My left foot was sliding on a stack of ancient phone directories, and the piano stool beneath me felt damp. One of my hands sat beside me on the stool; the other was curved around my belly, now swollen like a giant egg and resting on my thighs. From time to time I felt rubbery prods and wriggles from the two tiny bodies inside.

My lower back had long since started to ache. I shifted a bit to ease it, glancing longingly at the turquoise robe waiting nearby. The robe was the latest of my small but growing wardrobe, bought mostly from markets and Molehill. On it sat the plain blue glasses I'd chosen from the range of bargain frames at the optometrist. My hair, lush and glossy from pregnancy hormones, now fell to below my shoulders, but I'd pinned it up, because artists liked to draw the place where my head met my neck.

'How are you going, darling?' said Marianne, the teacher, earnest and willowy in her kimono-style dress. 'Let me know if you need a break, OK?'

'OK.'

Artists loved a pregnant life model. Since my bump started showing, I'd been offered so much modelling that I barely had to work in the café. Several teachers were hiring me on a monthly basis, to document the swell of my stomach. I now knew all the buses that wound through the mountains, and had started to learn how to drive.

Living with Freya and Brett made me feel as though I'd been transported to a different world. I woke every morning to birdsong and ferns, and ate the vegetables they grew in their back garden. In the daytime, I served soup and cakes to patrons at Molehill, or sat naked among artists, listening to paintbrushes tinkling into jars half-full of water.

Fran came to lunch every Sunday. For the first three Sundays she didn't mention Andrea, and I didn't ask. On the fourth Sunday she brought the university newsletter, which said that the Head of Women's Studies was laying charges against a male student who'd hacked her computer and vandalised her office. The suspect was thought to have seduced her granddaughter to pursue a personal vendetta.

I fumed, but the thought of confronting her in my condition was far too much to face. Instead, I told Fran to tell her I intended to do all I could to clear Ryan's name. Fran agreed, but warned me it could be two years before the case went to trial.

Ryan's number no longer rang when I dialled it. His department said he'd been expelled for misconduct, and they weren't allowed to issue contact details. I left a terse message for Shell and searched for mentions of him online, but as weeks turned to months he receded into myth. The only connections now between my world and his were curved lines of charcoal and the two squirming babies in my womb.

The timer beeped to mark the end of my twenty-minute pose. A couple of artists exhaled, as if they'd been holding their breath.

'Just beautiful, sweetie,' said a sixtyish woman with square, spotted hands. 'It's really special, drawing a pregnant model. How far gone are you?'

I'd been answering this question daily for about five months now. 'Eight months. But it's twins, so I look really huge.'

She unclipped her drawings and rolled them up. 'Boys? Girls? One of each?'

'I didn't find out. But I'll know soon. My caesarean's scheduled for next week.'

Her benevolent smile flattened with disapproval. 'Why a caesarean? Too posh to push?'

I put on my robe with an irritated sigh. My pregnant belly was a magnet for unwanted opinions and advice. 'Because it's twins, and one of them's breech.' In my last ultrasound, the babies had been lying head to toe, like the yin-yangs on Brett's favourite kurta.

The woman took a breath, preparing to mount her soapbox. 'You can birth a breech baby naturally, sweetie.'

As she launched into a diatribe on medical intervention in childbirth, something tightened below my popped-out navel, like the stretch of a thick rubber band. The feeling lasted for about twenty seconds and then dwindled away. Just a Braxton-Hicks contraction. I'd been having them for a few weeks now.

I nodded wisely and made my escape, pretending to look at the drawings. After eight or nine easels, I felt another contraction, strong enough to make me stop and catch my breath. The nearest artist brightened, assuming I'd stopped to look at his work. He was also sixty-something, with an eager face and a fringe around his domed pink scalp.

'Some really *great* poses from you today.' He peeled back the pages to show me his drawings. 'I reckon you've *doubled* in size since I drew you a few months ago. Take a look!'

He leafed through his sketches of models past. A cello-shaped woman reclining with a rose as if in a Rubens painting. A bearded old man with knobbly limbs and a spherical pot belly. A muscular woman with piercings and tattoos. A lean young man with a fountain of dark, springy hair.

My heart slammed into my rib cage. 'Hang on!' I said, but he'd already turned to a woman with braids pinned to her head.

'*Here* you are!' He beamed and tapped a drawing of me at four months pregnant. 'See how much you've grown since then?'

I almost snatched the book from his hands. 'Sorry,' I said, trying not to sound as frantic as I felt, 'can you turn forward a few pages? Please? I thought I saw … someone I know.'

He flipped back the way he came and my hand shot out and pinned the book open. Ryan looked thinner, and his hair was limper than I remembered, but it was definitely him.

'Oh, *that* guy. Bit of a misery guts, but he was a great model. I was going to hire him for the sculpture class I run at the community college.'

As he babbled on and on about his sculpture class, the tightening below my navel began again. At its peak it was strong enough to flush my cheeks and make me bend in the middle.

The man's enthusiasm stalled. 'Are you all right?'

'Yes, fine,' I said, in a breathless voice. 'Just a Braxton-Hicks contraction. False labour. About that model. Did you get his number? Because—'

'Are you sure it's false?'

'*Yes.* Look, I need to get hold of that man. Urgently.'

'Oh.' He tapped his chin thoughtfully. 'I was going to hire him, so I probably did take down his number. What's his name?'

'Ryan. Ryan Prince.'

As the man rootled in his satchel, the sixtyish woman bustled up. 'Did you say you're having contractions, sweetie?'

'Yes, but—'

'See?' She gave me a wide, indulgent smile, as if she'd won the argument. 'Your babies want to be born naturally. They can sense that scalpel coming, so they've decided to come early.'

The man finally emerged with an address book. 'What was his surname again?'

'Prince.'

'Hmmm.' He licked his finger and turned back through the book toward P, one frustrating page at a time.

The woman had taken out her phone. 'What's your husband's number? I'll tell him to come straightaway.'

'I'm not married.' My palms itched with the desire to snatch the address book and scour every page for Ryan's number.

'Your partner then. Come on, sweetie, you don't want to go through labour alone.'

'Hang on!' cried the man, tossing his address book aside. 'That was the class I did at Blind Creek! I didn't have my address book, so I wrote his number in my sketch book.' He flipped through the drawings of Ryan. 'Here it is! I'll copy it down for you.'

A fourth contraction, so powerful that when it ended I found myself folded in half and clinging to the easel. The entire class was open-mouthed and bubbling with anxious questions. *Do we take her to hospital? When's she due? Should we call a doctor?*

'Can I have the timer, Marianne?' The sixtyish woman again, speaking as if she was now in charge. 'I need to measure the time between her contractions.'

The timer went off. 'I'll get the number from you after class,' I said firmly to the man, waddling back to the stage. Pieces of masking tape had been stuck on the piano stool to help me reproduce my earlier pose.

Marianne caught my elbow, shaking her head. 'I can't let you keep on modelling, darling. Not if you're in labour. It's a safety issue.'

'But I'm *not in real labour*.' As I said the word *labour*, a pop in my loins sent a warm gush of fluid down my thighs. My heartbeats blurred into a deafening roar as a puddle grew beneath me. Clutching my belly as if it were bursting, I lumbered at speed toward the changing area.

Safe behind the curtain, I braced against the wall until the next contraction struck. When it ended, I put on my robe and grabbed my phone: a cheap, no-frills handset in a pleasant sage green.

'Hi, Freya.' My voice wavered under the weight of my news. 'I'm having contractions, and my waters just broke.' Freya had agreed to be my birth partner.

'I'll grab your hospital bag and be there in ten,' said Freya, and hung up.

The sixtyish woman pulled open the curtain. 'Come on, sweetie.' She seized my elbow. 'I'm taking you to hospital. Do you have a doula?'

I stared about wildly for the man with the sketchbook. He was zipping his portfolio folder. 'Have you got that number?' I called, an edge of hysteria in my voice.

'I figured you had more important things on your mind,' he said, with a maddening wink at my belly.

'*Wait!*' I shouted, but he headed for the door, with a wave and a call of 'Good luck!'

'Come on, sweetie,' repeated the sixtyish woman, bending to gather my things. 'You're having a baby. *Two* babies. It can wait.'

'No, it *can't* wait.' My voice started shaking. 'The man in that drawing's the *father of my children.*'

'And he left you when you were pregnant?' The woman sounded appalled.

'*No*, he …' Another contraction, so painful that I doubled over again, barely able to breathe. When I opened my eyes, the man was gone and Freya was standing in the doorway. She took in the situation, and shooed away the woman away with the cool authority she'd inherited from Fran.

'Ready to go?' she said. When I nodded, she picked up my bag and helped me to the door.

The man with Ryan's number was in the carpark, putting his folio in the boot. I clutched at Freya's arm and pointed. 'Freya,' I said, in low, urgent tones, 'that man has Ryan's phone number. We need to get it. Now. Before he leaves.'

'And you need an emergency C-section. I'll see to it later.'

Pain flooded me, not a contraction, but something deeper that I felt in every cell. 'Please, Freya. *Please.*'

Freya took out her mobile phone, photographed his numberplate, and unlocked the doors of her car. 'I'll find him, Sage. I promise. Now for God's sake, *get in the car.*'
She half-lifted me into the back seat, looped the seatbelt around my huge belly, and jumped into the driver's seat. I dug in my nails and gritted my teeth as the next contraction juddered through my body like a jackhammer.

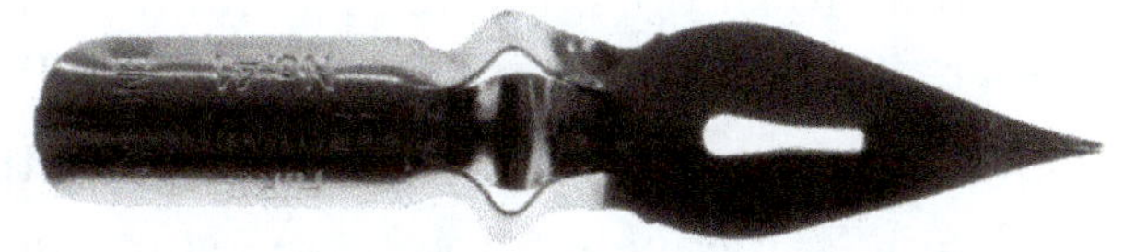

Chapter Forty-Three

Second Sight

The rattle of a trolley pierced my half-conscious brain. My sticky eyelids lifted. Everything in the room looked unnaturally sharp and bright, and a large rubber triangle was dangling over my bed. With effort, I deduced it was an aid to help patients who'd had stomach surgery pull themselves up.

'Sage?'

A female voice, kind but strident enough to rouse the dozy and drugged. Her face was apple-cheeked and rosy above her nurse's uniform, and she smelled of antiseptic and fresh linen. The photo ID around her neck on a lanyard read 'Marjorie'.

'How are you feeling?' she asked.

My throat produced a dry, wordless croak, and Marjorie nodded as if I'd said something insightful.

'The twins are doing really well. Your little girl's already out of the humidicrib, and your little boy should be out by this afternoon. Have you thought about names?'

Before they were out, my twins had never felt real enough for names. I shook my head and closed my eyes, reliving the surreal and wonderful moment when the obstetrician laid their wriggling bodies in the crooks of my arms. Longing for them filled me, and I tried to sit up, but it felt like lifting a building.

'Just lie back, dear. There's no hurry.' She angled up my bed with a foot pedal. 'Now,' said Marjorie, easing a tetra-pack of juice into my hand, 'someone's come to see you, but don't feel obliged. If you're not feeling up to it, I'll send him away.'

Him? Something burst in my chest, and memories of Ryan poured in. Comforting me. Dancing in a blindfold. Picking out my frames. Curled up and clutching his face on the floor before being wheeled away to hospital. All because of me.

Was it Ryan? Did Freya find him? Had he cared enough to come? I gripped the sheets beneath me for half a minute of silent uproar, then released them and crashed back to earth. Brett hadn't visited yet. It was probably Brett. Yet there was still a slight tremor in my voice as I asked her for his name.

'Ryan Prince.'

'Ryan?' I seized the rubber triangle and wrenched myself up with a crippling twang of pain.

With a firm, professional hand, Marjorie detached me from the triangle and lowered me back to the bed.

Anger took over as newer, darker memories bubbled up. Leaving voicemails, sending emails. Calling the hospital and the police. Trying to find out where Ryan had gone from the infuriating Shell. Getting bitched about at that party, then thrown out by Emmeline, being sexually harassed and fleeing that dreadful strip club. All that, while I was worried about how he was, and terrified he'd dumped me. And had just found out I was pregnant with his twins.

The events of that week brewed inside me, like a volcano about to erupt. Did he think that now the twins were born, he could saunter back into my life? Mouth some cheap apology, see his children and walk out? Let him try. I'd set him straight about the monstrous thing he'd done.

Marjorie was watching me with a cautious, questioning look. 'So,' she said carefully, 'would you like to see him?'

Would I? I forced the rage down to a simmer and weighed up the pros and cons.

If I said no, I'd be making a statement about what I thought of his desertion. Back when I was panicking and looking for him, he didn't even respond to my calls. How dare he turn up now the babies were born and expect a hero's welcome?

But refusing to see him could also mean my twins would never know their father. And I'd never learn why he vanished so completely after the night in Andrea's office.

If I said yes, on the other hand, what could happen? I'd be backing down and giving him a chance to say his piece. At worst, he might mumble some self-serving platitude and desert me one more time.

And at best? Unbidden, his soft expression when I was on Andrea's desk floated to the surface. The memory lodged inside me like a tiny, aching kernel, daring me to hang on to hope.

I shifted my focus to the twins. Whether or not Ryan wanted to be part of their lives, raising two babies was expensive. If he fled, I'd get a paternity test and force him to help support our children. If they had to grow up without a father, then at least they could do it with a bit more money.

But maybe, just maybe, Ryan was here to tell me he wanted in.

'Yes.' The word rang through my core like a bell. 'I do want to see him. Let him in.'

Marjorie studied me for a long, careful moment, then opened the door just a little to talk to Ryan while keeping him out of sight. 'Bear in mind she had surgery yesterday,' she said. She turned to me. 'Don't over-tire yourself. If you need me, I'll be just outside.'

She pushed the door further open and told Ryan to come in.

I'd intended to meet his eyes, stony faced, reserving judgment. But the sight of the man who shuffled in, eyes down, was like an icy slap across the face. Ryan was bright-eyed and vibrant. He had energy and zest, with his springy hair and screen-printed T-shirts. This man was pallid and broken, and his eyes were clouded and hollow. Even his signature fountain of hair drooped lifeless from his scalp. It was someone had reached inside the Ryan I knew and switched out all the lights.

Something nameless made of horror and compassion welled up, and I suddenly longed to hold and soothe him.

He shut the door behind him and looked at me as if afraid of what he might see. 'Hey, Sage,' he said, in an unsteady voice, with a weak imitation of his grin.

A spark of anger lit again at this inadequate greeting. *Hey, Sage.* Was that all he had, after dumping me and leaving me homeless while I was carrying his babies?

'*Hey*,' I said, my tone so sarcastic that he dropped his gaze back to the floor. I pointed at the chair beside my bed. 'Sit down.'

He perched on the edge of the chair, arms folded as though he was feeling cold. His face had shrunk around his cheekbones; his T-shirt was plain black, and hung like his shoulders were a coathanger.

'How much has Freya told you?'

'Not much,' he said. 'Just where you were, and that you'd just given birth to twins. Our twins.'

Our twins. At least that meant I could probably skip the paternity tests. My anger receded. What could have happened in just six months to put him in this state?

'I tried to get hold of you,' I said, pointed but more gentle. 'I left voicemails, I sent emails, I went to your house. What happened? Why didn't you get back to me?'

He lifted his hollow face. 'Because the police confiscated my phone.'

'*What?*' I tried to process this news, my mind reeling. 'Why did they do that?'

He gave a tight, bitter smile. 'To search for evidence. About our relationship, about what we'd been planning, to find out more about the keylogger. They never returned it, and in the end I just got myself a new phone, with a new number.'

The last of my anger burned a trail through me and died. All the voicemails I left him. All the photos Emmeline texted. And not one of them got through. Or they *had* got through, to whoever in the police force conducted the investigation?

He looked at me with shadowed, sunken eyes. 'Do you want the whole story?'

Feeling numb, I nodded.

'When I got to the hospital, they treated my eyes, and decided to admit me for the night. The next morning, they released me into police custody. The cops drove me down to the station, took my phone, and charged me with trespass, vandalism and criminal use of a computer.'

I'd known that Andrea would probably do this, but hearing Ryan confirm it made me flinch with guilt. He might well end up with a criminal record because he'd offered to help me find my mother.

'They interviewed me for ages about what led up to that night,' he went on, 'and told me I'd be summoned to appear in court. When they let me out at last, I couldn't face going home to Shell. So I rang my mother, and she drove down from the country. She took me home to grab a few clothes and things, and then took me back to her house. I called you, but at that point I thought you must have gone home with Andrea, so I left a message there with my mother's number.'

That would have been my second night at the penthouse, when Dirk came home, and Emmeline pretended I wasn't her daughter.

'The next day, my mum and I spend most of the day figuring out what to do about the charges. She rang up some lawyer friend, and it looked like my only option was Legal Aid. I called you again at your home and your office, because I didn't know where else you could be. Internet reception is dire up there, so I decided not to bother with an email until I got back to town. Besides, I figured you had a lot to deal with, and you might need some space before you called me.'

I smiled wryly to myself. He'd thought I hadn't called because I needed 'some space'. A full day after I'd been terrified that his failure to call me was his cowardly way of dumping me.

'On Monday morning, my mum got a call from the university to say I'd been expelled for serious misconduct. They told me my email account would be disabled, and my course fees for semester one were non-refundable. Sixteen thousand dollars, for a course I was thrown out of. And it wasn't me who'd paid it. My mum had paid the fees by taking out a second mortgage on her house. I'd promised I'd pay her back when I got a job as a teacher, but now I was never going to get one. Even if I could afford to do a teaching course somewhere else, once word got out about the hacking charge, no one would hire me.'

He put his face in his hands, in a gesture that reminded me how he'd clutched his eyes in pain in Andrea's office. The tiny, aching kernel I'd felt inside before returned and began to expand.

'I had to pay Mum back. And my rent and bills were due. So I made a snap decision, called Shell, and told her I was moving out. On the Tuesday, I borrowed Mum's car, drove to town, packed my room up and tried to track you down.'

Tuesday. The day I'd found out I'd been suspended.

'It was mid-semester break, so the buildings were locked on campus, but I sent you a note through internal mail and made a few more calls to your office. When no one answered, I went to Andrea's house and hung around. When you didn't show up, I left a note in the letterbox and drove back to my mum's place. The next day, Andrea must have come home from her conference and found all the messages and voicemails. So she rang my mum's place to tell me you'd walked out, and that if she heard from me again she was applying for a restraining order. At that point, I gave up.'

He fell silent, his face still in his hands, his body tense and trembling. Like mine, that day in the park when I cried and he stroked my hair and kissed me.

'After that, I decided to put everything I had into paying back those fees. I took all the modelling work I could get and found a full-time job.' His fingers stiffened, hooking his nails in his scalp.

'What sort of job?' I said, dreading the answer.

He lifted his head. His face was flushed and his mouth was taut with pain. 'Your everyday Arts graduate fallback,' he said, with a brief, savage smile. 'Answering customer complaints in a call centre. *Tower Bank customer service line*,' he recited. '*How can I help you today?*'

His face twisted and sank into his hands again, as if his head was too heavy to hold up. 'Angry, abusive callers on the line, eight hours a day. Commuting an hour and a half each way and working in rotating shifts. One week I'd be starting work at six in the morning, the next I'd be starting at midnight. Six months of hell, and then out of the blue some woman called Freya rings my mobile. To tell me you'd also been chucked out of your course, and that I'd vanished when you were pregnant with my twins.' His voice broke, and he hunched and closed his hands over his face, so I couldn't see him cry.

I pulled myself up, reached over and put my arms awkwardly around him. He tensed, too scared to let me in. Then he scraped the chair towards me and pressed his face into my thighs, clutching my surgical gown with both hands. I smoothed his limp hair with long gentle strokes as his shoulders shook and shook. When they finally stilled, he raised his head.

'I'm so sorry, Sage.' He smeared his tears with one hand. 'That you had to go through all that alone. That I wasn't there to care for you, and see the twins for the first time. I'm so sorry.'

His eyes filled again, and he put his face back in my lap. He cried, and I held him. And somehow, seeing him as fragile as this gave me strength.

'Have you paid back your mother?' I asked.

'Pretty much,' he mumbled.

'Then quit,' I said. 'Before it kills you. Find something else to do.'

He sat up. 'Like *what*, Sage?' he said, his eyes lit with something between frustration and despair. 'I have a degree in Visual Art and a third of a teaching diploma. What *something else* can I do?'

I plucked his hands from my surgical gown and held them in my own. 'Something you're passionate about.'

Ryan gave a hard, brittle laugh. 'I'm not qualified to be employed in something I'm passionate about.'

'I'm not talking about being employed. I'm talking about going back to your art. Reclaiming your vision.'

He laughed again, more brittle and bitter than ever. 'My vision's gone, Sage. I'm not cut out to be an artist. I can't even get a decent job so I can support you and our children.'

I gave a snort worthy of Andrea, and tossed his hands back in his lap. 'Who said we need you to support us? I've been supporting myself for the last six months. By life modelling, tutoring students in essay writing and shifts at my housemate's cafe. All of which I plan to keep on doing. I won't earn much, but I don't need much.'

Ryan looked down, and his lifeless hair slid down to hide his eyes.

'Besides,' I continued, 'I have my own passion to follow. And I've been working on a way to make it pay.'

He looked up again, his brows drawing together. 'Your own passion?'

'I'll explain later. But if I'm going to make it work, I'll need help.' I lifted my chin. 'Someone to care for the twins while I set myself up. Someone who'd love to live in the mountains. Exhibiting his work in a gallery cafe. Designing T-shirts. Writing and illustrating children's books. Someone that … someone I love.'

My eyes filled unexpectedly. I fought back the tears, but a single one managed to escape. Ryan watched it slide down my cheek, a strange expression on his face.

'There's not much market for any of those things,' he said, sounding cautious. 'Not enough people are interested.'

'I can think of two people who'll be very interested.' More tears escaped, and I tried to swab them away.

'Only *two?*' he asked, with a glimmer of his old humour.

'Down the corridor. In the hospital nursery. Waiting for us to give them names.'

I met his gaze, weeping but defiant, and something changed in his eyes. The dull, defeated look faded away, as if a cloud was starting to lift.

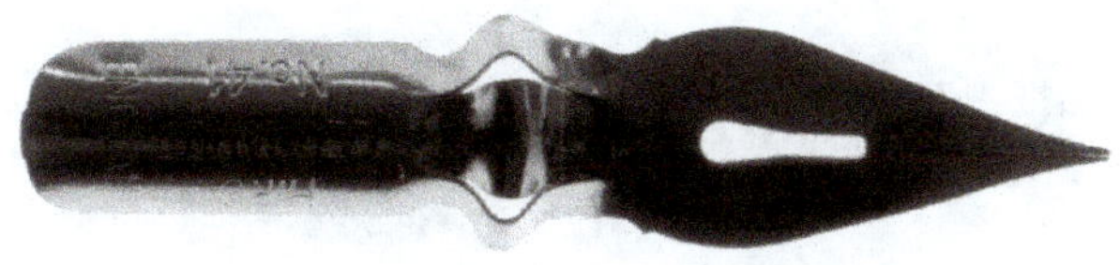

Part Four – The Castle

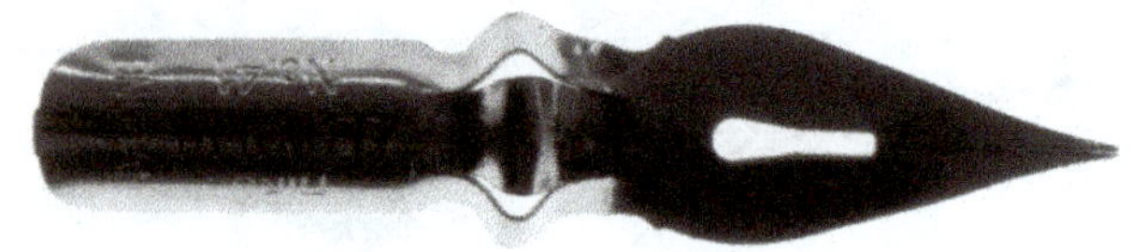

Chapter Forty-Four

Body of Work

Only a quarter of the girls in their mid-teens at Belfort College had their parents' permission to draw a naked woman. Still robed, I set up a circle of easels as they worked cross-legged on the floor. Freya and I had given them a grid of eight life drawings of women very different in shape. The girls' job was to comment on these in whatever way they wanted. In previous workshops, we'd seen girls make up biographies for each woman, rank their figures from 'best' to 'worst' and detail how each one should dress.

'Is everyone ready?' I said.

A murmur of assent.

'Who'd like to start?' said Freya.

The outspoken girl who'd talked the most so far shot her hand in the air. 'Angela?'

Angela stood up, pushing her hair self-consciously behind one ear. 'Um, yeah, so I thought I looked most like this one.' She pointed at sketch number three.

Number three was Josefina, who was twenty-five, with generous breasts and hips. Angela was busty, but the body in her too-short uniform was at least two sizes smaller.

'Can you explain why you chose number three?' I said.

'She's got big boobs, I guess, and they're sagging, like mine are starting to. I mean, God, I'm only fifteen, and they're *already sagging!* By the time I'm twenty they'll be down around my ankles!'

The other girls chuckled, with a nervous glance or two at the front of their uniforms.

'Then there's my hips. *Oh my God.* I swear they're taking over the world.'

Another chuckle as they looked for my response. 'Any thoughts on the other models' bodies?'

Angela gave a short laugh. 'I can tell you which body I'd *like* to have.'

'Which one?'

Angela rolled her eyes, as if this was too obvious to need pointing out. 'Number six.'

Most of the girls nodded emphatically. Two shrugged, as if to say they were above this sort of exercise. The remaining two looked at the floor, shoulders stiff and lips pressed together. Angela sat, and one by one the girls nominated the sketch they thought they resembled, describing their 'flaws' with such vehemence it was like watching someone cut themselves. Everyone cited number six as the body they wanted to have.

The second last girl sat, and we looked at Kim, who hadn't spoken yet. Kim was the largest of the girls, and so far she hadn't said a word. When we all turned her way, she hugged her knees to her face, as if she wanted to hide behind them. She'd placed the sketches face-down on the carpet. 'Do I have to answer?' she said, sounding on the verge of tears.

My heart ached for her. 'You don't have to,' I said gently, crouching at her side, 'but we'd like to hear what you have to say.'

'Well, I know what you're all thinking.' Her voice was hostile and trembling. 'You're all thinking number *seven*, aren't you?'

Number seven was Rose, a flamboyant woman who posed with feathers and flowers. She made her own clothes, which had a touch of the burlesque: jewels, fringed gypsy skirts and sequinned velvet dresses. She was at least size twenty-two.

'I hire number seven once or twice a month,' said Freya. 'She's a great model. She sews her own clothes and sells them in her online boutique. I'll put up a link to her style blog.'

Freya wrote Rose's URL on the whiteboard, and the other girls copied it down. After a minute or two, Kim uncurled and did the same.

'So,' I said, sitting back on the edge of the table. 'Everyone said they wanted to look like number six. Why's that?'

When no one volunteered an answer, Angela gave a worldly, knowing shrug. '*Everyone* wants to look like that,' she said. 'Blonde hair, long legs, tiny waist, perfect boobs. If you look like that, you can have anything you want.'

Freya raised an eyebrow. 'How do you mean *anything?*'

'You know, *anything.*' Angela's hands made an extravagant circle in the air. 'You could be a model or a movie star. Date the hottest guys on the planet. Marry someone rich so you can live in luxury and never have to work.'

I smiled wryly to myself. When the twins were born, I'd sent Emmeline a photo and told her she was welcome to visit. Since then she'd turned up a few times a year, with baby clothes and bright, defensive smiles. She'd taken up modelling again, playing mum in shots for department store catalogues. The last time we'd spoken, she'd met a new man, and was angling to move into his condominium. He played golf at the same club as Dirk, who'd replaced Emmeline with a younger blonde a few weeks after they split.

'Is that what you want to do?' I asked.

'Well, *yeah*,' said Angela, shaking her head at so stupid a question. 'Who wouldn't?'

Freya raised an eyebrow. 'What's it like, being a model or an actor?'

The other girls sat up, eager to fill us in. *You fly around the world and designers send you beautiful clothes. You get to be in movies and have any guy you want. Everyone looks up to you and wants to be you. Or be with you.*

'But that's not a *good* thing,' said Mia. She was small and determined, and rolled her eyes a lot, implying that her peers were silly children. 'That means fans hassle you all the time, and paparazzi follow you with cameras.'

'So you wouldn't want to be a rich, beautiful celebrity?' said Angela, with an eye roll of her own. 'Yeah, *right.*'

'Of course I don't want to be a *celebrity*,' said Mia, in scornful tones. 'Celebrities are bimbos with boob jobs and drug habits.'

Angela took an outraged breath, and I hastily stepped in. 'But you'd still like to look like one?'

Mia shrugged. 'I suppose so. Everyone wants to be pretty.'

I smiled to myself again and cranked up the data projector. 'Let me show you something,' I said. 'Model number six was me, four years ago.'

I clicked the mouse, and a picture from my photo shoot with Fabian de Carlo came up. In it, I was wearing Emmeline's polka-dot bikini and looking over one raised shoulder. The girls gasped, impressed and envious.

'I used to work as a fashion model,' I said, not mentioning that I quit my first job. 'I did a shoot for La Carina.'

They listened avidly as I told them about the shoot. How we'd posed outside in lingerie on a cold autumn morning, ogled and bullied by the crew. How I found a model their age crying in the toilets, convinced that she needed liposuction.

'Most fashion models are really insecure about their bodies. Everyone zones in on your looks and your weight, and one pound or pimple can mean you don't get work.'

I put up an ad from the shoot I'd taken part in, letting the girls think about what went on behind the scenes.

'Let's talk more about what you want in life. Who'd like to get married one day?'

All of the girls raised their hands, including Mia, who'd announced that she knew she was a lesbian at ten. 'By the time I want to get married,' she said, 'gay marriage will be legal everywhere in the world. And if it isn't, I'll fight until it is.'

Two girls applauded, three rolled their eyes, and one said, 'You go, girl!'

'How about kids?' I said, clicking back to me in a bikini and heading for the circle of easels. 'Who wants kids?' Eight hands went up, some more certainly than others.

'Great. Now. You see that photo? Six months later, I gave birth to twins.'

I threw my robe open, letting them take in my limp, hanging breasts, my stretchmarks, and the saggy, crinkled apron of skin that hung from my stomach into a full complement of curly pubic hair. These days I kept my legs and armpits bare, but I avoided Brazilians, because they were embarrassing, painful and gave me ingrown hairs.

A horrified hush descended. The changes in my body were a terrifying reminder that no matter how much you went to the gym and how little you ate, you were never safe. That even a beautiful young woman was only a pregnancy or a decade or two away from Not Being Pretty.

'Oh my God,' said Angela, whites showing around her eyes. 'I take it all back. I'm not having kids. Not *ever*.'

Ignoring the gasps from my audience, I put my hands behind me on the stool and leant back. 'Why not, Angela?'

'If it does *that* to your body, it's not worth it.'

'*Angela!*' shrieked one of the other girls, genuinely aghast.

Angela flushed, belatedly realising how this had sounded. 'I mean,' said Angela, trying to make amends, 'I'm not saying that you look bad now or anything, I just mean you … you were so beautiful, and … and …'

'Give it up, Angela,' said one of the others.

By now, every eye in the room was on me, waiting for me to cry, or flee the room, or at least tell Angela off. One or two girls had covered their faces, and the rest were making sympathetic faces and gestures, convinced I must be devastated.

I held up a calm hand. 'Let Angela finish.'

Angela bit her lip, almost purple with embarrassment. 'I just meant that if I looked like that, I'd do anything to stay that way. Exercise, surgery, abortion, *anything*.'

I lifted an eyebrow. 'You think my life would be better if I still looked like that picture?'

Angela opened her mouth, shut it, and looked at the floor. Around her, the other girls avoided my eyes, too uncomfortable to speak. Shocked as they were, they agreed with Angela. When they drew me, most would slim me down, remove my pubic hair, restore my shape to pre-baby perk. Photoshop by pencil. Some might even congratulate me on being so 'brave', or offer suggestions on how to regain my figure. But all of them had now seen at least one woman who was comfortable enough with her imperfect body to pose nude for people to draw.

'Looking like a model—' I gestured at the slide, '—didn't give me a wonderful life. I got a lot of attention, which was fun when I felt safe and confident, but creepy and stressful when I didn't. Sleazy, pushy men, staring and commenting and trying to touch me. Resentful women, making loud comments about how I was dumb and arrogant and probably starving myself. Now I have a career I'm passionate about, two beautiful kids, and a partner who loves me for myself. A man who wants me as a lover and companion, instead of flaunting me like a wearable sex toy. These things have made me much, much happier than looking like a fashion model.'

The girls sat in deep, fermenting silence.

'I won't lie to you,' I added. 'Pretty girls get unfair advantages. But life doesn't end at thirty, or forty, or whenever you can't play the pretty game any more. Less pretty girls can end up happier later on, because they learn a lot younger to base their relationships and confidence on things that last longer than their looks.'

Freya set the timer. 'OK girls,' she said, 'let's do some drawing. Sage is going to do four five-minute poses. Grab your pencils and I'll come around and give you tips.'

I settled into a pose that allowed me to study the girls' expressions. Two of them—beautiful alpha girls with long glossy hair—were ignoring me and talking, perhaps about the lame, preachy workshop the school made them do. One was checking Instagram on her phone. But the rest were looking intently from me to their sketchbooks, their faces unsettled but hopeful.

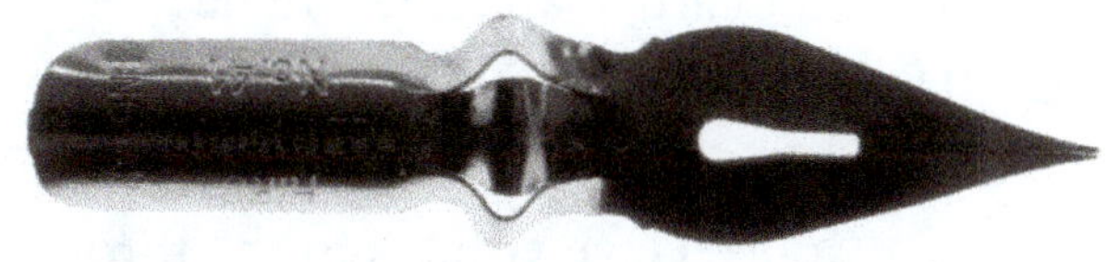

Chapter Forty-Five

A Man's Home

Our cottage was three blocks from Freya and Brett's, and backed onto the same forest. Instead of ferns, it was surrounded by fruit trees, with plums and apricots bobbing in the windows.

Between tutoring, life modelling and short shifts at Molehill, we'd scraped through our first year with the twins. When they turned one, a Colombian student began babysitting for us in exchange for help with academic English. Ryan started work on a portfolio for publishers; Freya and I designed body image workshops for girls in high school. Two years later, we were bringing in enough to run a car and rent a house of our own.

I opened the front door and the smell of baking pastry poured out. As I slipped my workshop folder on the sideboard, the twins came thundering down the hall. A child latched onto each of my legs, with an unselfconscious love that lit me up inside.

'Mum!' shouted Zoe, tugging at my finger. 'Look what Daddy made!'

I heaved my son on one hip, and let my daughter tow me down the hallway. Zoe had my surname and Ryan's buoyant hair; Lucas was a 'Prince', but his hair was fine and very fair.

'Hey!' said Ryan, bounding over. I just had time to register his King of Wands tarot card T-shirt before he grabbed me in an exuberant hug. 'How'd it go? Bikini shot still working its magic?'

'Like a wand.' I fitted my face into the crook of his neck. 'Why the King of Wands? Have you taken the throne?'

He hooked his arm through mine as if I were blind, his face suspiciously gleeful. 'All will be clear, sagacious girl. Close your eyes and I'll lead you to my masterpiece.'

I shut my eyes obligingly and he propelled me down the corridor.

'Open your eyes.'

The entire kitchen table was covered by a castle made from pale orange bricks of cantaloupe. The towers at each corner had figs on top, like edible minarets, and a moat made from blueberries encircled it. Beyond the moat he'd built a castle garden, with finely chopped honeydew grass. On this grew shrubs with grape leaves and strawberry flowers, and trees with kiwifruit trunks and autumn leaves made from apricot, among which wove a winding path of apple-slice cobblestones. It looked amazing.

'Fantastic,' I said with enthusiasm. 'We should start a business sideline in fruit sculpture. Did you take photos?'

'One from every angle,' confessed Ryan, and I chuckled.

Lucas pointed solemnly at a shrub. 'I helped you, didn't I Dad?'

'You did,' said Ryan, adjusting a piece of strawberry. 'You and Zoe picked all the grapes off the stalk for me.'

Zoe circled the table like a shark, uninterested in claiming credit. 'Can we eat it, Dad? I want to eat it *now*.'

'Not yet, Zoe. We'll eat it for dessert, OK?'

'O-K.' She rushed off to her bedroom, and Lucas picked up a picture book and settled on a beanbag in the corner.

I popped a leftover grape in my mouth. 'So what's baking?'

'A big, macho quiche. The type real men eat with their inch-thick steak.' He tweaked a fig and stood back to admire his handiwork. 'There's mail, by the way. Up on the kitchen bench.'

I inched around the castle to the oddly shaped parcel, and the old university logo caught my eye. Next to the parcel sat an envelope, with *Department of Womyn's Studies* printed in the corner. A twinge of apprehension flickered through me.

When the twins were two, Fran had passed on a letter from a lawyer, saying Andrea had dropped all charges. As a gesture of thanks, I'd told Fran to pass on my address, but we'd had no word until now.

I slit the envelope with a butter knife and pulled out a cream card embossed with swirly gold words that took me three stunned readings to take in.

'So what's the letter?' said Ryan, sounding mischievous. 'Best wishes from Andrea?'

'Actually,' I said, 'it is. Sort of. It's an invitation to her retirement party.'

I'd expected Andrea to keep on working until they wheeled her out in a coffin. The thought of her with cupcakes and a giant farewell card was so bizarre that I searched for a note to say it was a joke. But there was only the card, with no personal message, formal as a wedding invitation.

'She's *retiring?*' Ryan sounded as astonished as me, and he'd only met her once. Under less than favourable conditions.

'Apparently.'

'And she's invited you to her *farewell party?*'

'Not just me,' I said. 'Take a look.'

Next to the swirly gold *To* was printed *Sage Rampion and family*. We stood by the castle and boggled. I could understand why Andrea might invite me. I was a Women's Studies graduate, and knew lots of the staff and students. But in Andrea's one encounter with Ryan, she'd maced him, hit him, accused him of rape, and pressed criminal charges.

'I wonder who she'll appoint as her successor?' I mused aloud.

Of the two deputy Heads, Madhu and Hilda, Hilda had by far the better publication record. She'd published in every reputable feminist journal in the English language, and most of the German ones. She'd also exhibited her strange, menstrual collages in galleries all round the world. When I told Ryan about her, he'd laughed and said he should jump on the bandwagon, make a few collages from stubble and used condoms. So far he hadn't exhibited at a big enough gallery to satisfy him, but he had over 100,000 followers on Instagram, sales of his T-shirts were booming online, and he'd just got a deal for illustrating his first children's picture book.

Ryan reached for the oil and vinegar and started mixing a salad dressing. 'Fran might know. Or we could go to the party and find out.'

'Should we? It's 5pm Friday week.'

He grinned. 'Maybe we should. It's about time I saw my grandmother-in-law again. This time without a can of Mace in my eyes.'

'You might want to wear safety goggles, just in case.'

'Or dress in drag. She'd never dare to mace me then. That would be transphobia.'

We both laughed.

'God,' said Ryan. 'Why the hell has she invited *me?*'

I stuck the card to the fridge among the finger paintings, and came up with an answer to this question. Andrea had never been one for admitting she was wrong. Inviting me to her party and adding *and family* was the closest thing we'd get to an apology.

I picked up the other piece of mail, a parcel addressed to Zoe and Lucas.

'That's from me,' said Ryan. 'I ordered it from overseas.' He gathered some herbs from the pots on the windowsill, a housewarming present from Freya. Tiny purple flowers were blooming among the silvery leaves of the sage plant.

'Birthday present for the twins?' Their fourth birthday was a couple of weeks away.

'Partly for them, partly for you. To help you with an important motherly duty.'

The parcel was big, but felt light, and when I pinged it with my nail it made a metallic sound. I hacked through the layers of bubble wrap and pulled out a cake tin in the shape of a frog.

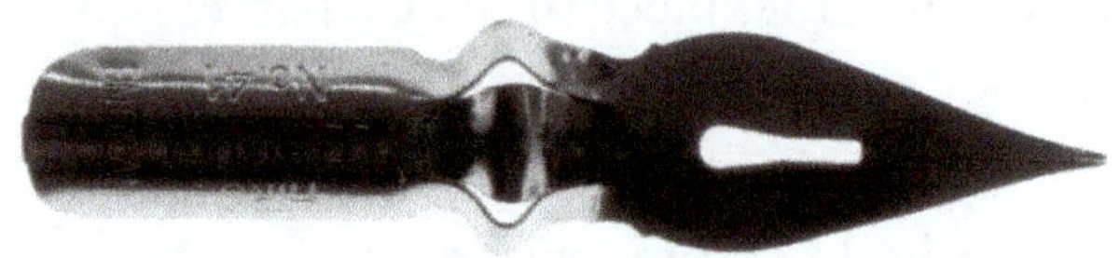

Chapter Forty-Six

Box Office

The courtyard at the foot of the Humanities building was filled with stackable chairs. In these, juggling wineglasses and paper plates of food, sat the students and staff of Women's Studies. Andrea was standing by a trestle table of food, surrounded by colleagues and awestruck young feminists. My body tensed, as if I were a long-paroled prisoner laying eyes on her jailer.

Ryan winked, gave my hand a squeeze, and led the twins to a sunny corner, a bag of books and toys dangling from one arm. I walked slowly toward the trestle table, in chic glasses, an ankle-length turquoise dress and longish, layered hair that hung loose around my shoulders. No one recognised me.

Some yards from Andrea, I heard a familiar voice. Zoe was trotting around the courtyard, loudly counting people's shoes.

'One, two, free, four.' As she said each number, she poked her small finger into Kate Cleaver-Murray's boots and her girlfriend's ballet flats. 'Five, six …' She poked Madhu Baghel's sandals. 'Seven, eight.' On 'eight', her finger hit the ground as a pair of clumpy Birkenstocks whipped beneath their chair.

'This is your child?' snapped Hilda Ziehler, indicating Zoe with a menacing jab of her fork.

Zoe reached toward her feet again to add them to her count, and I swept her up before Hilda stuck the fork in her hand. 'Sorry, Professor Ziehler.'

Recognising my voice, Hilda studied me with a dark, affronted scowl. 'So.' She spat the word as if it offended her. 'You are back. Maybe tomorrow Andrea will give you a lectureship. Next week, a professorship.'

'What's a pessa-ship?' said Zoe, who seemed fascinated by Hilda.

She reached for the chain on Hilda's glasses and I swiftly steered her away. 'Where's Daddy, Zoe?'

'Over there!' She pointed at Ryan, who was drawing a picture with Lucas.

I lowered her to the ground. 'Do you think you can catch him?'

'Yes!' To my relief, she scuttled off to join him.

'Or maybe Deputy Head!' Hilda impaled a falafel with such force that it split in two. 'Publication counts for nothing, so a PhD … why bother?'

Andrea must have chosen Madhu instead of Hilda to succeed her as Head of Department. Hilda stabbed one of the falafel halves, shoved it in her mouth and chewed with a festering menace. Seizing my moment, I said goodbye and made my way over to Andrea.

Even on the night I'd walked out, I'd known I'd see Andrea again. Her legacy was too powerful to cut her off without looking back, if only to see how far I'd travelled. I'd fenced off a stage in my mind, where Andrea and I acted out versions of this meeting.

In some I confronted her angrily; in others I crumbled—from fear, or from guilt. Yet now that the real Andrea was footfalls away, I was surprised by a faint pang of sadness.

In the years since we parted at the taxi stand, Andrea had aged about a decade. Her iron-grey hair had faded to white, and her once-square shoulders had developed a stoop, as if she'd been carrying too much. She was talking about gendered language to an admiring student, but even on this favourite topic her edge seemed dulled, as though worn by overuse. Unlike her fellow staff, she recognised me straightaway.

'Excuse us for a moment,' she said to the student, who scurried away, leaving me with my grandmother.

Andrea looked me up and down, a tired, diminished echo of the monster in my memory. She took in my appearance, like a general inspecting a court-martialled soldier. I stood without shrinking and let her look her fill, because I wasn't her soldier any more. She glanced at my left hand, and flicked back to my face when she didn't find a ring. Ryan liked the idea of an offbeat, creative wedding, but for me, getting married felt like a bridge too far.

'Sage,' she said, in a cool, wary voice. 'You seem well.'

'Thank you.'

'I hear you're running workshops on body image for teenage girls.' The same cool voice, but somewhere underneath I heard a hint of surprise. Surprise because I'd finally impressed her.

'Yes. For two years now. They've been really popular.'

Andrea nodded, and was about to say more when a platter of finger foods was thrust beneath our noses.

'Professor Rampion!' said a familiar voice that crashed my thoughts into a wall. 'Congratulations! I'm *so* freaked out to think of you retiring. Want a curry puff?'

The waitress jiggled her platter, shaking back curls from the rosy face of Jess. She was heavily made-up, in a black-and-white uniform with Premium Catering embroidered on the front. Eight-year-old memories resurfaced like dead bodies. Her admiration. Her betrayal. How her party woke a fear that I was worthless and contemptible because I didn't know the right things, or wear the right clothes.

I considered saying something cutting and rude, but looking at her wide-eyed expression, I realised I no longer cared enough to bother. 'Hi, Jess.'

Jess did a double take. '*Sage?* Oh my God, you look *great!* When did you grow your hair?'

As soon as I got home from your awful birthday party. 'Oh, a few years ago. I've had kids, too.'

Jess gasped. 'Is that cute little girl *yours?*' She looked across the courtyard at Lucas, who was combing his silky hair. It fell almost to his shoulders, because he reacted to haircuts like we were trying to amputate his ears. I located Zoe on Madhu's lap, being sung a song in Hindi.

'She's *such* a girl, your daughter,' went on Jess, still looking at Lucas. 'Look at her, combing her hair. Does she want to be a princess? My niece *loves* dressing up as a princess.'

I could almost hear Andrea bristling beside me. 'Actually, that's my son. My daughter's over there, with Professor Baghel.'

'Oh.' Jess blushed scarlet. 'I'm so sorry. It's his hair. And his T-shirt. I think of purple as a girl's colour.'

The purple T-shirt was Lucas's favourite. He and Zoe were both wearing navy shorts from Molehill; Zoe's top had red-and-white stripes.

'You should cut his hair shorter. You know, so people can tell.'

'Um, yeah, thanks for the tip,' I said, conscious that Andrea was ready to erupt. 'Anyway, Andrea and I were just talking, so …'

'Oh! I'm sorry, I'll leave you to it. Let's catch up *soon*, OK?'

Actually, let's not. Jess flounced away with her curry puffs, and before anyone else could interrupt us, Andrea said, 'Come with me.'

She led me to the foyer, and we caught the lift to the top floor without exchanging a word.

The carpet on the top floor corridor was as dense and deadening as ever. Solemn and silent as pallbearers, Andrea and I walked past the sequence of nameplates we both knew by heart. As she took out her keys with a familiar jingle, I saw the nameplate on her door, so new and shiny that the handle beneath it looked tarnished. Engraved on the nameplate was *Professor Frances Mackenzie, Head of Gender Studies.*

Andrea chose *Fran* as her successor? No wonder Hilda was furious. I looked at Andrea, a million questions swarming, but she avoided my eyes and strode in.

Both desks were empty, and all that remained of Andrea's career was the sag in the empty bookshelves and the boxes on the floor. On the carpet where Ryan's body had landed was the faintest of stains, half-hidden by a box.

Andrea placed another box on the desk that was no longer hers. 'For you.'

Inside was my wallet and a handful of books, which I lifted from the box. Underneath was a stack of manila folders. I opened one and everything went so still I could hear the clock in the corridor ticking. Mail from my mother. Everything she'd sent to Sadie Virtanen, in the twenty-two years between the day she left and the night I turned up at the penthouse.

'I always meant to pass them on,' said Andrea in a quiet voice, 'when you were an adult, and could think for yourself. It just never seemed to be the right time.'

With trembling hands, I opened the topmost letter. Inside was a photo of Dirk and Emmeline, wearing evening wear and camera-ready smiles.

I put the photo back and closed the box, not sure how to feel. Andrea had shut me away, cut me off from my mother, and put Ryan through the worst months of his life. Yet she'd also stepped in when Emmeline walked out, raising me in a way that she'd honestly believed was right. Despite everything, she was the only real mother I'd ever known.

I looked into Andrea's weary face, a treacherous sea of history between us. 'Would you like to go downstairs and meet your great-grandchildren?'

Her face went rigid, and something glimmered in her eyes. 'Yes,' she said unsteadily. 'I would.'

The silence as the lift went down was still guarded, but it felt just fractionally warmer. In the courtyard, Ryan was talking to Madhu, and Jess had put aside her tray and was playing with the twins. As Andrea and I approached, Jess tried to interest Lucas in a plastic truck from the toy bag.

'That's *Zoe's* truck,' said Lucas, with a sniff of disdain. He turned his back and picked up his comb.

Zoe hurried over and snatched the truck from Jess. She plonked it in the grass a few feet from her brother, her face affronted under her springy dark hair.

I laughed and glanced at Andrea to see her reaction, but she barely seemed to have noticed. Her eyes were on Zoe, who was using the truck to bulldoze a small clump of daisies.

'Do you think you'll raise her as a feminist?' said Andrea.

I hesitated, thinking of how Andrea had raised me. How she'd sheltered me so completely that I never learnt to question what she said. How she'd taught me to fear men, and look down on women who weren't her sort of feminist. How she'd turned me into a figure of ridicule and pity among my peers.

Then I thought about what I'd seen since. Emmeline, and her boob job and succession of sugar daddies. The shivering models at the photo shoot. The men at the strip club. The classes and classes of teenage girls, barely able to live with the shape of their bodies. And my children. My daughter, bold and full of energy, who hadn't yet been taught that women are only worthwhile if they're 'hot'. My son, reserved and sensitive, who hadn't yet been taught that men are meant to be emotionless sex machines. I found myself wishing for something to help them grow up strong enough to find their own voice. Not a tower to protect them, but a weapon they could fight with. I wasn't sure if I'd call that weapon feminism. But I knew that Andrea would.

I watched the twins, conscious of Andrea beside me, waiting for an answer to her question. Zoe abandoned the truck and ran to Ryan, who waved at us to join him. I waved back, and as I led my grandmother to my children, I turned to her and answered 'Yes, I will.'

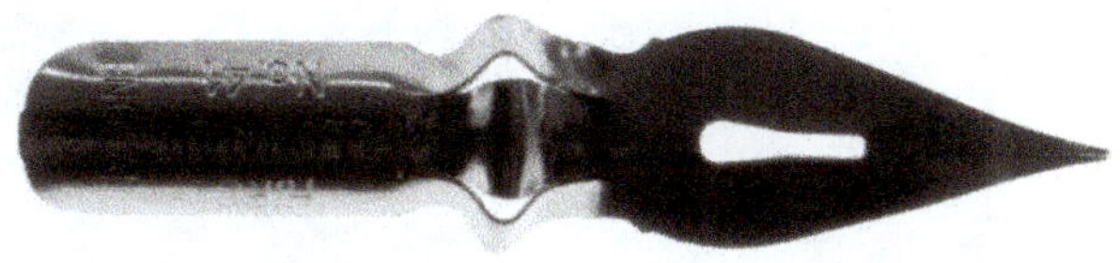

About the Author

Fiona Price fell in love with words at two, and has been playing with them ever since. By calling, she's a writer who's tried her hand at everything from screenplays to songs. She has long planned to retell fairy tales as contemporary novels, and hopes *The Ivory Tower* will be the first of many.

By career, she's a social scientist who specialises in cultural diversity. She runs workshops on cross-cultural communication and reads out names from all over the world at university graduations. At the moment, she is writing a fantasy trilogy and working on becoming a professional public speaker. She has an Australian father and a Chinese mother, and lives in Melbourne by the sea.